WANTING YOU

ALSO BY LESLIE A. KELLY

Hollywood Heat series
Watching You

WANTING YOU

Hollywood Heat Book 2

LESLIE A. KELLY

Best wishes —
Leslie A. Kelly

FOREVER
YOURS

New York Boston

Copyright © 2018 by Leslie A. Kelly
Excerpt from *Waiting for You* copyright © 2018 by Leslie A. Kelly
Cover design by Elizabeth Turner Stokes
Cover copyright © 2018 by Hachette Book Group, Inc.

Forever Yours
Hachette Book Group
1290 Avenue of the Americas
New York, NY 10104
forever-romance.com
twitter.com/foreverromance

First ebook and print on demand edition: July 2018

Forever Yours is an imprint of Grand Central Publishing. The Forever Yours name and logo are trademarks of Hachette Book Group, Inc.

The publisher is not responsible for websites (or their content) that are not owned by the publisher.

The Hachette Speakers Bureau provides a wide range of authors for speaking events. To find out more, go to www.hachettespeakersbureau.com or call (866) 376-6591.

ISBN 978-1-5387-6124-3 (print on demand edition)

ISBN 978-1-5387-6125-0 (ebook edition)

Sincere thanks to Caitlin Kelly for the brainstorming, editing, and plotting assistance;

to the Plotmonkeys—Julie, Karen, and Janelle—for helping to flesh out this whole series;

To Geoff Symon for the technical help;

and to my niece Christina, for the police procedural info!

Did Former Child Star *Really* Fall?

Hollywood Tattletale Reporter J. Federer

November 14, 2018

LOS ANGELES—Although actor Steve Baker's death was ruled an accident, questions remain about this summer's tragedy.

Baker's body was found in June at the base of a cliff directly below the home of actor-turned-director Reece Winchester. Though the reclusive star was questioned, police say he was not suspected of any crime and called Baker's death an accident. But some Hollywood insiders aren't convinced. Whispers of suicide, or even worse, still surround the case.

Baker, who starred in the sitcom *Dear Family*, was once a household name. Part of a teen supercouple, his career took a nosedive after his girlfriend, actress Rachel Winchester—sister to the famed director—fell to her death from a hotel balcony eighteen years ago. Although ruled an accident, no one really knows whether Rachel actually had committed suicide.

Six years ago, the actor's father, superstar agent Harry Baker, was brutally murdered in his home. The case remains unsolved to this day.

Did the series of tragedies prove too much for Steve Baker? Enough for him to follow his long-lost love and take his own life?

Or is something darker at work?

Some wonder if his fall was part of a revenge plot by

the Winchesters—a family known for carrying grudges, especially against those involved in the sad life and death of Rachel Winchester.

With one Winchester brother living in the house where the incident occurred, another a former Army Ranger and professional bodyguard, and a third a renowned detective within the LAPD, who knows how deep the conspiracy might go...or what else the powerful but secretive Winchester brothers might be concealing?

Chapter 1

Anyone interested in the many infamous murders that had occurred in Los Angeles knew the Cecil Hotel was worth a visit. More than one violent killer had called the building home, and brutal crimes had been committed within its walls. The place showed up on the city's murder tours and had even landed its own TV series on a cable network, even though it was now known by a different name.

For Evie Fleming, however, going to the Cecil wasn't about morbid curiosity. She made her living—a very good one— writing in-depth explorations about notorious crimes. As far as she was concerned, there was no better place to begin her research on the city's most brutal killers.

Right now, though, she wondered if that visit might have been a big mistake.

Because a man was following her down Seventh Street.

"Hell," she whispered as she heard his hard footsteps behind her.

She walked even faster toward the parking garage where

she'd left her rental car. The neighborhood was still, silent. When she'd arrived this afternoon, it had been crowded with busy Monday workers from surrounding office buildings. There were few shops, though, and the restaurants catered to the area's daytime employees, who'd left long ago.

She should have left earlier too. But her conversation with a talkative old maintenance man at the hotel had been fascinating, and she'd spent hours in his small office. Hours during which the night had grown late, the air had grown cold, and the street had grown menacing.

Knowing she was now within a block of the garage didn't offer much relief. The narrow entrance ramp was tucked in between two tiny stores. Even from here she could see they were dark and shuttered with security gates.

She'd parked on the third level. The elevator was in the back. The front stairs were completely enclosed—a vertical tunnel of privacy for anyone with crime in mind. None of this looked promising.

Maybe there's a twenty-four-hour cashier at the exit gate.

Or maybe it was entirely electronic.

There's probably a security guard.

But there might not be.

Damn it. By walking into it that garage she might be trapping herself with no way to get out.

The heavy footsteps on the sidewalk were getting louder. Although it didn't sound like he was running, he certainly wasn't strolling.

Maybe he was totally innocent, on an errand or meeting a friend. But she didn't think so. A creepy-crawly sensation danced up her spine, the one every woman felt when something told her she was being followed by danger. Her job—the constant immersion in the world of violent crime—made her more suspicious than most. She knew awful things could happen to anyone. At any time.

Should've Uber'd it.

Yes, she should have. But it hadn't seemed necessary. The LAPD headquarters building was only six or seven blocks from the Cecil. She'd walked to the station that afternoon, hitting the hotel on her way back. The neighborhood had seemed a little run-down but was still a busy, commercial one. She just hadn't seen the nighttime potential.

Big mistake.

"Okay, what are you going to do?" she whispered.

Did she go into the garage and call herself a paranoid fool when the stranger kept walking up the street? Did she turn around and confront him, knowing some guys would back off if they knew they'd been looked at and could be identified?

Identified. Another possibility flared in her mind.

Without missing a stride, she reached into her purse and pulled out her phone. Tapping the screen and thumbing for the camera app, she was prepared to swing around and take the guy's picture and text it to a friend. Just in case.

The footsteps pounded harder. The guy was getting closer. Maybe he'd seen the flash of light from the camera. Or maybe he'd realized they'd reached the darkest center of the street.

"Damn it," she muttered as she fumbled with the phone. Not even wanting to stop long enough to turn around, she lifted the camera high. She snapped what might have been a picture of her own shoulder, or the street in the opposite direction, and forwarded it in response to the last text message she'd received. Although she knew she should take another—one that she was sure actually showed the guy—her tension had quadrupled. Her heart thudded, her pulse roared, and her brain ordered her to move. *Now. Go now.*

Sensing she didn't have time to do anything else, she obeyed her inner voice and took off toward the next intersection. Broadway. It was seventy yards maybe. She just hoped she got there safely to give it her regards.

She ran. No, she flew, her long legs eating the sidewalk, her feet steady in her thick-heeled leather boots.

Although she'd anticipated it, the attack still shocked her. A hard form slammed into her, a powerful arm encircling her waist. Her phone flew from her hand as a strong hand yanked a fistful of hair and jerked her head back against a strong, alcohol-reeking body.

"Don't scream."

Of *course* she screamed.

He let go of her hair, slamming his thick hand over her mouth. Even as she twisted and struggled, he began to drag her toward a narrow service alley between two tall office buildings.

Evie wasn't stupid, and she wasn't helpless. She couldn't let him get her back there, away from any potential passersby. Obediently getting into the car, going into the back alley, or into the strange building was a common mistake victims made when confronted by an attacker. They might think it was safer to go along, but it wasn't. Because once an attacker got you out of sight and sound of anyone else, the battle was already lost.

She fought with all her strength, elbows hitting his gut, eliciting a grunt. Her nails clawed the hand over her mouth. Swinging her leg back, she caught his shin with the heel of her boot.

He winced but tightened his grip around her middle. His

other hand went to her throat and began to squeeze. "Stop struggling, bitch."

As if. So far he hadn't produced a weapon. That was fortunate. She just had to get away from him, or at least turn around to give herself a real fighting chance. Anything to prevent him from getting her in that alley. And to get his strong, powerful fingers off her neck.

Suddenly, she remembered a trick from a self-defense class she'd taken.

Evie picked up her feet.

Surprised at having to bear her entire weight, the attacker dropped her onto the ground. She rolled away quickly, knowing he would lunge after her and that he wouldn't be caught off guard again. Leaping to her feet, she swung around, preparing to jab her nails into his eyes, a fist into his throat, a knee into his crotch.

But he wasn't there. Rather than the attacker charging at her, something had come at *him*. A dark shape, powerful and broad, slammed into the other man, sending him flying.

Her ridiculous first thought was that Batman was real. Her second was that she was going to start carrying pepper spray. Her third was sheer, utter relief.

The attacker landed on the hard corner of a cement step and howled in pain.

"Police. Don't move," a deep voice growled.

A tall man moved toward the thug and pushed him onto his stomach. A gleam of moonlight on metal and a clanking sound told her he was putting handcuffs on her attacker.

"This is police brutality! I think you broke my arm."

"You're lucky it wasn't your neck. You think I don't know what you had in store for this woman?"

The words being thrown right out there made Evie shiver. So far, she'd held herself together. She suspected only the adrenaline roaring through her kept her from a more emotional reaction.

She might have been able to fight the guy off. But she might not have. And if she hadn't, she would probably, right now, be in that alley being robbed, beaten…maybe worse. Jesus.

Don't think about it. Just don't.

Once the handcuffs were in place, her savior looked up at her. His face was washed in shadow, only the dark eyes gleaming. "Are you all right, Miss…?"

"Fleming. Evie Fleming. And yes, I'm okay. Thanks to you."

She would have aches, pains, and bruises tomorrow from her fall. But all of those things were better than what she might have endured had the big cop with the intense eyes not come onto the scene.

Just like something out of a crime TV show, he sat the handcuffed creep on a cement step and read him his rights. Pointing an index finger in the guy's face, he said, "You move for anything other than to breathe, and you'll regret it."

The would-be mugger—*oh God, rapist?*—groaned. But he didn't move.

Pulling a radio off his belt, the police officer called in the crime. After he'd made the call, requesting assistance, he refocused his attention on Evie. "Are you sure you're not hurt? Do you want me to have them send an ambulance?"

"No, really, I'm fine," she said, meaning it. Everything—from her noticing she was being followed, to the jerk being put in handcuffs—had taken no more than five minutes. She might be a bit banged up because of her own maneuvers, but really, the only thing she felt was gratitude.

Now that her heart was settling back into a normal rhythm, the rush of danger easing out of her with every exhalation, she noticed more about the cop. First, that he was probably about six feet tall but gave the impression of being taller because of his overall *bigness*. Although he was still cloaked by night, she saw that his body appeared powerful—broad in the shoulder and in the chest, definitely no donut belly. He was in perfect shape. Good thing, since her attacker was probably a bit taller. But the guy wouldn't have stood a chance against someone this strong.

"You'll have to wait to talk to the local responders from Central. They should be here within a couple of minutes."

"You're not from there?" That surprised her. She'd figured she'd been correct in her initial assumption that this neighborhood would be well patrolled, given the location of headquarters up on Second.

"No, it was just dumb luck. I was dropping off some paperwork. Saw this jackoff start to follow you when I was waiting at the intersection and decided to cruise by and see what was going on."

"Thank goodness for me you did."

He shifted a little, probably uncomfortable with the praise, as many heroic types were. And she'd already pegged him as one.

As he moved, so, apparently, did some clouds overhead. Because a shimmer of moonlight emerged and cast light on him. *God in heaven.*

He had that kind of strong, angular face, all sculpted bones and jutting jaw, that made women take a second look. She catalogued the sexy close-cut beard, the thick, nearly black hair, and the swoop of equally black brows over dark, deep-set eyes.

The chin was hard, the jaw defined, the nose strong but not overlarge, the mouth…oh, Jesus, the man had *mouth*. A slow, involuntary shiver rolled up her body, but it was nothing like the shudders of desperation she'd been experiencing just minutes ago in this very spot.

"You're cold." He didn't wait for a reply, instead coming closer and whipping off a soft, worn leather jacket. He put it over her shoulders.

Funny, now that he was standing so close, cold was the last way she'd describe herself. The man put off more fire than a jet engine.

There was something else. He looked familiar.

Evie couldn't identify him, and she was almost certain they hadn't met in person. But she'd seen him somewhere. Maybe when researching one of her books—he was a cop, after all, in a city that had had more than its fair share of serial killer cases. She would figure it out eventually, of that she had no doubt. The man was simply too spectacular to be entirely forgotten.

"I'm fine, really," she said. "I think my senses are just a little heightened after what happened." That had to be why she was reacting so strongly to everything—the moonlight, his mouth, his broad, powerful body, and his *heat*.

"Completely understandable." He frowned. "You know, this isn't a great area to walk alone at night."

"I figured that out. It looked okay when I arrived this afternoon. I didn't realize how it would be once the businesses closed."

"Common mistake all over LA."

"First lesson learned."

"You're new here?"

She nodded. "As of yesterday."

He barked a laugh. "Welcome to the City of Angels, Evie Fleming."

"If he's a part of the welcoming committee, I prefer to skip the muffins and the glad-to-have-you-in-the-neighborhood basket." She managed a tiny smile. "I don't think I can handle any more of that kind of hospitality."

"Sorry about that. It's not a bad place. Like any big city, you just have to be aware of your surroundings."

"Understood. Honestly, I hadn't planned to be out this late—I lost track of time visiting the Cecil."

"*Oh.*"

Evie heard a tone, an unmistakably judgy one. "What?"

"Nothing," he said. He glanced over at the mugger to make sure he still wasn't moving, but still addressed her. "You're a horror fan, huh?"

"No, actually, I'm a murder fan."

He jerked his head back. "Excuse me?"

Seeing the way he gaped, she hesitated. Not many people understood her chosen profession. Her parents certainly didn't. They'd been happy having her work the local beat on a small Virginia paper, in a small Virginia town, reporting on bake sales and teen vandalism. They hated that she now immersed herself in violent crime, and especially hated that she sometimes interacted with violent killers. If they knew what she intended to do during this research stint in LA, they would lose their minds. Which was why she hadn't told them.

Lightning doesn't strike twice.

She couldn't possibly be repeating history by stumbling across a nearly invisible trail left by a serial killer. One nobody else in the world even realized existed. How could one person, a simple crime writer, come across two cases like that in her lifetime? No, it just wasn't possible.

And yet. Yeah. And yet.

She had questions, she saw connections, and while she was here in Southern California working on her contracted book, why couldn't she do just a little bit of snooping into this other matter?

Twelve women, their murders spread out over the last fifteen years, the crimes unsolved. Different jurisdictions played hell with investigations here in the sprawling Los Angeles area, and the crimes didn't leap out as being connected.

Maybe they aren't.

Maybe not. But maybe they were.

The cop who'd saved her stepped closer. "You sure you're okay, murder fan?"

Realizing she'd gone deep into her brain, she nodded quickly, and the arrival of a patrol car saved her from having to explain. The two police officers inside got out and hailed her rescuer, one calling him Detective Winchester. A crime scene investigator showed up ninety seconds later.

While the detective explained what had happened, Evie took a moment to look around on the sidewalk and found her phone. The screen was cracked, but the phone was still on, and she could see some of what was displayed.

Right away she noticed she had more than twenty text messages.

"Crap," she muttered, and she opened them, seeing a long string of "What's going on?" type questions from Candace Oakley, her agent and good friend.

Going back through the stream, she soon realized why. Candace had been the last person she had texted this evening as she left the hotel…and was the one who received the weird picture Evie had taken a short time later.

"Not bad," she murmured when she saw her own efforts hadn't been entirely in vain. She'd caught a digital image of her attacker looming out of the darkness, his face not clear, but possibly recognizable. She supposed there was some comfort knowing she might have helped solve her own murder if she'd had her throat slit in that back alley.

Enough, Evie, she thought, even while wondering what it would be like to have a normal job that didn't have her seeing psychopaths, sociopaths, and sheer monsters around every corner.

Then again, she had known psychopaths, sociopaths and monsters, and the guy who'd just attacked her could be one of them. Job or no job.

"The officers are going to take him in and book him. The crime scene guy wants to talk to you and will probably want to take some scrapings from under your fingernails. Judging by the marks on his hands, you scratched the guy, right?"

She nodded. "Can we can do it here rather than going in to the station?"

He hesitated, then slowly nodded. "I can probably arrange that, if you don't mind somebody looking you over right here on the street."

"Honestly, I'd prefer that than being paraded through a police station right now."

"It's usually done in a hospital. But since he didn't get any further than a grab, and you say you're fine, I've already convinced him that's not necessary."

That was a relief.

"But you will have to go in tomorrow."

"I have an appointment at Headquarters in the morning anyway."

The LAPD captain she'd met with today had been very gruff. He didn't know who she was or what she did and had resisted when she'd asked for specific old case files and reports. She was supposed to go back in the morning and hoped that with some pressure from her agent and publisher, she'd get the all-clear.

"Okay, then."

"Give me a second to send this message and then the guy can scrape away."

His brow went up and his mouth tightened. Figuring he thought she was some flighty social media type who was posting about her near-miss, Evie swung the phone around so he could see the image.

He leaned close, staring at the picture on the cracked screen. "Is that…"

"Yes," she said. "When I realized he was following me, I snapped a picture and sent it to a friend."

This time when his brow went up, he managed a small, lopsided smile. Good Lord, the man had a nice smile to go along with his oh-so-nice face.

"Very good thinking."

"Thanks. But the friend I texted it to is in panic/meltdown mode."

"Let her know you're okay, and then you can answer some questions. You're also going to have to turn over that phone."

"Of course."

She had a digital image of the man just before he attacked her. More solid evidence that would be used to put him away, she had no doubt.

She sent Candace a quick text that all was well, she was fine, and she would be in touch later. No way was Evie going to tell her that she had been attacked; the phone would ring a split second later, and she'd never get off the call. Candace had moved to California from New York when she married the owner of a talent agency two years ago. She was pretty jaded when it came to street crime. But even she would freak out if she found out somebody had tried to drag Evie into an alley.

After a couple of quick follow-up texts, she handed over the phone and allowed the crime scene analyst to do his job. While he studied her hands, her scrapes, and her clothing, she answered the questions posed by the responding cops. The detective who'd tackled the mugger—Winchester—filled in some blanks too. One thing she noticed: The other cops were deferential to him. Since he'd said he didn't work at their location, he must have a wide reputation.

As one officer put the suspect into the back of the patrol car, the other said, "Right place right time, huh, Cop Hollywood?"

Her incredibly sexy savior shot back, "Bite me, Bingham."

The other cop laughed. "You gonna make sure she gets safely to her car?"

"Yeah."

Evie hadn't really thought about that—about being alone with this man again or about walking into that parking garage. She'd assumed she would be fine now. What were the chances she would run into two predators in one night?

Tell that to the Beachside Butcher's last victim, who escaped captivity from her abusive boyfriend and landed in the hands of a serial killer.

One bad thing about Evie's line of work—she was an expert on brutal murder, and she had a damn good memory. Random tidbits of horror often popped into her mind without warning.

She only hoped she remembered who this Winchester guy was soon, because it was starting to drive her a little crazy.

"Where are you parked?" he asked.

She pointed to the garage.

"Come on, I'll walk you to your car," the dark-haired detective said. "Before you refuse, it's really no trouble, and I'd prefer to do it."

"I wasn't going to refuse, Detective Winchester." She didn't mention the Beachside Butcher. Some people were a little squicked out by her encyclopedic knowledge of murder. Given the way he'd reacted when she said she'd been at the Cecil, he could be one of them.

"Sensible."

"Actually, yes, I usually am, despite what you might think given what happened tonight."

As they stepped off the curb into the street, he put a hand on her arm. The touch was supportive, as if he feared she might still be shaky from what had happened, and there was nothing terribly intimate about it. Still, even through the leather of his jacket, which she was still wearing, she felt the strength of his fingers and the warm cup of his palm against her elbow.

"I'm sorry, I didn't mean to imply you were careless. You just didn't know."

"Hmm."

"What?" he asked.

"I caught a tone."

"I don't recall throwing one," he said. She thought his mouth quirked a bit.

"You did before. When I mentioned the Cecil."

They reached the garage and entered through the access door next to the ramp. No one was inside the stairwell, but it was full nonetheless. Full of garbage, dust, broken glass, dampness, and shadows. Her heart pounded. Despite the capable man at her side, she wanted to swing around and go right back out.

"Look, no offense, but ever since the TV show came out about that place, it's been a magnet for lookie-loos and thrill seekers," he said as the door swung shut behind them. He either hadn't noticed her sudden fear, or he was trying to distract her with normal conversation. "Which one are you?"

"I'm neither."

They began to ascend the stairs, shoes tapping on concrete, him still holding her arm. She probably could have managed with just the handrail—gross and germy as it probably was—but something about that completely innocent, yet somehow intimate, touch made her decide not to shrug him off. Evie had never felt like the type who needed anyone's protection, so the desire to stay close to him caught her off guard. Maybe it was because of the quiet. Or the smell. The dirty, rust-colored stains on the cement drew her eye, and the pitted handrail scraped against her fingertips. Smutty graffiti competed with smeary stains to cover the walls.

Evie's footsteps slowed. She was breathing heavier, despite being in good enough shape to take a few flights of steps without a gasp. And she was suddenly having trouble hearing—there was an echo in her ears, a pounding in her head.

"So why the interest in the place?" he asked, still focused on the hotel.

She swallowed, trying to find her voice. "It's research…for my job."

Even in the low lighting, she saw his mouth twitch. "Serial killer?"

"Not yet." Even to her own ears, the quip sounded weak and forced.

He glanced up and down the deserted stairwell. "Good thing for me."

"I think you could hold your own." But following his stare, seeing all those hollows of shadow and secrecy, she wondered if *she* could have.

Her stomach churned as she realized something. If she hadn't noticed the man following her, she might actually have been in here when the attacker had launched. No way would anyone have come to her rescue. The stairwell was tall and cement block-walled. Probably soundproof. She could have been dragged under the bottom-floor stairwell and...

Just envisioning it, she stumbled a tiny bit.

He immediately slid an arm around her waist and steadied her, pressing against her side as they reached the first landing. He was preventing her from taking a nasty fall, only that, but there was no doubt all her senses tingled at the contact of his hard, broad body against her own. It was almost enough to distract her from the dizziness in her head and the churning of her stomach, neither of which were dizzying or churning in a *good* way.

They were bad. All bad.

"You okay?" His deep voice held concern.

All light conversation was gone; he had noticed her tension. She sensed he had been aware of it all along, and the casual talk had been a mere cover as he waited for...something.

She nodded, swallowing hard, confused as hell about all the crazy signals her body was sending her. Her brain ordered her to remain calm, but every other part of her was on high alert.

Finally, her brain was too.

I was attacked.

Yes. She had been. She had just been assaulted, on a public street, in the late evening, by someone who'd intended to hurt her very badly. If not for this man's arrival, she couldn't even imagine what she would be going through right now. Or if she would even be alive to go through it.

"Oh God," she groaned.

"Don't picture it."

Swinging her gaze up to his, she saw the concern in his face. "What?"

"Don't let yourself imagine what might have happened. It *didn't.*"

Forcing a shaky laugh, she replied, "I am, unfortunately, pretty good at picturing things."

Dark things. Ugly things. Violent things. She had movies playing in her mind almost all the time, especially when she was working on an in-depth examination of a killer and his or her crimes. Police departments and the FBI gave her access to evidence deemed too violent and gruesome for public consumption. The stuff was nightmare-inducing, though she'd rarely suffered from nightmares.

Tonight, she just might.

Then there was tomorrow. And all the tomorrows laid out before her while she stayed in this city, writing her new book.

Intentionally or not, the research into the seediest, most brutal underbelly of Los Angeles had begun tonight…with her being dragged toward an alley by a strong attacker. It had set a dark pall over the work she was about to begin. For the first time since she'd proposed the new book to her publisher, she let herself acknowledge it was going to be more brutal than anything she'd done before.

Because it wasn't just one monster's crimes she would be focusing on.

It was many. So, so many.

She would soon immerse herself in a world populated by the dead, who'd lived their worst nightmares in the final moments of their lives. People victimized by single killers, by duos, by cults. Killers with catchy names the press so enjoyed: the Night Stalker, the Hillside Stranglers, the Grim Sleeper, the Lonely Hearts Killers. And some whose last name could conjure terror across the world: *Manson*.

She needed to be in complete control—dispassionate and unafraid—for what she was about to tackle. Not a near-victim.

That, however, wasn't going to be easy after tonight. Evie didn't know what her attacker had had in mind, but her darkest mental wanderings were certain to offer some possibilities.

Her shaking intensified. It started in her legs, and only her stiff leather boots kept her ankles from wobbling. Her knees did, though, practically knocking together, and then shudders rolled up her body. From out of nowhere, a thick lump of something jammed itself in her throat, suffocating her. Her teeth chattered, her eyes watered, and her stomach churned.

"There it is," he whispered.

Evie didn't understand his words. Besides, she wasn't hearing well, seeing clearly, reasoning at all. She couldn't breathe. Couldn't fill her lungs, couldn't draw air down her throat. She was spinning, reeling, tumbling into a truth she'd managed to hold back for an hour.

He caught her. "It's okay, honey. I've got you. You're safe."

She didn't so much fall as collapse against his body, all of her strength—physical and mental—gone.

He wrapped strong arms around her and held her close against his chest, one hand going to the back of her head to gently cup it as she buried her face in the crook of his neck.

Every drop of bravado and adrenaline had seeped out of her like a squeezed sponge. Energy and excitement had been holding her upright, and all of those things were gone now as reality filled every cell in her body. The could-have-beens lived in her imagination and chased away reason until all that remained was a weak, quivering, breathless, nauseous near-victim.

As tears burst from her eyes and sobs from her throat, she could only think about how very much she owed to this strong, handsome stranger, holding her so protectively in the night.

Chapter 2

Rowan Winchester had been waiting for the dam holding back Evie Fleming's emotions to break. Considering most would-be crime victims fell apart almost immediately after the police were on scene and they knew they were safe, this one had held herself together for a remarkably long time.

Now reality had set in. That reality had blasted down her defensive walls, leaving her exposed to the fear, rage, and helplessness her attack had almost certainly inspired.

"You're okay," he murmured, stroking the very pretty woman's fine blond hair as she cried away her tension and her fear. "You're going to be fine."

Although her arms weren't wrapped around him, she was leaning against him hard enough that he knew he was supporting her weight. Were he not here, she'd probably have collapsed onto the filthy concrete landing.

Of course, had he never been here at all tonight, he didn't even want to think about where she might be right now.

Had they been close enough to a bench or a car, he would

have lifted her onto a seat and held her on his lap like a kid, but they were stuck inside what must feel like a tomb to her. It was the worst place she could be. He kicked himself for not keeping her outside, where she wouldn't see corners where someone could be lurking and where the smell of sweat and desperation wouldn't have tinged every breath.

"Let's get out of here and have a cup of coffee," he said, not wanting to take her any higher up this stairwell that reeked of urine and vomit. "You shouldn't be driving tonight, anyway. You can come back for your car tomorrow when it's daylight and you're feeling a little better."

He didn't wait for her assent. Feeling the boneless way she still sagged against him and the wetness on his shirt, he made the decision for her. Bending down, he picked her up behind the knees and pulled her into his arms.

She jerked her head up, her startlingly blue eyes wide. "What are you..."

"Coffee. Fresh air. In the reverse order."

To his surprise, she didn't argue. She had enough sense to know she had to get out of this place pronto and probably also knew she'd fall on her cute ass if she tried to walk down on her own.

Being slim and of average height, she was easy to carry down a single flight of stairs. Hell, he'd carried heavier gear during training exercises. And she was a lot more pleasant—soft and smelling of cinnamony cookies.

Reaching the bottom level, he turned and pushed the exit door open with his hip to bring her right outside into the moonlit night. Los Angeles wasn't exactly the fresh air capital of the world, but it seemed like a tropical paradise compared to the miasma inside that stairwell.

Feeling her relax as she drew in deep breaths, Rowan lowered her to the sidewalk. He kept a steadying hand on her shoulder. "Better?"

She nodded slowly. Keeping her eyes closed, she brought herself back under control, one deep inhalation after another. Finally she whispered, "Was that an anxiety attack?"

"I suspect so."

"Me too." She rubbed her face with her hands, and then dropped them and finally looked up at him. "I've never had one before."

"I think you were entitled."

"I felt like I was being suffocated and having a heart attack."

"It happens even to people who *haven't* just escaped from a thug."

She winced. He kicked himself for bringing that guy up again. "Keep on breathing deeply," he reminded her, squeezing her shoulder. "You're doing fine."

"Getting there, anyway."

They fell silent for another minute, and he watched as she drew her focus inward, making herself come to grips with what had happened. Rowan wondered if she had any idea it would take a long time before she'd really be able to do that. What had just happened was the first step, but it wouldn't be the last one. He'd dealt with enough trauma in his own life to know that. And not just on the job.

Not moving far, he did edge back a little when he realized she was getting steadier on her feet. Right now, all her cylinders were sparking in every direction. As calmness came back in, though, she might realize she didn't want a strange man standing so close to her. He'd seen that reaction before in victims. So while he kept a light grip on her shoulder to keep her from falling, he also gradually inched away. Once she appeared completely still and straight, he dropped his hand and gave her even more room.

She remained where she was, still concentrating, and he watched her. Not for the first time, he found himself acknowledging just how attractive the woman was. He'd of course noted the just-below-the-shoulder-length hair the color of creamy coffee—dark blond with streaks of gold, amber, and brown. And of course those blue eyes. Now he studied the tear-stained oval face. Though it was cast in shadow, he'd already noticed the high cheekbones, the arched brows, the slim nose, and the pretty mouth.

He also noticed rough scratches and red marks that would become bruises tomorrow. Splotchy circles where ruthless fingers had dug in stood out on the soft skin of her jaw and throat.

Fuck. He wished he'd crammed that guy's head into a sewer drain. And then thrown the rest of him in after it.

With a low, deep sigh, she shrugged her shoulders and tilted her neck from side to side, stretching to release her tension and the last of her fear.

"*There* you are, Evie Fleming," he said, knowing she was past the anxiety attack and had regained her calmness.

"Here I am." She looked around, up the block and down it. Nobody was around, any onlookers interested in the police lights having gone about their business. "I owe you another thank-you for getting me out of there. I guess I wasn't really ready for enclosed spaces yet."

"No problem. I should have realized it sooner, after what happened."

"I don't think I was the only casualty tonight," she said,

looking up at him. Lifting a hand, she scraped the tip of her finger on his cheek, rubbing something away. "You're dirty, and that creep apparently got in one good punch."

"My cat punches me harder than that when I don't feed him on time."

She smiled a little. Not much, but it was something.

"So. Coffee?" he asked.

She nibbled a corner of her lip. "You know, I think I just want to go home, take a hot shower, and get into bed."

The images of a hot, wet woman and a bed quickly filled his mind, but he called himself an asshole and forced them away. Sexy as she might be, she had been through hell. Only a total prick would let the thought of soaping every inch of this woman's sweet body interfere with his need to help her.

"If you don't mind waiting with me, I'll call for a ride."

"No way," he said. "I'm taking you home."

"You really don't have to do that, Detective."

"I know I don't. But I'm doing it anyway."

He knew she wanted to argue—the flare of those midnight blue eyes revealed that. Again, though, her common sense outweighed any embarrassment. "I'd really appreciate that."

"It's not a problem. Protect and serve and all that."

"Well, you definitely protected and served tonight. I'm the one who will buy you a coffee…but not now."

"I'll hold you to that." And he would. Although his protective instincts demanded that he remain just a caretaker for now, he'd definitely like to see her again under better circumstances.

"I'll hold you to holding me to it," she said with the faintest of smiles.

He nodded, wanting to fist-pump the air with the knowledge of what that meant. She was interested. She was scared, tired, messed up, but she was also as interested in him as he was in her.

"You ready to go?" he asked, knowing that, attracted or not, the primary issue was getting her somewhere where she felt safe, warm, and comfortable.

"More than ready."

"I'm parked right down there."

Not taking her arm—initiating no more contact that might set her off again—he led her across the street. But before they'd gotten close to his car, which he'd parked so quickly it was almost on the sidewalk, another vehicle swung around the corner. It was coming fast, and he instinctively pushed her behind him.

"Where are they going in such a hurry?" he snapped when he realized the vehicle was a van from one of the local news stations.

Things became stranger when the van stopped, the side door slid open, and a woman holding a microphone hopped down. "Do you have any comment on tonight's attack? Was anyone injured?"

"Are you kidding me?" Evie groaned.

That was a good question, and Rowan wondered about it too. Muggings happened in LA all the time. How would a news team find out so quickly, and why on earth would they want to cover what was just another random act of interrupted violence in a city filled with them?

"No comment," he said. "Don't you have anything better to report on?"

The reporter wasn't deterred. "Is the suspect in custody?"

"I don't know what you're looking for, but there's nothing to see here. Excitement over." Noting the shock on Evie's face, he led her past the reporter, and a cameraman who'd followed her out of the van.

"Miss Fleming, do you have any idea why someone would target you?"

Rowan opened the passenger door of his unmarked sedan and ushered her inside, barely hearing the reporter.

"Do you think this has anything to do with the Joe Henry Angstrom case?"

Angstrom? What the fuck? "I told you, no comment," he snapped as the reporter tried to knock on the window of his car. "Now get that van out of the way before I cite you for reckless driving and illegal parking."

A veteran LA reporter probably would only have banged harder on the window. This one was young, fresh-faced, and not yet ready to take on a cop.

She stepped back as he walked around the car but didn't give up entirely. "Officer, can you give us any details at all? Do you know if Miss Fleming was a random victim or if this was a targeted assault?"

"How many times can I say 'no comment' in one conversation?"

His curiosity growing along with his annoyance, Rowan waved the woman off, got in the car, and jammed the key into the ignition. He was careful maneuvering around the newspeople but hit the gas hard once he had a clear path down the street.

"What the hell was that all about?" he asked once the van was in his rearview. His passenger huddled in her seat, his coat wrapped tightly around her. Rowan jabbed at the heater to warm up the car. "Are you famous or something?"

"No. Not really."

Meaning what? He racked his brain, trying to figure out if he'd ever heard her name before. It was pretty distinct and sounded a little made up. Not that he'd ever judge anybody for that—hell, his name was as fake as the Gucci bags peddled in Santee Alley. When his late mother had dragged him and his brothers to Hollywood after she'd divorced his father, she'd had their names changed to suit their big, bright, movie-star future.

Rowan had realized at a young age that he didn't want to be a superstar. His twin brother, Reece, and their sister, Rachel, had been the ones meant for the limelight. Rowan hadn't been sorry to leave that world behind and had thought about changing his name back. Unfortunately, George Franklin Winchester just wasn't a name he wanted to reembrace. So Rowan it remained. His brothers had done the same—Reece because he'd reentered the business. Younger brother Raine—whose given name was worst of all—just hadn't cared either way. And, of course, Rachel had died.

"Thank you for getting me out of there," she said softly, pulling him out of his thoughts. "I can't imagine how they found out so quickly."

"Well, you must have some element of fame. Somebody drawn by the police lights obviously recognized you and called it in."

She shrugged and looked out the window. "I'm just a writer."

"A famous one?"

Another shrug. So she was famous. Not being much of a reader, beyond the occasional police procedural, he supposed it was no wonder he hadn't heard of her.

"Kid's books?"

She jerked her head around and glared. "Why do men automatically assume a young female author writes children's books? I happen to write nonfiction."

Whoops. He had stepped in it there and realized he had definitely made a shitty assumption. "Sorry. My bad." He frowned. "I haven't heard of many nonfiction writers who are stalked by paparazzi."

She reached over and jacked up the heat. It was warm in the car, but he supposed after her evening, she was fighting off a chill that wasn't weather-related.

"They're making a movie of one of my books," she admitted. Clearing her throat, she added, "And talking about a TV show."

He nodded. That made sense. In this town, anybody who got a sniff of a new project always wanted to hover around the makers and the influencers. A nonfiction writer might not have a whole lot of input on any project made from her work, but it was possible she had some voice in casting. So he'd bet the hungry actors' agents who swam like sharks in Hollywood already had an eye on her. As, he would bet, did the movie-biz shows, tabloids, and websites.

Evie Fleming would be an especially attractive subject for them to cover. She was, after all, beautiful. Not just pretty, as he'd thought in that stairwell when she'd been shaking and looking ready to puke. But pretty damned stunning, in a brainy-sexy way. She would be entitled to attention for that alone. Add to it a movie and TV deal? The back-clawingly ambitious entertainment crowd was probably already trying to dig in their nails. Hence the media interest.

"What was that about Joe Henry Angstrom?" he asked, remembering what else the reporter had said. How Evie could be connected to an infamous serial killer who had terrorized the mid-Atlantic region a few years ago, he had no idea.

"I testified against him."

He jerked his head to look at her. "Seriously?"

She nodded.

"Holy shit. That must have been tough."

"It was." Her voice fell to a whisper. "His last victim was my roommate."

He sucked in a breath, remembering more details. Angstrom was one monstrous sonofabitch. He couldn't imagine how she lived with the knowledge of what her friend had probably gone through. "I'm so sorry."

"Me too. We had just finished college and were living in an apartment in Richmond. Angstrom owned an auto repair shop close to our place."

Right, mechanic. "I remember this—he used to copy house keys when people left their cars to be worked on."

Handing your whole key ring to someone who also had access to your car registration—with your home address printed right on it—wasn't wise. But it happened more than most people realized.

She sniffed. "Yes. That's how he got into our place. She was home alone."

He didn't want to think about what would have happened if she hadn't been. It was tragic about her roommate; Evie's presence, however, almost certainly wouldn't have stopped that murder from happening. It would just have meant two victims.

"It was my fault," she added in a low whisper.

"Don't."

As if she hadn't heard him, she went on. "I had a flat tire.

I waited right there in the shop office while he fixed it. It just didn't occur to me that he would make a copy of my apartment key while I was sitting ten feet away. She died because I was stupid and careless."

"It was *not* your fault."

It wasn't, of course. It was the fault of a psychotic monster. And hell, even Rowan had probably left his whole key ring in the car when getting a super-quick tire change while he waited. Angstrom had been good at what he did, and obviously very fast at key molding.

More, though, her words made him realize something else.

Evie had probably been the intended target.

"If I hadn't been dumb enough to…"

"Don't," he urged. "Do not do that to yourself. It is not your fault; it's that sick bastard's."

"So said my shrink for a couple of years afterward."

He wasn't at all surprised she'd needed professional help. "And now?"

"Now… I suppose my rational side accepts that it wasn't my fault. The emotional side isn't so sure."

"Let me be sure for you," he insisted. "Perps count on victims blaming themselves a lot of the time, but it's nobody's fault but the killer's.

"I still miss her," she said. "I'll do whatever it takes to keep Angstrom in prison."

"Must've been hard testifying against him with him sitting right there in the courtroom. Bet that caused a few nightmares."

"And daymares. I had so hoped that phase of my life was over, but it keeps getting dragged back up."

Considering heartbreaking death had touched his own life,

and the reverberations of it seemed to go on for years, he understood that. Maybe it had been a suicide, but nobody *really* knew how his sister had plunged off that high-rise balcony so many years ago.

Then there was the unsolved murder of Harry Baker, his childhood movie agent. For years, Rowan and Reece had believed their baby brother Raine had killed the man because Baker had molested their sister. Finding out they'd been wrong had been a shock. Guilt about that, as well as their desperate need to know the truth, had driven all three of the brothers into the most private of investigations.

They intended to find out what had really happened that night six and a half years ago when somebody had shot Harry Baker dead in his living room. No matter what it took.

"So what is it you testified to, leaving your car there?"

"That was only part of it." Clearing her throat, she explained, "I got a little obsessive about her murder and did some sleuthing on my own."

"Wow. Ballsy."

"Not really. I wasn't out there Sherlock Holmes'ing the case. It was more about doing a lot of Internet research and realizing there had been similar murders in several states. Then I remembered the license plates hanging on the wall of Angstrom's repair shop and everything sort of clicked."

"License plates?"

"One from each state of a previous victim. His souvenirs. I know some people do decorate with those, but it seemed odd that there were only nine of them, too few for a real collector, but obviously important enough to be displayed. I noticed what states they were from and remembered one of the personalized tags."

"That was pretty stupid of him."

"Yes, it was. I did a little search when I got home. Imagine my surprise when the tag showed up in a police report about a South Carolina girl who'd been murdered two years prior."

The implication sank in. "Are you telling me you were the first to realize there was a serial killer operating on the East Coast, *and* you identified him?"

She shrugged. Answer enough.

"Impressive. Did that lead you to a career in law enforcement?" He shook his head, remembering what she'd said before. "No, of course, you're a writer."

"I was a fledgling journalist at the time. Junior Girl-Friday type thing. I just wasn't going to give up trying to find out what happened to my friend Blair and I had a knack for research."

Rowan was fascinated, shocked a young journalist had put together a puzzle that multiple law enforcement agencies had not. Thinking about the Angstrom case and what he had done to his victims, Rowan could only think the world was a better place because of Evie Fleming's research abilities.

"I guess I should give you my address," she said, changing the subject.

He suspected she had to do that a lot. People were never pushier than when wanting details about a gruesome crime; he ran into those types every day. No way would he become one of them.

"Yeah, you probably should," he said, realizing he'd been on autopilot and was heading for his brother's place in the hills. He'd been staying there for a couple of weeks and just took the route for granted.

She gave him the address, and he frowned. She didn't live in a bad place, but it was in an older, beachside neighborhood.

There weren't a lot of security fences or gates, as there were in most upscale communities. That area was trendy, with crowds of partiers even on weeknights. Probably not the best atmosphere for a woman who had been attacked, and then had a microphone shoved in her face by a reporter. He only hoped they hadn't tracked down her address yet.

"What's the matter?" she asked. "Is there something wrong with that street?"

"No, it's not like downtown. Don't worry about that."

"So what *are* you worrying about?"

"Nothing." He shook off his concerns. There was no reason to think the mugging had been anything but a random crime of opportunity. And the news van was far behind them. "Forget it, I'm overanalyzing. Everything will be okay."

He didn't realize they would *not* be okay until he reached an intersection at the end of her street and stopped before turning left. "Oh, shit," he muttered.

She leaned forward and peered around him, letting out a low sigh at the sight of two of those news vans.

"How much do I win if I bet they're parked in front of your place?" he asked.

"I'm not going to take that bet," she said, throwing herself back in the seat.

He didn't make the turn, going straight instead. "Is it always like this?"

"Absolutely not," she said, shaking her head. "I'm a nonentity, seriously. But since this Hollywood deal came along and I moved out here, it's put me in a fifteen-minutes-of-fame spotlight." She fisted her hands in her lap, drawing his attention to her long fingers and trimmed, no-nonsense nails. A writer's hands.

Of course, he'd noticed those palms before they'd gotten into the car. They were scratched and scraped, and one of those nails was torn. He didn't imagine she'd be in any condition to type tomorrow.

He suddenly remembered something he'd heard in passing on the news a few days ago. "There's another reason you're in the spotlight, isn't there? Angstrom…his appeal has progressed a step, right?"

"Yeah. And if he gets a new trial…"

"You'll have to testify again."

"Exactly."

The situation wasn't unusual in today's legal system, with murderers and lawyers dragging appeals through the courts for years—or decades. Families and witnesses had to hold their breath, not sure if the torment would ever end.

Sure, everybody deserved a fair trial. The possibility of an innocent person being imprisoned or even executed for a crime he or she didn't commit made exhaustive appeals necessary. But Angstrom? They'd found a fucking slaughterhouse in his basement. If he recalled correctly, this latest appeal was on a technicality over a legal filing, not because the sonofabitch could be innocent.

Evie would have to be dragged back into the world of a deranged monster, not only as a random witness or journalist, but also as the friend of a victim. Christ, no wonder the media was on her trail. She had the whole Hollywood thing going on and was connected to the most brutal serial killer caught this decade.

"I wonder how long they'll stake me out."

Honestly? Probably until every one of Angstrom's legal options were exhausted and he took his place in the last chair in which he would ever sit.

"Depends on how slow a news night it is."

She rubbed a weary hand over her eyes. "God, I'm tired."

"What about a hotel?"

"Looking like this?"

Idling at a red light several blocks from her place, he glanced at her dirty, rumpled clothes. Her hair was tangled—twisted by a brutal hand. A red scrape and the beginnings of a yellowish bruise marred her jaw, and flecks of dried blood stood out against the pale skin. That alone made Rowan want to go back, find her attacker, and beat the shit out of him.

"Yeah, I suspected that's what I look like," she said, reading his expression.

"Sorry. You're beautiful, but you do look like you've been in a street fight."

When she sucked her lip into her mouth and looked down at her hands, he realized he shouldn't have made the beautiful remark. It wasn't exactly cop-and-victim appropriate. Then again, she had essentially agreed to a future coffee date.

Her throat worked as she swallowed hard before mumbling, "I guess that's fair, since I *was* in a street fight."

"I saw as I drove up. You handled that really well, fighting back and trying to get free. It could have been bad if he'd gotten you into that alley."

"And if you hadn't come along."

He didn't like the thought.

"Think if we go for that cup of coffee they'll be gone when we get back?"

"Probably not. I don't suppose you have any family in the area you could stay with?" Knowing she was a new resident, he seriously doubted it.

"No."

"What about the friend you texted?"

She nodded slowly. "I guess that's possible. But her new husband…"

Rowan's hands tightened on the steering wheel. "Bad guy?"

"Not really. Just a very ambitious one. She's my publishing agent, and he's my Hollywood one. He's always got an eye on deal making, and I suspect he'd love to use tonight's incident to get more media attention."

Just what she would not want. "Is he, uh, ambitious enough that he'd have tipped off the press about what happened? Or even shared your address?"

Evie started to shake her head, but slowly stopped moving. "He wouldn't have. He *couldn't* have."

"You sure about that? This town can bring out the worst in people."

"Can I borrow your phone?" she asked.

He nodded and pointed toward the center console. She took it, tapped some buttons, and then waited. In the dark interior of the car, he saw the screen darken and then, almost immediately, flash to life again.

"She swears it wasn't him," she said.

Huh. Maybe. "Do you believe her?"

"Of course I believe *her*."

Catching the inflection, he knew what he meant. But he didn't push it. Her opinion of her friend's husband was none of his business, though if he'd ratted her out to the press to gain some publicity, Rowan already couldn't stand the guy.

Thinking about her predicament a little more, he came up with another solution. He just had to word it in a way that didn't sound creepy.

"Look, I have a place you can stay for the night. My brother and his girlfriend are out of town and I've been house-sitting for them."

The light changed and he drove forward, thinking about the idea and liking it more and more. The house Reece had rented while his fire-damaged one was being rebuilt was entirely secure. That would probably make Evie feel better after tonight's experience.

"You want to take me home like a stray puppy?"

He laughed softly. "I don't think Cecil B would like that."

"Who?"

"My brother's dog."

"Cecil B…DeMille?"

"Of course."

"That's a Hollywood dog's name if I've ever heard one."

"He's the main reason I'm house-sitting. You're not allergic to dogs, are you? He's a slobbery golden retriever."

"No allergies."

"Perfect. The house is in the hills. It's gated and has security cameras everywhere. You'll be totally safe."

"Sounds that way. But, uh…"

Hearing her concern, he quickly explained. "You can have the place to yourself. I'll drop you off and go back to my own apartment to sleep. That is, as long as you don't mind letting C.B. out while I'm gone?"

"Of course I don't mind. But I can't ask you to do that."

"Believe me, I would enjoy a night in my own bed. There's only so much Hollywood Hills luxury my cop lifestyle can handle."

She laughed softly.

"Besides, Jagger would probably like a night away from the dog."

"Jagger?"

"My cat."

"You weren't kidding about the cat?"

"Nope. And he's an unfriendly terror. He's had about enough canine as he can stand. That's why I didn't just bring C.B. to my apartment while my brother's out of town. It's too small for them to retreat to their separate corners."

"Won't your brother and his girlfriend mind having a stranger in their home?"

"No. It's a furnished rental. His place in town is being rebuilt after a fire." He didn't want to get into specifics by mentioning the word *arson*—or, well, if Steve Baker's last words were to be believed *accidental* arson. "There's not a lot of personal stuff at the rental. I know they wouldn't mind."

"I don't know…maybe a hotel would be best."

"Sure, so a clerk can snap a picture and sell it to the tabloids?"

"I'm not that famous."

"In this town, it doesn't matter." Glancing over, he saw her nibbling on her lip and read her indecision. "Believe me, it's not a problem, but if it makes you feel better, I'll call my brother to be sure."

After a brief hesitation, she nodded. "Okay. I would feel better if you did."

No cop would use a cell phone while driving, and he was no exception. So he barked a familiar number into his Bluetooth. His brother answered almost immediately, his voice sharp and hard through the car's speakers.

"What's wrong? Is it Dad?"

Suddenly remembering the three-hour time difference, Rowan answered, "Sorry, dude, not an emergency."

His brother's low sigh held both relief and a hint of irritation. "Then why are you calling me in the middle of the night?"

Rowan quickly ran down the situation, trying to be succinct and careful considering Evie could hear every word being said. He didn't want her to feel more like a stray dog than before.

"Of course she can stay at the house." After a brief murmur in the background, Reece added, "Jess said to tell her to feel free to use or wear anything she needs."

The response didn't surprise Rowan at all. Reece might have been described as self-protective—even cold—a year ago. Since falling for Jessica Jensen, a sexy, sassy redhead, however, his icy walls had been blown all to hell. She had him eating out of her hand, and the rest of the family couldn't be happier about that.

Ending the call with a promise to get together when Reece and Jess returned to California in a week, he glanced at Evie and said, "Okay?"

"Just like that?" she asked, her eyes wide. "They're really fine about you bringing a complete stranger to their house and letting her stay there?"

"You heard him."

"I don't know whether that says more about your brother or about you."

"Meaning?"

"Meaning either he's very trusting overall, or he has complete faith in *you*."

He barked a laugh, picturing his brother, the poster child for self-protective, reclusive Hollywood mogul, being overly trusting. Reece might have been named the *Sexiest Man Alive* a few years ago, but more than one starlet also privately called him the biggest asshole alive. He'd been an immovable mountain of cool calculation…until Jessica.

"Of course he has faith in me. We're twins."

"Oh my God, there are *two* of you walking the streets?" She immediately gasped and put a hand to her mouth, as if angry at herself for having made that remark, which was when he realized she was paying him a compliment.

He hid his amusement. "Fraternal. *Some* people actually think he's the good-looking one. Can you believe it?"

He might have heard the tiniest snort, but didn't push. He liked that she was actually relaxed enough—and no longer arguing about where she was going to be spending the night—to laugh about something.

But as he watched her, seeing the dashboard lights make art out of her profile, watching her stretch to make herself more comfortable, noticing the soft curves of her body as she settled back for the ride, Rowan realized he might have made a mistake. A big mistake. And not just professionally.

He had invited a crime victim to come home with him. Worse, she wasn't just a crime victim; she was a woman to whom he was incredibly attracted.

Maybe a hotel would have been a better idea.

Maybe he should take her out for coffee and then try to go back to her house in an hour.

Maybe they should have tried going over a neighbor's fence into her yard.

Maybe…anything.

Anything other than going home with a woman he most definitely could not take advantage of, but who he wanted more than he'd wanted anyone in a very long time.

* * *

Parked on Evie Fleming's street, one block down from her house, the dark-cloaked figure jerked awake with a curse, angry at himself for having drifted off. He quickly peered up the block to make sure the situation hadn't changed.

All was the same.

Three local news vans were parked in front of the small house, right where they'd been since he arrived. Had there been news to report, had they caught up with their quarry, they would have been gone by now, or else in the midst of shoving cameras into her face. So he almost certainly hadn't missed her, and didn't give himself too much of a hard time about falling asleep. Judging by the dashboard clock, it had only been for a couple of minutes.

He slunk back down in his seat, hiding in shadow, parked away from any streetlights for even more concealment. Other cars stood at the curb, so he didn't fear standing out, but it would be stupid to take a chance on being seen and remembered. His SUV was dark, nondescript, and dusty. And he'd taken the precaution of removing the license plate. Were he pulled over, he could always claim it was stolen. Anyway, it was worth taking the risk.

He just hadn't counted on the damn press.

"Assholes," he muttered, staring at the vans, willing them to just go away. But he knew they wouldn't. They were waiting for the same person he was—a snotty writer who needed to be taught to mind her own business. Or else to shut right the fuck up permanently.

"Where are you, nosy bitch?"

He began to wonder if she was going to come home at all.

Little pigeon was probably so scared after tonight's attack that she'd checked into a hotel. She would be afraid of things that went bump in the night for a while and probably on guard once she did get home, which made things a little harder for him.

Not that much harder, though. He could be very quiet when he wanted to be.

He would get to her. Sooner or later, he *would* get to her.

He reached for a cigarette, but decided against it. The tiny flare of a match might be enough to draw the attention of a neighbor looking out a window to see what the excitement on the street was all about.

Thinking about going home, figuring tonight was probably a bust, he realized there was another possibility.

"Did you sneak home, Ms. *New York Times* Bestseller?"

Had she gotten here before he or the press had arrived, and was she now playing possum inside her house, keeping the lights off and blinds closed?

Possible.

He could go check. It would be the easiest thing in the world to go over to the next street, creeping through lawns, over fences, until he reached hers. He could be in her place in ten minutes, easily finding her bedroom.

Easily finishing what that idiot downtown had started.

You just couldn't trust anybody these days. If you wanted anything done right, you had to do it yourself.

The more he thought about it, the more he liked the idea. He hated sitting here with his thumb up his ass, risking exposure just by staying still.

"Yeah, do it," he muttered, liking the idea of creeping into her home and silencing her when there were cameras and reporters set up right outside.

But not from here. There was no point risking it.

He started the engine and put the SUV in gear. Not turning on the headlights, he drove slowly toward the intersection and turned, going to the next block. Just as many cars parked on this side. Just as easy to blend in.

And much easier to go through a neighbor's yard so he could get into her house and end this once and for all.

Chapter 3

The drive back to his brother's place was silent. Evie had fallen asleep, her slow, steady exhalations the only sound in the car. He'd looked over too often, at least until they hit windy Laurel Canyon Road and he had to pay closer attention to his driving.

It hadn't helped, though. Every glance before that had reinforced what he already knew.

She was beautiful. She was smart. She was strong.

And he wanted her.

Dropping her off and going home, going home, going home.

When they arrived at the exterior gate and he stopped to enter the code to open it, she yawned, sat up straight, and looked around. As everyone who went up the driveway did, she gasped when they hit the sharp curve in the driveway that appeared to miss a deadly-steep drop-off by mere inches.

"Wow, nice view," she mumbled.

He shrugged. "Too close to the cliff for my taste. I was

worried during the mudslides over the summer. A place a mile away slid right down into the canyon."

"Scary."

"Yeah. I'll be glad when their house is finished and they move back in there. It's closer…and no cliffs."

Just childhood "friends" with grudges who liked to throw alcohol around and then light a match.

Let it go. Steve Baker had plunged into the canyon as ruthlessly as that house up the street had. With equally deadly results. Whatever debts Steve owed had been paid by that plunge…so much like Rachel's all those years ago.

Not that she'd had any debts. At sixteen, she had barely started to live, even though her childhood had been cut short by Baker's sick, abusive father Harry.

As always, memories of Rachel—and Harry Baker—hit him like a club to the head. He had to force away the images that haunted him, knowing if he thought too much about them they'd revisit him in his darkest nightmares.

"Let me show you how to use the alarm, give you a quick tour of the place, and then I'll be outta your hair."

Once inside, he entered the code to shut off the alarm system, then showed her how to reengage it. With the animals inside, only the exterior motion sensors and window alarms were on, but she looked pleased to have that much security. Given what she had been through earlier tonight, he wasn't surprised.

Cecil B knew the drill and had been patiently waiting for Rowan to finish. As soon as he had, the dog bounded over to offer a slobbery greeting. Jagger, meanwhile, watched with paw-licking disdain from atop a nearby bookshelf.

"Wow. Your brother and his girlfriend must be pretty

successful," Evie said as she glanced around the airy, open common areas of the house.

With its high ceilings, tiled floors, upscale furniture, and a wall of windows looking down on the city and the Hollywood sign, the place was pretty impressive.

But Rowan wasn't into fancy furniture that was uncomfortable as hell to sit on. Nor, as he'd said, was he a big fan of heights; he rarely went out on the patio to enjoy the view. Whenever he came to visit and sat out on the patio with his brothers to smoke a cigar or drink a scotch, Rowan always chose a chair closest to the house. He didn't like looking over and seeing nothing but empty air and huge rocks below. Especially now that he knew firsthand what a body hitting those rocks really looked like.

Cecil B had finally noticed they had a visitor and went over to check out Evie. She stood calmly and quietly, letting him sniff her to determine if she was friend or foe. A lick of her hand soon gave the answer. That wasn't surprising considering golden retrievers in general—and Cecil B in particular—loved everyone. Standoffish, snooty Jagger would be the better guard dog...if he was a dog and could bark or growl. He did have a wicked hiss, though.

As if knowing he was being thought about and wanted to prove he was both omniscient and bipolar, the black cat leapt down from shelf onto an end table. He rubbed against Rowan's side, meowing loudly.

"Jagger, I presume?"

He stroked the cat behind the ears, not sure if he'd get a purr or a scratch. Jagger must be happy to have him home, or sick of having just a dog for company, because he wound around Rowan's hand, his body rumbling in satisfaction.

"You said he was a monster cat," Evie said, her tone accusing.

To make Rowan look like more of a liar, Jagger sauntered over to their guest and rubbed against Evie's arm, demanding attention.

"Crazy feline," Rowan muttered.

"He's a sweetheart," she insisted, bending over and scratching the animal's back. When Jagger grew restless, his fur hackling a bit, Evie dropped her hand and stepped away, realizing he'd had enough attention.

Good with animals. Something else to add to the *why-I-want-her* list.

He quickly fed the dog and the cat, and then led Evie to the guest room where she'd be sleeping tonight. Pushing open the door and flicking on the light, he waited until she went in and then told her where to find the bathroom.

"How many bedrooms are there?"

"Three."

"Then why do you have to go home?" She turned around to face him. "Seriously, you don't have to drive all the way back to your apartment. I was assuming you offered because the place was a one bedroom."

"Aren't you uncomfortable sharing a house with a strange man? Especially after what happened downtown?"

"You'd think that, wouldn't you?" She slowly shook her head. "But for some reason, I don't think of you as a stranger. And I trust you, especially given the way you saved me more than once tonight." She ticked off her fingers, one by one. "You stopped my attacker, you carried me out of that stairwell, you got rid of the paparazzi, you enabled me to avoid going home, and you are giving me a place to spend the night."

All five fingers spread, she lifted her other hand and ticked off one more point. "And those animals really like you, definitely a point in your favor."

"They like you too."

"So I guess that's a point in mine?"

"Yeah," he said, smiling down at her.

Here in the bright interior light, he got a better look at her perfectly shaped face, her full lips…and the bruise on her jaw that was darkening by the second.

He put his fingertips on the bottom of her chin and lifted her face to examine it more closely. He held her gently, not wanting to add any more fingerprint-shaped marks to her beautiful skin, like the ones that marred her neck and throat.

"I should've broken his hands," he muttered.

She stared up at him, those big eyes bluer than the Pacific on a calm day, and licked her lips. A hint of color flushed her cheeks, and her mouth opened a tiny bit as her breaths deepened. They stood close together, her soft body brushing against his in a few places. Not intimate places…but the touch was intimate just the same.

It was a cool night, but heat suddenly spiked through him, as if he'd been blasted by an open furnace. Rowan had noticed how attractive she was right away. Now, however, he was slammed in the chest by pure sexual need.

The peach-pie fragrance of her shampoo filled his head every time he inhaled. Color rose in her cheeks, and her throat trembled as she swallowed hard. He suspected she was just as affected by the sudden heat rising between them.

The urge to catch that soft mouth and kiss her until all her dark memories of tonight were obliterated nearly overpowered him.

So much for the hero.

Rowan dropped his hand, gritting his teeth to keep himself from cursing for being weak enough to even *consider* kissing her.

Evie Fleming had been attacked a few short hours ago. She was a victim in need of safety and security. Not a come-on from a guy she barely knew.

He stepped back and swiped a hand through his hair.

Evie swayed a little, as if her legs had grown a bit unsteady.

"Uh, you probably want a shower or a bath—"

Jesus, don't think about her naked, wet, pink, and so goddamned soft.

He jerked a thumb toward a closed door. "The master bedroom's right there. There's a big sunken tub with jets. Feel free to take advantage of it."

"Isn't that your room?"

He shook his head quickly. "No, I've been staying in the other guest room. Speaking of which, I oughta grab my stuff."

To leave. To go home. To remove himself from temptation.

"You're sure, Detective?"

Sure? Hell yes he was sure.

Hell no he wasn't sure.

His brain and his body just couldn't seem to come together to make that call.

One thing was certain, though: If he was this wound up about a stranger—a woman he was supposed to just be protecting—he needed to get out more. His recent assignment had played hell with his sex life, and it had obviously been far too long since he'd been laid.

Yeah, that was it. Being near any attractive woman would cause the same churning low in his gut and the tension shooting in waves throughout his body.

You are so full of shit.

His inner voice was both amused and disgusted. Maybe if he kept telling himself he was just an average guy who hadn't had sex in a few months—pretending it didn't have anything to do with her big blue eyes, that ashy-blond hair, the angel's face, and the curvy body—he'd start to believe it.

"You really can stay here, you know." She gazed up at him, visibly trusting, still seeing a nice cop and not recognizing the horny wolf in sheep's clothing.

Decent guys do not take advantage of crime victims.

Right. Time to go.

"Thanks but now I'm looking forward to a night in my own bed."

Don't think about beds, Jesus, man.

"I'll pick you up in the morning and take you back to your car."

"I hate to put you to more trouble. I've been nothing *but* trouble to you."

He shook his head. "I'm glad I was there, Evie."

"So am I," she whispered, stepping closer to him. "Very glad."

Her tongue swept out to moisten her lips, and just like that, with that miniscule movement, he knew he wasn't going to be able to sleep again until he'd tasted that mouth. It made no sense, it wasn't wise or particularly noble, but that mouth had been driving him nuts for hours, and he just had to kiss her.

So he did.

He didn't think about it, didn't really plan it, didn't worry about what would come afterward. He simply touched her chin again, lifting her face, and then brushed his lips against hers.

Soft, slow, and easy. A kiss that wasn't really going anywhere—couldn't go anywhere, not if he ever wanted to think of himself as a decent guy again. No, it had no particular destination, but was a hell of a nice way to get there.

If she'd flinched, if she'd reacted with any lingering fear because of what had happened to her earlier tonight, he would immediately have stepped back. But she didn't. It was as she'd said—she already trusted him.

She sighed and her lips parted, her tongue sliding out to delicately touch his. Every movement was molasses slow, no thrusts and frenzy, all soft and sultry. She tasted sweet, almost like those peaches he smelled in her hair.

Knowing he could get lost in that kiss, which would be a very bad idea right now, he slowly ended it. Their mouths parting, they stared at each other for a long moment, close enough to share each breath, strangers to each other mere hours ago, but now connected by a moment as tender as it was delicious.

He cleared his throat. "Uh, that was unplanned."

"Don't say you're sorry," she warned. "I needed that…needed something good to think about."

Good? He sensed they could be *great*. Their chemistry screamed it.

But he just wasn't wired to take advantage of someone in his debt or in his power. Right now, tonight, they were on unequal footing. She probably felt like she owed him something, and he wasn't about to go any further while she felt that way.

She might be strong enough to pretend she was okay now, but he doubted she really was. Just like when her emotions had slammed into her in the stairwell, he suspected she would be hit by delayed reactions for some time to come.

Rowan wasn't a game player, wasn't a seducer, didn't plan five steps ahead before taking step one. His twin was the king of the long scene, a storyboard always playing in his mind. Rowan tended to live moment by moment, but always by his own personal code. That code said it was time for him to go.

After that kiss, though, he knew one thing. Their coffee date couldn't come soon enough.

"Okay, I have to leave."

"You really *don't* have to," she said, the tiniest tremble in her voice. "I mean, I trust you."

"Maybe you shouldn't," he admitted in a gruff whisper.

"You don't fool me. I know a good guy when I see one."

Maybe. But tonight he wanted her *bad*.

"I'll see you in the morning."

She huffed a breath, obviously realizing he wasn't going to change his mind. "I really do hate that you have to go home and then turn around and come right back in eight hours."

"It's fine. I'll need to bring Jagger back anyway. He might not like being stuck with a dog all day, but he likes being alone even less. I have the scratched-up furniture to prove it."

"All right, Detective...You know," she said with a soft laugh, "I just realized I don't even know your first name. You rescued me, took me in, and I am still calling you by your official title."

He smiled. "It's Rowan."

One of her delicate brows shot up. "Rowan?"

"I know, I know," he said with a sigh, used to people reacting to his unusual name. He was pretty sure his mom had picked it out of an Irish history book.

Her eyes twinkled. "That sounds more like a stage name than a cop's one."

"I get that a lot."

As if her words had sent an arrow of realization into her brain, she immediately gasped and jerked away from the wall to stand straight.

"Oh my God. Rowan Winchester."

He hid a frown.

"One of *the* Winchester brothers."

Yeah. And no matter how many cases he closed or how many bad guys he brought to justice, people would still immediately associate him with fast-food commercials and guest spots on *Law & Order* and *Home Improvement*.

Shit, maybe he should just go back to being George Winchester. Nobody would mistake a George for being a part of a Hollywood dynasty.

Tell that to Clooney, dumbass.

Well, that he couldn't do. Clooney wasn't in his circle—despite the two-episode arc Rowan had done on *ER* as a dying kid. Nowadays, though, mingling with the top-tier movie star set was Reece's gig, not his. Oh, and Raine's, considering their kid brother ran a bodyguard company specializing in protecting famous child actors.

But Rowan? Shit. He was far more comfortable staking out a gang banger in south LA or downing a few beers with his brothers in blue at a popular cop bar. If not for the fact that every surviving family member he had lived here, and he liked his job, Rowan would have gone back East years ago.

"Rowan Winchester, I just can't believe it." Evie stepped past him, returning to the living room, but then quickly spun around. "Oh my God, is this your brother Reece's place? Of course it is. He's your twin, right? He's the one you called from the car!"

Following her, Rowan crossed his arms and leaned a shoulder against the wall. He would not have pictured Evie Fleming as the starstruck, go-gaga-over-a-movie-star type. Especially not since the movie star in question was his own damn brother. Damn it all.

Rowan and Reece didn't really compete over women. Rowan was fully capable of getting just about any woman he wanted, all on his own. But his brother had the fame, money, and reputation to win nearly any battle. So they rarely engaged in competition, though they often joked about it.

When it came to Evie, though, he was not laughing.

If she decided to sleep in the master bedroom in an effort to get up close and personal with the famous actor's bedsheets, he might just have to punch a hole in one of the walls of this house.

He wasn't jealous of his twin. Not ever. Reece's life hadn't exactly been easy, despite his fame, success, and money.

Right now, though, hearing a woman to whom he was incredibly attracted gush about his famous brother, he could picture himself punching Reece in his perfect jaw, but making do with the cream-painted plaster instead.

"I'm right, aren't I? That was Reece on the phone earlier? He lives here?"

"Yeah. Him and his girlfriend," he muttered, already looking out for the spunky redhead who Rowan already considered his sister.

"I can't believe this. A Winchester brother came to my rescue tonight."

"I'm just a cop now. Reece is the movie star," he bit out, hoping his tone sounded normal, not that he was, at this moment, jealous and pissed off.

Evie turned to face him, her blue eyes gleaming. For the first time, he realized her excitement wasn't a product of starstruck awe, but something else. Something he couldn't quite identify...until he *did* identify it.

It was determination. Narrow-eyed, laser-focused, totally serious, she looked like a woman on a quest.

"I know that, of course, I should have recognized you sooner. I was aware you joined the LAPD, Raine is a bodyguard, and Reece is in the movie business."

Damn. This was going from bad to worse. He'd never have pegged her for a tabloid-trash follower either, but it sure sounded like she had an interest in his family. And she'd said she was a writer, hadn't she? A nonfiction one.

God, had he brought a Hollywood trash-talking tell-all scandal-mongerer right into his brother's house?

"Look, Reece is very private," he said, seeing what he'd put in motion here. He'd brought an enemy spy right into the home camp.

If Rowan hadn't stumbled across Evie being assaulted, he'd almost wonder if the whole thing had been a setup. But it wasn't. The cuts on her face, the bruise on her jaw, and, oh Christ, her terror and near-hysteria when she'd finally broken down, confirmed that. This one just had to be chalked off to shitty luck and worse coincidence.

"I hope I don't have to even ask you to respect that privacy and not take any pictures or anything," he said.

She flinched. "I'm not a member of the paparazzi, you know."

"You said yourself that you're a nonfiction writer. It sounds like you, uh, have an interest in my brother's career. You can't blame me for being on edge."

"Actually, I have an interest in your whole family."

He stiffened.

Licking her lips and clasping her hands together in front of her, Evie looked like she was preparing herself to say something he wasn't going to like. Rowan couldn't figure out what that might be.

Until she opened her mouth.

"I'd hoped to get to speak to one of you. You see, the current book I'm writing is about infamous Hollywood murders."

Oh shit.

"And your family is certainly connected to a fascinating mystery."

No, no, no. Not this. "My sister is off-limits."

She gasped and stepped closer, lifting a supplicating hand. "Oh no, of course I wasn't talking about your personal family tragedy." Her head tilting in confusion, she added, "And her death, well, it was classified as—"

"Don't," he snapped.

Don't say suicide. *Don't say* accident.

Because nobody knew for sure. No one knew precisely how the beautiful teenage starlet had ended up on the ground far below that hotel suite in Atlanta. Nobody except the two people who had been out on the balcony that night, both of whom were long dead. Rachel Winchester and Harry Baker.

As for the third person who'd been in the hotel suite that night, his kid brother Raine, well, his childhood memories were hazy and he'd been in the bedroom when it happened. He honestly didn't know if Rachel had jumped, if she'd fallen…or if she'd been pushed.

They would never know.

"I'm so sorry," she said, dropping her hand and standing

respectfully a few feet away. "Of course I would not intrude on a private family matter like that."

"Then what do you want?" he asked, knowing another shoe was about to drop. What would otherwise explain her excitement at finding out who he was?

"I want to know about your former manager."

His heart skipped a beat.

"My new book will include unsolved murders. Harry Baker worked with your family for several years, correct? And there are rumors…"

Fearing what those rumors were, he managed to spit out a word from between gritted teeth. "About?"

She swallowed, and her face pinkened. "Well, um…that he was involved with your late mother?"

Rowan's jaw dropped. "Excuse me?"

She nibbled her lip before rushing on. "I'm sorry, like I said, just rumors."

Rowan's head was spinning at the claim that his mother had been involved with Harry Baker. If it wouldn't have been so difficult to explain, he probably would have let a dark, jaded laugh spill from his mouth.

My mother was not his type.

No, she was about thirty years too old for that sick, twisted bastard, who preferred his female companions exceedingly young and vulnerable.

"That is definitely not true."

"I'm sorry." Swiping a hand through her silky hair, she muttered, "I'm usually not such a bumbling klutz. I work with words—you'd think I would know how to say something clearly and concisely."

He could have let down his guard and given her a break. But

this was his family she was talking about. His family. Their secrets. No outsiders allowed.

"So be clear and concise," was all he said, ignoring the slump in her shoulders and the regret in her eyes.

She took a deep breath and obviously strove to be clear and concise in her reply. "I thought that since your family was so close to Baker, maybe you could talk to me a little about his life and his death. I'd hoped you could give me any insights you might have about the man, and possibly share any suspicions."

"Share…suspicions?" he managed to mumble.

"Yes. I think the story is pretty fascinating, and I included a chapter on it in my outline. I'd really like to dig into the case and see if I can find out anything that hasn't been discovered yet."

Like the fact that all three of the Winchester brothers had been in Baker's house the night he died and had suspected each other of killing the man who'd abused their sister?

Right. Sure. Let me just go ahead and fill out arrest warrants right now.

"Maybe you and your brothers could help me with that?"

Fat fucking chance.

He and his brothers had *finally* started talking to each other about Harry Baker's death—his murder. Raine had been as stunned to learn his brothers had believed he'd killed the man as they had been when they realized he had *not*. No way were any of them going to talk to a stranger—a writer—about it.

"Absolutely not," he said, stepping closer to her, edging her in between the wall and the bookshelf. He was shaking, furious at himself for having invited this drama into their lives. Out of what, some ideal of nobility? Or was it because he had wanted her from the moment she fell into his arms in that stairwell? "Don't make me regret trusting you."

She flinched and jerked back. Realizing he was crowding her—her, the woman who'd been attacked by a ruthless bastard tonight, he staggered back. "Jesus Christ, you are messing with my head."

"I'm sorry."

"I have to go." He needed to get out before he opened his mouth and said words that needed to remain unsaid, either revealing ones or downright rude ones.

"I'm sorry, I really didn't mean to pry." She wrapped her arms around her middle. "Again, I've been very clumsy about this. It's just been a strange night."

True...but it hadn't been his strangest. Not by a long shot.

Ignoring her, he grabbed Jagger. For once, the cat seemed to recognize that Rowan was in no mood to put up with any crap, and he didn't try to squirm away as Rowan put him into his carrier.

"Can we please talk about this?"

"No."

"Rowan, you can't believe...you have to know this was just a coincidence." She straightened and said with simple dignity, "I never intended to entrap you or insert myself into your life. I can call a cab to take me to a hotel."

"Forget it," he said.

"I can see you're no longer comfortable having me around."

He drew a deep, steadying breath. Lowering the cat carrier to the floor, he turned and looked directly at her. "Look, I'm glad you're okay. I'm fine with you staying here, and so is my brother. But you need to know, some things are off-limits. And Harry Baker is one of those things."

"But—"

"I'll pick you up at eight a.m.," he said, cutting her off. There were no *buts* about this topic. Not a single one.

Evie Fleming needed to stay out of the Harry Baker case.

Not just because the Winchester brothers were in it up to their eyebrows, but because whoever really had killed the man was still out there. She'd drawn the eye of one murderer in her life and had testified against him in court. Damned if she needed to come onto the radar of another one.

"Rowan, wait—"

"Good night, Evie," he said.

Without even a glance back, he stalked out of the house to his car, got in it, and put the cat carrier on the passenger seat. He drove too fast down the steep driveway and the windy road as he headed back toward the city. But the speed didn't distract him as dark memory intruded.

For over six long years, Rowan and Reece had believed their kid brother had killed Harry Baker. Raine had just turned eighteen, was drunk, leaving for boot camp the next day, and he'd found Baker attacking a young girl. Like a sledgehammer bashing into his brain, the memory of Harry fighting with Rachel the night she died had come back to him, driving the teenager a little crazy. It had made sense to the twins that, with such justification, Raine could have done something he never would have while sober or in his right mind.

And so they'd done what they believed family *should* do.

They'd protected their brother.

They'd cleaned up the scene and hidden evidence of Raine's presence.

For his part, Raine had wondered over the years if his older brothers had gone over to Baker's house that night and finished delivering the beating Raine had started…and had gone too far.

None of them had ever confronted the others, until Steve Baker, Harry's son and Rachel's teenage boyfriend, had told them things that made them question their beliefs about that night. The fact that a witness existed who'd seen Harry Baker, bloody but alive, screaming on the front porch as Raine staggered away had been news to all of them. And it had proved Raine's innocence.

Finding out they had *all* been innocent had shocked the hell out of the three of them, and they'd spent the last few months trying to atone by getting to the bottom of the mystery. Quietly.

Now a famous writer wanted to dig into the case, expose what she found, and blow the whole thing wide open? And he'd brought her right into the heart of the family? God, what the hell had he done?

He honestly didn't know. He was only certain of one thing.

His brothers were going to fucking *kill* him.

* * *

Despite what people might think, Raine Winchester was not the strip club type. Yeah, he was former army. Yes, he ran a security firm. He was usually armed, had a few tattoos, dressed in dark T-shirts and camo pants, and usually looked pissed off.

But he didn't party. He rarely drank. He didn't particularly like to talk to people other than those closest to him, and he'd never needed to buy *anything* he desired from a woman. So there was no reason for him to ever come to a place like the Lusty Lady club in southeast LA.

Still, here he was, sitting at a table in the corner that provided a broad view of the garish purple interior of the place, sipping a club soda and trying not to touch anything.

He wasn't watching the dancer. Nor was he interested in seeing the glazed-over eyes of a bunch of skeevy dudes with their hands in their laps as they drooled over the gyrating thrusts of a brunette who looked barely legal.

He pitied the girl. The men just repulsed him.

He hated places like this and was here for only one reason.

Her name was Marley.

He'd been looking for her for a couple of months now, and this was his latest lead to her current location. Already having ascertained that she was not the dancer performing, nor any of the skimpily clad servers, he knew he would have to ask some questions. Not exactly a popular thing to do in places like this.

His opportunity came quickly. A performer appeared beside him, her legs bare down to her scuffed spike-heeled shoes, and only a string of hot pink satin covered her hip.

"Hey, sexy, my name's Candy. Wanna buy me a drink?"

He lowered his glass to the table and glanced up at the woman—girl, really—who'd approached him. Her G-string looked like it could be removed with a quick flick of the wrist. Tiny, star-shaped spangles on her nipples were, he supposed, meant to entice clients to pay more for a private dance during which he could see the whole package. Her red hair was dank and stringy, and she was filmed with sweat.

"You interested, hot stuff?"

No, he really wasn't interested in what she was obviously offering. Instead, he did what very few men in this place probably ever did—he really *looked* at her.

There was much more to see if you actually took the time to pay attention. Like the purplish-yellow bruises on her hip and thighs, showing through whatever concealer she'd put on to cover them. The shadow beneath one eye was darker than the other—again, a poor concealment job, this time to hide the fact that somebody had punched her in the face. She tried hard to keep her arms bent at her sides, but he'd seen the telltale marks that said if she wasn't living in heroin-land yet, she was on a fast train to that destination.

He wanted to grab his jacket, throw it over her, and carry her out of here. She should be living at home with her parents while she went to community college or something. Not working for grimy dollar bills held out by the groping hands of men old enough to be her father. Christ, he hated thinking about the desperation that would push a barely-out-of-high-school-aged girl into a life like this. Considering Raine worked day and night protecting children from being used, abused, or hurt in any way, this "exotic dancer's" precarious position hit him hard.

"You're hot, baby. I'll give you a discount if you wanna go somewhere private and let me put on a real special show for ya."

He said nothing but reached for his wallet and pulled out a hundred-dollar bill.

Her eyes went round, and she licked her lips. "Now we're partyin'!"

"I just want five minutes of your time."

She slid her fingers through his hair, bending down to wag her breasts in his face and cooed, "You can have longer than that, sugar. I'll even let you have a taste."

Pushing his chair back, he stood up. "Five minutes. And I only want to talk."

She frowned, and looked around the club. The bouncer was watching them closely. The bartender, who pretended to be drying a glass—as if the things were actually washed between customers—gave her a warning frown that Raine easily read as *Close the deal, bitch.*

She tucked the money into her G-string and said, "Come on, this way."

He followed her into a small velvet-draped booth. In it was a chair, a mirrored wall, and some grimy carpet that would probably set off alarms if tested by a hazmat team.

The girl pulled the drape, enclosing them in the five-by-five space that smelled of sweat and other bodily fluids. Reaching for a button on the wall, she jacked up the volume of the song playing on the main floor of the club. She stepped close to say, "What do you want with me, mister? You here to cause trouble?"

He held up his hands—*no harm no foul.* "No trouble. I'm looking for someone."

"You sure you ain't found her?" the girl said, lifting her hands to his shoulders and digging sharp nails into his muscles. "Not often we get hot young meat willing to spend real dough in here. Usually it's all bachelor party pussies who get too drunk and are thrown out, or flabby old fucks who try to touch without paying."

"No, thank you." He reached up and disengaged her hands. "I'm trying to find Marley."

The girl's mouth tightened.

"She used to work here," he continued.

"I don't know nobody named Marley."

"I'm sure it's not her real name; she could have been using another one. She's young, probably around your age. Petite, pretty. Has a scar down the side of her face."

Candy's eyes widened quickly, but then narrowed. Her mouth tightened and she sneered. "Yeah, I knew her."

Knew. "She doesn't work here anymore?"

"Nope. Goody Two-shoes wouldn't give A.J. what he wanted, so he kicked her ass out."

"A.J.?"

"Owns the place. Samples all the merchandise. But she wasn't havin' it, so out she went."

She'd slipped away again. Every time he thought he was narrowing in on the mysterious Marley, he found she had pulled one step away.

"How long ago was this?"

"'Bout a week or two. She wasn't calling herself Marley, though. Everybody called her Sugar. But if you ask me, she wasn't very sweet. Uppity, that one."

"Hell," he muttered, rubbing a hand over his weary eyes. This off-the-books investigation had been eating up a lot of his time. He'd been putting in seventy-hour workweeks with his regular job at his protection agency and then following leads to track the always-moving stripper during every other waking moment.

Marley—Sugar, or any other fake name she might be using now—was the only one who might be able to help solve the mystery that had been plaguing him and his brothers for more than six years.

The night Harry Baker died remained a mystery that haunted them all. Until it was solved, he didn't think he, Rowan, or Reece would be able to have a normal life, though

Reece appeared to be at least trying to with his new girlfriend. But how could any of them really find normalcy when a sword of Damocles was hanging over their heads?

Although Raine had been the last Winchester to see the bastard alive, he had very little memory of Baker's final hours. He'd been a teenager, he'd been drunk, and he'd been beaten up by the man he'd always thought of as a jolly uncle.

Mostly, he'd been fucked in the head. His memories of the night his sister Rachel died had exploded back into his mind with the power of a heat-seeking missile.

Because history had repeated itself. He'd awakened to the sound of a young girl crying out for help, just like when he was a six-year-old kid in a hotel room with his teenage sister.

Screams in the night. Awakened from a drunken stupor. Staggering out to see what was wrong. Seeing Uncle Harry hurting a young girl. Rachel? No, not his sister; she'd been dead for twelve years. This was another girl, probably not even fifteen.

She looked terrified. Harry was on top of her. Hurting her.

At that moment, all the repressed memories of Rachel—and what "Uncle" Harry had done to her—had erupted from the hiding place in the corner of his brain where they had lurked for so many years. Raine had been enveloped in a black rage, striking out, fighting brutally with the bigger, heavier, much-older man. Raine had been young and strong, just turned eighteen, but Harry had been a beast and stronger. The girl whose attack had prompted his sudden recall had run out, disappearing into the night...or so he thought.

Bloodied, bruised, and battered, Raine had eventually staggered away from the house, Harry alive and well behind him. Yet no more than ninety minutes later, when his brothers had gone back to confront the man, they'd found him dead on the floor, a bullet in his brain. And thinking their brother was a killer, they'd cleaned up the crime scene for him.

Which was why the case had never been solved.

Harry had been a monster. Not one of them was sorry he was dead.

But they all regretted the part they'd played in letting a murderer get away scot-free.

The three of them were trapped in that secret, wrapped up together in the lie. What had happened in those ninety minutes, who had killed Harry—whether the girl had come back to take revenge or whether it had been someone else—was a mystery that taunted them all. And it had to be solved if they wanted to find any peace and get any closure.

"Listen, baby, Sugar ain't got nothin' on me. She didn't know how to show a man a good time, but believe me, I do."

The stripper wrapped her arms around his neck and ground into his body. Sliding a leg between his, she humped his thigh, rubbing up and down, faking little sounds of delight. A performer going through her usual act.

Raine disentangled himself, putting her away from him. Then, reaching into his pocket, he pulled out a business card and a fifty. "I know the house will take most of that hundred. Can you hide this?"

She nodded. He didn't ask where, not really wanting to know.

"Okay." He handed her the card. "This goes with it. You call me if you hear anything about this Sugar, okay?"

She glanced at the card, reading the name. "Hollywood Guardians, huh?"

"Yes."

She plumped up her breasts and slipped her fingers under the tassels, popping them off.

"You sure you don't wanna be my guardian angel, sweetie?"

Feeling nothing more than pity and sadness, Raine shook his head. "Listen, keep that card, okay? Whether it's about Sugar or not, if you ever find yourself in a bad spot, you give me a call."

The girl's mouth fell open, and her eyes rounded. It was as if she wasn't used to anybody wanting to help. Like it had been ages since anybody had even been kind to her.

God, this city was ruthless.

He left the booth feeling both sadness and anger.

And wondering just how many more places like this he would have to visit in his search for the mysterious Marley/Sugar, who might hold the key to the questions that haunted his family.

Chapter 4

True to his word, Rowan Winchester picked her up promptly at eight the next morning. Although not as dark and obviously angry as he'd been when he left, he seemed in no way like the friendly, upbeat—*sexy, oh so sexy*—guy she'd been getting to know before she'd spoiled everything by asking him for a scoop.

She'd been so stupid to react to the knowledge of his family's identity by leaping onto what had to be a really difficult memory for them. Of *course* Harry Baker's death would be a hard one to revisit. Hadn't their agent been a close family friend when the boys were young? She'd found interviews in which they called him Uncle Harry. Whether he was involved with their mother romantically or not, there'd been a very close relationship.

To make matters even more tangled, the man's own son had apparently committed suicide right in front of Rowan's brother a few months ago. Plus Steve Baker had been their long-lost sister's teenage love.

The Baker name must be an Achilles' heel for the Winchester boys.

And she'd poked that heel with a sharp stick.

"I owe you an apology," she said as they drove toward downtown. "You were wonderful to me last night, and I repaid you with intrusive questions."

He shrugged. God she hated the strong-and-silent stuff.

"So, I apologize."

"You said that."

"No, I didn't. I said I *owed* you an apology. Actually apologizing requires an additional step."

A tiny grin might have appeared on that strong, masculine mouth. "Most people don't recognize that distinction or take that step."

"I'm not most people."

And neither was he. Good Lord, no.

He was different from anyone else she'd ever met. How many child-actors-from-Hollywood-dynasties-turned-LA-detective could there be in the world? Especially ones who looked like the guy sitting right beside her in the car?

None. Zero. Zip. And she'd run right into him, or, actually, he'd run into her, courtesy of a violent attack that could have gone *really* badly for her.

"So you're seriously gonna write a book about Harry Baker?" he asked, the words sounding like they'd been pulled out of him with a hook and chain. She suspected he'd pondered that question all night long.

"No, not about him," she quickly replied. "It's a fresh look at several infamous murder cases in the Los Angeles area."

"Which is why you were at the Cecil last night? Ramirez, right?"

"No book on Southern California murder would be complete without coverage of the Night Stalker."

"Obviously. Black Dahlia too?"

"There's no proof she actually stayed at the Cecil. I think that's a myth."

He grunted. As a cop, he had to know just what rumors and whispers could do to an investigation. Even more than seventy years later, the murder of Elizabeth Short still fascinated, and her legend never seemed to die, so the questionable stories—like that she'd been staying at the Cecil—had grown into urban legends.

"Manson?"

"Rewind and listen to what I said about Ramirez."

"Pretty dark stuff."

"I know."

"Some would say twisted."

"Did you just call me twisted?"

"No, but some might say your job is."

So much for casual conversation. He obviously still had a bug up his ass about what she did. She supposed that wasn't too surprising coming from a detective to a journalist. Even though they did have a symbiotic relationship, with a lot of quid pro quo, the trust never went far either way between cops and reporters.

"Maybe it is. Or maybe I'm just good at solving mysteries and at writing."

"You think there's more to solve about Manson and the Night Stalker? Haven't those cases been covered enough?"

She kept her patience, though she had to grip it with her teeth.

"That's true. But in the solved cases, I can peel from the

outside in, killer to victims. Unsolved ones mean going from
the core—victim—out to the killer, which is much more difficult."

"You're tellin' me."

She almost slapped herself on the forehead, remembering
who she was talking to. "Sorry, Detective. I imagine you've
solved your fair share."

He merely grunted.

"I just don't seem to know what to say to you. Maybe my
brains were rattled when I hit the ground last night."

"Forget it." He went back to the subject. "So you're only
looking at cases that were solved? Then why…"

She knew what he didn't say. He was wondering about Baker
again; he just didn't want to bring it up. The memory must be
very painful. Having lost someone she cared about to brutal
murder she could certainly empathize.

"Although I'll spend more time on the really famous ones
that were solved, I do intend to bring up some unresolved
mysteries that never resulted in convictions," she explained,
not saying Baker's name either, in an effort to keep the peace.
"This town has seen a lot of them. George Reeves, Bob
Crane…"

"The Simpson and Blake cases?"

"Yes."

"Sounds like your stay in sunny California is gonna be pretty
friggin' dark."

"That's not exactly unusual."

He hesitated, as if not wanting to get too personal, but then
asked, "How do you deal with it on a day-to-day basis? With
that darkness?"

He'd opened a door into a real conversation, sounding

more concerned than curious, and he was right in assuming she had a process to protect herself from her work. Her whole professional life had been dark for several years, but she had ways of dealing with it. After being immersed in the details of horrific crimes committed by the worst humanity had to offer, she found ways to pull herself out of that thought-dungeon.

"When I'm *not* working on a book, I read upbeat books, I take cooking classes and fail miserably. See my family, spend time with friends, go shopping. Normal stuff." She added, "Oh, and I spend a lot of time watching romantic comedies on Netflix. I don't Netflix and chill; I Netflix and laugh."

He chuckled. Progress.

"That reminds me, gotta finish the first season of *Mindhunter*," he said.

"Me too."

He eyed her. "Now? Thought you were hip deep in horror and looking to laugh."

"I said I want lightness and happy comedy when I'm *not* working on a book."

"Okay, remind me not to put on a Disney marathon when we hang out."

"Are you kidding?" she asked with a snort. "Have you seen *Bambi, Dumbo*, or any of the other dead-parents-brigade movies?"

"Oh yeah. Raine used to cry and turn the TV off when the mama elephant got put in the clink."

Given what she knew about the youngest Winchester now, she found that amusing. She'd seen pictures of Raine standing protectively beside various child stars, looking fearsome and dangerous. She could hardly picture him being sad about a cartoon. Or, for that matter, smiling.

Funny, she had the same impression of older twin Reece. He had a reputation as a cold, calculating jerk. Which made Rowan's mostly easygoing nature surprising, especially given that he was a cop, that he was a protector, and that he was so damn sexy.

Something he'd said suddenly flared up in her brain and started circling. "Wait, you think we're going to hang out, huh?"

He shrugged. "Stranger things have happened. I guess it depends on what, exactly, you're working on."

She caught the hard tone and knew what he was referring to. The Harry Baker case. Yeesh, he really did not want her digging into that. Frankly, his persistence made her more curious to find out what he knew. Not that she was about to tell him that.

"I'm quite busy working on the major chapters."

"Can't imagine what's going on in that brain of yours. LA has had more than its fair share of nightmare characters."

"Probably no more than any other major city. But the stories do tend to linger."

"So what do you do when you're in the throes of it?" he asked. "Do you just suffer nightmares, bad thoughts, and darkness for a couple of months? Because that's a hell of a shitty way to live."

"Yes, it is," she admitted. "And it was like that with the first book."

He knew what she meant. "Was Angstrom's book at least cathartic?"

"In some ways. But yes, the others, the criminals who weren't within one degree of separation of me, were easier to research and write about." She had to clarify. "Though not *easy*. Believe me, there's a lot of wine involved."

"No doubt." He glanced out the window at the clear blue sky. "What kind of car did you rent? If it's a convertible, you should add drives up the coast to your decompression techniques."

"Mind reader."

He nodded in approval. "What else? Any pets?"

"No, though having met Cecil B and Jagger, I'd really like to change that."

"Well, Cecil B anyway."

"Don't be mean."

Grunting, he explained, "I thought Jagger would be thrilled to be in his own home for a night. Instead he got pissed off and used my shower as a litter box."

She bit her lip to hold in a laugh.

"What about relationships?" he asked, his voice lowering. "It'd probably take a certain kind of person to understand what you're usually thinking about."

"Yes, it would, and no I haven't found anyone who really gets it."

Not for lack of trying over the years. She'd been in a few long-term relationships. Not lately, though. As he'd suspected, few men really dug the idea of going out with a woman who saw serial killers around every corner and had examined autopsy and crime scene photos that would cause many people nightmares for months.

The last guy she'd been involved with had started calling her Wednesday Adams. She'd ended up calling him Cheating Asshole.

"You sure your work is worth it? Sounds like you live under a little black cloud most of the time."

Maybe. But the accusation stung. "Do you live under a box of Fruity McTooties cereal?"

He stiffened before emitting a loud laugh. "Touché. I swear, to this day if I even see the stuff in the grocery store I wanna throw up."

Mention of the commercial he'd starred in as a child seemed to have finally lowered the brick wall he'd had in place since last night. God, she liked his smile, liked the way it made his eyes crinkle in the corners. He was looking ahead, at the road, not at her, so she couldn't enjoy that amused twinkle she'd caught sight of a couple of times last night, but she knew it was there.

Despite the book, despite her job, despite all the reasons she was here, and the way she'd questioned him last night, she would really like to go back to where they'd been before she'd found out who he was and put on her researcher bonnet. He'd been just a hot, sexy cop who'd saved her from a violent assault. He'd scooped her up into his strong arms when she'd finally collapsed in delayed reaction. He'd taken her home to keep her safe and out of the spotlight.

He'd kissed her like they were meant to be lovers…but not yet. He had not taken advantage of that kiss, or the situation, recognizing that her nerves and emotions were a jangled mess.

Honorable was this man's middle name. She hated that she'd put him on guard by being so intrusive.

"Look," she said, broaching the subject that still hung between them, "I'm really sorry about being so nosy last night. I appreciate everything you've done for me. Please just forget about my request for help on the case."

He cast her a quick, surprised look. "So you're not going to include Baker's murder in your book after all?"

She could say that, and perhaps it would end up being true if she couldn't find anything unique or interesting to say about the cold case, but Evie was no liar, and she was no coward. "I'm not sure yet, but one thing I do know is that I don't need to drag your family into my research."

His jaw, that rugged jaw, its masculinity highlighted by the short beard, hardened.

"That's as far as I'm willing to go," she said.

After a tense moment, he nodded once. "Okay, we understand each other."

She snorted, catching his eye again. "I am not about to claim I understand you, Detective."

But she'd like to. She'd very much like to get to know him better and was almost disappointed when they reached the downtown area, nearing the parking garage where she'd left her car.

He didn't turn into the entrance. "Listen, I have to go up to headquarters again this morning. Why don't I take you straight there so you don't have to deal with getting your car out, fighting traffic, finding a place to park, and then doing it all over again to go home?"

"It's no trouble?" she asked, not disappointed at the thought of having to spend a little more time with him, even if it was only the fifteen minutes it would take to crawl along the mile or so to their mutual destination. And she'd thought East Coast traffic was bad.

She also didn't mind putting off returning to that dank, dark garage.

Then there was the idea of having to relive last night's ordeal with the investigating officers, who had left her a voice mail first thing this morning asking her to come in for a lineup.

Ugh. It sounded ridiculous, since the guy had been caught red-handed, but she would do it, even if it was just a formality.

"No trouble," he insisted.

"Then thank you, that would be a big help," she said.

As they idled at a stoplight, she cast a quick glance at the alley in which she'd almost ended up last night. The gate stood open, revealing some tipped-over cans, strewn trash and leaves, and broken glass on the ground. She couldn't see farther than a few feet into the narrow, shadowy space, and an involuntary shudder jerked through her entire body, from head to toe.

A strong hand reached across and covered hers. "Don't."

"I know."

Another shudder.

"Really, don't do this to yourself. It didn't happen, Evie."

"So close…if not for you…"

"I'm just happy my spidey-senses started pinging."

"Not as happy as I am, web-slinger."

They shared a quick smile, and then the light changed and they crawled through the intersection. The slow traffic enabled him to look over again. He cleared his throat. "Speaking of that, are you okay?"

She knew what he meant. "I'm fine, thanks. That bath helped."

"You had everything you needed?"

"Definitely. I borrowed your brother's girlfriend's bathrobe while I washed my clothes. There were even new and un-wrapped toothbrushes in the guest bathroom. It seems as though she thinks of everything."

He chuckled. "I suspect that stuff was left there by the owner of the place. Jessica's focused on her work right now."

She thought about it, remembering the last time she'd seen Reece's image on the front pages of the tabloids. "Is she the stunning redhead pictured coming out of the limo with him a few months ago?"

"Yeah. She's fantastic. She's definitely shaken up Reece's life."

"I suspect he needed it."

She didn't want to insult Rowan, but from what she'd read, it sounded as though his twin could be a real jerk.

"Yes, he did. He's a new man, happier than I've seen him in years."

The traffic eased a bit, and they reached the tall and glassy downtown headquarters building. Rowan parked the unmarked car and walked her inside. Evie was on a visitor's list, since she had an appointment with Captain Avery, someone she'd met yesterday, and Rowan waited with her while she was cleared to go in.

"The investigating officer you have to meet is on the second floor," he said.

Evie nodded. "Yes, but I have a meeting up on six first. I called from the house this morning. The lineup isn't scheduled until ten a.m., so I shouldn't have any problem getting there on time."

"You gonna be okay with the lineup? You know it's just a formality, right? I mean, I did catch the guy literally in the act and he was never out of my sight. We just believe in dotting all *i*'s and crossing all *t*'s here, so some slippery defense attorney doesn't get the bastard off."

"Yes, I'll be fine," she said, though a tiny tremble did make her limbs quake. "As long as we're separated by a glass wall, I'm surrounded by police officers, and we're in the middle of one of the biggest police buildings in the country, I should be okay."

"Definitely," he said. "I wish I could be in there with you, but I'll have to stay outside since I'm not investigating it."

"I understand," she murmured, wishing he could be right there beside her. She knew and trusted Rowan already. How could she not, considering all he had done for her last night?

He stopped her, putting both hands on her shoulders and facing her. "It's going to be fine, Evie. Once you've identified him, and his attorney tells him there's no real defense since he was caught in the act, hopefully he will realize he's got more to lose by going to trial and will agree to a plea, so you won't have to testify."

"Let's hope. I've testified enough to last me the rest of my life."

Having to tell her story in open court about her assault last night wouldn't be pleasant, and she'd prefer to avoid it if possible. Worse, though—far worse—was the prospect of sitting on a witness stand in a packed courtroom and again repeating everything she knew about Joe Henry Angstrom. She still shivered at the memory of the monster watching her with those soulless eyes from the defendant's table.

Last night's attack had been bad, and she wouldn't soon forget it.

Angstrom, though…he had slaughtered her best friend, in their own home, and had cast a shadow over Evie that had lasted for nearly a decade.

Forcing a weak smile to her mouth, she nodded up at Rowan, looking into his dark eyes. She wondered if he could see the tiniest hint of fear in hers, and if he would think she was merely nervous about the lineup. She hoped so. Frankly, she preferred to shove all thoughts and conversations about Angstrom into the next millennium.

"You were so brave last night," he said.

Obviously he *had* seen it and was offering reassurance. His tone wasn't exactly intimate, more professional cop to victim, but it was kind.

"It's amazing what you can do when you're not given any other choice but to fight."

He nodded. "That's exactly right. *You* were exactly right. Too many people think it's better to go along than to resist, but with someone like *him*, you'd have regretted it forever if you hadn't tried to get away."

"And then you were there," she whispered, staring into that strong face, unable to look away from the warm mouth that had kissed her with such sweet and tender passion the night before.

God, how could there be so many facets to one man? He'd been brutal with her attacker, professional with his colleagues, firm with the press, commanding when figuring out what to do with her. He'd been thoughtful, accommodating, noble, and sexy as hell. And then so angry at her. All in the space of a few hours.

What, she wondered, might she learn about the man given more time?

And how might she *get* that time so she could find out?

"So why did you have to come back here again for this early meeting?" he asked as they resumed walking toward the bank of elevators.

She pulled her stare away and ordered her thoughts.

"I need access to some sensitive files on some of the cases I'm writing about."

He snorted. "That'll be fun."

True. The case files for a lot of these crimes were simply

revolting. It took a lot of fortitude—and sometimes liquid courage—for Evie to really dig into them.

"Anyway, I came in yesterday to plead my case and got some resistance. Fortunately, one of the members of the police commissioner's board is a fan of my books, so I suspect word was passed down that I should get what I want. But I don't think the captain I met with—Avery—is very happy about it. He's making me work for them."

Rowan chuckled as they entered the elevator. "He would. Guy's old school. He'll put you through hoops before letting you look at a single thing."

Although she assumed he had other business in the building, and she would see him for the identification later, Rowan accompanied her up to the sixth floor. They walked together to the Administrative Services offices, to Captain Avery's door. The man's assistant, a uniformed officer, ushered them inside, announcing them to the captain. Avery, a broad-chested African American man with short graying hair, sat behind his desk. Opposite him sat another cop, this one maybe in his midthirties, tall and good-looking, with sandy-colored hair and green eyes.

Evie recognized him, though she couldn't remember his name. Carter? Connor? Cooper? Something like that. She'd met him yesterday afternoon when she came in before going down to the Cecil. He had insisted on escorting her out of the building when she left, his attitude more flirtatious than informative.

The blond-haired cop walked over, extending his hand. "Miss Fleming, I'm so glad I get to see you again. I was just talking to Captain Avery about your project."

"Can it, Carlton," barked the gruff captain.

Right. Lieutenant Carlton, that was his name. One thing she did easily remember about him was that he was trying way too hard to be friendly and had made her uncomfortable. That had been *before* last night's assault. Right now, the only man she felt completely comfortable with was Rowan Winchester, so she really wished Carlton would go away.

Avery gestured toward another empty chair. "Take a seat, Ms. Fleming." Then he turned his attention to Rowan. "Winchester, what're you doing here?"

A quick glance at Rowan told her he was tense for some reason. He wasn't heading off to tend to his own business but was instead staring at Carlton, who was staring at Evie. The vibe was noticeable, and uncomfortable.

"He's actually with me," she said to Avery. "Detective Winchester came to my aid last night and got me out of a very bad situation."

"What happened?" Carlton asked, leaning closer to her. His hand dropped onto hers, which rested on the armchair. "Are you all right?"

She cast a quick glance at Rowan and saw the way his brow was pulled down and his eyes were narrowed. He didn't like the other man, that much was obvious.

"I'm fine, thank you," she said, sliding her hand free.

"I heard about what happened," the captain said, leaning back in his seat and crisscrossing his hands to rest on his chest. She suspected he was not one to give praise, because he sounded grudging when he added, "Good job, Winchester."

"Not a problem, sir."

"That doesn't answer my question, though. How'd you end up here with our illustrious visitor this *morning?*"

Rowan opened his mouth, then closed it again. She could almost see the wheels churning in his brain. Taking a crime victim home with you and putting her up for the night probably wasn't in any LAPD instruction books. So, before he could answer, she quickly explained.

"Some reporters showed up last night and were pretty persistent. Plus I was a little shaky and didn't feel capable of driving, so the detective drove me home."

Not a lie, since she didn't mention *whose* home.

"He had to bring me back to view a lineup, which is scheduled for later this morning."

Avery nodded, accepting the explanation. "So, Miss Fleming, Lieutenant Carlton here was just offering to help you with your project."

She stiffened. Carlton had not done or said anything inappropriate. Far from it—in fact, he'd been overly friendly and charming. Which, to be honest, kind of creeped her out. Ted Bundy had supposedly been pretty charming too.

Her instinctive reaction didn't surprise her given what she did for a living. The research she'd done on dark crimes perpetrated on helpless victims lurked deep in her brain, leaving her far more cautious about strangers than most. Which made it even more unusual that she'd let Rowan take her back to his brother's place last night. Funny how quickly she'd trusted him.

Maybe someone saving you from assault made the get-to-know-you phase of a relationship—*friendship*—easier to skip over.

"I really don't need any assistance. I've done a lot of investigative research. Plus I'm sure Lieutenant Carlton is too busy to waste his time babysitting me," she said.

"It truly isn't a problem, Miss Fleming—Evie, isn't it?"

She ignored the pushy cop, still staring at the captain.

"I wasn't sure about giving you access to so much material," said Avery. He cast a hard stare at Evie. "And then I realized it didn't matter what I say. This morning, I was informed from above that you are going to get what you want whether I liked it or not."

Feeling a little like a kid sitting in the principal's office, she merely gulped.

"But with this incident last night, and the reporters—damn vultures—I'm not so sure how to handle this." He cleared his throat. "I did some checking up on you last night and saw what's going on with the Angstrom case. No wonder you're in the spotlight." Another throat clear. "Nice work there. Took some guts to do what you did."

It was a grudging compliment, but she greatly appreciated it coming from the gruff, no-nonsense man. Despite the gruffness, there was something likable about him.

"Anyway, nobody wants anything else to happen to you."

Nobody meaning his superiors?

"I am going to make sure you are looked after."

"I really don't think—"

"It's not up to you," he said, piercing her with a stare. "I don't know what other police departments you've worked with, but we're not in the habit of handing over access to just anyone. This is a highly secured building, and you will have to be escorted at all times."

"I can help Ms. Fleming with her research and make sure she comes to no further harm," Carlton insisted.

"Who's gonna do your job, Carlton? We're talking about more than a couple of days in the file room." Avery frowned again. "I heard this morning that your research will also include visits to some crime scenes that are still available. It sure would give the department a black eye if something *else* happened to you while you're in town."

Am I gonna get detention or expulsion?

"We can reassign Burke to cover my work for a week or so, I'm sure."

Carlton was nothing but persistent, and he was turning her off more by the moment. Evie couldn't help casting a quick glance at Rowan, who stood in the doorway to the office, though there was no real reason for him to have remained. He still wore the glower. Now, though, his thick arms strained against the sleeves of his shirt, and she saw the way his hands clenched and unclenched into fists.

He looked furious…at Carlton.

His dislike of the other man rolled off him in powerful waves. Which made Evie even less anxious for Carlton's help with her research. She really didn't want to spend a lot of time in a musty room, a car, and crime scenes with a man who was so deeply disliked by someone she already trusted.

"You know there's some sites that're gonna be off-limits. People live in some of those houses now," Avery said.

"I know that."

"Some places were torn down—good riddance."

"Yes, of course, but I have made contacts with a few current owners, occupants, and former investigators, and have gained permission to visit and interview some of them." Seeing his face redden, she hurriedly added, "And I would like to go out to Spahn Ranch."

Avery's frown deepened. "Not very easy—or pleasant—ground."

"Sir, really," said Carlton, his tone cajoling, "this isn't a problem for me."

"I'll do it."

"If need be, I can take some of it as time off."

"I'll do it."

Carlton's voice rose. "You might not know this, but I'm really interested in writing and might be able to help. Plus I know a lot about the historical crimes in the city."

Oh God, a wannabe writer? This was worse than when she'd feared he was flirting with her. Other writers tended to want to pick brains, soak up knowledge, and ask intrusive questions. *How much do you make? Where do you get your ideas?*

Then there was the oh-so-frequent *I'm gonna write a book someday and make boatloads of money.*

She was often tempted to reply to the dentist, or the pilot, or the engineer with, "Oh, you know, I've always wanted to perform a root canal/fly a 747/design a car."

"I'll do it."

Evie suddenly realized she'd been hearing those words faintly repeated. They simply hadn't registered in her mind, so focused had she been on arguing Carlton out of the job.

"What was that, Winchester?" Avery barked.

Yeah, what was that, Winchester?

Evie swung around in her chair and looked up at him, her mouth circled, her eyes wide. Had he *really* said what she'd thought he said?

He crossed his thick arms over his chest and growled, "I said I'll do it."

"Why?" she asked. Seeing his mouth tighten, she quickly added, "I mean, I appreciate the offer, but can you really afford to take the time?"

She didn't ask the more obvious question: Why would he want to? Despite his kindness, she still had the impression after what had happened last night that he wanted to get away from her, and stay away. Now he was offering to be her babysitter while she worked on a project he obviously disdained?

Avery chuckled. "Good idea, Winchester. Just the thing."

If anything, Rowan's frown deepened when the captain agreed with him.

"I mean, you being Cop Hollywood and all, and Miss Fleming being an out-of-town celebrity. I'm sure you'll have a lot to talk about. I heard you fell into that trafficking case by accident and need to get off the streets for a while anyway, right?"

His jaw hard, Rowan nodded once.

"I volunteered first," Carlton insisted, rising from his chair.

Nanny-nanny-boo-boo much?

Avery put a hand up, palm out, to stop the other man. "No, this is perfect. Let's give it a week for now. Winchester. You help Miss Fleming with her research and see to it that nothing happens to her when she's visiting these sites."

Rowan nodded once, his eyes the tiniest bit narrowed. "Yes, sir."

"That's done, then."

Done. She'd just gained a nanny/bodyguard, neither of which she needed.

But honestly, deep down, she couldn't deny the tiniest hint of excitement that Rowan had volunteered for the job.

"Is that all, Captain?" Rowan asked.

Avery nodded and waved a hand. "Yeah." But before Rowan's hand even hit the doorknob, he added, "Hey, since you're not gonna be dealing with junkies and pushers for a while, how about shaving that crap off your face?"

"That an order, sir?"

Avery grunted. "I'll call your captain and get you temporarily reassigned."

"Fine," Rowan said.

Evie looked back and forth between the three men, not entirely understanding what had just happened, why it had happened, or the undercurrents in the room. The only thing she knew for certain was that Rowan was going to be by her side while she was working on this project. They'd have to spend a lot of time together, at least for the next week.

That meant she didn't have to try to come up with a reason to see him again, which she'd been trying to do all morning.

So while Carlton looked ready to snarl, Avery looked ready to laugh, and Rowan just stood there all big, brawny, silent, powerful man, Evie offered the three of them a bright smile and said, "Wonderful. We'll get started right away."

* * *

Now his brothers were *really* gonna fucking kill him.

Had he really done what he thought he'd done? Was he actually going to help the beautiful blonde he'd had wild, sexy dreams about last night with a book that could destroy his family?

"I must be outta my mind," he mumbled.

"You said that, not me," said Evie from the passenger seat beside him. She didn't even look up, continuing to peruse the thick folder on her lap, which contained copies of old black and white photos, reports, and newspaper clippings.

They were the first words they had exchanged since they'd gotten into the car.

After leaving Avery's office, the two of them had walked in

silence to the elevator. While Evie had done her interview and lineup with the assigned detective on her assault case, Rowan went for a second debriefing with the head of the Detective Support and Vice division. The drug case he'd been working, which had led into a human trafficking one, had caught attention way up the ladder. Rowan knew he was being looked at now and that he'd probably be offered a promotion.

Frankly, he would rather keep doing what he was doing at the 77th. But having gotten far more involved than he'd expected to in the trafficking case, he knew that might not be possible. He'd been down in the dregs for weeks; it might be hard for him to regain the relative anonymity he would need to go back to doing his regular job hunting down street dealers.

"So do you really think the suspect will plead guilty to avoid trial?" she asked, still not looking over at him. He sensed she was trying to break the ice between them, ice that had existed since he'd made his insane offer up in Avery's office. So much for the relaxing of tension between them this morning on the drive in. He and Evie seemed to be a yo-yo on a string, going up and down, never quite steady.

Remembering the way she had been shaking, her face completely pale when she came out of the viewing room after looking through a one-way glass panel at a group of men, one of whom had brutally attacked her less than twenty-four hours ago, he went along and tried to move past the tension.

"Yeah, I really do. The guy's rap sheet could wallpaper an entire house. With his record of violent assault, he'd be crazy to go in front of a jury."

She made a tiny sound. He glanced over and saw her throat work as she swallowed down that tidbit about her attacker.

Shoulda kept his mouth shut about Frankie "Firecracker" Lee's history. *Smooth move, jackass.*

"And he won't get out on bail until then?"

"If a judge gives him bail, it'll be so high he'll never be able to come up with it." He changed the subject. "You sure you don't want to go get your car and take it back to your place, maybe change clothes?"

"I told you I washed these," she said with a shrug, not sounding like she cared at all.

Although she looked good—stylish, if he was any judge of such things—she wasn't matched head to toe. He doubted that kind of stuff mattered to her. He would bet she spent more money on books and travel than she did on clothes and shoes.

"And the car is fine where it is. I really don't want to waste any time."

"Okay, you're in charge."

As they had walked to his car from the headquarters building, Evie had silently handed him a list of the sites she wanted to visit, intending to get started right away. Rowan believed he'd mumbled something reasonable in response, though he wasn't sure since he'd still been in shock over his own impulsive offer.

Damn Carlton. The creepy bastard couldn't keep his crawling eyes off Evie, even in front of his own boss.

And damn Avery with his obnoxious sense of humor and old-school way of dealing with things that pissed him off. As, obviously, the Evie Fleming situation, Carlton's pleading, and apparently Rowan's beard, had.

Now here he was, because of his own stupidity, knowledge of Carlton's sleazy reputation, and some weird protective instinct he had for a woman he barely knew, heading to the scene of a crime that took place decades ago.

"So Glassell, huh? Starting right with Ramirez?"

She didn't ask how he knew they were going to the apartment of a Night Stalker victim. Some LA crimes were so infamous, every cop knew the details of them, even from a distance of decades.

"The manager agreed to show me around. Somebody lives in the first victim's original apartment, but another ground floor one that's on the opposite side of it is vacant."

"What do you expect to find after all these years?"

"I don't expect to *find* anything, at least not as it relates to that case. I'm looking more to just understand the person who once lived there. How the apartment was laid out, the position of the windows, the doors. The vibe."

"The vibe?" He rolled his eyes. As far as he was concerned, the only vibe the place could possibly hold was the depression of the building's tenants about how much they paid in rent.

"You volunteered for this," she pointed out.

"Don't remind me."

After a slight hesitation, she asked, "Why'd you do it?"

His response came out of his mouth before he could think about it. "I have no friggin' idea. I must be a glutton for punishment."

She sucked in an audible breath, and he realized how that must have sounded. Like being with her was a punishment.

Well, it was, but not in the way she was thinking.

Frankly, being stuck in a car with her, or in a cramped room to research old case files, was going to be agonizing because every minute he spent with the woman increased the churn of hunger in his gut.

He'd left the house last night cursing who she was. That hadn't stopped erotic dreams about the woman from wrecking his sleep, however. And this morning, when he'd seen her in broad daylight, the California sun shining on that soft blond hair, the breath had been pulled right out of his lungs as a sheer wave of attraction washed over him.

He wanted her. Badly. Wanted the woman who was on a mission that could destroy his life, and the lives of his brothers.

If she got too close, she could blow up his entire world.

And with his impulsive offer, he'd inserted himself into hers instead.

He cast a quick glance at her, seeing the way she'd dropped her head down as if staring at her folder, her hair swinging forward in a curtain to conceal her face. She was obviously avoiding looking at him.

"I didn't mean it that way," he muttered.

"Forget it."

"Evie, look," he said, trying to think of an excuse, something to say other than the truth. Finally, he settled for *some* of the truth. "You're incredibly attractive, you know that, right?"

This time, her gasp was different, more feminine. She jerked her head up to look at him and pulled a hand to her own chest. "Excuse me?"

"You heard me." He tightened his grip on the steering wheel as he changed lanes. "Carlton—well, he's a real piece of work."

"I noticed. Get back to me being attractive and why you're a glutton for punishment."

Damn, the woman didn't pull any punches.

"I meant, I guess I've already fallen into the habit of taking care of you."

She harrumphed, obviously dissatisfied with that answer. "And I very much appreciated that last night. But I'm not in the grip of a violent criminal trying to drag me into an alley anymore. I don't need you to physically protect me."

"I know that. But when I thought about you getting stuck with somebody like Carlton, who wants—"

"I know, he wants to be a writer."

"I don't think he even knows how to spell *writer*, much less become one. The only thing he wants to hear from you is the word *yes*. The guy's a slimeball."

"I noticed that too."

"Then you understand why I did it."

"Um, you offered to be my police guide because you were, what, protecting my virtue or something?"

That did not sound right. "Of course not."

"Then what?"

Jesus, she was persistent.

"I didn't like the way he was looking at you, okay? That piece of shit would have harassed you, which would've caused all kinds of trouble."

"Oh, so you were protecting the LAPD from a sexual harassment claim?"

He was torn between wanting to laugh and wanting to growl. Instead, he bit out, "I didn't want him touching you."

She still didn't let it go, didn't accept the very true explanation. "So you were playing a boy's game of claim-the-toy-by-putting-your-hand-on-it-first?"

"God, you're pushy. You shoulda stuck with being a reporter."

"Answer the question."

Stopped at a stop sign, he turned his head to look at her. "All right. I put my hand on you first."

Despite her huffy annoyance, her eyes gleamed in feminine satisfaction at having gotten him to admit it.

But he wasn't finished. "I put my hand on you when I hauled you out of the frying pan last night, and the last thing I wanted was to watch you dive headfirst into the fire this morning."

Her triumphant expression faded. "You really think Carlton's that bad?"

Did he? Was he really concerned for Evie's safety with the other cop, or was that just a justification for what Rowan had done?

He thought about it, but he honestly couldn't say for sure.

"I don't know. But I do know this. There's more to him than his kiss-ass, brown-nosing façade. He's at headquarters, in an office job, not just because he's ambitious, but because he has family connections that he took advantage of to get ahead. Worse, it's because nobody trusts him enough to work with him on the streets. I didn't want him around you. And that's the truth."

Not the whole truth, not nothing but the truth, but it was as far as he was willing to go right now. No way could he tell her he was incredibly attracted to her himself. Kissing her last night had probably made that indisputable, but he was hoping she would forget about that crazy encounter, just as he intended to.

One of these days.

Memories of the taste of her notwithstanding, he was determined not to act on that attraction, oh hell no. He had to be on guard, walking a tightrope between assisting her with her research and preventing her from digging into anything that could incriminate his family. That meant letting her know he still wanted her would be a very bad idea.

And actually letting something happen between them—like the kind of hot, wild, sweaty, outrageous sex he wanted to have with her—would be sheer insanity. He needed to keep his hands—and all his other all-too-interested body parts—off her.

She nodded slowly, her vividly blue eyes still locked on him, gauging, judging…accepting. "All right. Thank you. I appreciate it."

"You're welcome."

He just hoped he didn't live to regret his protective instinct.

When they reached their destination, Rowan went into cop mode and immediately began assessing the location and possible threats. The area wasn't bad—the neighbors were certainly quiet, considering the place was very close to a cemetery. The apartment building itself was small and old, two story, brown and beige, and gated. An on-site manager was waiting for them and immediately came over to greet Evie. He was holding a hardcover book in one hand and a clanking ring of keys in the other.

Not sure what, exactly, his part in this play was, Rowan simply stood beside her, listening, as the other man gushed about her books and asked for an autograph. She gave it while asking and answering a few questions, smoothly managing the man and getting exactly what she wanted: private access to the apartment.

Making a mental note to stop by a bookstore and pick up a copy of one of her books for himself, Rowan went with her into the vacant unit, which smelled like old shoes, bleach, and lemon.

"So how's the vibe so far, murder fan?" Rowan couldn't help asking as he followed her through the one-bedroom space, which looked just like any other small, old apartment.

"Hmm," was her only reply as she studied the ancient refrigerator.

"I don't think that was here in 1984. It can't be more than thirty years old, tops."

Another *Hmm*. Evie was absorbed, lost in her own thoughts, taking notes, measurements, and pictures. In the bathroom, she got on her hands and knees and peered into the under-sink cabinet. She was on all fours. His mind went right into the gutter.

Lord have mercy.

He turned around and walked out of the bathroom, waiting for her near the front door, wondering why he was so attracted to someone who was so wrong for him in every way. Not only because she could put a key in a lock his family had been keeping over the Harry Baker case, but because she was very different from most other women he went for. He liked beer-drinking sports fans, brunettes usually, young, energetic, and sunny-dispositioned.

This woman was not at all like that. Thirtyish Evie was blond, cool, brainy, and detached. Obviously successful, with fame from her books and potential Hollywood connections, he suspected she had a fairly large bank account. Her mind was constantly churning with the darkness from her work, the world that she'd chosen to embrace for her career. He doubted the sun penetrated that exterior very often.

Maybe in a different life, she'd be right for him. Or, rather, he'd be right for her. Before he'd ever thought about becoming a cop, he'd been enrolled in law school. It was only after the Baker incident that he'd dropped out and applied for the LAPD, feeling the need to atone for what he'd done by walking a beat, not by becoming some rich, successful attorney.

That guy—the lawyer Rowan with money, prestige, and higher-level tastes—might have been a match for the woman snooping through the musty apartment. The one he was now, with the small apartment that still broke his bank every month, a beat-up old Mustang, and a savings account in the low-four-digit range definitely was not.

The truth didn't stop the wanting.

"Fuck," he mumbled, wishing he could stop thinking of her like a woman he wanted and merely like a threat he needed to block before it achieved complete Winchester destruction.

He was able to console himself with one small fact. If he was working closely with Evie, he should be able to steer her away from anything regarding Harry Baker's murder, or Steve's suicide. She already knew he didn't want anything to do with that case, and since Steve had been so publicly involved with his poor sister, Rachel, and he'd put that topic off-limits, too, maybe it wouldn't be too hard to keep this situation under control.

Just make sure you keep your dick in your pants, he reminded himself.

Right. Because if he got personally involved with her—had sex with her—it would be a lot harder to tell himself he was do-ing this for legitimate reasons.

The illegitimate ones would be so much nicer.

It took several minutes for her to finish what she was doing and find whatever the hell it was she was looking for. When she returned, she was mumbling to herself and tucking her phone and notebook into her oversized purse.

"It doesn't matter that this isn't the right unit?" he asked, his curiosity aroused by her single-mindedness. He'd gotten into this for dumb reasons of his own; now he was actually getting a little interested.

"No, the manager said it's a mirror image." She tapped lightly on an interior wall. "It's right there." A tiny shiver shook her slim form, as if she felt some taint in the very air that lingered from that long-ago crime.

Rowan felt nothing.

He had been to plenty of crime scenes for his job…and a couple not for work. He'd even cleaned them up—once for his intoxicated mother when he was just a little kid. Another for his brother, who he'd feared was a killer.

Seeing the evidence left behind at a crime scene affected him. Seeing the victim definitely did. But this, and the apartment on the other side of that wall? They were just rooms. Just places. Places removed from the dark past by decades' worth of moments, of breaths, of meals, of sleep, of sex, of tears.

Evil wasn't a tangible force that lingered in a single spot where something awful had happened. Evil was a man-made malevolence. Something that found dark and fermented soil in which it could swell and grow in hearts and minds and deeds every single solitary day.

"Okay, I think I'm finished here," she said.

Shaking off his thoughts, Rowan straightened and opened the door. "Did you get everything you needed?"

She nodded, eyeing him. "What, no quippy comment?"

"Are you calling me quippy?"

"If the quip fits…"

"Nobody uses the word *quip* in real life."

"I do."

"You would. You're a *writer*."

Reaching the car, he opened the door for her. Before she got in, she said, "You really should be careful, you know."

"Of what?"

A smile. "As you said, I'm a writer. If you don't watch out, I might just have to include you in this book of mine."

Rowan's heart pounded and slid down to his feet. Somehow, though, between the time he closed the door on her side and walked around to his own, he pulled it back, forced it into a steady beat, and built a wall of silent self-protection.

He couldn't lower his guard toward her. She might be kidding now, but if she found out the truth and published it, his sister's memory and legacy would be tarnished, and he and his brothers would be in the spotlight for all the wrong reasons.

Chapter 5

"Tell me everything," Candace Oakley said, scooting her chair closer to Evie and lowering her voice. "What have you been up to?"

Evie and her agent sat in a crowded restaurant during the weekday lunch rush on Thursday afternoon. They had met at a place near Candace's office so they could catch up without being interrupted before Evie set off for another crime scene visit later today. And because Evie didn't want to go to the office and see Candace's husband, Marcus.

It wasn't that Evie actively disliked her movie agent. It was just that he was...a movie agent. He was a slick California stereotype. Although handsome and successful, he had little personality and less charm. She still couldn't comprehend what, exactly, about him made Candace pick up and leave New York for LA, a city she'd once claimed to hate.

"Come on, give me details," Candace whispered.

Considering her work wasn't exactly appropriate for restaurant conversation, she assumed that was the reason for the super-spy routine.

"Tons of research, reading, and taking notes. The usual early days of a book."

"And, um…your *side project*?"

The "side project." That was one way to put it.

Another way was the potential new serial killer case.

Candace knew about Evie's suspicions. She was the *only* person who knew. She was fully on board with Evie doing what she could to connect the dots on the Southern California murders of those twelve women whose cases remained unsolved and mostly forgotten.

"Everything's fine. Thanks for the help. If you hadn't called in some favors, I might have been stuck sitting in a room in the Archives and Records Center begging for crumbs from every file. Having access anytime from the private office they set up for me at headquarters is a real blessing."

Candace waved a hand. "No worries. Marcus knows lots of people, and the member of the board of commissioners really is a fan of yours." She dropped her voice into that rough whisper again to ask, "Were there any questions about why you wanted cold case files from so many random, unsolved murders in addition to the more well-known, closed ones?"

Evie shook her head. "I asked for so much information, I don't think those particular files would stand out much. Nobody has said anything."

Hopefully the lead detectives who investigated those cases weren't too suspicious either. Six of them were still members of the LAPD, another was dead, and four were retired. Considering they hadn't connected the murders before, she didn't imagine they would be on the phone comparing notes about her requests for interviews now.

She didn't doubt that Rowan would eventually catch on and would want an explanation. So far, she'd been focusing on the infamous crimes, reserving her research into this longshot idea for when she was at home alone. But if she wanted to really dig into the files, she would have to do it at headquarters, which meant Rowan would probably be on hand. And curious.

Of course, since she had made arrangements to talk to a retired detective who'd been the lead investigator on two of the murders tomorrow, and since Rowan would be with her, as her "bodyguard," he would likely be demanding answers sooner rather than later.

"So how's the rental house? Everything okay there?"

Evie hesitated, but then nodded.

"What's wrong? More press?"

"I've managed to dodge them. I suspect they've lost interest. They haven't shown up at my house since Tuesday." Evie still wasn't sure she totally believed Candace's assurances that Marcus hadn't given out her home address to the media.

"But there's something else." Candace wagged her index finger. "Come on, what is it?"

Evie shrugged. "I'm being stupid. A little paranoid after what happened, it's nothing."

"*What's* nothing?"

Breathing deeply, Evie replied, "I just…I suddenly feel uncomfortable there."

"Well you haven't been here a week yet."

"I know, I mean, well, the other day when I came home, the day after the attack, I just felt very tense." Realizing she'd admitted she had not gone home that night, and not wanting to answer any questions about where she'd been all of Monday night, she rushed on. "I was uncomfortable as soon as I walked in the door. I kept thinking things had been moved around, very subtly. And a window was unlocked. I thought for sure I'd latched it. The milk was gone, but I don't remember finishing it, and the pillows were reversed on the bed. Things like that."

Candace tapped a brightly painted fingernail on her mouth, appearing concerned. "Was anything missing?"

Evie shook her head. "No, nothing. I know I'm being ridiculous. If anybody had broken in, it would have been an easy thing to grab my iPad, the jewelry off the dresser, and a few small bills lying on the bedside table."

"Exactly."

"Forget I said anything, please."

Reaching across the table, Candace covered her hand and squeezed. "Sweetie, you went through a terrible trauma. It would be surprising if you weren't overly on guard. It's natural."

She supposed so. Remembering the days after Blair's murder, she was pretty sure Candace was right. Her apartment had been a crime scene, of course, so she couldn't move back in. But she hadn't been able to keep living downtown on her own, either. Although she'd sworn it was the last thing she would ever do—that she'd never be one of those college grads living in Mom and Dad's basement—that's exactly what she'd done for a few months. This current reaction was similar, just on a smaller scale.

"I'm sure you're right," she said.

"You know you're always welcome to stay with us."

"You're very kind, but I'm fine."

Evie considered her agent a friend, but she would never have accepted. Not with Marcus there. That didn't mean she didn't appreciate the offer, however.

"So what else is going on? They still want you to have a police escort on your field trips, right?"

"Right," she said, but then fell silent again.

She didn't want to talk about Rowan to the other woman. She feared she had already revealed her personal interest in him when she and her agent talked on the phone. If his name came up now, in person, she didn't doubt her astute friend would ferret out the truth that Evie felt something other than professional appreciation for the man.

What that might be, she didn't know.

Well, attraction, yes, she knew that. But over the past two days when he'd been chauffeuring her around, waiting patiently as she took pictures and drew sketches of buildings, of bridges, of hillsides, of empty lots, she'd begun to like him a lot too.

Yes, he was still reserved with her. No, he hadn't completely reverted to that warm, friendly guy she'd met the night he'd rescued her. He certainly hadn't kissed her again.

But oh, God, did she want him to.

"Have you found any particularly interesting angles, fresh ways to look at old cases?"

"Yes, actually. It's really going well." If you could call being immersed in some of the worst crime scenes, forensics, autopsy reports, and photos in history *going well.* "I might be able to shine some new light on some old blood."

Wincing, Candace said, "I don't know how you do it. Better you than me, honey."

"I know, I know. You ran out of the theater screaming when Scar killed Mufasa."

"Come on, that was fucking brutal."

"Meanwhile, I was rooting for Mufasa to whip out a claw and scratch the crap out of Scar's face," she said, pausing as their server topped off their cups of coffee.

"So," Candace said when they were alone. "Everything okay with LA's finest?"

"Yep, all good."

"The cops are being cooperative?"

Evie turned her gaze toward her cup and slowly added sugar, watching it dissolve. Finally, she murmured, "Very cooperative."

Yes, cooperative. Professional. Respectful.

Not personal, though. Nothing *truly* personal had occurred between her and Rowan since he'd volunteered to be her police escort during her research mission.

Actually, no, the strong vibe between them, the heat and the awareness, had come to a screeching halt the other night at his brother's house. When she'd made herself appear to be just as bad as the paparazzi and reporters, who still tried to get her on camera whenever she was spotted, though they had, at least, stopped staking out her house.

"What aren't you telling me?" Candace asked, her tone sharp and her gaze piercing. "I know you. There's something you're not saying."

Although Evie trusted Candace, she knew that as a newly-wed, still infatuated with her six-years-younger husband, the woman might not be the excellent secret-keeper she had once been. So although she might otherwise like to have confided in someone about the frustrating attraction she felt for Rowan, who was trying so hard to treat her like she was a client and he a bodyguard, she just couldn't do it.

"No, seriously, everything's fine. I've been to several sites already. Spahn Ranch is right after lunch. My police escort is picking me up here soon. Should be a really interesting day."

She only hoped Rowan did not come into the restaurant when he arrived. She didn't want Candace meeting him. Her agent had an eye for good-looking men, and Rowan would be impossible for her to ignore.

Candace wrinkled her nose, recognizing the name of the ranch where the Manson "family" had lived. And, supposedly, killed. "Ick. The way your mind works, woman, you kinda scare me sometimes."

"I get that a lot," she grumbled.

She scared a lot of people, or at least made them look at her strangely. Maybe that was one thing that so drew her to Rowan. He didn't eye her and see a ghoul…just a nosy writer.

"Sorry," Candace said, looking a little sheepish. Her warm brown eyes, the same shade as her short hair, shifted toward her purse. "Speaking of scary things…" She opened her Gucci bag and retrieved a white, letter-sized envelope.

As Candace slid it across the table, Evie saw the stamped notice across the front.

Notice: Forwarded from the Virginia Department of Corrections.

Angstrom.

Swallowing hard, she put her fingertips on the letter, drawing it closer. Seeing that the top of the envelope had been slit open, she took no offense at the invasion of her privacy. Evie didn't give out her contact information, having everything sent through her agent. Candace's staff opened and copied all corre-

spondence, including the infrequent letters from the murderer
Evie had helped put away. It was a cautionary measure, one she
appreciated.

"Do I want to read it?" she asked with a shrug, feigning
nonchalance she definitely did not feel, even with Angstrom
locked up in a maximum-security prison thousands of miles
away.

"Same charming guy," Candace said with a sneer.

"No threats?"

"Not in so many words. Were you expecting any?"

"Not in so many words."

Ever since she'd gotten the news that there might be a new
trial, Evie had been waiting for Angstrom to make his move.
He would almost certainly try to prevent her from testifying
against him. Her testimony in his first trial had been pivotal,
and she'd already been told by prosecutors that his attorneys
wanted her excluded for some BS reason.

She had already begun to suspect that if legal maneuvers
did not work, Angstrom wasn't above trying less legal methods.
Like threatening her…or even, the prosecutor had warned her,
sending someone to find her and make her cooperation even
less likely.

She had little doubt that Angstrom, despite being a monster,
held a fascination for a certain kind of lonely, needy individual.
Some people believed in his innocence, some didn't. Some with
equally twisted minds applauded what he'd done and wanted
his approval for their own adventures. Some wanted to cure
him, some to learn from him.

Would any of them, she wondered, be crazy enough to do his
bidding and eliminate witnesses against him?

Despite the warm California breeze wafting in through the

open doors of the restaurant, she couldn't contain a chill as an invisible, icy finger slid up her spine.

"You don't have to read it now," Candace said, trying to take the letter back.

"Begun is half done," she murmured, quoting something her grandmother used to say. "I'd rather get it over with."

She slid the single sheet of folded paper out of the envelope, opened it, and quickly scanned the words from the monster who'd brutally murdered her friend.

Dearest Evelyn—

Hope this letter finds you well. I hear you're in California working on a new book. Can't wait to read it! A fan sent me one of those new ebook devices, so you can count on me to download it the day it comes out. Can you believe I've turned into such a reader? Funny how your tastes change when you have lots of time on your hands and nothing else to do. I miss my old activities…hope you're keeping up with your oil changes and checking your air pressure. Sure wouldn't want you to get a flat out in the middle of nowhere!

How do you like California? I used to go there sometimes. An old buddy of mine lives there, and I always liked to visit. Maybe I should hook you two up so you have somebody to make friends with.

Getting out much? Remember what they say, all work and no play makes Evie a dull girl! Be careful on that sunny beach—your skin is pretty fair, as I recall. So pretty with that blond hair of yours.

I guess you heard I might be getting a new trial.

Between you and me, I really hope I don't see you there.

Stay well,

J.H.A.

Having felt the blood drain from her face, Evie lowered the paper to the table and reached for her water glass. Her hand trembled as she picked it up, and cool liquid sloshed onto her thumb. Ignoring it, she brought the glass to her mouth and drank deeply.

"Why don't you throw it away?" Candace said gently. "I made a copy for your file."

"I can't." She lowered her glass. "Someday I will. For now, I'm keeping all the originals...just in case."

Just in case he got a new trial. Just in case her world went red with blood again. Just in case she was dragged back into his insanity.

Just in case he came after her.

Just in case.

Joe Henry Angstrom had been writing to her since shortly after his conviction. Chatty letters, with pointed references she would understand while censors might not. Like the line about his hobbies and her car maintenance. He blamed her for his capture, and undoubtedly wanted to keep himself in the forefront of her mind. She'd done a pretty fair job of ignoring his continued existence for a couple of years now. With the potential of a new trial, however, that was becoming harder and harder to do. His letters were coming more frequently, and the press had been pressing her more diligently.

God, she just wanted it to be over.

"Frankly, I think he's been reading too many Hannibal Lecter books on that e-reader of his," Candace said with an eye-roll. "He's got delusions of out-eviling the biggest literary devil in history."

"Yes, delusions. He's not a genius-for-the-ages. Smart, yes, but certainly not a mastermind. And I am no Clarice Starling."

Angstrom had been a mechanic with sick proclivities whose own arrogance had helped Evie figure out what he was up to. He'd been a fool to keep and display trophies from his victims.

Of course, he hadn't been careless enough to put *her* license tag on the wall of his shop, not when she was a customer and Blair's roommate. That would have been just begging to get caught.

If not for that weakness, his need to see and remember what he'd done, to flaunt proof of it in front of anybody who came into his shop, she never would have connected him to the murders. He might still be out there, doing the monstrous things he did.

"Are you okay, hon? You're not worried, are you? There's no way he could get to you."

"I know. I'm really fine."

"What happened the other night, though...the mugging..."

She waved a hand. "Random crime of opportunity."

Her friend nodded in agreement. "I think so too. Lord, I almost had a heart attack when I got that photo text from you. I screamed so loud Marcus thought somebody was breaking in."

"I'm sorry, I wasn't thinking very clearly. It was my first impulse."

"It was a good one. I knew right away you were in trouble. If I hadn't reached you, Marcus was going to go out and look for you since we could just barely make out a sign on a business across the street."

"That's kind," she said, glad Candace's husband hadn't come to the rescue. Knowing him, he'd have wanted to call a press conference right on the spot.

"Hey, there are my girls!"

Speak of the devil and he shall appear.

Candace's husband—tall, impeccably dressed in a designer suit and spit-shined shoes, with perfectly styled hair and a closely shaved face—strode to stand beside the table. Without waiting for an invitation, he grabbed a vacant chair from a nearby table and pulled it up close.

Evie found herself wishing they'd met somewhere far away from the agency office instead of right across the street.

"What are you girls up to? Gossiping?"

Candace looked embarrassed by his intrusion. "Shop talk. The book, the…"

"Hey, what's the deal on the guy who attacked you?" Marcus asked, interrupting his wife, who dropped her lashes and looked away.

"He couldn't make bail, so he's still in jail," Evie responded, not happy that her lunch with her friend had been intruded upon, and even less happy at his casual rudeness toward his wife. Marcus might be a superstar Hollywood agent, but he wasn't a very thoughtful husband.

"That's good news." Marcus glanced out the open sliders toward the street, and then back at Evie. He smiled. "How's the new book coming? How are you liking California? When are you coming over to see the house?"

Fine. Okay. Never if I can help it.

She couldn't help it, of course. Candace was her friend, Marcus was Candace's husband and Evie's Hollywood agent. She had to play nice, whether she liked the man personally or not. And that would be a very big *not*.

"Soon," she promised. She smiled at Candace, seeing the other woman shifting uncomfortably, obviously embarrassed that her husband had shown up and inserted himself into their lunch, and into the conversation. "I look forward to seeing what you've done to the place."

Marcus draped an arm across the back of his wife's chair. "She's a born decorator," he said, his huge smile revealing those perfect, expensively capped teeth. "I keep telling her she's in the wrong business. She should become a designer and start supporting me for a change."

Cringing inwardly with embarrassment for the extremely successful literary agent, Evie sipped her coffee. But she did notice Marcus looking again out the doors toward the street.

Suddenly, he looked outside again, and his eyes gleamed. She suspected what he was seeing one second before she heard someone at the next table whisper about the arrival of a news crew from a local channel.

"Son of a bitch," she muttered.

Candace jerked and started. Marcus merely smiled.

"Did you set this up?" Evie asked, not trying to hide her anger and dismay.

"Now, don't get upset. Keeping you in the news can only help in our negotiations with the studio. A little competitive interest due to some hot press is a good thing, believe me."

Evie rose from her chair, letting her napkin fall to the floor. She quivered with rage at having been cornered like this by someone who was supposed to be a member of her team. She had known Marcus was ambitious, but she'd just never imagined he would pull a stunt like this.

"Oh my God, Evie, I'm so sorry," said Candace, starting to rise from the table as well. Marcus's hand on her shoulder pushed her back down in her chair.

For that alone Evie wanted to slap the man.

The news media van made her want to kick him right between the legs.

"Evie, come on. Back door."

Shocked to hear a familiar male voice, she looked across the restaurant and saw a broad, brown-haired figure watching her from behind dark sunglasses. Rowan was weaving between tables, moving quickly and deliberately, almost gracefully for a man so masculine and strong.

"Let's get outta here."

She grabbed her purse. He took her by the arm.

"Thank you."

"Who the hell are you?" Marcus asked, trying to step in their way.

Not even slowing, Rowan elbowed the other man out of the way. They hurried toward an emergency exit in the back of the café even as she saw a reporter enter through the front.

Rowan's dark sedan was illegally parked in the alley behind the place, blocking a Dumpster and a delivery truck, whose driver was honking in annoyance. Flashing his badge at the irritated man, who immediately stopped yelling, Rowan unlocked the door, watched her get in, and then joined her in the car. Two minutes later, they disappeared into LA lunch hour traffic, leaving the restaurant, the press, Candace, and her jerk of a husband behind them.

Evie finally relaxed enough to lean back in the seat, close her eyes, and take a slow, deep breath. Her heart had kicked up its pace when Marcus had appeared. When she'd spied the media outside, the quickening beats had roared like a freight train.

"You okay?"

She nodded, not looking at him, content merely to sit close to him, soaking up the warmth and security that the man always gave off.

"I pulled up outside to wait for you and saw the news van arrive. Did a quick run around the back to try to get you outta there before they got the microphone in front of your mouth."

"Thank you," she said, turning her head to look at him. "This is getting to be a habit, you showing up in the nick of time to save me from creepy men or stalking reporters."

He glanced over at her, concern in his dark eyes, a tender smile on his mouth. "I saw the reporters. I take it the creepy man was the dude in the shiny suit? He looks Hollywood."

"He is Hollywood." She wrinkled her nose, explaining about her lunch with Candace and Marcus's unexpected arrival. "I still can't believe he did that."

Rowan whistled. "So you really think this guy intentionally called the reporters to ambush you when he found out you were having lunch with his wife?"

"Yes, I do."

After a brief hesitation, Rowan murmured, "Okay, I know we talked about this the other night. But with what just happened, have you rethought the possibility that he really was the one who sicced the press on you given how easily they tracked you down after you were attacked?"

Evie stiffened in her seat. "Candace swore he didn't. I have such a hard time imagining somebody doing that," she said, spacing her words slowly and carefully.

Because she could. She *could* imagine it. Although they hadn't gotten an interview, there had been some film footage of her hurriedly getting into Rowan's car at the scene, along with brief details about the attack, which was being called a mugging.

Huh. She suspected the creep was after more than her purse.

With the coverage, Marcus had a new angle to take back to the studios. He had almost certainly pointed at the story, reminding them that she was a figure in the press. That she attracted danger. That a serial killer might be after her—that was one news station's take on it.

Whatever details they hadn't gotten from her, they'd simply made up.

God was she ever glad she'd left journalism after a very short-lived career.

"Did you tell your friend where you were when you texted that picture to her Monday night?"

"No, but she said they had a rough idea of where I was because of the background," she slowly admitted.

"Uh-huh. And then you texted her later to tell her you were okay, right?"

"Yes, I told her what neighborhood I was in." A throbbing started in her temple.

"And the press got there maybe an hour later? How coincidental. Just like today—when he actually admitted he set it up."

Yes, he had. The night she was attacked, he would have had just enough time to make a call providing the tip, and likely *would* have lied about it to Candace. "That bastard."

"Doesn't sound like your friend has very good taste in men."

No, she did not. Candace was twice divorced, and often

said the third time was the charm. Frankly, Evie had thought three strikes and you're out to be more appropriate, but she hadn't wanted to butt into something that was none of her business. Candace had never asked Evie's opinion of her new husband, and, to be honest, Marcus did talk a good talk. He had convinced Evie he could get her career going in Hollywood, and so far, he appeared to be making good on his word.

That didn't mean she didn't thoroughly dislike the man.

If he was the one who'd put the press on her tail the other night, could he also have given out her home address? She'd moved into the furnished rental less than a week ago. How else could they have gotten to her place before her if her movie agent hadn't told?

If that were the case, she would soon be shopping for a new movie rep.

"Know any good Hollywood agents?" she muttered.

He snorted. Yeah, with his brother's connections, he probably did. She hadn't even considered that.

"I believe he did it, but I *can't* believe it, you know? It's so sleazy."

"Welcome to Hollywood."

"I know, I know."

"Want me to plant heroin in his car and throw him in the slammer for you?"

Her mouth fell open. Rowan's widened into a big smile.

"Smartass," she said, chuckling, wondering how the man managed to catch her off guard and bring her out of a bad mood right into a pretty good one.

He was funny. Not all the time, certainly, but she saw flashes of wit and mischievousness. She never would have associated those things with a tough, powerful, hard-ass cop, but now she knew better.

Rowan defied expectation and stereotype. There was much more to him than the muscles, the badge, and the courage. Frankly, he wasn't like anyone else she had ever known.

"Okay, while we're on kind of unpleasant topics about shitty men, there's something you should know."

She stiffened. "Am I going to want to hear this?"

"Probably not."

Her heart started to beat faster. "Is it about Angstrom?"

He grabbed her hand, squeezing lightly. "No, God no. I'm sorry, I should have said that up front."

Her pulse might have slowed down by .01 percent, but it might not have.

"Then what?"

"It's Franklin Lee."

It took her a second, but then she remembered the name on the paperwork she'd signed at headquarters. Franklin Lee was the man who had attacked her Monday night. How funny—in a this-is-so-not-funny way—that she hadn't even thought about the creep who'd assaulted her earlier this week. Her mind had gone only in one direction. Which probably showed just how much she'd been worrying about Joe Henry Angstrom and his appeal.

"What about him?"

Rowan hadn't removed his hand. She curled her fingers into his, not only because she sensed she was going to need to grip something, but also because she just liked the feel of his rough palm against hers. They were strong hands, man's hands, rugged and powerful. Hands a woman could rely on, connected to a man a woman could fall hard for. *If* he didn't distrust her and wasn't determined to keep an emotional wall between them.

"Lee didn't make a deal with the prosecutor on the case. He was offered a pretty fair one, but he turned it down and is rolling the dice with a jury."

Shit. So she was going to have to testify at another felony trial.

"Wonderful," she mumbled. Something else occurred to her. "Was he granted bail?"

Rowan shifted uncomfortably, which gave her the answer before he opened his mouth.

He nodded. "Yes, but even if he did get out—a huge if—he'd never come after you. It was a crime of opportunity. I bet you he'll end up agreeing to a plea when he gets closer to the trial and the likelihood of doing fifteen to twenty."

Maybe. But nothing was ever certain. Certainly life wasn't. Just look at Blair.

"All that aside, even if for some crazy reason he did try to track you down, he wouldn't be able to find you."

"Unless good old Marcus takes out a billboard and plasters my address on it to make sure the press can find me to get some good, juicy shots."

He gripped her hand tighter, and she shook her head slowly, knowing she was being overly dramatic. That wasn't like her. She was usually pretty cut and dried, down to earth and realistic. But realizing someone had betrayed her the way Marcus had, all to earn a bigger buck, had rocked her deeply. It was a trust broken, one she didn't think she was going to be able to move past. It might mean finding another literary agent as well. That would be really hard, considering the close, personal friendship she and Candace shared, but whatever the case, she was finished with Marcus Oakley.

"It's a moot point, I swear. He's not going to be on the streets to even try to track you down. His bail was set really high, Evie. I don't see how a street thug like that is going to come up with even ten percent of it. He has no property. No family, no gang affiliation—i.e., no deep-pocketed trafficking buddies to put up the cash or security. He'll be sitting in there until trial, I almost guarantee it."

Almost. Not her favorite word, that one. But she supposed it was the best she could expect or hope for right now.

"Okay," she said, not unlooping her fingers from his. He seemed to have forgotten they were linked, and she wasn't going to make the first move to un-entwine them. "Thank you for telling me."

He nodded, still staring at the road. After about thirty seconds of silence, though, he added something low under his breath. "And if he tries, I'll make sure he regrets it for the rest of his days."

She shivered lightly, hearing the darkness and intensity in Rowan's voice. It wasn't there often. She'd heard it when he tore Lee off her the other night, but not since. Sure, he'd been serious most of the time.

This, though. This sounded dangerous. A promise, not a threat, and she pitied anybody who didn't recognize the determination in that voice and get the hell out of the man's way.

Not wanting to talk anymore about her troubles, she changed the subject. "So, you have the trail maps to find the areas I'm interested in at Spahn Ranch?"

He got the message and, to her disappointment, pulled his hand away and put it back on the steering wheel. "Got 'em."

"I appreciate you going with me," she said, "though it wasn't absolutely necessary. I'm sure I could have figured it out on my own now that it's part of a state park."

"Not a problem, since I'm officially assigned to you for now," he said.

She licked her lips. "Been meaning to ask, is that a problem for you? Was your own boss mad when Avery asked for the reassignment?"

"Nah. Until the trafficking ring I put on the task force's radar forgets my name, it's not a bad idea for me to stay in another part of town."

"I suspect there are other things you could be doing."

"There are, but this assignment has proved to be…different."

She searched for resentment but didn't see or hear any. He was just stating a fact; he no longer seemed annoyed about it. In fact, since they'd sat together in the office the LAPD had set up for her, going through old files and reports, she suspected his interest had been piqued, probably against his own will.

She didn't blame him. Some of what they were looking into was truly fascinating. Originally, most of the old LAPD documents had been stored on microfilm, but the agency had transferred almost everything to digital storage. That was fortunate, considering it was still hard to read the scratchy handwriting of a 1940s detective as he described a murder scene *after* it had been digitized and enhanced. The originals would be a nightmare.

"I probably know I shouldn't ask, since I'll get the same answer, but are you sure you really need to go out to the ranch?"

"What answer are you expecting?" she asked, tilting her head in curiosity.

"I need to see the angles, feel the vibe," he said, pitching his voice up in a bad imitation of hers.

She had to laugh, noting that the nice, playful, sexy guy was back. Who'd have believed ninety seconds ago she'd been thinking how dangerous he was.

"Shut up."

"Your words, honey, not mine."

"Ha-ha. Actually, I want to take some geographical measurements from famous spots immortalized in old photos," she said. "The cave being number one."

He glanced over at her, taking in her lightweight blouse, jeans, and ankle boots. "Um, you know it's a hike, right?"

"I know."

"Those boots are not gonna do it."

She stared at her feet. "Why not? They're not spike heeled or anything. It's just a wedge."

"I don't care what they're called, they look like shoes-to-trip-in to me. Even sneakers would be better than those things. There's some climbing, rough sections of rock...I just don't trust what you have on."

She could have argued, but Evie had always been the sensible type, and she took no offense. "I do have one other pair of boots. They're knee-high, and a little more East-Coast-winter style, which is why I didn't wear them. But they do have rugged soles and they're flat."

"That would be better."

"Guess we have a stop to make," she said, wishing she'd thought more carefully about the shoes. She hated putting him out even more.

"Wanna remind me of your address?"

He'd been near her place only once, the night they'd met, so of course he wouldn't remember the exact location. The idea of having him come inside her home to wait while she changed shoes gave her the tiniest shiver of expectation. Since the other night when she had so bumblingly questioned him about the tragedy that had touched his family, he'd been nothing but respectful. Sometimes coldly so, but lately, more friendly. But there was always a distance.

Today, though, she'd felt a shift. He was more relaxed, teasing, as if the tension over the Baker case had finally eased. She only hoped it stayed that way.

And she wondered what it would take to go one step further than just an easing of tension, like right back into his arms for another of those glorious kisses like the single one they'd shared at the mountain house.

Not to mention all the things that could come after it.

Before she could come up with some other bit of light conversation to take advantage of his good mood, or, she considered, even asked him if he was ready to schedule that coffee date, his cell phone rang. He eyed it, saw the name, and frowned. The phone was on a dash holder, facing him and not her, so she couldn't see who it was.

But when he answered, snapping, "Raine? What's up?" she knew.

"Got a lead, bro. Need to talk to you."

She could see his muscles bunch up under the T-shirt he wore. His arms thickened and flexed, his hands clenching on the steering wheel. The thighs stretched against the loose cotton jeans, and she had to close her eyes to stop herself from gawking at all that masculine power.

"I have someone in the car with me right now," Rowan said, his tone stiff.

"Oh. Call me when you're free, okay?"

"Is it, uh…important?"

Hearing the hesitation in his voice, Evie knew he was being very careful because she was unable to help listening. He didn't even feel comfortable talking to his brother while she was around. Such a change from that first night when he'd so freely called Reece in front of a perfect stranger.

Despite today's progress, he really hadn't regained his faith in her. Which made something in her heart twist and clench. They hadn't talked more about his family or Harry Baker, but she knew that was behind his sudden cold front that had blown into the car.

He didn't trust her. He might have let down his guard again a little while ago, being the chill guy he was. Chill for a cop, anyway. But just the sound of his younger sibling's voice had him freezing up so fast she almost shivered.

Looking out the window, she focused on the road, not on the driver. Even before he finished the brief call, she knew what was going to happen. The veil would fall again, the formal layer of aloofness he wore around her whenever he remembered he wasn't supposed to like or trust her.

Funny, she'd thought at first that his antipathy toward her was completely instinctual after she'd revealed her interest in his family's connection to Baker. Now, though, having seen him transition back and forth from the teasing guy she'd seen a few times back into the rigid, cold cop who was settling into the seat beside her, she had to wonder if it wasn't entirely deliberate. It was as if the phone call had reminded him he wasn't *supposed* to let his guard down around her. Wasn't *allowed* to relax.

Every time the barriers began to slip, and he started to forget about the reasons for shutting her out, she saw the real Rowan again. Then something would happen to remind him, and he'd force an almost tangible wall between them.

That bothered her as a woman.

As a writer and a researcher, though, she had to admit it also interested her.

What wound, she wondered, had she opened up when she'd pricked that Achilles' heel of his Monday night? Was there more to the story about the Winchester's relationship with their late agent than she'd suspected? What secret was Rowan hiding about Harry Baker that made him pretend he felt nothing for her when she knew damn well he did?

Most of all…was it more important for her to pry his secret out of the depths of his family's history? Or do whatever it took to make Rowan Winchester trust her enough to really let her into his life?

There was really no way to ask him those questions outright, of course. She just had to hope that the more time they spent together, the more of those I-trust-you times there would be.

On this particular day, she definitely had to trust him. Because after a quick stop at her home to get a change of boots, they reached the Santa Susana Pass state park, whose land included what had once been the Spahn movie set, and she realized it would have been far more difficult to find her way around on her own. He knew exactly where to park and which guardrail to step over. The ranch certainly wasn't on any trail map. But once they were near it, there was a trail. Lots of Manson lookie-loos still came out here. The dead cult leader's mystique had lingered for decades and would probably continue to linger on for many more.

"Everything's pretty well gone, isn't it?" she said as they explored scrubby, empty land where old-fashioned stores and saloons had once stood, serving as backdrops for some famous Hollywood Western films and TV shows.

"Yeah. All the set buildings burned down in the early '70s."

"Yes, at the same time the trials were taking place."

The fire was not long after Charlie and his "family" had gone on their reign of terror. Although the cause was a spreading wildfire, she couldn't help thinking locals probably would have happily set it themselves, torching the blighted land from which so much evil had sprouted.

It didn't take long for Evie to learn the layout of the "town." There were no scraps of metal or wood, nothing that hadn't been scavenged by Manson fans long ago. It was just dusty, empty space. Nearly fifty years after its last human inhabitants, the area had been reclaimed by Mother Nature, which was for the best, as far as she was concerned.

"I looked up how to get down to the cave," Rowan said once she indicated she was finished up here. "It's going to be a little iffy. You'll probably be glad you changed your boots."

She was already glad. The last thing she wanted to do was fall around here. Not just because of the jagged rocks, some hidden beneath tall scrub, but also because of the poison oak. Not to mention the rumored snakes.

Less than five minutes later, she discovered that the rumors were true.

When she spotted the curled-up rattlesnake lying almost directly at the entrance to the overgrown trail that led down to the infamous cave, she let out a surprised little shriek.

"It's okay," he snapped. "Be quiet."

After that one squeal, her vocal cords had stopped functioning, so being quiet wasn't a big problem. Of course, her feet had stopped working too. And she might have come close to peeing her pants.

The snake—a big one, as far as she was concerned, but what

snake wasn't?—had spotted them. Its head rose from its coiled body, and it stared and hissed. The tail sticking out the bottom of the wound-up pile of teeth, venom, and slitheriness began to quiver, making that unmistakable sound that had also somehow been deemed appropriate for little baby toys.

"Back up slowly," he murmured, taking her arm and pulling her with him.

"I hate snakes, Rowan," she whispered.

"You're okay. He's more scared of you than you are of him."

"I seriously doubt that."

"He's just protecting his territory."

The animal could become king of the ranch as far as she was concerned.

When they were about fifteen feet away from the creature, it lowered its head and settled back down into its sunny spot, but it kept looking in their direction. Evie had the feeling it had no intention of going anywhere. It wasn't like they'd scared it out of their path, but he'd definitely scared her out of his.

"You okay?" he asked, turning and placing both hands on her shoulders. His expression and tone were concerned.

"Yeah, I think so. But I've seen enough. Ready to go? I could really use a corn dog. Or pizza. You want some pizza?"

He stared at her, a tiny smile on his lips. "You really are scared of snakes?"

"Um…"

"I didn't think you were afraid of anything, Evie Fleming." He shook his head. "You go up against a serial killer, you fight with a mugger, but a three-foot-long animal who hisses at you sends you running?"

Glaring, she replied, "Everybody has one weakness, okay?

My stupid brother dragged me to see *Snakes on a Plane* when we were in high school. I never recovered."

"You have a brother?"

She nodded. "Two actually, one older and one younger."

"Wow, so do I. One seventeen minutes older, one six years younger."

Smirking, she said, "Yeah, I've heard."

"To think I didn't know that about you."

"There are plenty of things you don't know about me. But that's okay, I don't know a whole lot about you either."

"Except what the entire world has seen in every tabloid on the planet since I was six years old."

"But then almost nothing since you left Hollywood when you were, what, twelve? Thirteen?"

He nodded.

She had always assumed the death of his only sister was what had driven the boys out of Hollywood. Although he had only mentioned Rachel once or twice, she suspected the bond had been very tight and that none of the brothers had ever truly gotten over the loss. Her brothers were a pain in her ass sometimes, but she didn't even want to think about losing them.

"I don't think cops rate tabloid covers."

"Not unless they've done something really awful," she said.

"Thankfully I've avoided that."

"But there are a lot of things I don't know about you after you left acting." Licking her lips, she went on. "Maybe we'll start letting each other in on some of those things."

He met her eyes and she knew he heard her unasked question. She wasn't flat-out saying he should just tell her whatever it was he didn't want to get out about Harry Baker. But she'd like to think there might be a chance for them to someday be more open with each other.

Frankly, it was about time *she* was open with *him* about her side project. And she would be. Tomorrow.

"We'll see, Evie," he finally replied. "Now, you ready to go, great snake chicken?"

"Oh shut up. Everybody's got an Achilles' heel. You watch for the snakes. If we see a tarantula along the way back, I'll take care of it."

He visibly shuddered before he could stop himself.

She laughed out loud. "You're scared of bugs?"

"Tarantulas aren't bugs. Haven't you heard? They're mutant creatures from another planet."

"Uh-huh."

"And once they're all here, a sun flare is going to blow them all up to the size of swing sets. There'll be intergalactic wars and we're gonna need Will Smith and Jeff Goldblum, and we better just hope water burns their skin."

Her laughter turned into a peal of giggles. He managed to maintain a serious tone despite his ridiculous words.

"Swing sets?" she asked, that one image having popped foremost in her mind. "Why the size of swing sets? Why not cars or something?"

"Because Reece once threw a spider down my shirt when we were on the swings. And that's when I learned their whole plot."

Her giggles continued.

"I've been watching for swing sets outside of playgrounds everywhere I go."

"You said they'd be the *size* of swing sets, not that they'd disguise themselves as them."

"It is a perfect disguise, you have to admit. All those legs."

"I think if every spider blew up into the size of a swing set, they wouldn't be too worried about being disguised. The secret would pretty well be out." She smiled brightly at him, knowing he'd intentionally teased her out of the snake mood, not to mention the darkness of what they'd come here to do. And it had worked. Damn, the man was likable. "So we have a deal. You watch for snakes, and I'll watch for spiders."

He stuck out a hand. She shook it. And they grinned at each other.

"Just remember," he said once they let go. "Spiders come in all sizes, and you agreed to take care of them. I threw up in the theater when that crazy-ass one rolled Frodo up in that web, so if we see him, just so you know, I'm running my ass off."

"And if I see a snake as big as the one in *Anaconda*, I'll be standing on top of your head to get away from it."

"Okay, 'cause I know you have had enough of these mother-fuckin' snakes on this motherfuckin' trail."

"Ack! Don't ever quote that movie to me again."

They started walking, and she soon heard him mumble, "Snakes. Why did it have to be snakes?"

"Would you please shut up? If not, I am going to have to feed you to the giant spider from the woods near Hogwarts. I think she's even bigger than the one Frodo got webbed by."

On that note, with the darkness of the project fading away, and a new kind of warmth between them, they began heading back toward the road. Their strides matched, their arms swung together, their hands almost brushing. He was actually whistling, and she knew that beneath those dark sunglasses, his warm eyes were undoubtedly twinkling to rival the stars in a kid's lullaby. It was the most relaxed and comfortable they'd been with each other. The attraction that always lurked beneath the surface was still there, but now it wasn't concealed beneath tension, fear, or anger. It was light and playful, and she liked it very much.

And then his phone rang.

Rowan pulled it out, glanced at the name, and mumbled, "My brother."

His steps slowed, but between one and the next, he moved farther to the left side of the path. Farther away from her. The smile was gone, the mouth was tight, and a veil of tension dropped between them like a blanket had fallen from the sky to drape him.

Evie suddenly found herself glad for Rowan's sunglasses.

Because she had no doubt that twinkle was gone.

Chapter 6

This is your lucky day, Franklin. I guess one of your scumbag druggie pals came up with the money to post your bail."

Frankie P. Lee, known on the streets as Firecracker, smiled and nodded as a fat, swaggering pig let him out of the cell he'd been locked in for four nights. He'd been waiting for this ever since the motherfucking judge had set his bail at two hundred and fifty grand.

He'd known somebody would bail him out. And he knew who had done it. Mighta taken the dude all week, but he'd obviously gotten the money here first thing this morning, because it was barely sunup and Frankie was soon gonna be a free man.

An hour later, after he'd walked out of jail and a couple of blocks away from the federal courthouse, he got a burner phone and confirmed his suspicion with a text. *It's me. Took you long enough, boss man.*

The answer came fast. *UR lky I got you out. U scrwd up bad.*

Screwed up? Shit, man, he didn't screw up. How was he

supposed to know an off-duty cop would show up? *Toldja we shouldn'ta done it so close to LAPD.*

Took only a second or two for the reply. Dude musta been waitin' by the phone for him to reach out.

Had to look rndm.

Yeah, yeah, so the guy who'd hired him had said.

They dnt cnnect me?

Nah. Didn't have nothin on me for them to trace. Dumped cell before. Cash stashed.

U dnt talk?

He thought about how to answer. Then thought, *Screw it,* and typed, *Not yet.*

This time the text back didn't come so fast. He started walking up the street, wondering if he'd made a mistake. Maybe he shouldn'ta pushed the guy. But damn, the fucker wouldn't listen when Frankie told 'im they needed to find someplace else to take the bitch.

A place that *wasn't* a couple o' blocks from the downtown home of the cops woulda been easy. The plan was good. Drag the bitch into the alley. Do what he wanted. Finish her off. Make it look like a street crime. Collect some serious money.

Fuckin' cop showed up and ruined everything.

Firecracker rubbed the back of his hand where the woman had scratched him. If she hadn'ta put up a fight, he'd probly'a gotten her behind that gate before the cop saw anything.

Bad luck. Super bad.

Maybe it was his own fault, not 'cause he did anything wrong, but for trusting a dude he knew better than to trust.

Well, that wasn't gonna happen no more. He typed out another text. *I ain't goin' down for dis and ain't takin' you down neither. But you gotta get me outta town. I need cash.*

I kno. Got ur bus ticket. Cash. New ID.

Firecracker breathed a sigh of relief, knowing he shouldn'ta worried. The dude was a pro. He had everything handled, just like he said he would when he hired Frankie to do this job.

Fan-fuckin'-tastic.

Dude responded with a warning. *Nvr com back.*

Got it. Where it at? He suspected he knew, but waited for the answer.

Same place. Bus at 8 tonit. 7th St.

Just like he figured. *Where'm I goin?*

Who cares? Jst go.

Where?

The guy who'd hired him, bailed him out, and was how gettin' him outta town with money and a new identity finally answered. *Florida.*

Awesome. Far away, still sunny. He could dig that. Bitches prob'ly be wearin' bikinis and shit on them Florida beaches. Already too cold here.

Cool.

We good?

Whistling as he walked down the street, he typed one more message. *Yeah, we good.*

Hopping on a city bus, Firecracker headed for Boyle Heights, knowing right where he was going. They hadn't done any of this in person. Firecracker had gotten a burner phone and all the plans were made over text. They'd arranged a drop spot for a first payment in an old abandoned house in the Heights, one of a shit-ton of flophouses in the area. Rich people were buying them places up and doin' that gentrification shit, but it was slow goin'. Meantime, there were lots o' old, abandoned buildings you could crash in, or use for drop spots for drugs, money, whores, just about anything you wanted.

Getting off the bus, he walked the couple of blocks to the house where he'd picked up the first wad of money—a deposit—a week ago. Boss man had picked the place, and a thousand bucks cash had been waiting right under an old bathroom sink, as promised.

His new ID and even more money than that just *better* be in the same place today.

Reaching the street and turning the corner, Firecracker frowned to see a ragged old woman pushing a shopping cart up the cracked, weedy driveway of *his* place.

"Where you think you're goin', old whore?" he called.

The woman looked at him and hurried up into the house.

Motherfuckin' cow better not even go near that bathroom or Frankie Lee was gonna be leavin' behind a pile of rags and old bitch bones in that house when he left.

He picked up his pace, jogging and then running to the house. Hunks of glass broke beneath his booted feet as he stomped through the knee-high weeds in the yard. Reaching the front door, he kicked it open and bellowed, "Old woman, this is my place."

"No," the bag lady whispered. "No, please."

"Get the fuck out of here."

"Don't want no trouble," she said.

He followed the sound of her voice and stepped into a hallway leading to the back of the house. To the bathroom. To his shit.

She was standin' right there, shakin' in her taped-together sneakers, her raggedy dress almost fallin' off her.

"Get away from that bathroom and get out this house, old woman, or I'ma put you out."

His fists bunching at his sides, he walked toward her, each long step slamming hard onto the cracked and rotting wood floor. The old woman didn't race toward the back door, as he figured she would. She looked around all scared and shit, like a rabbit with no place to go.

Then she did the one thing he'd told her not to. She jumped into the bathroom.

Firecracker charged forward, but he didn't get two steps before a massive explosion rocked the entire house.

Heat roared outta the bathroom and hit him in the face. He couldn't hear a fuckin' thing and felt shit hittin' him, stabbin' into his skin. He saw nothin' but smoke and flames and bits and pieces of old woman splattered on the walls.

"A trap, a trap, you motherfucker, a trap," he muttered as he staggered back toward the front door. He fell onto the ground out front, coughing and choking.

People came outta a couple of houses; the explosion had made the street shake like an earthquake. Still on his back, he shimmied away from the building, feeling bits of burning ash on his front, on his face, in his hair. He smacked at it, killing the sparks. But he also kept backing up, not knowing if that piece of shit had planted more traps.

Boss man wanted him dead. Dead so he couldn't testify about who'd paid him to do the hit on the writer. And he'd set a trap to take him out. A fuckin' bomb.

If the old woman hadn't gone into that bathroom, Frankie woulda set it off and it'd be his guts and brains splashed all over the burning walls of that place.

Fury and fear raced through him. He wanted the double-crossing prick's throat between his hands, wanted to rip him apart. He just wished he knew where to find him.

What if he's here, watchin'?

He might be. Might be hidin' around the corner to make sure his trap worked.

Don't got no knife, no gun.

He usually carried a blade, but the cops hadn't given that back this morning.

He was hurt, unarmed, lying out here in broad daylight.

And somebody wanted him dead. Somebody who didn't have any problem with a woman getting beaten up and killed right in downtown LA. Somebody who knew how to set bombs.

Firecracker rolled onto his stomach to put out the tiny bits of spark and flame. He got to his knees and then to his feet. A woman in a bathrobe yelled something from across the street. He couldn't hear her; his ears were fucked up.

He didn't call for help or even try to answer, much less wait for the ambulance or the fire department. He just started to stagger away from the house that was now really in flames, burning up the walls, the floors, the old woman, and any evidence that Frankie had picked up cash here from his client last week.

Gotta go, gotta get outta here.

Dude who did this shit was crazy. Had to be. You don't go blowin' up houses in an LA neighborhood. Guy planted a bomb to keep Frankie's mouth shut. He found out Frankie survived, he'd be tryin' again.

His legs was shakin', he hurt all over, he could barely hear.

But he could run. And he wasn't gonna stop runnin' until he was far away from that psycho who'd hired him to kill that writer.

* * *

Rowan was supposed to pick Evie up at 8:00 a.m. Friday for a meeting she'd arranged with a retired detective—he didn't know the reason for the meeting, assuming she'd fill him in on the way. But knowing traffic would be a bitch, he'd left Reece's place super early and had shown up on her street at 7:30. He'd thought about just waiting in the car but didn't want to freak out her neighbors, who had already bitched to her about the reporters and strange cars lining the block the other night.

Parking in front of her small house, he reminded himself to be cool today, totally professional. He could do it, just like he had yesterday during the hours they'd spent at Spahn Ranch, at least up until the snake incident.

Before that, though, they'd hiked, they'd explored, they'd stopped for her to take notes and pictures and compare places to old pics from the 1960s when a "family" named Manson had called the place home. She'd given him a history lesson on the case that he hadn't particularly wanted to hear.

He'd been Mr. Police Escort. Mr. Representative of the LAPD. Mr. Lapdog.

Not Mr. Interested, Attracted, and Horny.

It had taken every molecule of willpower he had, but he'd done it.

He'd been polite, sure. He hadn't once grabbed her and kissed the taste out of her mouth like he wanted to. The few times they'd touched, when he took her arm to steady her on a climb or something, he'd let go as soon as possible.

Yay for him, gold star and a merit badge for the Boy Scout

who'd ignored his hard dick and his watering mouth and had been totally cop and not at all seducer.

Not, he suspected, that she needed to be seduced. He saw the way she looked at him. The attraction was mutual. He was the only one making sure they didn't do anything about it.

Damn it, why did she have to be so single-minded about that book and the cases in it? Was it too much to leave out one story of one murder in a city with a long and storied history of them? When the tension had eased and they'd actually talked, joked, and laughed together, when they talked about their families, he'd *almost* asked her. Almost let it come up.

And then Reece had called. When Rowan saw his brother's name on the screen of his cell phone, he'd felt a stab of guilt, as if Reece had been watching, wondering why the hell Rowan was letting down his guard with "the enemy."

Not that Evie could ever be his enemy. Oh God, no.

But if she went ahead with the focus on Baker, he wasn't sure he could call her friend, either. And definitely not lover.

Somehow, he'd managed to maintain a balance between the aloof escort and the casual acquaintance that evening when they stopped at a Mexican restaurant for dinner. She'd had a margarita; he'd had water. She'd talked a lot; he'd mumbled as few answers as he could. Her soft laughter was all he could hear in the crowded place, while he'd probably looked like a humorless jerk as he tried to maintain distance. He wouldn't allow himself to let down his guard and just enjoy being with the woman. He kept coming close to that before he was yanked back to reality with a reminder, like the calls from both his brothers earlier in the day, at different times, that had been veritable slaps upside the head when he started lowering his guard.

The knowledge that he still had to tell them what was going

on—*they're gonna fucking kill me*—was a constant reminder to keep up the effort. At dinner, he'd focused on his own food; he hadn't once leaned over and opened his mouth for a sample of her fajitas just so he could wrap his lips around her fork. Watching her own mouth on the damn thing had been bad enough.

By the time he'd brought her home, walking her to the door and seeing that she got inside safely, he'd been as tense and stiff as an ironing board, and she'd been quiet and a little withdrawn. She'd actually shaken his hand good night and thanked him, not even smiling.

What, no good night kiss?

"No way," he reminded himself.

Cold vibes sent, message received, and all's well.

So why did he feel like such utter shit about it?

Why did he hate that he'd spent the past three days with her and hadn't revealed—as far as he knew—that he not only liked her more and more, but he also fucking wanted her with carnal need like nothing he'd ever experienced before?

Every husky laugh, every irritated thrust of her hand through her hair when it fell into her face, every drop of sweat on her brow when they'd been outside yesterday, the freckles the sun had brought out on her nose, the curves under the jeans, even the cute feet she'd stuck into the boots...everything about her appealed to him. Not to mention screwing with his mind, twisting his guts, and practically making him break the zipper of his jeans.

And here he was, about to spend another glorious day with the woman he wanted an insane amount but had to pretend he did not.

"You got this," he mumbled as he locked his car and went to

her front door. "Totally professional. You did it yesterday, you can do it again."

Mr. Cool, that was him. Mr. I-am-not-going-to-do-anything-to-make-this-even-worse-or-harder-to-explain-to-my-brothers.

He had all those great intentions. And then she opened the goddamn door, wearing a short, silky robe that revealed twenty miles of bare thigh, and his intentions went up in smoke.

"Jesus, Evie."

She tilted her head in confusion. "What?"

He pushed past her into her little house and kicked the door shut behind him. "You always answer the door like that?"

She looked down at herself. "Like what?"

"Almost naked?"

Rolling her eyes, she said, "For heaven's sake, this is a beach cover-up."

Well it looked like friggin' lingerie to him. It was way too short, and way too clingy on that feminine body. He had an endless view of those legs that he'd dreamed about having wrapped around him. The sash emphasized the slenderness of her waist and those curvy hips. The crisscross front didn't reveal a huge amount of cleavage, just a tempting curve or two—*two, definitely two*—but it was enough to make him have to close his eyes and remind himself of everything he'd been saying right before he knocked.

"Get some clothes on," he said, knowing he sounded like a gruff asshole but unable to stop himself.

"You're early," she pointed out, crossing her arms in front of her chest.

That just plumped up those perfect breasts closer to the top of the robe. The fabric tightened against her body, revealing her hard nipples. His mouth watered to taste her, his hands itched to hold her, and the rest of his body just roared to be allowed to get up close and personal with the woman.

"Evie?" he bit out.

"Yes?"

"What time is your appointment this morning?"

"Nine a.m. Why?"

"Because I'm trying to decide whether I have time to go back home and take a cold shower or not."

Her jaw fell open. Rowan should have smacked himself in the head for being so blunt, but frankly, his brain was a little scrambled. He'd been doing a pretty damn fine job of staying aloof from this woman, but no man was a frigging island. And that "beach cover-up" had one purpose in its silky life, and that was to be torn right the fuck off.

"Oh, so you like me again?"

He rolled his eyes. "I've always liked you."

More than liked. *Wanted* would be another way to put it.

Desired. Hungered for. Dreamed about.

But until she was ready to put down her pen, which could be mightier than even the Winchester family's lawyers, he couldn't do a thing about it.

"But you don't want to."

He shook his head. "I don't want to."

"Even after the way you kissed me Monday night."

"That's right."

She actually clenched her fists at her sides and shook them. "Why do you have to be so stubborn?"

She was pretty cute when she was angry. Not to mention sexy, especially given the way that robe slid down to bare one shoulder as she gave in to her frustration. There was nothing underneath it. He'd bet that could be said for every other inch of her body beneath the slick fabric.

"It's all about my book, isn't it? You have to make sure you don't let your guard down for too long because of a stupid, unimportant chapter in a book."

He gritted his back teeth. "If it's so unimportant, why do you need to write it?"

"Why do you care so much?"

They glared at each other for a second. He could see her pulse fluttering in her neck and the way her breasts rose and fell with her inhalations. His own breaths were deep and fast too. The tension rose, and he waged a serious battle to stop himself from just saying to hell with it, pushing her against the wall and kissing her long, deep, and hard.

And wet. Oh, God, wet.

The internal battle raged. He held on to his self-control like a skydiver might cling to a parachute that failed to open, just praying it would come through in the end.

But doubting it. *Seriously* doubting it.

"Enough of this. Are you going to kiss me or what?" she snapped, stepping closer, until her robe brushed his leg, and her bare foot slid between his shoes.

Say *"or what."* Say *"or what."*

Before he could say anything, however, she took the decision out of his hands, throwing her arms around his neck and pulling him down so his mouth slammed onto hers.

Well, then.

His self-control hadn't failed. He didn't have to admit to his brothers that he'd kissed her again. After all, *she* was kissing *him*.

So he let her. Oh, Christ, yes, he let her and then some.

Rowan met the deep, hungry thrusts of her tongue, taking her demands, answering them, and raising the stakes. They tilted their heads to fit better, their mouths glued so tightly even air couldn't come between them. He dropped his hands to cup her waist, his fingers digging into her soft hips. His fingertips rested on that perfect ass, and she was practically wrapped around him right there in the foyer, with the door open and the neighborhood free to watch.

He didn't give a shit. And he suspected she didn't, either.

They just continued to devour each other.

She tasted like bananas and toothpaste. An odd combination. And the best thing he'd ever tasted. Her curves melted into all his angles; they fit together like two pieces of a puzzle.

And then she abruptly ended the kiss, stepped back, and lifted a shaking hand to her mouth. He took a half step toward her, but she turned that hand around and slammed it against his chest.

"You ready to end this ridiculous argument and tell me why you are trying so hard to dictate what I can and cannot do in my writing career?"

He wanted to. Hell, he wanted to tell her to write whatever she wanted, about whomever she wanted. If it were just him, he'd roll the dice. He sensed she—they—would be worth it.

But it wasn't just him. His brothers were involved in this. And fuck if he was gonna do anything that could land them in jail for murder...especially not when they were completely innocent.

"Are you ready to stop digging into stuff that affects me and my family?"

She gaped. "How does it affect you and your family? I told you I wouldn't ask you any questions or try to involve you."

"Look, Evie, do you really think the murder of a man who was once like an uncle and Steve's plunge right in front of my brother make us just uninterested parties? Christ, the tabloids are still printing articles practically accusing Reece of murdering Steve. If the whole thing wasn't on video, it could have destroyed Reece's life. I don't want this shit dragged back up, and neither do my brothers."

"I wouldn't—"

"It doesn't matter what you do or don't do," he said, his frustration growing because he couldn't tell her the whole story, and she wasn't accepting the most basic one. "We will get sucked in. Frankly, I have quite enough old tragedy shoved in my face every year when some asshole points a microphone at me for the standard it's-the-anniversary-of-your-famous-sister's-death-how-do-you-feel-about-it? bullshit."

She didn't argue this time. Didn't open her mouth to promise nothing she wrote would affect him and the rest of the Winchesters.

Maybe she finally got it. Maybe she finally understood that with a family like his, there really was no way to fly completely under the radar, and just about anything could thrust them back into the most unforgiving spotlight.

Or maybe she was just tired of arguing about it, didn't think something personal happening between them was worth giving up a chapter in her book and hadn't felt like they'd just shared a mind-altering kiss.

"I should go get dressed," she said in a low voice. "I'll be ready to go soon."

He sighed, wishing things were different. Wishing he didn't have to hide something from her, wishing she wasn't so determined to pick at wounds. He had no right to ask her to give up something important; he knew that. But was one single story really that critical?

Maybe it was. Maybe he was being an asshole.

But he just didn't see any way around this issue between them.

He couldn't get romantically involved with someone who might be working to bring down his family, whether intentionally or not. And he supposed *she* shouldn't get involved with somebody who was so intent on keeping secrets from her.

Talk about a mismatch—they were wrong in every way, destined to failure before they even started.

But damn. That kiss.

"I need coffee," he called after her.

She didn't turn around, pointing to her left, toward what he knew, from yesterday's quick visit for her to change boots, was the kitchen. "Help yourself."

Today wasn't starting out very well. Okay, that wasn't true—that kiss had been one hell of a good way to start a Friday, especially if it could be followed up with a romantic Friday night dinner, a weekend at the beach or exploring the coast under sunny California skies, and having hot, wild sex whenever the mood struck them. Which, he had no doubt, would be often.

"Coffee, asshole," he muttered, putting all thoughts of sex and banana-and-toothpaste kisses out of his mind.

Evie had one of those one-cup-at-a-time makers, so he opened cabinets until he located some coffee pods. He made two cups in a row and poured them together into a travel container he'd found in the pantry. He had the feeling he was going to need it. He'd been with her for five minutes and already every pat on the back he'd been giving himself about how well he'd been handling things had swung around and become a punch in the gut.

She came back out in ten minutes, dressed and ready to go. He didn't think he'd ever known a woman who was more low maintenance. She'd obviously swiped on a little eye makeup, and her lips were shiny, but the hair was simply loose and brushed, and her clothes casual. Yet she managed to look stunning.

God, he was in trouble. This assignment was getting harder and harder by the day.

And so was he.

Damn you and your sick life, Harry Baker. You got what was coming to you; did you really have to bring my family down with you?

"You finished with the coffee maker?" she asked.

He lifted the travel mug. "Full. Hope that's not a problem."

"Not as long as you left me two pods too," she said with a faint smile, going over to repeat the same coffee-making process he'd just walked through. He watched as she opened the cabinet directly above the coffee maker, appearing confused. "Where's the coffee?" She cast him a quick glance over her shoulder. "You holding out on me? Because I need caffeine. You wouldn't like me when I'm decaffeinated."

"I put them right back where I found them," he said, walking to a cabinet on the other side of the kitchen.

Her frown deepened. "Seriously? Or are you kidding?"

Opening the door, he retrieved the box and brought it to her.

"That's crazy."

"What's wrong?"

Sighing heavily, she shook her head and took the coffee. "I swear, I must be losing my mind. I'm so distracted, I'm obviously sticking stuff in the first place I can find and then forgetting where I put it." She nodded toward the nearest cabinet, which contained mugs and coffee supplies. "They are supposed to live in there."

"That's what I figured," he admitted. "I was kinda surprised to find them with the plates and stuff."

"I am just so distracted this week," she said with a slow shake of her head.

"Not without reason, Evie," he said, standing close beside her. Close enough to smell her clean skin, close enough that her arm brushed against his when she moved. Close enough that he forgot to breathe.

He wanted her. Lord, how he wanted her.

She spun around and went to the fridge to get creamer. Rowan returned to his chair and swigged from his own mug, wishing he'd gotten a big glass of cold water instead. Frankly, he was tempted to walk the couple of blocks to the beach and dive into the Pacific. After that kiss, he needed a cool-off big-time.

While she finished making her coffee, he asked, "So have you heard anything more from MarcSleazy who set you up for a media ambush yesterday?"

She frowned. "I haven't figured out how to handle that yet. Candace has called me four times and has texted me even more than that asking me to get in touch. But I told her I was busy and needed some time. Guess I'll call her tonight or tomorrow and get it all out in the open."

"What will you do if he admits he was also behind Monday night's setup?"

She pulled an elastic out of her pocket and swooped her silky hair back into a soft ponytail. On Evie, the simple hairstyle didn't look jaunty and casual, but rather classic and feminine. Damn, she made everything look good.

"I don't know. That's why I haven't been able to call Candace back yet. If he is behind it, I can't keep working with him. Not if he gave out my home address. Not when…"

He waited. She swallowed and turned back to the coffee maker. Her hands were shaking, and he immediately realized something had happened.

Getting up, Rowan walked over to her, standing a few inches from her back. "Not when *what*?"

She didn't turn around, stirring cream into her coffee hard enough to break either the metal spoon or the plastic travel mug.

He reached around her, took the mug, put it down on the counter, and then turned her around to face him. "What aren't you telling me?"

She shrugged. "It's nothing. Nothing I haven't gotten used to dealing with over the past several years."

"If it's nothing," he said in a soft, even tone, even as he tried to ignore that peach scent rising off her swooped-back hair and the pink gleam on her lips, "why don't you just spill it?"

Gesturing toward her unzipped purse on the counter, she said, "Just another letter from my friendly neighborhood death-row pen pal."

He gritted his teeth and let out a low growl. "Angstrom."

"Yes. Candace gave me his latest cheerful correspondence yesterday at lunch. I can't deny I spent a lot of last night tossing and turning, wondering how freely Marcus might be giving out my home address."

He hadn't even paid much attention to the asshole yesterday. Right now, though, he wanted to go over to this Marcus dude's office and dangle him out a window until he confessed about whether he'd been selling out Evie's location to anybody who would pay the price.

Glancing at the letter, he said, "May I?" He figured she was giving him permission to read it by pointing to it, sticking right out of her bag. If she said no, he wasn't sure he wouldn't grab the damned thing anyway.

"Go ahead."

He retrieved the letter, quickly scanned it, and almost growled. He remembered every word she'd said about Angstrom, including how the bastard had copied her house key—because she'd had a flat tire. There were hidden messages throughout the whole poisonous page. He'd aimed it directly at Evie's heart, and her imagination, and let it fly.

Fucker.

"He writes you often?"

"Not often. Maybe a few times a year."

"You don't have to read them, you know. You could leave them unopened and forward them right to the DA handling his case."

"I always scan them and send him a copy. And my agent keeps a copy. Lots of backups and everyone in the know."

Smart. Of course, he would have expected no less.

"And the originals?"

"I have a file."

"Is it stamped Rubbermaid and lined with a big, green plastic bag that comes in a box marked Hefty?"

She forced a tiny smile.

"How about made out of brick, covered with wire mesh, and filled with flaming logs?"

He realized his hand had tightened and was crumpling the vile letter only when she tugged it from his grip.

"It's okay, I won't ever look at it again. But I do keep them…just in case."

He hated that expression—*just in case*. Just in case what? Just in case she needed a reminder that a fucking monster had tortured and murdered someone she cared about? Just in case she ever started to forget that she'd crossed paths with a psychopath who'd wanted *her* to be the one under his knife?

"Let me file it for you. I'll find the perfect place."

Like a mail drop that fell directly into hell.

Come to think of it, he'd happily put Angstrom in a box, mark it *Warning: Forwarded from the Virginia Department of Corrections*, and send it right down that chute too. The sonofabitch was going to end up there anyway; he would happily save the state the cost of feeding the walking piece of filth.

"Forget it, okay?" she said, dropping the letter into a drawer and slamming it closed. "It just got to me a little because of everything that's happened this week." She spun the lid onto her travel mug, sealing it. "It was bad timing to hear from him. I'm not completely used to this place and I'm jumping at shadows."

"You're the least shadow-jumping woman I've ever met, Evie Fleming."

He'd been telling himself that kiss this morning was the end of it, the final moment of intimacy that they could share. So why did he suddenly want—no, need—to take her into his arms and hold her close?

He didn't know.

But he did it anyway.

"C'mere," he said, putting his hands on her hips and pulling her to him.

She didn't resist. Rowan wrapped one arm around her waist and cupped her head in his other hand, holding her tightly. She relaxed into him, her face buried in his neck, her warm breaths softly whispering against his skin. He felt the faintest trembles rocking her body, up and down, and back again, and recognized the brave front she had been putting on. She was not as calm about this letter—and her address being leaked—as she'd let on.

"It's okay, Evie. I'm here, and I'm not going to let anybody get to you."

If he had to sleep in his damn car outside, with Jagger and Cecil B fighting over who got shotgun, he would do it.

Bodyguarding wasn't in his job description. He was just supposed to be her assistant, her escort. But tough shit. She didn't just have a lot on her shoulders this week; trauma was landing on her head like a shower of rocks. The mugging, the press intrusion, the betrayal by her agent, the goddamn letter like a bloody fingernail from the past scraping her out of the darkness.

Most women—most people—would probably already have packed their bags. Or at least they'd be a whole lot less calm than she was right now. But that faint tremble, the rapid heartbeat he could feel against his chest, and the quickening exhalations hitting his throat were all that revealed the turmoil that was going on inside her head.

He'd held her in his arms just fifteen minutes ago, wrapped in a hot embrace and indulging in a sinful kiss.

This was completely different. She needed support, someone to lean on, someone to remind her she was not alone.

And he needed to be that someone.

Yeah, different. But pretty damned nice too.

"Thank you," she said as she pulled away. She took a deep breath, lifted her chin, and added, "I'm okay."

"You sure?"

Her answering smile was obviously forced, but she got points for trying. "Yes."

"Okay."

"Ready to go?"

Right back to work, as if they hadn't already kissed like they were gonna spend the day in bed, and then hugged like she was gonna break down and weep. That was Evie.

Glancing at the time on his phone, Rowan hesitated. Before they left the house, he wanted to understand what this morning's field trip was all about. All the other names and places on the list she'd emailed him a couple of days ago had made sense in the context of her work. Today's interview? Not so much.

Remaining at the table, he asked, "So why is Phil Smith on your list?"

"Do you know him?" she asked quickly.

He shook his head. "No, but I've heard of him. Got some commendations before he hit his twenty-five and got out."

"Yes, I've read up on him. I was just hoping you might have a personal relationship. I'm not entirely sure he's going to be open with me."

"I don't remember him working on any of the cases you're covering in this book."

She didn't respond right away, instead busying herself cleaning off the counter, putting away cream and sugar. She didn't once look at him.

This didn't feel like a few minutes ago, when she was worried about the letter from a serial killer. It felt more like she had something to say but didn't know how to say it.

"What's going on, Evie?"

She hesitated, and then walked over to sit in the other chair, facing him.

"So," she said slowly. "You probably know about the traits of serial killers."

"Well, I did a guest stint on *Profiler* once. Does that count?" he replied. Jesus, did the woman really not remember what he did for a living?

"I'm sorry, that was stupid." She lifted a hand to her face and rubbed her temple. "I just, I'm trying to figure out the best way to explain this."

He nodded, knowing he'd reacted a little too quickly. Probably because he was still distracted thinking about the hug, the kiss, and that damned sexy lingerie she'd been wearing when she opened the door.

Beach cover-up my ass.

"I'm trying to lay the groundwork here. I mean, you know the basics, what the studies say about serial killers?"

"Sure. Usually white males. Bed wetters as kids, probably abused animals, fire setters. Targets one type of victim, almost always of his own race. So-called organized killers have jobs, lives, friends, and are highly intelligent."

"Like a Bundy or a Gacy."

She didn't say like an Angstrom, though thinking about it, he knew that monster would have to be classified as organized. He ran a business, he socialized with customers, he planned well in advance, he copied keys and got addresses.

But no, he was absolutely not going to use him as an example to one of his own victims. He hadn't killed her—thank God—but Evie was one of the man's victims nonetheless.

Seeing a shadow cross her face, and figuring her mind had probably gone there, too, he quickly went on. "Disorganized or sloppy killers aren't necessarily that smart. They don't plan as well, they act on impulse, they don't usually even try to hide their crimes. Like that Sacramento vampire guy."

"Yes. You know about signatures?"

"Sure. Serial killers usually have them. Something unique about their crimes that distinguishes it from others. It's usually psychological need, not something strictly required to accomplish the murder."

"Yes, and it's often how investigators are able to string cases together." She swallowed and her lashes fell over her eyes. "Angstrom's license plate collection was his trophy case, but not his signature because he didn't leave it at the crime scene. His signature was the…the…"

He reached across and took her hands in his, clenching tightly. He'd read up on Angstrom after he and Evie met. He knew exactly what that sick fuck had done to her roommate and to so many others, beyond kill them. "Stop. I understand."

She squeezed his hands back and didn't pull away. Rowan knew he was disobeying his mental rules, but there was just no way he could let go. Not when she was so obviously in need of human connection.

He wanted to continue to be what she needed. At least for right now.

After taking a few deep, steadying breaths, Evie squared her shoulders and continued. "Sometimes that signature is pretty subtle. It's not always easy to associate crimes with each other, especially if they take place in different jurisdictions, with different investigators. None of those jurisdictions views their case, their piece of the pie, as part of a whole—a serial crime—because they don't know there are others spread all across other areas."

"Which is how the Night Stalker got away with what he did early on."

"Precisely. His preferred target was older women. He often broke in through first-story windows—which made for a long, hot, miserable summer for the city of LA since everybody started closing their windows at night. That was all part of his MO, despite his change-up of the means, since the method was so different in many cases. But it wasn't *always* that way, and he attacked all over the region."

"All over the state, actually," he murmured, knowing Ramirez had taken a field trip up toward San Francisco before his reign of terror had ended.

Yeah, terror.

He'd heard about that long, frightening summer and could envision the entire area gripped with fear. This city seethed when it got hot now. He didn't even want to imagine what that had been like back then.

"But he also left a pentagram at his crime scenes—that's a signature," she explained. "Practically a literal one."

"Right. So, back to Smith. You haven't answered my question yet," he said.

But even as the words left his mouth, a possibility blossomed in his mind.

Evie was a researcher. She was out here looking into serial crimes. She had dug her way into the middle of one once before. Now she was talking about it as if…

"No," he snapped.

She blinked but said nothing.

His hands tightened. "Tell me that's not what you're really doing here."

Her eyes shifted. "Of course it's not. I'm working on a book. Want to see my contract for it?"

"Don't sidestep. Tell me you aren't Veronica Mars'ing your way onto another serial killer's radar."

She sucked in her bottom lip. Rowan froze.

"I'm right? You think you've found another Angstrom operating here in LA?"

It wasn't at all far-fetched that there could be another monster loose in a city this size. He knew the stats, knew the FBI believed there were as many as fifty active serial killers in the U.S. right now. And LA was a prime spot for sociopaths to find the perfect victims. Filled with runaways, drug addicts, underage prostitutes, undocumented workers...Along with the starry-eyed dreamers, the stars, and the millionaires were the hungry, the desperate, the broken. The City of Angels was an ideal hunting ground, which was why it had attracted more than its fair share of serial killers in the past. So no, he could muster no surprise that another one might be working the streets of LA right now.

But damned if he wanted Evie Fleming to have anything to do with it.

"Let it go," he demanded. "Write up your notes and I'll make sure they get to the right person. Then you bow out and forget everything you know or suspect."

She reacted only with a slight tensing of her body.

"You can't get involved with this, Evie."

"Nor can I convince anyone I'm onto something with just suspicion."

"So tell somebody your suspicions and let *them* investigate it."

"The LAPD isn't busy I guess? They don't mind journalists-turned-authors telling them what to do without having a shred of proof? Rich, spoiled Hollywood TV show type tells one of the biggest police forces in the country that they've overlooked a serial killer in their midst, but can't say how she knows other than a suspicion? That'll go over so well."

"Damn it," he muttered. "You might be right."

Sure, a good cop would always look into tips, but without any evidence, and coming from somebody like her, it might not make it to the top of somebody's already heavy caseload.

He sighed, let go of her hands, and got up to make himself another cup of coffee to drink right now, rather than hitting the travel mug. Partly to stall for time to think, partly because he suspected he was going to need all the coffee. Like, *all* of it.

"Okay," he finally said, "what are we talking about here?"

"You'll really listen?"

"Of course I'll listen." He wasn't promising to believe, much less to help, but he was fair-minded. Not to mention curious.

"I've found what I believe are twelve connected cases that nobody else has put together."

Twelve.

He didn't react, merely saying, "Go on."

She did, filling him in on names, locations, dates. As she spoke, he had to lean back against the counter, bracing himself with a flattened palm on the countertop. He kept going back to her first sentence.

Twelve.

Going back fifteen years.

How the hell? It was crazy, right? If twelve women had been murdered by the same killer in this geographical area, surely *somebody* would have linked the cases together by now.

Somebody other than a writer with a dark and vivid imagination.

"Why are you so convinced of this?" he asked once she'd finished describing the cases. "What makes you the expert, seeing what nobody else has ever seen?"

"It's not that nobody else could have seen it," she insisted, rising from her chair and standing stiffly. "It's that nobody else would ever have really looked."

"Bullshit," he said.

"I didn't mean that they wouldn't have cared to," she quickly explained, realizing she might have sounded offensive. "I mean, these cases were spread out over a decade and a half, and, with the exception of the fourth and the seventh, they all took place in different jurisdictions."

Ramirez. The Night Stalker's name flashed through his mind again.

But that had been decades ago. Police methods and communications had advanced by leaps and bounds since then. Which was exactly what he told her.

"Of course, you're right. But these crimes were spaced out so very far apart, and there were definite variations in MO. One detective might have been looking into the shooting death of a woman in Glendale for months. He gets nowhere, the file goes to the bottom of his pile. In this city, there's always another case to investigate."

That much was true. Murder rates had fallen in recent years, but violent crimes were definitely on the rise.

"A year later, when another woman is found dead— strangled—in Redondo Beach, why is he going to connect it to his case in a metro area the size of this one? It's not like Ramirez when they were all happening in a compact period of time. And, like with Ramirez, the means of death varied."

She was making sense. He crossed his arms and nodded for her to continue.

"I don't blame anybody for not catching on to it."

He thought about what she'd said. "How'd you put it together? What's the link?"

"Honestly, I was just researching crime statistics, neighborhoods, and victimology. The number of Caucasian women between the ages of twenty and twenty-five murdered over the past fifteen years seemed higher than I would have expected. So I dug into them to find out why."

"And you found something they had in common, other than their age?"

She nodded slowly. "The signature."

Ah. That's why she'd made sure he had a primer on serial crimes.

"Aside from the victimology, the age, the race, the sex, and the fact that these women were all killed at home, there is what I think is a very clear signature, Rowan."

He waited, but she didn't go on. His curiosity was aroused now, his investigator senses pinging. She'd caught him; she'd interested him.

He wanted to know more.

Finally he prodded, "So what is it? What did you see?"

She mumbled something.

"What did you say?"

Looking out the window toward her small backyard, she murmured, "Flowers."

He wasn't sure he'd heard her right. "Flowers?"

She nodded.

"That's the big reveal?"

Her jaw clenched a little. He dropped the attitude.

"Okay, help me understand this."

"I'll try." She licked her lips and swiped a strand of hair off her brow. "So, as I said, each one of the women I've singled out was killed in her home. And each one had a vase of perfectly fresh flowers, in bloom, on her bedside table."

Her seriousness told him she thought that was very significant, but frankly, Rowan just didn't get it. "Don't all women like flowers?"

"Yes, most do. But we don't all have fresh flowers in vases in our bedrooms *all the time*. A birthday, Valentine's Day, Mother's Day, an anniversary, maybe. But none of these crimes took place around any such holiday. So why would *every one of them* have fresh flowers sitting in their homes for no reason at all? One, sure, easy to write off. Maybe two. Hell, Rowan, maybe five. But *twelve*? All of them murdered at home, Caucasian, and around the age of twenty-five?"

His heart skipped a beat. Jesus, when she said it like that, it really did raise his hackles.

He started to think like a cop and not like a protector of a woman who managed to get herself into some really bad situations.

"So you think the killer poses as a flower delivery guy?"

"No, I don't."

He blew out a breath.

"If that were the case, I'd think there'd have been a broken vase or a crushed stem somewhere along the way. There hasn't been. The flowers mean something else."

Realizing why she'd felt the need to carefully go over the basics of serial killers, he started to catch her meaning. "You think he's leaving the flowers as part of his own ritual…his *signature*."

She nodded, looking relieved. "Yes."

He let the theory sift through his mind, tossed it around.

And couldn't come up with an immediate reason to decide she was wrong and change the subject. So he kept going. "All the same type of flower?"

She nibbled her lip and slowly shook her head, admitting, "No, all different."

He frowned. She could be right about the flowers. It did seem strange, though not entirely out of the realm of possibility. If they'd all been orchids or roses or something, it would be easier for him to believe. The killer might be leaving *particular* flowers at the scenes of his crime because that flower had a certain meaning to him.

Right now, though…well, it was curious. Suspicious even. But enough to grab the attention of an overworked detective crew? Or, make that twelve of them?

No, it probably wasn't enough. Not under these circumstances.

"Did the police reports mention whether they looked at where the flowers came from?"

She flew out a frustrated breath. "A couple looked for any records of a delivery but didn't dig too deeply. Several of them didn't even note the flowers at all."

"How do you know—"

"I spotted them in the crime scene photos, once I knew what I was looking for."

Christ. She was very serious. And very thorough.

"Okay, I understand why this has caught your attention. It's…it's weird. Interesting. But you know it's all circumstantial."

"I know." She came closer, looking both sad and determined to get through to him. "Do you see why I want to look into this a little more myself before I potentially go cry wolf to the police, claiming they're overlooking a serial killer? I could be wrong. I might be way off base."

She took another step, putting a hand on his chest. He felt

the heat of it burning through his clothes, right to his skin. There was such an intensity about her, such fervor as she added, "But I have had this feeling before, Rowan. I've felt this intense certainty down deep inside. And I have to do what I can to see if I'm right."

Their stares locked. Her blue eyes were clear, her gaze steady. She absolutely believed every word she was saying.

And, God help him, he believed *her*.

He covered her hand with his. Their fingers entwined.

Finally, he said, "Okay, Evie. I'm in."

Chapter 7

Retired LAPD detective Phil Smith lived in a modest bunga-
low in Westlake, on a quiet, neatly kept street lined with similar
homes. His place looked exactly what a working-class retiree's
place should look like, but Smith didn't look exactly how she
would picture a retired cop.

"Hey there. Miss Fleming, I presume?" the sixtyish man said
as he opened the front door.

The voice was gravelly, a little phlegmy. The heavyset man
wore sweatpants, a baggy T-shirt, sneakers, and had a thin oxygen hose resting on his upper lip. A portable oxygen tank stood
at his side. The handle was raised for easy grabbing, like a rolling
suitcase. He likely had to walk around all the time with the
thing.

He extended his left hand. The right one, she noticed, was
curled in against his chest, and swollen, with visible bulges at
the knuckle that told tales of arthritis. What a shame.

"Yes," she said, extending her left hand, too, a little awkwardly. Funny how much the world discriminated against left-

ies. "Please, call me Evie. And this is Detective Winchester, who is assisting me while I'm doing research for my book."

Smith reached out for a handshake with Rowan. She couldn't help noticing how careful Rowan was with the ritual. His grip was brief and appeared gentle. He'd noticed the condition as well and had immediately reacted with thoughtful consideration. The way he did with anyone and everyone, as far as she had seen. Including her, for the most part.

Except when his late agent's name came up.

"Come on in, folks," Smith said with a big smile. "Not often I get visitors these days. I've made some fresh iced tea."

He led them into a small family room decorated with an old tweed sofa, two well-worn recliners, and some knobby pine furniture. The only self-indulgent thing in the place was a huge flat-screen TV, which was tuned to a sports channel but muted.

Immediately, she noted several things, made several impressions.

He'd made the tea—he lived alone.

He didn't have family nearby—he wasn't used to visitors.

He was frugal, cautious with his retirement income because he'd been forced to retire earlier than he'd planned due to his medical conditions.

He was very neat; the place wasn't immaculate, but it was tidy, like the front yard.

The details painted a picture in her mind, and she found herself feeling a little sorry for the man. She didn't know if he was divorced, widowed, or had never married, but she had no doubt his life now was very lonely.

"Have a seat," he said, gesturing toward the sofa. "I'll get the tea. It's presweetened, hope that's okay. Had to give up some of my vices, but I just can't do without *all* my sweets."

"Sounds delicious," Evie said with a smile.

Rowan nodded as well.

She sat down, as invited, but Rowan walked around the room. A nicked and slightly warped bookshelf stood in a corner, and he walked over to read the plaques and framed commendations that stood on it. There were several.

The only photograph in the room was a framed eight-by-ten that stood in a position of pride on the coffee table. A black and white, it depicted an older woman with a beehive of dark hair on her head. The hairstyle and fashion hinted that this wasn't a late wife, but probably Smith's mother. That added to the picture of a lonely lifelong bachelor.

Smith returned with a tray holding three glasses, as well as a plate with some prepackaged cookies. The gesture again hinted he didn't do much entertaining.

"Help yourself," he said. "I can't do the cookies on account of my blood sugar, but you go right on ahead."

"Looks like you were very busy on the job," Rowan said, nodding toward the bookshelf as he walked over to sit down.

Smith shrugged, modest as she'd found many police officers to be. "Like any job, you do the best you can."

He sat in a recliner, extended it to lift his feet, saying, "Sorry, gotta keep 'em elevated for the diabetes."

Good grief, the poor man didn't have it easy.

"That's fine," Evie insisted as she sipped the icy cold drink, which was delicious.

"So," said Smith, "you say you wanna talk about a couple of my old cases from when I was still on the job?"

Right to business. Once a cop, always a cop.

"Yes, as I said when I first contacted you, I am writing a book on older crimes in the Los Angeles metropolitan area."

Smith snorted. "Lots of material there, missy."

No doubt.

"Two murders that you worked before you retired caught my interest."

"Lemme guess," he said, piercing her with a sharp glance that revealed the inquisitive, determined mind that still lived in the sick man's body. "One of 'em's gotta be Felicity Long."

Evie lifted a brow. He'd nailed that one. "It is."

Shaking his head, Smith looked at Rowan. "Always a couple of cases that haunt you, am I right?"

Rowan was sipping his drink and swallowed quickly, coughing a little, before answering. "Oh yeah. They keep turning up like…"

"A case of herpes!" Smith laughed at his own joke, then grew serious again. "That one stuck. She was young, a wannabe actress I think."

Evie opened one of the two files she'd brought along. "Yes, she was trying to break in to the movie business." Like so many others in Hollywood.

"Strangled in her own bed." He closed his eyes and winced. "Such a sight, never stopped seeing it in my mind's eye."

She had seen the crime scene photos and understood.

"Pretty red hair," the older man mumbled.

She turned to another page in the file. It was the victim's picture, likely a professional headshot taken when she was going on auditions, full of hopes and dreams.

Seeing it, Smith nodded slowly. "Yes, long and red. Such a pretty girl."

She had been. So had all the women Evie had connected to this mystery killer. No connection as far as hair color or body type went, but they'd all been very pretty.

"Really bothered me that we never caught her killer. I hated goin' out with that one still open, on the books. I spent the first few months of my retirement digging into it, on my own dime, ya know. Till I got too sick. Never did see anything new. No prints, no sign of forced entry, nothing stolen, no usable DNA."

Just like all the other cases she was pursuing. If this was the same killer, he was very good at covering his tracks.

Rowan leaned forward, dropping his elbows onto his knees. "How does somebody go into a house, commit a violent murder, and not leave a single hair, fiber from his clothes, or a drop of spit, sweat, or tissue anywhere?"

"Your guess is as good as mine," Smith said with a shrug.

"There were a few other cases you worked on that remain unsolved," Evie pointed out.

The former cop stiffened a tiny bit.

"I'm sorry, I'm not being critical," she quickly explained. "Your record is outstanding. I just mean, there was one other murder of a young woman that you worked on fourteen years ago that remains in the cold case file."

Frowning, he scratched his slightly grizzled, graying chin. "Can't remember 'em all. Sorry, but it's a myth that we remember every victim forever. In this line of work, you just can't afford to hold on to every single case, every single victim."

"Of course not," Rowan said.

"Fourteen years you say? Similar case?"

Evie nodded, opening the second folder. "Another young woman, same age, found murdered in her apartment, about ten blocks from where Felicity eventually lived, but eleven year earlier."

She turned the file around and lifted it to show him the other picture. He leaned forward in his chair to get a better look.

"Hmm, yeah, she looks familiar." Another chin scratch. "Wait, GSW to the chest, right? In her kitchen? What was her name?"

"Amy Nolan."

"Right, Nolan," he said, nodding. His brow was furrowed as he obviously tried to remember. Then he snapped his fingers. "Oh of course! That was not long after I transferred into the Central Bureau. Rampart. Pretty sure it was the first murder case I caught there."

"That one remains unsolved as well."

"Well, yeah, but I always knew the ex-boyfriend did it. She had dumped him a week before. He'd been following her, calling, showing up at her house."

Evie had read all of that in the investigation notes. "But he had a solid alibi. He was on an overnight trip to Las Vegas with his friends to try to get over the breakup."

Smith rolled his eyes. "Four-hour drive. He coulda ditched his drunk friends, driven back here, killed her, and gone back to Vegas overnight with nobody the wiser."

She knew that wasn't the case. There were a lot of witness statements from the owner of the hotel-casino where they'd stayed, plus surveillance images of the ex-boyfriend playing blackjack and talking to every sexy "single" woman on the floor. He'd ended the night with a prostitute.

But with an unsolved case of a pretty young woman, maybe the old cop preferred to think he had mentally solved the case, even if he'd never made the arrest. Perhaps it made it easier to swallow. He just hadn't had a similar explanation about Felicity Long's murder, which was why her case was the one that haunted him while Amy Nolan's did not.

"Did you have any other theories?"

He frowned, looking irritated that she hadn't bought his explanation. "No."

She sensed his back was up. Worried he might stop talking, she went right to what had brought her here. "What about the flowers?"

He stared at her, shaking his head, mumbling, "Flowers?"

Evie quickly reminded him that in his own report on the first murder he had mentioned a vase of fresh flowers in the bedroom and had speculated that the ex-boyfriend had brought them to her to pretend he had come to make up.

He considered, scrunching his brow. "Oh yeah, right. Roses I think. Typical take-me-back-or-I'll-kill-you gift."

"They were carnations."

He shrugged. "So the guy was a cheapskate."

"Felicity had the roses."

"Whadda ya mean?"

Beside her, she felt Rowan grow very still. Here was where the path got more slippery, the steps more tricky. She didn't want to make another comment that annoyed the sick man enough that he clammed up. Hinting that he had missed something by not even mentioning the flowers in Felicity's case file might do just that.

"There was a vase filled with roses on Felicity's dresser. They were visible in the crime scene photos, but I didn't see anything about them in the report."

"Lemme see the file," he snapped.

She got up and brought the documents she'd printed out over to him, placing them on his lap to avoid him having to use his gnarled hands any more than necessary. Going back to her seat, she waited while he glanced at the crime scene photos. He stared at the two with very clear views of the roses for a long while.

Then, finally, he crossed his arms over his chest, tucking the twisted fingers under his armpits. "It was a couplea days after Valentine's Day, right?"

"Yes, it was."

"No big deal about red roses on Valentine's Day. I guess I didn't note them because they didn't seem relevant."

"But she wasn't seeing anyone, was she?"

"So what? Don't single women buy themselves flowers once in a while?"

"Oh, of course they do," she murmured.

But not usually red roses, at least in her experience. They were just too closely connected to romantic love. It was the same reason why when she bought her mother roses—her favorite flower—for her birthday or Mother's Day, she always chose yellow or peach. Never red. It was just too weird to give red roses to a friend or family member who wasn't your significant other.

Or to buy them for yourself.

Not impossible. No, definitely not. But unlikely.

Plus, in going through the scans of banking records and receipts found in Felicity's purse and her home, there had not been a mention of a florist or even a grocery store flower purchase, anywhere. She'd found the same lack of evidence in the Amy Nolan case. Actually, the retired detective had noted it himself in the first murder.

"It's just," she went on, speaking casually, as if she were merely curious and not deadly focused, "it seems a little funny that two women around the same age were killed in their homes and unexplained fresh flowers were found in their bedrooms."

The folder resting on his lap, Smith sipped his tea, staring at her. His brown eyes, sharp and youthful, unlike the rest of his body, were narrowed, piercing, as he considered.

Finally, he said, "You tryin' to say you think those cases were connected?"

"Do you think it's possible?"

His jaw flexed. "No. You think I'm a bad cop or something? You think if they were at all alike I wouldn'ta noticed it?"

She leaned forward, matching Rowan's pose. "No, not at all," she said, trying to calm him. "The cases were almost a decade apart! One victim was shot, one was strangled. There's no reason they would have come together in your mind."

He nodded, appearing a little mollified.

"I'm just asking if *now*, looking back on both cases from a distance of time, do you think there's any chance they were connected?"

Although he still didn't look pleased with the line of questioning, Smith appeared to think about it. One hand resting lightly on the file folder, he stared into the distance, rocking his recliner the slightest bit. The silence stretched on, save for the tiny squeak of the chair every time it came forward. At one point he closed his eyes. For a second, she wondered if he had fallen asleep. But finally, he sighed heavily and returned his full attention to her.

"Okay, I'll admit it," he said, not sounding pleased about it. "Yeah, looking back, it's possible the cases were connected all along. And I missed it. That what you wanna hear?"

Smith's hands were painfully clenched now, and she suspected he was starting to accept her theory and wondering what his part in the unsolved murders might be. It wouldn't be easy to accept that he might have missed something critical while investigating those two crimes.

"Detective, I didn't come here to accuse you of anything, or to insult you," she said, hoping she hadn't mortally offended the man. He didn't appear to have much of a life, and his memories of his glory days as a decorated police officer were probably the most important thing in the world to him. She would never want to stain those memories. "You were obviously an excellent detective, and I know this is coming at you from a very long time ago."

Smith hesitated for just a second, and then finally shrugged. His tense body relaxed a little bit. "No, it's okay. I guess because the Long case always stuck with me, I'm a little mad at myself for possibly missing something. Not your fault for pointing it out." The older man lowered the footrest and leaned forward in his chair. "How'd you come up with this, anyway?"

"Pure luck," she insisted. "I'm doing research on unsolved crimes, and these caught my eye. I have no official capacity."

He nodded, and then looked at Rowan. "You on these cases now?"

"Nope. Just tagging along."

"Bodyguardin'?" He looked back at Evie. "I know about the Angstrom thing. You watchin' your back?"

Evie's brow went up. Of course she wasn't surprised the retired officer would have investigated her before this meeting. She was just surprised that he'd so quickly zoned in on the fact that Angstrom might pose a danger to her. Then again, he was a former cop with twenty-five years investigating crimes and criminals; maybe it did make sense.

"I'm fine, thank you very much."

Seeing the way he winced as he shifted on the lumpy old chair and had to suck in a slow, deep breath, Evie realized he was in physical pain from more than his hands. And they'd worn him out. She imagined the theory she'd laid out for him hadn't helped with his heart any, either.

She rose to her feet, as did Rowan. "Thank you so much, Detective Smith. I truly appreciate you taking the time to meet with us."

The older man shifted by an inch and slowly got to his feet. "S'okay. Just wish I could be of more help. Wish I coulda helped those girls more too." Looking down for the handle of his oxygen tank, he mumbled, "Pretty red hair."

"You helped a great deal," Evie insisted. "And mostly, you cared."

He eyed her curiously, but it was Rowan who explained.

"You kept working Felicity's case long after you retired," he said. "I hope I'm that diligent when I go out."

Evie nodded. "Plus you were professional enough to admit there might have been something you overlooked."

Smith's brow furrowed. "Hate to think somebody else stumbled over something so obvious all these years later." He actually sounded angry. With himself, undoubtedly. "You'll keep in touch, right? I'll want to hear where this goes."

Evie nodded as Rowan put a gentle hand on the man's shoulder.

"Thanks for your service, Detective," he murmured. "I hope to live up to your example someday."

Out of his pocket came a yellowed handkerchief. Phil Smith blew his nose in it and wiped some sudden moisture out of his eyes, and then bid them goodbye.

Evie and Rowan walked out toward the car, and as they did, she thought about what Rowan had said. She knew he was a good cop—brave, smart, and hard-working. But she also knew he was single, lived alone, and didn't appear to have ever had a wife, certainly no children.

Her heart twisted. She thought about Smith's life, and about Rowan's future.

God, she did not want him turning out like the other man. Lonely, old before his time, in pain, with nothing but the memories of his work on the force to keep him company.

Being a police officer wasn't easy work. Not on the body, on the mind, on the spirit. Not on spouses and on families. Smith was not a very unique example of a "lifer" as police retirees sometimes called themselves.

She couldn't stand the thought that Rowan Winchester—a sexy, friendly, thoughtful, funny, and protective man—might someday join that rank. He was far too good to spend his life alone with only his job to think about. Of course, he had his brothers, to whom he seemed close. He'd fondly mentioned his father and his aunt. And he had his persnickety cat.

But love? Did he have that? Did he even want it?

She suspected he did. He was too warm to want to be alone forever.

Which made her wonder what kind of person would be the one who gave him that life? Who would welcome him home at night with open arms and a bright smile? How many kids would be bounced on those broad shoulders? What lucky woman would share the anniversaries, the holidays…and the sultry nights in his hot bed?

You're being ridiculous.

Of course she was. She hadn't even known the man a week yet; he'd done nothing more than kiss her. So his future long nights of sex, not to mention the rest of the crazy-curious questions, were no business of hers.

Still…she couldn't stop wondering.

* * *

It had been a hell of a day. Not one to waste any time, Evie had set up meeting after meeting with the lead detectives who'd worked those twelve murders that had caught her eye. From Smith's house, they'd gone to a division in Anaheim, to a mall in Laguna where one worked part-time as a security guard. Back to another station, then a retirement home.

In nearly every case, the detective remembered that particular victim. All commented on the brutality of the crimes, the location—in the victim's own home. The age, the vulnerability, the lack of any physical evidence whatsoever.

In every case, as soon as Evie laid out her interest in the flowers in the bedroom, each detective hemmed and hawed and then finally admitted they'd either overlooked the significance of them, or else barely tried to get any information about where they'd come from. Fresh flowers in a woman's bedroom just didn't seem to make an impression, any more than a pizza box in the fridge, tampons in the bathroom, or new shoes in the closet. Women bought things, they figured.

Well, most of them figured. One officer had really dug in to try to find out where they'd come from. It had been a female cop, who was now a captain in Long Beach.

"You never mentioned to any of them except Smith that you think each individual case might be connected to others," Rowan said as they pulled into the parking lot of a steak restaurant. He needed some protein, and she had readily agreed to a hearty dinner. It was almost eight p.m. and they had only grabbed drive-through food for lunch, having a lot of road to cover and a lot of people to see.

"Smith was the only one who had worked on two of these

cases. I had to mention both, meaning he would instantly know I'd connected them somehow."

"You didn't think the others would believe the similarities?"

"On the contrary, I suspect they will."

He doubted she was trying to hoard the information, keep it for some future scoop. There had to be some other reason, knowing Evie.

"What do you mean?"

"I mean, I wouldn't be surprised if one or more of them goes looking through cold case murders of women that somehow involve flowers." She smiled. "It shouldn't be hard to find what I found, and maybe this whole thing will be blown open without me having to be the one to bring it in."

"Ahh," he said as he got out of the car.

That was smart thinking. He'd seen the spark of interest in the female captain's expression and would lay money that she was going to revisit the file. Once she spotted what Evie had, he didn't doubt that she would make sure somebody took a second look at the case, which would almost certainly lead them down the same path Evie had followed. And then Evie could get back to just being an author researching a book, and not a serial killer bloodhound at risk of putting herself into the sights of a monster.

He went around to open her door, but Evie was already in the parking lot, her arms raised above her head as she tilted side to side in a stretch. They had spent a lot of time in the car all week, especially today. He shared her discomfort. Rowan had spent a lot of his free time lately running with Cecil B out in the canyon; he wondered if she'd been hitting the beach.

"You need a day off," he insisted.

"Gotta strike while the iron is hot."

"Yeah, but if you're not careful, you might get burned."

"There you are being all quippy again."

"Don't call me quippy."

"I think the expression is don't call me Shirley."

Recognizing the cheesy old movie line, Rowan had to laugh as he opened the door to the restaurant and followed her in. Evie was more relaxed tonight than he was used to seeing her. Maybe because she suspected her plan to get the cold cases evaluated by fresh eyes looked like it might actually work.

He just wished she'd filled him in on it. And told her so.

"Honestly," she said as they followed a hostess to a booth, "it wasn't my plan going in or anything. What we talked about this morning about me being the messenger really resonated."

"I'm glad something has."

She cast him a quick look from between lowered lashes but didn't respond. He hadn't exactly been talking about Baker... except yeah, he had.

Once they were alone at the table, she continued. "As for today, I really was playing it by ear. After we talked to Bingham in Anaheim, and he looked pretty thoughtful as we were leaving, I knew it could work. There are enough of the original detectives still on the job that one of them is surely going to stumble across this angle."

God, he hoped so. He did not want her continuing to be involved in this.

After they'd ordered drinks, Rowan heard his phone buzz and checked the text. "It's Avery. I need to step out and call him back."

"Sure. I'll be sitting right here drinking my wine. After today, I need it."

Going outside to avoid being overheard, he called the captain back.

"It's Winchester, sir."

The gruff captain got right to it. "Franklin Lee made bail."

"Oh hell," he muttered, immediately recognizing the name of Evie's attacker.

He'd practically given her his word that the guy was going to rot in jail until he changed his mind and took a plea. Now he was out, walking the street?

"Who bailed him out?"

"Local bondsman. No clue who put up the ten percent to hire him. I guess Frankie does have some friends out there with deep pockets."

"Damn."

"You still seeing Miss Fleming regularly?"

He did not volunteer the information that she was seated thirty feet away inside a restaurant, waiting for him to finish this call. "Yes, sir."

"Good. Don't think this punk is stupid enough to come after her, or that he could find her. Frankly, I think that bondsman is gonna be hunting this guy down because I don't doubt he's gonna try to skip. But you never know."

Right. You never knew. He might instead decide to try to get rid of the witness against him. Or, hell, witnesses. Rowan wasn't at all worried about himself, but he was the one who'd caught Lee right in the act.

One thing was sure, it was time to find out for certain if Evie's movie agent, Marcus Oakley, had been free with her home address. And, if so, who he had leaked it to.

"Understood, sir."

After a moment's hesitation, Avery said, "One more thing,

Winchester. I got a message a couple hours ago from a Captain Sanchez outta Long Beach. The message mentioned you. Any idea what this is about?"

He immediately recognized the name of the female captain who had worked one of the flower murders. He suspected Sanchez was calling to get more info on why Rowan was temporarily assigned to Avery's group. And he hoped it was because she had done some digging through old records as soon as they had left her office this afternoon.

"It's, uh, a little complicated, sir."

Avery grunted. "I can handle complicated."

"It's probably better discussed in person."

Now that he knew about Evie's suspicions, and she was bringing them to detectives all over the Los Angeles metropolitan area, he needed to report everything up the chain of command. He doubted Evie would like it, but this was incredibly serious. It needed to go by the book. He wasn't about to do anything to jeopardize any future prosecution…or anything to put Evie in any more danger than she already was.

Avery harrumphed. "All right, fine. Be in my office first thing tomorrow to *un*complicate it for me before I call her back."

Working on a Saturday. Well, that wasn't anything unusual.

"I'll be there, sir."

Disconnecting the call, he went back inside and returned to their table. His beer was waiting for him. Sliding into his seat, he lifted it to his mouth and swallowed deeply. Although he, like Captain Avery, didn't think there was much chance Lee would do anything to get rid of Evie, Rowan still had to tell her the prick had made bail.

She obviously saw something in his expression. "What is it?" she murmured. She lifted her wineglass to her mouth. He saw the way the golden fluid sloshed in it and realized her hands were shaking.

Knowing what had inspired her sudden tension, he cleared up one thing immediately. "It's not Angstrom."

She let out a small, audible sigh, and then sipped her wine. She watched him over the rim of the glass, her blue eyes bright and inquisitive, and she no longer looked nervous.

He hated that Angstrom had the power to do that to her from the other side of the continent and from inside a maximum-security prison.

"Okay, fill me in," she said as she lowered the glass.

He did, seeing her hand clench around the stem of the glass. She didn't otherwise react.

"I'm sorry as hell about this."

"I thought he wasn't going to make bail." There was no accusation in her tone, merely curiosity. Well, maybe a bit of worry too.

"I can't believe he did. His record didn't show any close family or affiliations with gangs that look after their members. No money, no assets. I have no idea who would come forward to put up ten percent of his bond." Rowan took another deep swallow of his beer before adding, "Whoever it was is gonna be out some serious money, because I have no doubt that sonofabitch is already at the border, trying to cross into Mexico."

She licked her lips. "Or staking out my house."

He was shaking his head before she finished speaking.

"No way." He understood the concern but wanted to make her see it the way he did. "Look, Evie, an off-duty LAPD detective caught him in the act. I *saw* the assault, I dragged him off you."

"Thank heaven," she mumbled into her glass.

"He was never out of my sight from the second he came at you until he was put into the police car and taken to headquarters. No room for him to weasel out of it. There can be no argument about mistaken identity or anything else. Lee was caught about as red-handed as a cat with canary feathers in its mouth."

"Or a man with a woman's throat in his hands."

He grimaced, not wanting to think about that. "The point is, you're not the only witness, and as witnesses go, I'm a pretty damn good one. That's why any lawyer would advise him to take a plea deal." He shook his head, really not understanding. "I still can't understand why he didn't. Unless he *knew* somebody was gonna bail him out and that he could make a run for it."

"That makes sense," she said. He saw that some of the tension had eased out of her stiffly held body. "And I think you're right. I was just a random victim; he might not even know my name. He won't stick around; he'll hightail it out of here."

She was so sensible, so smart. One of the things he liked best about her.

"But, of course, that doesn't mean I'm not going to sleep with a crowbar under my pillow for a while."

He laughed, as he knew she'd meant him to.

If things were different, if this damn book weren't casting its shadow over them, he would like to think he could be right there in her bed at night. He'd be much better than a crowbar at keeping her safe.

But he couldn't do that. And he couldn't take her back to Reece's place with him. When his brother had called yesterday, it was to let him know he was coming home for the weekend for some meetings and planned to stay at the house. He was probably there now.

Rowan had already been dreading coming face-to-face with his brothers and telling them what he'd gotten mixed up in. He definitely couldn't do it if Evie was right there.

"Listen, my apartment's empty," he finally said, thinking of another option. "If you'd feel better staying there, you're more than welcome."

She was already shaking her head. "No, it's fine, really. *I'm fine.*"

"You're sure? I mean, with your address being given out..."

"I talked to Candace about that late last night," she said. "She put Marcus on the phone. He swears he did not give anyone my home address Monday night." She let out a disgusted sound. "Though he did admit calling the media to tell them about the attack, which *is* how they got there so quickly."

He frowned. "Do you believe him?"

She hesitated, and then slowly shook her head. "No, I really don't. I think he said what he thought he had to in order to get Candace off his back and to keep me from firing him."

Yeah. That's what Rowan suspected too.

"But that doesn't mean a parolee with a record of violence would be able to find out where I live," she said, sounding quite reasonable.

"No, it doesn't."

"You want to hear something crazy?"

"Crazier than anything else you've said to me since the minute we met?"

She flicked his hand with her middle finger. Hard.

"Ow. Okay, what?"

"The thought of Franklin Lee walking on the streets free and clear doesn't bother me nearly as much as the thought of Angstrom getting a new trial. I'd rather come face-to-face with a mugger any day than *ever* have to sit in a courtroom across from that psychopath again."

Rowan had testified in his fair share of trials. Never one involving a soulless monster like Joe Angstrom, though. He couldn't imagine how hard it must have been for her, especially given what he'd done to her friend.

"Okay, then," he said, glad she wasn't stressing too much over this. "Let's just focus on dinner and not spare another thought for either of the bastards."

He'd be thinking of them later. Tonight. When he staked out her house, watching over her from his car. She might be comfortable with just a crowbar for protection.

He, however, was not.

Raine might be the professional bodyguard of the family, but Rowan had done more than his fair share of stakeouts. He knew how to sit in a car all night watching for trouble.

Tonight, the mission would be very personal.

He wasn't going to let anybody get near Evie Fleming, be it a serial killer on the East Coast or a street thug right here in LA.

Nobody was getting past him and into her house.

Nobody.

Chapter 8

Evie Fleming! Just the person I wanted to see," a male voice said Saturday morning as she sat in the room in headquarters she'd been given to use for research. She was alone, or she had been until the door had been pushed open and a man had come in.

It wasn't Rowan. He'd made an appointment to see Captain Avery and had followed her in this morning. She'd found the overprotective man sitting in his car right in front of her house. Judging by his clothes and the redness of his eyes, it didn't take much to figure out he'd been parked there all night, her own private bodyguard.

God, she wished he had just come in and spent the night. This stalemate between them was infuriating. It was time she did something about it.

But first she had to deal with *this*.

"Hello, Lieutenant Carlton," she said, offering him a small, polite smile. And definitely no encouragement.

He didn't need any, or even an invitation. Ignoring the fact that she was obviously working, a pencil stuffed behind one ear, her reading glasses perched on her nose, and a highlighter pen in her hand, he sauntered in. The center table on which she was working had reports, maps, photos, and files strewn over every inch of its surface. He pushed some charts out of the way so he could sit on the table's edge directly in her line of sight.

She had no clue why men did that. There were several perfectly good chairs in the room. What was the point of balancing on the edge of a table right in front of a woman's face? Just to try to get them eye level with whatever magnificence they had in their pants? Men obviously just did not understand women's brains and how to pique their sexual interest. A point proved every time any man anywhere sent an unsuspecting woman a dick pic.

"I've been watching for you all week, but I kept missing you. Guess you're going in and out a lot, huh?"

Maybe, but she had spent long stretches of hours in this room. Plus, every time she entered the building, she had to sign in. It shouldn't have been that hard for him to find out she was here working, if he'd cared to look. Though why he would have wanted to, she didn't know.

Frankly, she was glad he hadn't. But it was confusing that he now acted as though he'd been staking out the door. Could it be, she wondered, that he hadn't come into the room before now because Rowan was almost always in there with her? And had he approached her this morning because she was alone? Hmm.

"Um, so what did you need to see me about?"

"Huh?"

"You said you were watching for me all week. Does Captain Avery need something from me?" She started to rise. "Oh, of course, he probably wants me to come into the meeting with Rowan…er, Detective Winchester."

"Oh, no, it's not that."

She waited. He smiled a smarmy smile.

"Is there something I can do for you, Lieutenant?"

"Well, you could start by calling me Carl."

Carl Carlton. His parents must have disliked him at birth.

She maintained her polite expression but did not reply. After a long moment, he finally said, "Actually, I was wondering if we might go out for dinner tonight."

"I'm afraid I—"

"Or lunch. I wanted to talk to you about something."

Oh, here it comes. Will you read my writing?

"I was wondering why you were looking into some old case my uncle worked on way back in the day. It wasn't connected to a serial crime, so I'm not sure why you would be including it in your book."

Evie barely managed to stop her jaw from hitting the tabletop. Pushing her rolling chair back, she rose to her feet to get a better view of the man that didn't involve his crotch.

"Your uncle?"

"Yes. Jack Slaughter is my uncle."

Slaughter. The name rang a bell. "Wait…Phil Smith's partner?"

Carlson nodded. "Yeah, those two were together for a couple of years. Then Uncle Jack got promoted here to headquarters and worked his way on up." He grinned, appearing self-satisfied, and pointed to the ceiling. "His office is on a very high floor."

Rowan had hinted at Carlson's family connections the other day. She just hadn't realized where Carlson's relative had worked his way up *from*, and who he'd been partnered *with*.

"Did Detective Smith call your uncle?"

Carlson tilted his head in confusion. She suspected it was a look he wore often. "I don't think so."

"Then how did you know what I'm investigating?"

He chuckled, looking pleased that he had caught her off guard. "I saw the files you requested, including that one, which was just a standard old unsolved murder of some chick from a long time ago."

Standard murder. Some chick. Wow.

While his words and attitude were gross, his explanation did make sense. On her very first day here, last Monday, when she'd come in to see Avery, she'd had to fill out a lot of forms about her request for information from Avery's office. Those had included a list of what she was requesting and why. She'd included the twelve murders that had captured her interest but hadn't gone into detail about why she'd wanted them, merely listing them as research material for her work of nonfiction.

Carlson worked for Avery, though she wasn't sure what his duties were. Maybe he reviewed those types of requests in an official capacity. At least, she hoped so. The man had made her uncomfortable from day one; she hated to think he'd dug into the records just to get more information on her, especially since her address and phone number were right there. Since the guy hadn't tried calling her, she had to hope he hadn't gotten access to that stuff.

"So, what should I tell my Uncle Jack?"

"Why would you need to tell him anything?"

"Well, he wants to know why you're digging into his..." Carlson drifted into silence, and his eyes grew round. He had been just about to say something he shouldn't have.

She quickly put it together. If his uncle wanted to know why

Evie was looking at one of his old cases, *someone* must have shared that bit of information with him.

Who else could it have been but his nephew?

Maybe it wasn't a state secret. Maybe it didn't violate any confidentiality rules. Maybe it wasn't even against departmental policy.

But it was really unprofessional, and it really ticked her off.

"You told your uncle about my confidential information request?"

Carlson opened and then closed his mouth. "Uncle Jack and Captain Avery are good friends."

"Oh, so are you accusing Captain Avery of doing it? I guess he's the one I'd better talk to, then."

His face losing all its color, Carlson said, "No, Captain Avery wouldn't do that."

But Carlson would?

"I don't know the public information laws here, so maybe my request is not private. But don't you think if someone used their position in the administrative offices, it might have been a tiny bit unprofessional to take it right to a family member?"

"I...I wouldn't think it was that big a deal."

"Maybe not to you," she said, her tone cold. "What is Captain Avery going to say when your good old uncle Jack mentions that you shared information like that?"

"Oh, he won't tell him!"

Bingo. Confirmed.

Carlson must have realized that too. He immediately launched up and strode toward the door. "I have to go."

"Yeah, I'm sure you do," she said, wondering who else the annoying man had talked to about her and her work. Jeez, first Marcus, now this guy. Was it too much to ask for a little privacy from people who were supposedly trustworthy?

The door opened, but before Carlson could walk out into the corridor, he was blocked by a big, solid body.

Rowan.

"What the hell are *you* doing here?" he asked as Carlson froze in his tracks.

"Uh, nothing. I was just stopping by to offer Miss Fleming some assistance."

Jesus, did the cop think she was deaf? Had he forgotten she was standing right here? Or was he just so used to talking bullshit that he'd forgotten other people might actually call him out on it?

"Actually," she said to Rowan, smiling sweetly at Carlson as he swung his head around, "the lieutenant stopped by to tell me he'd been talking to his uncle about my request for information on one of his old cases. One he investigated with his partner, Phil Smith."

Rowan's shoulders bunched, and he frowned darkly.

"It's okay, though," she added. "Now that I know Captain Slaughter has been made aware of my interest, he might consider making room in his schedule to see me."

Carlson looked horrified, but it was his own damn fault. He's the one who had talked about her research. The least his uncle could do was open his office door and lend his insights on the Amy Nolan case. She had been focusing on the lead detectives in the cases, but there was no harm in talking to other investigators. Maybe Slaughter would recall something Smith had not. It was worth a shot anyway.

Once the lieutenant scurried out, leaving them alone, Rowan came over and put a hand on her shoulder. "Are you okay? He didn't...upset you, did he?"

"Of course he did. That jerk talked about me and revealed what I was investigating to his uncle. That upset me."

He nodded, having already heard that much. "I mean, personally. Did he…do anything?"

Evie's brow went up. "Um, other than being kinda gross and flirtatious, no."

Seeing him sigh in relief, she couldn't help asking, "What is it you so dislike about him? I mean, I know you said he was untrustworthy and used his family connections to rise in the department." *Yeah, good old Uncle Jack.* "But is there something else?"

Rowan tensed and walked over to look at the papers strewn on the table. A couple of them had been pushed off when Carlson had just plopped down on them. Bending over to retrieve them, Rowan said, "I know he was investigated for dating teenage girls several years ago. Nobody would testify, so he got off with a finger-wagging, and his uncle made sure everybody forgot about it."

Wrinkling her nose in disgust, Evie bent to take some papers too. "So Sleazy McSleazeface is what I will now officially call him."

She and Rowan reached for the same sheet of paper, which showed a photo of a murder victim from about five years ago. Only fifteen years old, she had been very pretty, with long dark hair and a very sweet smile. She wondered if that was why Rowan had grown still, if he was thinking about Carlson's ugly history and relating to this poor lost soul.

Their fingers brushed. He looked up at her, and she saw his eyes were glistening, gleaming with emotion. Although it could have something to do with the obnoxious man who'd just left, something in her told her it did not.

She clasped his hand in hers. "What is it?" she asked, knowing something else had deeply affected him. "Talk to me, please."

He didn't reply, a silence stretching between them in the quiet room. Neither of them got up, both crouched near the table, their hands still clasped.

Finally, he spoke. "Tomorrow would have been Rachel's thirty-fifth birthday."

She immediately recognized the name of his only sister. "Oh, Rowan, I'm so sorry," she whispered. "I can't even imagine what you're feeling. I honestly don't know how you ever get over a loss like that."

"You don't. Not ever."

The pain in his voice cut her to her soul. Despite how much they'd annoyed her when they were kids, she adored her two brothers and couldn't even fathom the thought of losing one of them.

Rowan, as just a young child, only about twelve years old, had not only lost his older sister, but also it had been under such tragic, and very public, circumstances. Rachel Winchester had lived in the spotlight, as had her brothers. Rumors about her drug use and her subsequent death had filled the tabloids and gossipy Hollywood shows for weeks after her death. How did you grieve a loved one when everybody in the world was talking about her, speculating about her, asking about her? Especially when you're just a kid?

"It must have been hell."

He hesitated again, only briefly, and then replied, "It drove my mother insane."

"That's completely understandable."

"No, I'm not speaking figuratively. She had, uh…issues. After Rachel, well, she couldn't deal with them anymore. She spent the last years of her life in a private mental hospital and died there thinking her Academy Award–winning daughter was coming to visit every single day."

Oh God. Feeling tears sting her eyes, Evie blinked rapidly. "So much pain. How did you survive? You were so little."

"Don't feel sorry for me," he said, slowly rising to his feet, drawing her with him. "My brothers and I had—*have*—an awesome father who has always been there for us. And my aunt was more than happy to mother us if we'd let her. Mostly Raine, since Reece and I were older. He was so little, only six when our mom had her, uh, breakdown."

She took back the snotty thought she'd had about the youngest brother. If anyone had a reason not to smile much, it was him.

"Losing my mom to an institution was just like another death, within just a couple of years of losing Rachel."

Mother and daughter. So tragic.

Rachel. Beautiful, lost Rachel, so full of promise with a long life to live, had been cut down at such a young age, maybe any mother would go mad from the grief. But with three other young children to care for, she couldn't help wishing Rowan's mother had been strong enough to get through it, for the boys' sakes.

She glanced at the page in her hand as she put it back on the table. Spying the picture of the victim again, she realized what had likely caused Rowan's disquiet. The girl was probably about the age his sister had been when she died. She was similarly colored, with a sweet smile.

"She must—"

"Evie, there's—"

They smiled faintly. They both waited for the other to speak. Finally, he did.

"Look, there's something you should probably know," he said, the words slow and halting, as if hard for him to get out. "Something that has, uh, affected me and you. *Us.*"

Incredibly curious, she dropped a hand onto the back of the chair she'd been sitting in. She didn't even know why she reacted that way, but something about his expression told her this wasn't going to be easy to hear. How he'd drawn a line connecting his lost sister to *them* she had no idea. But it appeared she was about to find out.

"My sister didn't just fall in with a wild crowd and become a reckless drug addict."

She would never have said such a thing, though she knew that had been the regularly reported story all those years ago. Evie had been just a kid, but she'd been a big fan of the teen star, and she'd been very disappointed to hear about her spiral.

"Rachel went a little wild, yes. She started doing drugs. But it wasn't because she wanted to party with the in-teen-crowd in Hollywood."

His throat worked as he swallowed hard. Although they were no longer touching, she felt the tension in his powerful body. It almost rolled off him, filling the small office with anger, with grief, with pent-up emotion.

"She was being molested."

Sucking in a shocked, horrified breath, Evie tightened her grip on the chair, squeezing it almost painfully.

"By somebody who the entire family trusted. None of us even knew about it until after she was dead. Once we found out, it, uh, brought everything into focus."

It took no more than five seconds for the truth to burst into her brain. Suddenly, the tears that had been building in Evie's eyes burst from them, spilling down her cheeks. "Harry Baker."

Rowan nodded.

"That monster," she whispered, knowing very well what the man's relationship with the Winchesters had been like.

He had never been just a business associate. He had, it appeared, insinuated himself deep into their family. She'd thought it was because of the rumors about his involvement with the mother. This was so much worse. Absolutely insidious. Evil.

She'd seen many pictures of the man when researching his death, and a lot of them had been with his child clients, especially the Winchesters. There was an entire spread in a teen magazine about the Winchester kids in Disneyland with their ultra-glam mother and their "Uncle Harry" who had put them on the rides. In one, little Raine had been on the man's broad shoulders, and Rachel had been holding his hand trustingly. There'd been shots of him on film sets, in back lots, one showing him smiling broadly, his arms around Rachel and Reece as they showed off their Kids' Choice Awards. His big, jowly face was always creased in a smile that made him look something like a jolly, beardless Santa Claus.

He'd been a sick, twisted monster instead.

"I can't even stand to hear his name," Rowan admitted, staring at her evenly.

She caught the underlying message and closed her eyes, shaking her head. "And I kept throwing it in your face." Stepping close, she lifted a hand and placed it on his chest, touching lightly, offering tenderness and support and not demanding anything at all from him…as she had since the night they'd met.

"I am *so* sorry, Rowan. I promise you, I will never mention him to you again."

He caught her hand in his. "Do you understand *why* I didn't want him in your book at all?"

Of course she did. "Because it will stir up interest in him all over again."

"Yes. And one of these days, somebody's going to find out what was discovered on that bastard's computer—his ex-wife and son managed to get that kept out of the press."

She could muster no surprise that he hadn't stopped at one victim. Filth like that never did.

"He was a slime and a pedophile, and yeah, he deserves to be remembered that way. But if that comes out, then what he did to Rachel will come out too."

She caught her lip between her teeth and nodded. Of course they wouldn't want their sister's secret trauma to be dragged out of the vaults of history and splashed all over the news. Rachel was resting in peace and had been for almost twenty years. Was there really any reason to disturb her memory by exchanging it for a wild-child who overdosed and fell off a balcony to a sexually abused victim who, she strongly suspected, might *not* have fallen?

"Maybe someday one of the other victims will want to come forward. This past year, with all the Hollywood revelations, I've almost held my breath, waiting for it."

He was probably right. Baker had managed many child actors, some of whom were still in the business and successful. Some of whom weren't and had probably ended up making the same choice Rachel had—to drown the pain in drugs.

"And you and your brothers," she murmured. "You were so close to him as kids, you'll get asked a million questions all over again."

He nodded. "Yes, we will. Our relationships with Harry got

very...ugly once we knew the truth. I might be willing to talk to you about it, but it's not my call. And I've probably already said too much. The thing is, this affects everyone in my family. So you see, Evie, I just can't do it. I can't help you do something that could hurt my brothers."

Hearing what he was really saying—that he *did* know more than he was letting on—she found her journalistic curiosity going to war with the tenderness she already felt for this man. She looked up into his handsome face, seeing the furrowed brow, the rigid jaw, the downturned mouth, the genuine sadness that had lasted for years, and...tenderness won.

Emotion won.

Rowan had finally opened up to her about some of what drove him.

And it had only made her care for him more.

Her hand rose to cup his cheek. "I understand. I won't do anything that could hurt you, Rowan. My book doesn't mean more to me than your family's well-being, or your sister's memory."

He sighed in relief. Without waiting for him to respond, she rose onto her toes and brushed her lips across his, catching him, she knew, by surprise.

But not for long. Only a second after she touched her mouth to his, he dropped his hands to her waist and pulled her close, kissing her back. Softly, gently. It was achingly sweet and tender, but also, as always, evolved into something so much more.

Their lips parted and their tongues met and twisted in a slow, fiery duel. Thrusts and tangles, heated breaths and soft sighs only increased the tension. The excitement.

They had kissed before, but each time had been followed a fight, or a reminder of why they couldn't possibly go any further.

Now, though, the cards were on the table. Rowan had revealed what he'd been hiding from her...or at least most of it, other than that which affected his family.

Which meant now there was nothing standing between them.

"Please tell me you're not going to end this kiss and stomp out," she whispered as he moved his mouth to press hot kisses on her jaw.

"Not a chance."

He pushed her back toward the table and lifted her onto it. This time she didn't give a damn about the papers spilling off. Not when she was finally in Rowan's arms, finally sure in the knowledge that this kiss wasn't going to end in an angry argument or an icy wall.

"God, you've been driving me crazy," he murmured as he scraped his tongue along her earlobe. His hands twisted in her hair, holding her tight, and she loved the power of it, knowing he was driven by passion and need, and not by a need to control.

Not even thinking about it, she spread her knees and moved closer to him, welcoming him to step between her legs. He didn't hesitate, coming to her like he'd just been waiting for the invitation. She twined her limbs around his, tugging him even closer, indulging in the feel of that hot, male body right where she had wanted him since the night they met.

She'd known Rowan's body was remarkable, his chest wide, shoulders broad, and arms thick and powerful. Now she was able to appreciate his lean hips, and those strong thighs whose muscles flexed under his jeans.

Not to mention what else strained at those jeans.

He was erect—huge, hard. Hungry.

She whimpered and rocked into him, loving the pressure as they came together, as close as two people could when clothed.

"I hate jeans," she muttered as he thrust against her, the pressure unbearably delicious yet also frustrating.

"Ditto," he said as he tasted a path from just below her ear back to her mouth. He kissed her again, this time his tongue plunging hard and fast. Their bodies rocked together, catching the rhythm of the hungry dance of their mouths, and she could only imagine what it would be like if there were no clothes between them.

But there were. *And* they were in the headquarters building of the LAPD, a fact of which she was reminded when she heard voices passing the closed office door.

Rowan heard them too. With a deep groan in his throat, he dropped his hands from her hair. He ended the kiss. He stepped away from the table, sucked in a few audible breaths, and tried to adjust his pants.

There was no hiding *that*. Not right now.

The realization made her wish more than ever that she had a key to the door. Headquarters and eleven stories worth of cops and officers be damned. She wanted him, right here, right now, on top of the table or up against the wall or any place she could have him.

She hopped off the table and approached him.

Rowan threw a hand up, palm out, to stop her. "Uh-uh."

"Spoilsport."

One side of his mouth curved up, though he didn't look very amused. "I want more than anything to rip your clothes off and lose myself inside you for at least the next forty-eight hours."

She quivered.

"But this isn't the time and it sure isn't the place."

She knew that, logically. Her body wasn't very happy with the answer, however.

"Aside from which, I am supposed to be off today, and I agreed to meet my brothers for an early lunch."

"Reece is back? Does that mean you need another place to stay?"

She wasn't suggesting anything, wasn't inviting him to stay with her.

At least, she probably wasn't.

Liar, liar.

"He's back for the weekend, so I'm staying at my own apartment." He grinned. "Can you believe Jagger meowed all night, walking around looking for Cecil B?"

"He's a big softie."

"Remind me to show you the scratch on my chest where he punished me for not being a dog."

She licked her lips and smiled wickedly. "Feel free."

He took another step away from her, as if not sure he could trust himself not to reach for her and pull her back into his arms, which would have suited her just fine.

Then another voice intruded, and she was again reminded of time and place.

When the footsteps in the hall paused in front of the door, she swung around and began neatly restacking the papers on the table. Rowan was still standing a few feet away, and hopefully the person who swung the door open and walked in didn't notice their posture, their expressions, or the hot smell of sultry kisses and some serious dry humping in the air.

"Captain Slaughter," Rowan murmured.

Oh dear.

Carlson was responsible for this, she had no doubt. He had

probably left here and called his uncle, demanding that he cover the loudmouthed lieutenant's butt about this situation. Maybe he even thought he was doing Evie a favor by getting Phil Smith's former partner in here to talk to her, but she preferred to set her schedule herself. She liked to be prepared, to have all her files right in front of her, to at least not be breathless, with messy hair and swollen lips, after a heated encounter with the sexiest man she'd ever known.

"Detective Winchester," the older man said as he entered the room and pulled the door closed behind him. He was about twenty years older than his nephew, probably in his mid to late fifties. His once-blond hair was now mostly gray, but his face was youthful and his dark eyes piercing. She knew he'd worked at a desk for several years, but he still looked fully capable of chasing down a bad guy in the street, his form tall, lean, and athletic.

"Miss Fleming I presume?"

She took the hand he extended and shook it. "Captain Slaughter. This is a surprise."

He gave her a disbelieving look. "Really? You didn't expect my irresponsible nephew to race to a phone and beg me to cover his ass after he told me about your document request?"

She hid a smile. "I can't deny I wondered if he might. I did intend to make an appointment to talk to you."

"I figured I'd come down here and save you the trouble." He pulled out a chair and sat at the table, casting a quick glance at the files and documents she'd been examining. "Pretty grim."

"Yes."

He crossed his arms over his chest, sitting stiffly in the chair. "You think you have something new to say about one of my old cases, I hear."

How would he have heard that? she wondered.

He must have seen her confusion. "After my idiot nephew talked to me this morning, I called my old partner. He told me he heard from you."

That made sense. "Yes, we visited Detective Smith yesterday."

Slaughter shook his head and frowned. "Damn good cop, Phil. Strong, smart sonofabitch. He shoulda had another ten years. Shame his arthritis took him out of the game."

Well, his arthritis, his diabetes, his probable emphysema... she didn't imagine the retired cop would have been on the job now even if his hands hadn't twisted like gnarled limbs on an ancient tree.

"Did he tell you why I went to see him?"

Slaughter nodded once. "Amy Nolan. You think there was some issue about flowers being found in her place?"

Although it wasn't the ideal time, she wasn't going to waste an opportunity to interview another detective who'd been active in what she suspected was a flower killer case. So although she didn't have her files and notes at her fingertips, she did begin to ask him some of the same questions she'd asked Phil Smith the previous day.

He listened, nodding once or twice, but didn't appear terribly interested. In fact, at one point he even yawned. Standing in the corner of the room, Rowan glowered at the man, though she didn't think Slaughter could see him.

"Look, Miss Fleming, I really don't know what you want to prove here. A murder victim from more than a dozen years ago had some flowers in her house. Okay. So what? Really, what difference does it make? Even if whoever killed her brought them, or used them as a ruse to get in, what kind of help is that going to give us now?"

"The vase," she murmured, determined to remain calm. "It could have had fingerprints."

"Look, Phil and I talked about this. There were no unexplained prints anywhere in that place."

"Including on the vase?"

"Including on the vase."

"What about the flower petals?"

He looked down at her, obviously trying to make her feel stupid.

"Look, I know it's not common, but it's not impossible, is it?"

"You think we shoulda dusted some flowers for prints," he said, sounding not just surprised but a little annoyed.

She wasn't about to retort that they could have at least made the effort. He was already on edge, and so was she. She didn't like how the interview was proceeding, and again cursed this man's nephew for forcing it on her before she was ready for it.

"Look, if you can figure out who killed that girl, great. I've always felt bad that we didn't close that one. But if you think you're gonna solve it because of some flowers, I think you have a lot to learn about police work."

"But other—"

Before she could finish her sentence, telling him other victims had had unexplained flowers in their homes, she caught Rowan's warning shake of the head. Quickly realizing she had been about to reveal something she hadn't wanted to, a connection she hadn't mentioned to any of the other detectives she'd interviewed, she slammed her mouth shut.

"Now if we're through here, I have to go." He glanced at a clock on the wall. "I was supposed to be on a golf course this morning."

His tone was cold, laced with annoyance.

"I certainly hope you didn't alter your plans because of what your nephew told you." She didn't imagine he needed the reminder of who, exactly, was at fault for him being here, but couldn't regret doing it all the same.

"No," he said, getting up and heading for the door. "Good luck with your book, Miss Fleming." His hand on the knob, he stopped to say one more thing. "I do hope you don't get carried away with these questions of yours. That case was a long time ago. I barely remember it. Obviously my idiot nephew didn't."

Not following, she asked, "You mean Lieutenant Carlson?"

"Sure. Kid was a rookie and was one of the first responders on that case. I'm pretty sure he threw up when he saw the body."

She thought she heard Rowan grunt but didn't look over, not wanting Slaughter to stop speaking.

"Anyway, I'm sure Phil didn't have much to offer either. Best to just let it go if you don't have any real, concrete evidence to add."

At least Smith had expressed some genuine sorrow for the victims of some of the unsolved crimes in his past. Slaughter seemed more like his nephew—heading for the top no matter who got in his way. Having a "nosy" writer digging into an unsolved case that stained an otherwise almost pristine career would not please a man like this. And judging by the dark look he gave her right before he walked out the door, he was definitely displeased.

"Nice guy," she mumbled once they were alone again.

"Sure, in that special Death Eater way."

She grinned, feeling better about the interview. Slaughter had treated her like an interloping kid who had no clue what she was digging into. The captain was the first she'd interviewed who'd done that. Some of the detectives she'd spoken to yesterday had been a little aloof, some confused, some very interested. None had been really scoffing, until today.

"You okay?"

"Sure."

He glanced at his watch and frowned. "I hate like hell that I can't stay here and help you, but I agreed to meet up with my brothers. Since Reece leaves town again tomorrow, I don't want to bow out."

"No, don't be silly," she insisted, waving a hand. She got up and started reorganizing her files, tucking her notes and laptop back into her satchel. "I think I've had enough for today too. Frankly, I need a mental break."

He fingered a strand of her hair. "Wish I could take you on that drive up the coast in your convertible, murder fan."

That sounded heavenly. But he had family obligations, and she had...well, nothing else to do but read a good book and listen to the ocean.

And think about what might come next between her and this amazing man now that the barriers between them had, by all appearances, been knocked down.

"I think I'll take advantage of living a few blocks from the beach. I'm gonna go home, grab a book, and sit on the beach this afternoon."

"That sounds like an excellent idea." He leaned in, still touching her hair, and brushed a soft kiss across her lips. "But, Evie?"

"Yes?" she whispered, wanting him to lean in and kiss her again.

More soft kisses on her cheek, her temple, and in her hair. She was a quivering mess by the time he whispered, "Don't wear that damn bathing suit cover-up in public, okay?"

Laughing softly at what sounded like jealousy in his voice, and remembering the way he'd reacted when she'd opened the door yesterday, she said, "I bought it in a surf shop, not a lingerie store."

He slid his hands to her hips and kissed her again. "Maybe. But on you, that thing might as well be in a Victoria's Secret catalog."

He kissed her again, long and hot, with unspoken promises of what was going to come after such kisses from here on out. Once they were out of this building. Once it was the right time and the right place.

She could hardly wait.

Finally, they drew apart. "Come on, let me at least walk you to your car," he said. "I hate like hell to be walking out on you today."

"Don't be silly. Go, go! Enjoy some time with your brothers."

He helped her pack up the rest of her things, and she did a quick mental inventory. She didn't want to forget something, considering an armed escort had to open the door for her every time she went in.

Leaving the room, they went down the elevator and out to the parking lot together, saying little. Evie suspected he had as much on his mind as she had on hers.

Everything felt different. They'd argued and danced around this powerful attraction between them all week. Now that the barriers appeared to have been swept away, she suddenly felt a little nervous. Ridiculous really—she was no inexperienced girl. But the certainty she felt that she and Rowan would end up in bed together soon, maybe even tonight, had her trembling like a virgin at the homecoming dance.

"Okay, Rowan," she said when they reached her car. "Have a good lunch, and hopefully I'll see you later."

He brushed his knuckled against her chin. "You can count on it."

Just before she got into a car, she said, "Oh, wait, I forgot something."

"What?"

She licked her lips and smiled at him. "I forgot to tell you…while I really did buy that beach cover-up at a surf shop…I have a Victoria's Secret account. And I use it a lot."

Seeing him close his eyes and let a low breath ease between his lips, Evie smiled and got into her car. He was still standing there as she backed out of her space, and she gave him a cheery little beep as she left the parking lot.

Yeah, she definitely had the feeling she'd be seeing him sooner rather than later.

* * *

Last night's local news channel had confirmed human remains were removed from the ruins of an abandoned house that had exploded in Boyle Heights yesterday. He'd slept well, glad the issue of Firecracker Lee was taken care of. Nobody could connect him with the hired thug who'd botched the murder of the writer who just couldn't stay out of other people's business.

Then came today's news over the car radio.

"Authorities say the victim was likely a homeless woman taking shelter in the abandoned house."

Woman? Fuck!

"Although police haven't revealed the cause for the explosion that rocked this quiet neighborhood, neighbors are saying they saw a man running out of the house just as it exploded. Witnesses have given descriptions of the man, and police are searching for him now."

Double fuck.

He'd thought he was taking care of his problems, ticking off the checklist of any ties that might lead back to him. But it appeared he'd been the one to screw up this time.

It had been his intention to kill Lee no matter what. He'd expected "Firecracker" to succeed in getting rid of Evie Fleming, making it look like a random city crime. With Frankie's experience and complete lack of conscience, it should have been easy. Knowing guys like Frankie would always try to make a deal the next time they got picked up on another charge, he had intended to then take the hit man out too.

But everything had been screwed up right from the start.

The writer was still alive. Lee had gotten caught in the act and would almost certainly have talked if he wasn't bailed out quickly. So he'd had to get the cash and make that happen.

"Oh, shit," he muttered, remembering the other thread that needed to be snipped.

The bail bondsman was the only one who knew who had posted the 10 percent for the bond. Although he'd used a fake name and ID when delivering the $25K, he could still be physically identified, which was no good.

"Can't deal with all this shit," he said aloud. It was all spiraling, when it should have been pretty simple. How hard could taking out one dumb broad be?

"Winchester," he seethed.

That asshole was nosy. He'd been at the wrong place at the wrong time and was still sticking to the bitch like he was a piece of gum on her fuckin' shoe.

Everything was a mess.

He hated messes, and he wasn't going to be able to rely on anybody else to help clean them up…not unless he wanted to drag in even more potential witnesses.

He had to find and eliminate Frankie, deal with the bail bondsman, and cover all his tracks.

And somewhere during all of that, preferably sooner rather than later, he had to deal with the writer. He'd stopped by to visit her a couple of times this week but had never found her home. The bitch kept odd hours.

He hadn't entirely minded. Messing with Evie Fleming's head by slipping into her house and moving things around, knowing she would wonder if she was losing her mind, had actually been fun. Now, though, with the Frankie situation, he couldn't fool around anymore. All of these issues needed to be taken care of. "Toot-friggin'-sweet," he mumbled.

It was time to take her out. Starting today, he was gonna watch her house, make sure she was home, and then go finish what his hired help had started last week.

Chapter 9

Reece is gonna fucking kill you, man."

"Would you please stop saying that?" Rowan glowered at his kid brother, who was eyeing him from the other side of the booth in the crowded fast-food joint.

No pretentious lunch for the Winchester brothers. Reece had been out of town for weeks, and the only place he'd wanted to go was an In-N-Out Burger. Surprisingly, he was usually able to blend in at places like this, where he was least expected to be. He'd probably show up in a baseball cap and jersey or something, and should be able to fly under the radar.

Of course, with all three of them together, it might be a little tougher. But even the pitfalls of fame couldn't win in a battle against a delicious, greasy burger.

"Sorry. But you know he is," Raine said with a shrug as finished off burger number one.

The two of them had gotten here around the same time. Reece was late. They'd grabbed their food, knowing their brother might well have been held up at one studio or another and wouldn't make it at all.

But in case he did come, and knowing Reece was probably the one who was going to lose his shit over this whole Evie situation, Rowan had carefully explained everything to their younger brother, hoping for an ally.

As was his custom, Raine didn't react much either way. His jaw went hard enough to crack a bowling ball, but he'd been pretty quiet other than predicting Rowan's impending doom.

He'd probably predicted correctly how Reece was going to react when he found out his twin had brought a journalist into their lives by accident and had compounded the mistake by then inserting himself into hers.

Maybe that could be understood, even forgiven since he'd been telling himself he was in a perfect position to keep the Winchester family secrets from falling into her hands. Now, though, he'd fallen for *her*, something his kid brother had recognized as soon as Rowan mentioned Evie's name. How was he going to convince them they could trust her? They might suspect she was trying to seduce their secrets out of him.

Which, to be fair, she probably could.

But she wouldn't need to. Because she wasn't writing about Harry Baker. End of story.

"How bad is it?" Raine asked as he chomped more crispy fries. "You told her anything?"

"Nothing about that night." Definitely not. "She knows just enough to know how hard bringing all that up again would be on our family. So she's not going to."

"You're sure about that?"

"Believe me, she's got enough to worry about without trying to trick me into spilling something for a book."

The mugging, the mystery she was trying to solve, and Angstrom, who was always hanging in the back of her mind like a noxious ghost that never went away. He cast one hell of a long shadow. She'd been living under it for years, trying to inch away as time passed. Now it looked like he was throwing it over her again, a caustic blanket of darkness and contamination.

Christ, how he hoped she didn't have to go through any of that shit again.

Frankly, when pictured what she might have to endure if the bastard's conviction was overturned, and the possible danger she could be in if Angstrom reached out from behind bars to try to silence her, he found himself not giving a shit about his family's secrets. Not much else mattered other than keeping her safe.

God, he must be losing his mind. But that didn't make his feelings any less true.

"Okay, you know her and I don't. I trust your judgment."

Nice compliment coming from his usually very quiet kid brother.

"But you know Reece is still gonna fucking kill you."

"Why, exactly, am I going to fucking kill him?"

Hearing his other brother's voice, Rowan jerked his head up. What shitty luck. His Dodgers-cap-wearing, ex-movie-star brother had walked up to their table just in time to overhear.

Across from him, Raine was smirking. He'd probably seen Reece come in, the little shit.

Well, not little. Raine was the tallest of the three of them. Not to mention the broadest. That army stint had changed him from a scrawny eighteen-year-old into a candidate for the next Incredible Hulk movie.

"So, am I gonna need to eat my food before I hear whatever

it is you've been up to?" Reece asked. "I mean, if you make me nauseous and I can't enjoy the burger I've been fantasizing about for weeks, I might kill you at that."

"Get your food," Rowan muttered.

Reece headed for the counter. Raine leaned across the table.

"Postponing the execution?"

"Don't you have some snotty six-year-old movie star to play Barbies with?"

"See what you know. Barbie is *out*, dude. It's all about the American Girl dolls."

He chuckled at his brother's knowledge, but his laughter grew wistful as he murmured, "Rachel had one of those. I remember she wanted the one with the prettiest dresses."

Raine didn't smile back. He rarely smiled whenever Rachel was mentioned.

That probably wasn't surprising considering Raine had been the last member of their family to see Rachel alive. And in those final moments before her fateful fall, she'd been trying to get away from the fucking bastard who'd been molesting her. Her six-year-old brother had borne witness, though the memory had been locked in his brain for years. Until he'd seen Harry Baker reenacting his crime with another young girl.

Yeah, it was no wonder Raine wasn't much of a smiler. His happy thoughts had died when he was six years old. And despite a flash of a normal, happy guy here and there, for the most part, it had never come back.

Reece returned and grabbed a chair, pulling it to the end of their booth, his back to the rest of the restaurant. That was probably a good thing. There'd been a few murmurs and whispers, and Rowan had the feeling some customers had a suspicion about his identity. Only the fact that they couldn't really

believe an Oscar-winning actor/director would be sitting in an
In-N-Out burger in Glendale prevented anyone from coming
up to ask for an autograph.

Reece took a couple of bites of his burger, sighing in satisfaction, and then took a big gulp from his water bottle.

"Okay," he said. "Why am I gonna kill you, Rowan? What
the hell is going on?"

Knowing from experience that, with Reece, it was better to
pull off the Band-Aid and let him get all shitty and mad, and
then talk him back down off the ledge, Rowan spilled it. He
told his twin about stopping Evie from being mugged, reminding him that Reece and Jessica had both invited her to stay at
their place.

"Yeah, I know all this." Reece smiled a little as he reached for
his burger. "Just FYI, Jess was very curious about this new friend
of yours. She snooped around the house last night, looking for
some evidence of what happened."

"What did she think she was gonna find? Evidence of an
orgy in your bedroom?"

"Dude, please, I'm eating." Finishing one burger, Reece un-
wrapped another. "She was looking to see if she could figure out
where everybody, uh, slept. But I guess that new friend of yours
is a neat freak. Beds were stripped, trash cans emptied."

"That was me," Rowan mumbled. What'd they think he was,
a savage?

Reece ignored him. "Jess's robe freshly laundered and folded.
She was pretty disappointed."

"So sorry to disappoint your girlfriend…"

"Fiancée."

Rowan dropped his fry. Raine jerked back in his seat. Reece
just smiled.

His twin, aka the bomb-dropper.

"*Seriously?*" Raine asked.

"Yep."

"Congratulations! Why don't you tell a person?" Rowan asked.

"I believe I just did."

"You are one lucky son of a bitch. You know you don't deserve her, right?"

"Oh yeah, I definitely know that."

Reece had that crazy-in-love look on his face, one Rowan used to think he'd never see on the emotionally rigid man. And he couldn't be happier about it.

Smacking his brother on the back, Rowan smiled broadly, and not because he was temporarily off the hook with his whole story. He liked Jessica a lot. Mostly he liked the changes his future sister-in-law had brought out in his brother, who had at times been one of the biggest assholes in the universe. Now Reece was in love and engaged to marry a beautiful, kindhearted, funny young woman who didn't take herself too seriously...and didn't take *him* too seriously either. He needed someone who wouldn't take any of his shit, and Jess was that person.

"She's fantastic," Rowan said. "I really am happy for you. But I hope you did it right and didn't just toss a ring at her and inform her of the date and the church address."

Reece was a director, always planning out the scene. Jess swore she would break him of that if it took a lifetime. And it sounded like she was going to have her chance.

"Bite me. Believe me, I planned it all perfectly."

Curious about the satisfied tone in his twin's voice, Rowan couldn't help asking a question that would probably be more likely asked to a future bride by her future bridesmaids. "So how'd you do it? What does the ring look like?"

Across from him, he saw Raine roll his eyes. But tough shit. Rowan wanted to know.

Not because he was thinking about getting married or anything, hell no.

But he *was* thinking a lot about one certain woman.

And what it might be like to really let himself go for it with her.

He wasn't exactly a love-at-first-sight kind of guy, and his first sight of Evie had elicited rage and concern, not love-everlasting. Every sight since, though, had brought a storm of feelings like he'd never experienced before. Admiration, liking, confusion, irritation. Attraction—hell, yes. Plus a desire to make sure she wasn't hurt, that nobody got to her, that no evil monster ever laid another finger on her, or played psycho mind games with her.

He wanted to see her smile all the time and wanted to hear that joyful laugh she very seldom let escape those perfect lips. He wanted to kiss the taste out of her mouth and wanted to have sex with her more than he wanted to live until Christmas.

Was that love?

Fucked if he knew.

"It's a ruby. Not traditional, but Jess loves rubies. And she's not very traditional either."

"Well done," Rowan said. "Where and when?"

"We went to New York last weekend to see *Hamilton*."

"No wonder she said yes," Rowan muttered.

"The show was just an excuse."

"You didn't really have tickets?" he said, his eyes rounding. "You're lucky she didn't turn you down, you asshole."

"Of *course* I had the tickets. Jesus, pay attention. I meant the show was the excuse for the trip. The truth was, I wanted to take her out on the town, in a limo, show her a fantastic time, and then propose somewhere really special."

He had to ask. "So? Where was that?"

"Uh…" Reece suddenly wouldn't meet his eye. His unflappable brother was so seldom at a loss for words that even Raine suddenly looked interested.

"Where?" their younger brother asked.

"Well…we never actually got out of the limo."

Rowan barked a laugh and even Raine chuckled.

"Dude, you took her to New York to see the hottest show, like, ever, and planned to propose, lemme guess, on top of the Empire State Building?"

"Rainbow Room," Reece muttered before shoving more fries into his mouth.

"And you never even got out of the damn car."

"What can I say? She likes limos."

Reece wasn't at all the kind of guy who kissed and told, but his expression was pretty damned self-explanatory. Obviously he and his fiancée had ridden around New York City in a long stretch limo all night long, boning and getting engaged.

"Nice," Raine said with a grin.

"Has she forgiven you for not taking her to see the show?" Rowan asked.

"I took her the next night."

Knowing what not one but *two* sets of tickets to that production must have cost, Rowan whistled. He sometimes wondered what it would be like to have the kind of money his brother did. He didn't envy him, of course, knowing the kind of shit Reece dealt with because of his very public lifestyle. In the spotlight was not an easy space to live, as evidenced by the stalker who had really made his life hell earlier in the year.

No, Rowan didn't miss Hollywood stardom, not that he'd ever been as good as his siblings. But if he'd stayed in law school, how different might his life be now? He certainly doubted he'd be living in a crappy apartment, driving an old muscle car. He wouldn't be at Reece's level, but he didn't doubt he'd have done pretty well for himself.

Strange, he could barely remember the young, right-out-of-college guy he'd been when he'd started at Stanford, determined to graduate at the top of his class.

He'd been well on his way to fulfilling that vow. But within a year of finishing, he'd dropped out. That had been right after he and Reece had hidden evidence of what they thought was Raine's killing of Harry Baker.

He just couldn't stand the hypocrisy of it, becoming a lawyer and arguing in a courtroom while carrying the weight of something like that. Maybe it had been crazy to then join the LAPD instead, but it had made sense to him at the time. He couldn't tell anyone what he had done, or why he'd done it. So he couldn't practice law. But walking a beat, catching genuinely evil criminals and taking them off the street? That had sounded right. He wasn't going to get rich doing it, but he wouldn't feel like as much of a fucking hypocrite either.

And he could do some good. He could atone.

No, he didn't regret that Baker was dead. But he did regret that his actions—and Reece's—had enabled a killer to get away with the crime.

"Okay, back to the point. Why am I gonna kill you again? And can I put it off since I want the two of you to stand up for me at the wedding?"

Before Rowan could answer, his phone rang. He glanced at

it, just in case, and was surprised to see a name that tugged at his memory.

"Candace Oakley," he murmured. Then he remembered. Wondering why Evie's agent would be calling him, he held an index finger up to his brothers and answered.

"Detective Winchester? This is Candace Oakley. I'm Evie's—"

"I know who you are. What can I do for you?"

"I can't reach her." The woman sounded anxious, nervous and tense. "I've tried and tried. She kept the same number when she replaced her phone, right? But she's not picking up."

"She said she was going to the beach," he explained. "She must have left it at home."

"Are you with her?"

"No."

"She's all by herself?" Her voice was no longer just tense; she sounded almost fearful.

Rowan's heart started to thump in his chest. Something was very, *very* wrong. And he sensed it wasn't anything as simple as her Hollywood manager outing her to the press.

"She *is* alone. Now, do you want to tell me what, exactly, is going on?"

"It's bad."

Bad. Like Evie needed more of that in her life. "Tell me."

The woman did. And she was right.

It was bad.

* * *

As much as Evie liked the cold weather back home when the holidays drew close, there was something to be said about lying on a sandy beach, soaking up the sun, just a week or so before Thanksgiving. She had walked the few blocks here to a quiet beach used mostly by people in her neighborhood. There was no big public parking lot nearby, so it seldom drew outsiders. Today, it was practically deserted, the temperature probably just a tinge too cold for the locals. For an Easterner like her, it was just perfect.

Spreading her blanket, she'd planned to just lie here and read a book. But she'd been so comfortable, so relaxed, that she ended up closing her eyes for an afternoon nap. The churning of the surf and the cries of seagulls overhead provided the perfect background noise, lulling her, easing her stress. She felt the tension leave her body. Here, with the breeze on her skin, the sand between her toes, and the sunshine falling warmly on her face, she could *almost* forget there was such a person as Angstrom, or as the mugger. Or as the flower killer, whoever he may be.

She was almost there, almost completely boneless and devoid of thoughts of anything except how she wanted to spend the coming night—in Rowan's arms—when she heard footsteps crunching in the sand and felt instant coolness on her face as a shadow fell over her.

She opened her eyes. Rowan stood above her, staring down at her, but not wearing that sexy, mischievous smile she'd already grown to adore.

Trying to moisten her suddenly dry mouth, she swallowed and licked her salty lips. She had hoped to see him today, but she'd thought it would be later. That she'd have a chance to wash her hair, to put on something sexy and prepare to seduce and be seduced. Instead, here, she was sweaty, sandy, windblown, and smelled of coconut.

"So what's up?" she asked, pretending she wasn't a complete mess.

"Hope you're wearing sunscreen. It might be too cool to swim, but you can still burn."

"SPF 50 and plenty of it," she said with a grin.

He didn't return it. Whatever was going on, it had definitely affected his mood.

"Um, what are you doing here?"

"I need to talk to you."

He had that serious tone. The cop voice. Not the cold, aloof stranger one he used to try to put up barriers between them, but the professional, no-nonsense one he used when on the job.

The first tinge of genuine disquiet pinged in her brain.

Maybe this wasn't a social call. Perhaps it was a professional one.

She shimmied up into a sitting position, scooting over on the blanket to make room. He took the seat she offered, stretching out his long, powerful, jean-clad legs beside hers.

"You don't have your phone with you," he murmured.

"No. I left it at home. I know I shouldn't have, but frankly, I was *desperate* to disconnect this afternoon. Why?"

He was staring out at the water. "Your agent called me. She's been trying to reach you."

She could tell by his tone that he hadn't sought her out to tell her Candace had sold her next book at auction for seven figures.

"What is it, Rowan?" she asked, reaching over and putting a hand on his leg.

"I have news." He dropped his hand over hers, squeezing tightly, as if bracing her for what was about to come. "You're not going to like it."

She stilled, thoughts whirling, and then the truth slammed into her brain. "Angstrom?"

Rowan nodded, still looking out at the waves crashing against the beach. Nobody was in the water, only two or three sun worshippers lying anywhere in sight, but even in this vast, empty space, Evie felt the world crowding too close, rushing in, suffocating her. She hauled in a deep breath, fighting off a chill that had nothing to do with the November breeze.

"He's getting a new trial?" she managed to whisper.

Rowan nodded.

She let out a little sound of dismay that might have been a half shriek, but she would call a gasp. Rowan, thoughtful as always, grabbed a bottle of water from the small cooler she'd brought down, opened it, and pressed it into her hands. She sipped greedily, wanting the claustrophobic sensation to disappear, especially since it made no sense at all. She was in a huge open space, in the bright sunlight, with the wind in her hair and salty spray on her bare skin.

So why did she feel like she was the one who'd just been tossed into a prison cell, the door slamming behind her with a deafening clang?

"I guess somebody in the DA's office finally thought about you and contacted your agent to try to get ahold of you."

"Oh my God, oh my God, oh my God," she whispered as she handed back the bottle. "Blair's parents...the other victims' families. Let this be a bad dream. Let me wake up."

"I'm so sorry, Evie," Rowan said, putting an arm around her and pulling her against his side. She curled up close, burrowing into him, taking his warmth, his strength, and his *goodness*. When so saturated in ugly crimes and evil minds, she sometimes forgot that there were genuinely decent, caring, honorable men out there.

She was very glad to have found one, and she hoped that

the attraction that had flared so suddenly between them was already turning into something else. It *certainly* was on her part.

She'd been incredibly appreciative of him the moment they'd met. She'd been incredibly attracted to him the moment she'd calmed down and really looked at him later that night.

She'd wanted him as soon as they'd kissed at his brother's place.

In the days since, she'd gotten to know the real man, and everything she'd already been feeling exploded exponentially. Yes, he'd driven her crazy with that wall of never-gonna-trust-you that he'd erected early on. But even with that wall, she'd gotten to know the real Rowan. The kindhearted one who was so gentle when shaking a sick man's pained hands. The smart one who had believed what she told him and agreed to help her on this very tricky case. The loyal one who so obviously loved his family, living and dead. The good-natured one who was able to laugh at himself and make her laugh with him. The one who was scared of spiders but not of snakes, who hummed off-key to the car radio.

The sexy one who kissed like she was the most perfect thing in the world and he wanted only to be lost in her mouth forever.

"Oh, Rowan," she whispered, shaking her head slowly.

"I've got you, honey," he whispered as he stroked her hair. "I've got you, and I'll do anything you need me to do to help you get through this."

She pulled away enough to look up in his handsome face. He pushed his sunglasses up so he could meet her stare, and the warmth she saw there, the compassion, the concern, the *emotion*, was enough to calm her completely. Her heart stopped thudding, her stomach stopped churning, and her thoughts stopped skittering.

She drew in a few calming breaths, sucked up warmth from the man beside her, and focused on the bright and sunny now, not the dark and bloody then.

She was not the same woman she had been. Not by a long shot.

As a frightened twenty-two-year-old, she'd faced Angstrom in his shop even after she'd begun to suspect he had slaughtered her best friend.

She'd faced him again in a courtroom, when she'd been only a little older than that, still terrified, with nightmares and anxiety that held her in a relentless grip and nightmares that woke her with screams filling her mouth every night.

Now, though, she was no longer a new college grad who'd barely started living in the real world. She was a thirty-year-old professional with several books under her belt, a *New York Times* bestseller in front of her name, and the confidence to know she could make a difference.

Plus determination. A whole lot of it that far outweighed any residual fear of the monster who'd shaded most of her adult life with his vicious presence.

He'd been the monster in the closet, the terror of her dreams, the creak in the night, the evil grin in the crowd, the hand emerging from the darkness.

But no more. No longer.

She wasn't afraid of him. She couldn't be, not when faced with the possibility that he might actually get out of prison. She would find whatever strength it took to keep Blair's killer right where he was. Forever.

"What can I do, Evie?"

She slowly rose to her knees, and he came up with her. The breeze blew her hair into her eyes and her thin dress hard against her legs. The salty ocean spray landed on her lips and her eyelashes, and she wished it was warm enough to go swimming. "Go for a walk with me?"

He smiled gently. "I'd like that."

They left the blanket and the cooler. Nobody was around; she didn't think anybody would be interested. She slipped her sandals off and carried them, walking barefoot with him a few feet from the lapping edge of the surf with its white foam breaking on the sand.

They held hands. It wasn't something they discussed; he simply reached out and took hers between one stride and the next. She twined her fingers between his, and they walked in silence, heading away from the few people on the beach, toward a rocky curve in the coastline where the surf pounded wildly and where even no surfers would dare to try catching a wave.

It suited her mood. The wildness of it. The coolness of the wind, the crash of the waves, the whistle of the breeze through the rocks. There were no swimmers, no joggers, and no sunbathers. No boats in the water or planes in the sky or mansions up on the cliff. It was a self-contained little world, as darkly dramatic as it had been for hundreds of years, she imagined.

Here there was no anxiety. No serial killer to think about, no book to write, no confusion about how she could go on living when the past kept trying to reach out and grab her.

There was just wild beauty, and the man walking beside her. They went around the base of the cliff, onto a small stretch of beach surrounded by high cliffs, where the wind whistled and blew more wildly, and the surf roared.

She moved closer to him, and he slid an arm around her waist. "Are you okay, Evie?"

"I'm fine."

"Not too cold?"

"No. Actually, I love this weather." She stopped, turned toward the water, closed her eyes, and lifted her face toward it. Breathing deeply, she inhaled all that clean air, liking the sensation of cold droplets landing on her skin, making her feel...alive.

Completely alive.

After a second, he asked, "How about emotionally. You all right there too?"

She looked up at him. "I am. I've been dreading that news for a while, but now that it's come, I can stop worrying about it and start moving into the I-can-do-this phase."

Cupping her cheek, he murmured, "Yes, you can. And I'll help you in any way possible."

"Why would you do that?" she asked, genuinely wanting to know. "You've known me for less than a week."

"I know enough," he told her with a simple shrug. "I know I'll rip apart anyone who messes with you, and I'll fight whoever I have to in order to keep you safe." He leaned down and brushed his lips across hers. "I know you're special. I don't want anything to happen to you."

If there was any remaining anxiety flowing through her, it melted under the vow he'd just made. She hadn't asked him to. She would never ask anyone to put her first, to think only of her safety, her needs. But the fact that he'd just made that promise made something inside her melt.

She was used to being on her own now, accustomed to taking the bull by the horns and doing what needed to be done, whether it was interviewing a murderer on death row or fighting for a better contract. But this...his gentle strength and support just offered because that was the kind of man he was made her *want* to give up everything about herself, to get lost in his strength, his tenderness, and his warmth.

Dropping her shoes, she snaked her arms around his shoulders, tunneling her fingers in his short, dark hair. She leaned into him, rose on her tiptoes, and whispered, "Thank you." Then she touched her lips to his, sweetly, underscoring her thanks.

He dropped his hands to her hips. Circling her waist, he gently stroked the small of her back as he licked her lips apart, then slid his tongue between them. She sighed, tilting her head to deepen the kiss, savoring the slow strokes as he explored her mouth.

They'd walked by a few people on the beach. But right here, right now, in this special, wild little cove, where she felt sheltered from the storm swirling all around her, and inside her, nobody else even existed anymore.

For all the crazy feelings she'd had about the man since he'd literally rescued her from a violent attack, Evie hadn't expected that it would be pure tenderness and emotion that would finally bring them together. But it was. Without saying a word, without even ending the kiss, they slowly reached for each other's clothes.

He slid her loose, flowy dress off her shoulders and Evie let it fall to the sand with her shoes. Rowan looked down at her, his eyes growing darker as his gaze lingered on her breasts pushing up over the top of her bra, her bare waist, and her plain bikini underwear.

She wasn't dressed like the Victoria's Secret model she'd planned for tonight. But judging by the way his breaths sped up, his eyes turned into dark pools of hunger, and his hands actually shook as he touched her, she suspected it didn't matter much.

"You are beautiful," he muttered, stroking her from her shoulders, down her front, his fingertips riding lightly across her skin. Her skin was goose bumped with cold, but just the faint scrape of his fingers set her on fire. When he reached her cleavage, he continued that light, easy glide, not giving her the pressure she wanted, leaving her nipples aching for attention and making her want to rip off the last of her clothes.

She didn't need to worry about it. Without a word of warning, he moved his fingers to the front clasp of her bra, flicked it, and the thing fell apart, freeing her breasts. A tiny shrug of each shoulder and the lacy thing landed on the sand with her dress.

"Christ," he groaned as he pulled her back against him.

He caught her mouth again, and this time there was no hesitation. Their tongues met and mated, pushing and pulling, taking and giving. There were no more questions, only answers. No more hesitation, only sweet, sultry desire.

The feel of her bare breasts brushing against his shirt made her feel weak. Her nipples ached at the sweetly rough scrape that simply wasn't enough. She wanted skin on skin, wanted to become part of him, to wrap herself around him and bring him into her body.

Evie tugged his shirt free of his jeans, pulling away from his kiss long enough to push it up and off. Reaching for his belt, she unfastened it and unbuttoned his jeans. But rather than going on the way she was dying to, rather than freeing that thick ridge she could feel pushing up toward her fingers, she just *had* to step back and look at him the way he had looked at her.

So she did. And her breath whooshed out of her lungs at the sight of him.

His body was beyond her wildest dreams of what a man could look like. Rowan was broad and strong, she knew that.

But he was also just *beautiful*. A work of art in physical form, all rippling muscles, taut skin, and raw masculine power. Just enough dark hair swirled over his chest, and down a perfectly formed six-pack, trailing in a thin line down...down. She couldn't help following the trail with her gaze, noting how lean-waisted and slim-hipped the man was. His unbuttoned jeans had slid down a little, revealing a glimpse of dark cotton underneath the bulged that strained for release.

"You looked enough?"

"I don't think I could *ever* get tired of looking at you," she swore, knowing it was true.

He stopped her heart, made her mouth water, and made her wet just by standing there.

"Come 'ere," he said, reaching for her waist and pulling her back into his arms. Evie stroked his thick shoulders, then caressed her way down his hard chest, delighting in the textures of his body and the heat of his skin. He moved his mouth to her face and skimmed her jaw, her cheek, and her lips. He nipped, he tasted, he gave her crazy-sweet kisses that made her quiver.

While she tangled her fingers in the wiry hair on his chest, he delicately felt his way from the sides of her neck down each of her arms, the tips of his fingers barely touching her, providing just enough pressure to drive her mad with the need for more. Then he moved lower, kissing his way down her throat, to its hollow, where he stopped to take a deep breath, as if inhaling her very essence. Evie arched back, offering herself to him. When he lowered his mouth to the curves of her breasts and tasted them, she moaned. He was holding her around the waist, supporting her weight, and she leaned back, silently begging for more.

"So beautiful," he mumbled as he caressed her soft breasts, arousing her more by the very spots he was avoiding.

"Please, more," she whispered.

"No problem." He finally stroked her nipple that was puckered with cold and with heat, but mostly with heat.

"Oh yes," she groaned as he caressed her, squeezed her, lifting his other hand to her other breast to continue to play with her. When he bent to lick at the top curve of one breast, she moaned. And when that mouth moved to the very tip and sucked, she lost her strength and fell back.

He caught her, his powerful arms slowly lowering her to the damp sand. He came with her, kneeling between her bare legs, staring down at her with a hunger so obvious it was almost a physical, tangible thing that existed outside both of them. It was matched by her own need, and she knew they were creating something altogether new, this mating of want and hunger forming an invisible connection that she felt down to her toes.

"Are you all right?" he asked as he stroked her hips and her thighs. "It's cold and not very comfortable. It might kill me, but we could get dressed and go back to your place."

"If you do that, *I* might kill you."

He smiled, then reached for his zipper. She watched him tug it down, having to swallow as her mouth flooded with actual hunger for him.

"I want this so much. I have since the night we met," she admitted.

"Me too."

Before pushing his jeans off his hips, Rowan reached into the pocket and pulled out a condom. The sight of it shocked her for a second. She'd never in her life forgotten protection, but she had today. It was a very good thing he had remembered.

Tossing the condom on the sand, he shoved the jeans and undershorts down, and Evie gasped, closed her eyes, and then opened him again.

She trembled. She twisted. She gaped.

She should have known. Of course she should have.

He was, after all, big and powerful everywhere else.

"I want you so much, Rowan Winchester," she managed to say, still staring at that big, powerful erection jutting out from a thatch of dark hair.

"Same, Evelyn Fleming."

But rather than put the condom on and *take* her, Rowan instead kissed his way down her body, gliding his tongue across each rib. He dipped in to taste her belly button, scraping his bearded jaw against the elastic of her underpants. His warm breaths were a shocking contrast to the cool air rolling in off the water, and she quivered and arched toward him, wanting what he obviously intended to give her with a desperation that bordered on frenzy.

"Still warm enough?" he asked as he began to tug at the hem of her panties with his teeth. He brushed his lips back and forth across the curls there, but didn't go farther.

"I am burning up, you rotten tease."

Laughing softly, Rowan took hold of her bare hips, squeezing her ass, then tilting her closer to his waiting mouth. She tensed the tiniest bit; then all tension slid away and she became a boneless heap of sensation as he licked into the folds of her sex, finding her clit and slowly stroking it with his tongue

"Oh my God," she whispered, overwhelmed by the pleasure of it. She'd been thinking of wild, hard, pounding sex. She hadn't even considered all the other amazing, delicious, delightful ways Rowan could make her so very glad she was a woman.

He toyed with her until she trembled, bringing her close to the edge. Rather than taking her over it, however, he moved away at the last possible second. She groaned in frustration, at least until she felt that hot tongue gliding lower, into the wet folds of her sex, dipping in, teasing her, driving her wild.

She gasped. "Can't take much more of this."

"Yeah. You can. I have faith in you."

His laughter was wicked. So was his mouth. Oh God, so wonderfully wicked.

Sliding his hands around her thighs, he parted them, further settling between them and making slow, deliberate love to her with his tongue. He savored her like a starving man at an all-you-can-eat buffet, leaving her helpless to do anything except lie there and love it.

Evie vaguely remembered they were on the beach, lying on rough sand. She barely processed the sound of the waves crashing near their feet, barely saw the rays of late afternoon sun slanting across their little cove. She just…enjoyed.

"Oh, Rowan," she groaned, tangling her fingers in his hair. "I need to—"

"Shh. I've got you."

She couldn't think, couldn't do anything but lie there as all the sensations came together and her senses took in every bit of it—the sky, the sun, the sand, the lapping waves, the unbelievable ecstasy of his mouth on her clit—and she shook into a shattering climax.

Evie let out a little scream. The ocean breeze caught it and carried it out to sea.

She hadn't even caught her breath before he was there, covering her mouth with his. It was strange—tasting herself on his lips—but still so incredibly erotic. She grabbed his hair and held him so she could thrust her tongue against his.

He grabbed the condom and moved back between her parted legs. She stroked his taut butt, arching up in delight at the feel of warm skin between her thighs. His erection lay hot and huge against her belly, and she started shaking again in pure, unadulterated want.

He tore open the condom with his teeth, but Evie shook her head. She needed to touch him, to stroke that velvety skin before he covered it in latex.

"Wait. Let me help you."

He looked into her eyes and must have seen the need there. Rolling onto his side, he guided her hand until they were both touching the tip of his cock. She sighed as she stretched her hand wide, stretching to grasp him, and stroked.

"Oh, Evie," he groaned. "I love how your hands feel on me."

She intended to see how he liked having her mouth on him, but knew the need was too much for the both of them now. She had to have him inside her, and that's where he had to be.

Although her hand shook, she was able to roll the condom down, her fingers lingering, her touch obviously driving him wild.

"Evie," he warned when she slid her hand lower, to the base of his shaft...and beyond. When she cupped his balls, he let out a guttural groan. "If you don't want me coming right in your hand, you'd better let me set the pace," he said. He immediately pushed her onto her back, settling again between her thighs.

"Set the pace, take control, do whatever you want," she said, now nearly desperate to feel all that rock-hard flesh buried inside her. "Just do it *now*, Rowan, *please.*"

He didn't hesitate, driving in, driving hard, driving deep. He stretched her, filled her completely. And it was such a relief, after so much waiting, she needed to shout out loud. So she did. She shouted, she groaned, and when he began thrusting, short and quick, then long and so deep she thought she'd split in half, she screamed again.

"People up the beach are gonna think you're drowning," he muttered.

He quickly covered her mouth with his, kissing her deeply to shut her up. She didn't mind, kissing him back with wild hunger. Twining her arms around his shoulders, she arched up to meet every slow, deliberate thrust, taking all he could give her and demanding more.

Rowan tried to keep it slow and deep, and at first, she let him, loving how she could feel the glide of every spectacular inch. But soon her body caught the pounding rhythm of the waves. The tide was coming in, and suddenly the water lapped over their feet. Cold, foamy, splashing a little bit higher with each subsequent wave.

The wildness leapt into her blood, and she scratched his back, groaning with pleasure when he responded with the kind of thrust that drove her deep into the sand. The hunger took over and there was no more control, no more measured touches, they simply poured themselves into the connection, pounding, giving, taking.

And enjoying every single solitary second of it.

Until the seconds were done, they were both utterly spent, and completely satisfied.

"Want a drink or something?" she asked. "I have some beer in the fridge."

"Sounds good," he said.

"I'll be just a sec."

She walked toward a doorway that led into what he thought was her bedroom. She didn't walk through it, though. Instead, she froze, staring toward something in that room, her face a mask of confusion.

"What is it?" he asked, instantly on alert.

Not waiting for her to answer, he strode over and moved in front of her to eye the room. It looked normal to him—a tall dresser, a TV mounted on the wall, neatly made queen-sized bed. The cream-colored spread looked more to her taste, and when he spied a pile of garishly bright linens piled up on a chair, he knew she'd redecorated at least this little corner of her space.

"The window," she murmured, pointing to the one that looked out into the backyard. The curtains were pushed back, the window raised several inches, enough to bring a slight breeze into the room. "It's open."

He heard what she wasn't saying. *She* hadn't opened it.

"Stay here," he ordered, pushing past her into the bedroom.

The room was pretty sunny and uncluttered, with no nooks or dark corners in which anyone could hide. He could easily see into the attached bathroom, and a quick glance into the walk-in closet confirmed it contained nothing but clothes and shoes. He double-checked under the bed and did one more pass of the entire room.

Pushing past her, he went to search the rest of the house. He opened the kitchen pantry door, lifted the tablecloth, peered into closets, and pulled back the shower curtain in the guest bathroom. There was no attached garage, no other open windows, and the whole house was probably only a thousand square feet.

Nothing. Other than the two of them, it was completely empty of life.

Nor was there any evidence that anyone had been here and had left. Robbers usually didn't bother with closing cabinet doors. They weren't careful not to knock over furniture. They didn't overlook computers on the kitchen table, electronics in the living room, or even a handful of coins left on her dresser. When he'd been to robbery scenes before, he usually found intentionally damaged belongings, broken glass, sometimes graffiti, not to mention clothing strewn all over the floor as the thief dug for hidden valuables.

This place was simply pristine.

"There's nobody here," he said as he rejoined her.

But he saw the expression on her face. Evie still stood where she'd been before, her arms wrapped around her waist, her creamy-complexioned face a little pale, though she'd been rosy with sunshine and passion just a little while ago.

He knew she was worried but had to ask, "Are you sure you didn't leave the window open? Maybe you got up during the night to let in a little fresh air and just forgot?"

She was shaking her head before he finished speaking.

"No, never. What happened spooked me so bad I made a mental note to ask the landlord if she minded if I put up some of those cheap little window alarms. I would never leave them unlocked, much less open."

"Okay," he murmured. Seeing her dismay, he couldn't resist lifting a hand to brush back a strand of her soft hair. "I understand why you're so cautions, Evie. But you know he's not gonna come after you. I'm sure Frankie Lee is somewhere in Mexico by now."

She stared into his eyes, appearing confused. Then her mouth fell open. "Oh, no, I don't mean that. I'm not worrying about *him*."

"What do you mean, then?"

She swallowed, her slender throat flexing. "I mean, when I came home the day after that, I found that same window open then too. And some of my things were…moved around. At least, I think they were. It's happened once or twice since, but it's so subtle, I just haven't let myself try to puzzle it out."

"Explain," he barked, going back on high alert.

She pointed to the bedside table. "The clock. I've turned off that alarm every morning since I've been here, and it's always been on the right-hand nightstand."

It was now on the left. The time was accurate, the numbers gleaming red. It was perfectly positioned to be seen from the bed. And it had been moved?

Gesturing toward her dresser, she went on. "My hairbrush was right there. I used it when I dried my hair this morning."

If it had been, it wasn't anymore.

"It's like, things have been moved and touched—doors left open, a glass left in the sink that I know I didn't use, things like that—but it's all almost under the radar, stuff a person who wasn't always on the lookout for anything out of the usual might not even notice."

"But you did notice."

"Yes."

"Why haven't you said anything?"

She pushed her windblown hair back. "I have been so stressed, so distracted, I've just been figuring I was becoming forgetful."

"The coffee," he whispered, remembering how it had been out of place in the kitchen.

"Exactly."

His *danger* instincts were pinging. Evie was a cautious woman, with good reason given her history. She might forget one or two things, but this sounded almost like a campaign to make her doubt her own senses and memories.

It sounded very—*very*—deliberate.

Going to the open window, he glanced out into the small, fenced backyard and saw nothing out of the ordinary. Closing it, he tested the lock. He latched it—or thought he had—but when he tried to lift the window, it came up easily.

"It's broken," he said, now not just tense but on high alert. High enough to make him wish he had his backup service weapon in its regular place on his ankle.

The windows weren't original to the house. They had obviously been replaced within the last few years. There was no reason for the lock not to work, as far as he could see.

He bent down and examined them. The plastic latches at the bottom that were supposed to snap into place and lock it down had been carefully trimmed across the back, shaved flat. It wasn't something anyone would notice from the front, unless they carefully examined them. Evie obviously hadn't even noticed as she closed it, not realizing there should have been a click when they attached.

"How much do you trust your landlord?" he said with a glower.

"She's a little old lady who lives with her widowed daughter in Laguna," she whispered. Then, with a visible shudder, she added, "Angstrom."

"No, baby." He walked over to take her into his arms. "He can't get at you."

She was lost to dark imaginings. "He warned me he has friends here. Maybe they started out trying to scare me so I'd already be rethinking testifying if he got a new trial. Now he has."

He held her even tighter. "No way, Evie. He is not gonna get anybody anywhere near you, I swear to you."

After she stopped quivering, he said, "Let me secure that window and then we'll get out of here, okay?"

She nodded, watching as he went and broke off a short metal bracket from the closet. He positioned it in the track of the window. It wasn't great, but it should hold for now until real locks could be put back on. In the meantime, he wasn't leaving her alone in this place for a single second.

"Oh my God," she whispered.

Looking over, he saw Evie standing near the bed, her arms wrapped around her middle, her mouth hanging open. She looked like someone who had just had a major shock.

"What?" he snapped, instantly at her side.

She nodded toward the pillows sitting on top of the neatly spread comforter. One was fluffed up. The other, on the right-hand side, where she usually slept given the preferred location of the clock, had an indentation in the center. As if a person had just been sleeping on it.

Then he saw what was in that indentation. And knew why she was so horrified.

"Pack a bag."

She remained frozen, her stare locked on the horrible sight.

"I mean it," he insisted, going to her closet and yanking the door open. He began to haul out clothes and toss them on the bed. "Take whatever you need for now. I'll come back and get the rest later."

"I can't just—"

"Evie, listen to me." He came over to her and put both hands on her shoulders, gripping tightly. "You can't stay here. You weren't imagining things. Someone *has* been in your house, using that window as a highway to invade your privacy."

He didn't even want to think about whether that person had been standing here, right in her bedroom, standing over her while she slept. Nor did he want to imagine what that person might have done tonight, now that word had gotten out that Angstrom actually was getting a new trial.

She was a key witness. The serial killer's "friends" already had her in their sights. They'd probably just been waiting for the word to go. And somehow, Angstrom had gotten it to them.

Rowan, meanwhile, had been completely oblivious, barely paying attention when she'd told him the coffee was in the wrong place. He prided himself on being observant, and he'd failed to even notice that someone he greatly cared about was in danger.

"You're coming home with me."

She didn't react. She wasn't surprised. She just finally had someone else to confirm what she already suspected.

"Now let's get your stuff, just enough to get you through, and we'll get out of here."

She didn't argue, instead going right to the closet and pulling out a suitcase. She took the clothes he'd already grabbed, rolled them up, and stuffed them in. A quick visit to the bathroom and she had her toiletries as well. Adding a few pair of shoes, she nodded that she was finished and he helped her zip the bag closed.

"We'll get you someplace safe, and then I'll have this whole place checked out, top to bottom and get whatever else you left behind. You will not be moving back in."

He thought about how her mind-game-playing visitor had gotten her address so easily. He suspected she had her miserable excuse for a Hollywood agent to blame. He'd given the address out to the media, who'd staked out her house and shown the exterior. It was entirely possible there'd been a street sign, something recognizable in the shot. Or hell, that bastard might have just given it out to anybody who called looking for a story on the famous writer.

Rowan was gonna have a private talk with that man. Soon.

"Thank you, Rowan," Evie whispered.

He knew she wasn't thanking him for lifting the suitcase off the bed.

She cast another glance toward the pillow.

So did he.

What he again saw there made him take her by the arm and practically carry her out of the room, straight to his car.

He didn't want to think about what might have happened if he hadn't shown up at the beach, if he hadn't walked her home. It was very possible whoever had been inside had seen him pull up and park out front, and then walk off toward the beach. Probably fearing Evie would not return alone from the beach, he'd escaped through the back window.

But not without leaving a souvenir.

There had been a single strand of hair in that hollowed

pillow, carefully positioned and curled into a near heart shape.

It was very long.

And very dark.

Not blonde.

And most definitely not Evie Fleming's.

Chapter 10

Although Evie had assumed they would go back to his brother's fancy house, Rowan had instead taken her to his own place. He'd warned her she'd find no luxurious sunken tub, private pool, or magnificent views, but frankly, she liked it better. The one-bedroom apartment was comfortable and homey. With brown leather sofas, rich, dark-wood tables, and just a few prints of mountain scenes on the walls, it reminded her a lot of its occupant. Warm, unpretentious, and masculine. It suited him. Which suited her.

After they had arrived late Saturday afternoon, they'd showered, and then he'd left again. Eliciting her promise not to open the door for anyone, he'd headed over to meet a cop from the police station closest to her rental house.

She'd known it had to be done and hadn't objected. But she couldn't help being anxious for him to return. Not because she was nervous about being alone, save for the persnickety cat who had suddenly decided he did *not* like her. But for Rowan. She didn't want him going back to that place, where someone had obviously lurked, intent on doing her harm. If that person came back when Rowan was there, he might target him instead. Bad enough that she'd dragged him into her drama. If she also put him in danger, or caused him to be harmed, she would never forgive herself.

So she watched the clock and wished time would pass. She couldn't concentrate on work, and the cat was not interested in being scratched today.

Suddenly she remembered she did have one thing to do. Knowing how Rowan had found out what had happened, she placed a call to Candace to let her know she was okay.

"Oh my God, Evie, I was so worried," the other woman said, sounding tearful.

"I'm fine, I promise." She did not get into what had gone on at the house. Frankly, it would be a long conversation, and she just didn't want to have it right now. "How did you find out about the court's decision?"

"I got a call from someone at the DA's office yesterday afternoon. They were trying to reach you. But I didn't even listen to the voice mail until this morning. I'm so sorry! As soon as I heard it, I started trying to track you down."

And she hadn't had her phone, wanting to "disconnect." Given what had happened between her and Rowan on the beach, she couldn't regret that. She was also glad she hadn't had to hear the news on the phone and that he had been the one to break it to her.

"It's all right. My fault for being out of reach. But I got the word."

"Thank heaven. Are you...all right about it?"

Good question. She wasn't sure she could call herself all right, but she was managing, which was probably all she could ask for. Which was what she told her friend.

"Look, I'm not staying at the house right now," she also admitted. "I just…well, I felt a little uncomfortable."

"That's probably a good thing." Clearing her throat, Candace quickly added, "He didn't give out your address, Evie. I feel really sure of that."

She could have been nice about it, but right now, with everything she was facing, including the fact that someone had been in her house, she just wasn't in the mood. "Look, Candace, he admitted he called the press twice last week to try to get me some attention that I really did not want. Especially after being attacked on the street."

"I know," her agent said. "It was awful, and I know he feels bad. It's just…well, to be honest, business isn't so great. It's hard for Marcus."

Yeah. Right. So hard for poor Marcus.

"I think he feels like he has to wow you to make sure you don't regret taking him on because he's my husband."

"About that…"

"Oh, Evie, please don't. Give him one more chance."

"I know you trust him. But after what he pulled, how can I?"

Candace was a proud, strong woman. But there was almost a plea in her voice when it came to her sleazy husband. Which simply proved that love really was blind.

"If I find out he really did give out your address, I'll fire him for you," Candace said. "But in terms of the press, well, that's how it's done out here."

"It's not how I want it done," Evie said, still not sure of what to do.

"Oh, he knows that. He won't ever pull that kind of stunt on you again."

She hesitated and then finally sighed. "All right. For now."

"Thank you!"

Not finished, Evie added, "But I swear to you, if I find out he has given anyone—*anyone*—my home address or phone number, we're done. The end."

"I completely understand." Candace's voice grew softer. "I know you're worried about Angstrom, honey. He won't be able to get to you."

"I'm not worried about him doing it *directly*."

Angstrom's multiple-murder conviction might have been overturned, but it wasn't as if they were going to let him out of prison to wait for his new trial, because he was *also* serving a sentence for kidnapping and robbery, from other cases. He was going nowhere.

"I don't know how on earth any of his psycho fans would find you."

Knowing somebody already had, somebody who'd been having a grand old time messing with her mind for the past week, she wondered if she was going too easy on Marcus.

Maybe he hadn't given out her address. But if he had…

"Listen, can we meet for lunch or something in the next day or two? I have gotten the marketing plan for the new book and I think there are some things we should discuss."

"Okay. I'll come by the office on Monday."

"Good. Wait, where are you staying? Do you want to stay with us?"

"Oh, no, I couldn't do that. I'm okay. I'm staying with a…friend."

After a moment's hesitation, Candace chortled. "It's that hot cop, isn't it?! I knew there was something you weren't saying about him the other day. As soon as I saw him, I realized the man is pure catnip for pussies everywhere."

Evie chuckled despite herself, able to picture Candace's eyebrow wag. Her sly, risqué sense of humor hadn't been much in evidence since she'd married. Evie suspected Marcus didn't appreciate it. One more thing not to like about good old Marcus.

"We'll talk on Monday," she said, wanting to get off the phone.

"Okay. I want details!"

"No."

"Spoilsport."

"Bye, Candace."

Ending the call, Evie got online and started looking at other rental properties. She appreciated that Rowan had brought her home, and she would very much like to spend some of her nights here. Or a lot of them. But she couldn't just move in with the man. She needed her own place.

This time, she would find something with better security.

And woe to anyone who gave out her location.

Growing discouraged from the Craigslist and Realtor listings, she flicked on the TV and turned to a cable news station. Within a few minutes they covered the Angstrom case. The man's crimes had been shocking and had caught the attention of the entire country, so of course his appeals had too. That this one had succeeded was probably giving nightmares to everyone who knew his name.

"Oh hell," she muttered when a picture of *her* appeared on the screen. She was coming out of the courthouse, flanked by her parents on one side and a police officer on the other. She looked small, pale, young, and terrified.

She was no longer that girl anymore. And while today's incident had rattled her badly, she wasn't going to let anyone scare her off. She'd been strong enough to face down Blair's killer at only age twenty-two. Damned if anything would stop her from doing it again now.

She turned off the television before the news cycle could roll around again to repeat the exact same story again. Wanting something to eat, Evie nosed around in his pantry and fridge. Both were well stocked; it didn't look much like a bachelor's kitchen, and she suspected he actually knew how to cook. Probably better than she did. But she gave it her best shot, chopping chicken and vegetables to make up a stir-fry when he got home.

Which was at about eight o'clock.

As soon as he walked in the door, she went and wrapped her arms around him. "I'm glad you're back."

"Sorry it took so long. You okay?"

"I'm fine. It was you I was worried about."

He pressed a soft kiss on her mouth, and then rested his forehead against hers, holding her around the waist.

"Did you find anything?" she asked.

Rowan lifted his head and looked into her eyes. "Not really. No prints on the window or sill, inside or out. There was one pretty clear footprint in the very back of the yard, right behind a bush that backs up to the fence. Not sure what'll come of it, but it was collected." He frowned. "The landlady should have cut that shrub back. The bushes are really high and overgrown. They provide too much screen to anyone coming over from the next street."

"Not my problem anymore," she said with a light shiver.

"No, it isn't. I made sure everything was secure before we left," he told her. "I should have asked you before I went over there if you wanted me to get any more of your stuff."

"I grabbed my laptop but left a big box of my files. But I think it will be okay until I find another place to rent."

"You can stay—"

She cut him off. "No, I can't. I can't just crash in on you permanently."

He raised a brow. "Who said I was going to suggest that? Maybe I was going to suggest you stay at the Motel 6 around the corner?"

"Were you?"

"No."

"Okay, then."

"They're not cat friendly."

She didn't follow. "I don't have a cat."

"I do. I can't leave Jagger behind."

"What are you talking about?"

He snorted. "You don't *really* think I'm going to leave you alone, do you? If you go to a hotel, I'm getting the room next door. If you rent a house, I'll be parked in your driveway every night."

"Or you could just be in bed with me," she said with an eyebrow wag.

"Whatever you think is best."

His feigned piety was funny, but his message wasn't a joke. He was deadly serious. As he'd said earlier, he fully intended to watch over her, to make sure she was okay.

"Look, I appreciate the offer," she said, both warming under the thought of having his undivided attention but also feeling guilty as hell for the same reason. "But you're not responsible for me, Rowan."

"Actually, I think according to some old legend, I am."

"Huh?"

"Save someone's life and you then have to take care of them forever."

"That sounds very counterintuitive."

"I know, but I'm pretty sure that's the rule."

"I'm pretty sure it's not."

He kissed her, murmuring, "Just go with me on this."

She sank into him, soaking up the heat of his body, inhaling his sexy-musky scent. He was tempting. So very tempting. What woman wouldn't want a man like him by her side at all times? But not like this. Not because he felt the need to protect her.

"If you can let me stay for a night or two, until I find another place, that would be great."

He stiffened, obviously not pleased, but didn't argue. She suspected he thought he could talk her out of the leaving part. He couldn't. She'd had her momentary meltdown today, but she knew from experience that she couldn't rely on anyone else to take care of her. It then became too easy to rely on others, to not reclaim her life and regain her power over it.

That's what had happened after Blair's murder.

"I know you're trying to help," she said, pulling away and going into the kitchen to continue working on dinner. "But I can't let this derail me. Angstrom gained a lot of power over me, even after he was arrested. I will not let that happen again."

"I know," he murmured. He came into the kitchen and went to the fridge, grabbing a bottle of nice white wine. He lifted it questioningly.

"Yes, please." Finding some rice in his cabinet, she put water on to boil. "After what happened to Blair, I went home and lived with my parents for almost a year. I wouldn't go out unless one of my brothers was with me. I didn't work, I didn't see anyone. The longer I stayed, the harder it was for me to even be a part of the world. They were so protective, so terrified at the what-could-have-beens that nobody noticed I was becoming a shadow of myself. Not even me. I was scared of living the life I'd always wanted."

Carrying two full wineglasses, he came over and offered her one. "It's called PTSD. You went through a terrible trauma. Anyone would retreat from life for a while after something like that."

Maybe. Maybe not. "My point is, it's in the past now. I want it to stay there. I don't ever want to feel like that helpless girl again, the one who couldn't stop someone she cared about from being killed and who had nightmares for months."

Rowan sipped his wine, eyeing her over the top of the glass, his eyes dark and his expression inscrutable. "I understand," he finally murmured. "Believe me, I do. That kind of trauma—coming back from losing someone who died a violent death—is hell."

Evie had just taken a sip of her wine, but suddenly gasped when she realized what he was talking about. She coughed out some wine, lifting a hand to her mouth.

"Are you okay?" he asked, quickly taking her glass.

"Fine," she choked out with another cough. "Just tried to breathe my wine."

"Never a good idea. Just ask that English king or duke or whatever he was who was drowned in a big barrel of the stuff."

He was trying to distract her, make her laugh or something. But he wasn't going to get away with it, not now when she'd figured out just who he had been talking about a moment ago.

"I'm so sorry, Rowan. I must sound like the most self-absorbed person on the planet. I *have* thought about the way your sister died, about how young you were, and what it did to your family. You're the last person I should be complaining to about loss."

He put a strong hand on her hip and pulled her close. "Grief isn't a team sport. There's no competition and no winning. We all deal with it in our own way, and that is whatever way enables you to get up in the morning and go on living."

She looked into his handsome, serious face, not seeing that twinkle or a glimmer of his beautiful smile. He was utterly serious, speaking truths about loss that she understood completely.

"I'm so sorry about what happened to Rachel," she said, meaning it completely.

"Me too." He hesitated, his eyes shifting, and then added, "Someday…someday we'll talk about it. There's a lot more to the story than anybody knows."

She sensed it wasn't an offer he made often or lightly, and felt honored that he had made it to her. "Whenever you're ready."

He nodded and then bent to kiss her again. This kiss lasted longer, went deeper, was hotter and wetter than before. He didn't even disengage as he reached to the stovetop and turned off the burner that was set to boil the water for rice.

"You're not *that* hungry, are you?" he asked, nibbling the corner of her mouth.

"I can think of a lot of things I'd rather do than make dinner."

"Do any of them involve me?"

She twined her arms around his neck. "Every one of them involves you. And that nice, comfortable, non-sandy bed."

Rowan kissed her again, and without separating his mouth from hers, picked her up by the hips. She wrapped her legs around him and he carried her to his room, following her down onto his huge bed.

There was no sand. No surf. No squawking birds or whistling wind or blowing salt spray.

Just sexy, attentive, amazing Rowan...who made her forget about food and investigations. Not to mention everything else in the world.

Including the danger that seemed to be building around her more by the day.

* * *

Firecracker needed money to get outta town.

Since the motherfucker who'd hired him had tried to take him out, he hadn't been too surprised to find out there was no ticket to Florida waiting for him at the bus station the other night. And if there'd been any money in that house, which he doubted, it had blown up along with that old hag who'd gone in ahead of him.

Hell, he shouldn't think of her that way, he guessed. She had, after all, saved his life. If she hadn't gone into that bathroom first, he woulda been the one to set off that bomb. Meaning he woulda been the one who ended up splattered all over the inside of that crappy old house.

"Sorry, Frankie, but she says you gotta go tomorrow."

He looked at his friend Winkie, who had taken him in off the street and gave him a place to crash while he figured his shit out. "Who runs this house? You or that bitch?"

Winkie had been a badass when they met. Now he was a pussy-whipped daddy who worked at a bottling plant. Some shit like that.

"Don't talk 'bout my wife like that. She let you come in, let you sleep on our couch, even though we both know what kind'a trouble you're in." Winkie had settled down some since the old days, but he still flew off the handle pretty easy, and right now he was bunched up and ready to defend his bossy-ass wife.

"No, no, man," Frankie said, holding both hands up to make peace. "Sorry, you done me a solid. Both of y'all. I'll get outta here tomorrow."

It pissed him off to play so nice, but he knew Winkie was a changed man. His wife hadn't even wanted to let Frankie walk through the door when he'd come knocking, half deaf and bleeding from the explosion. He'd been allowed in on the condition that he not go upstairs to the kids' rooms and he had to be out by Monday—now tomorrow.

He'd taken the offer, not having any other options. He couldn't go to his place; the guy trying to kill him knew where he lived. And so did the police. He didn't have many other friends who'd take him in, other than Winkie. But he knew that wasn't gonna last for long, and he had to figure out a way to get away from Southern California. Far away from the charges pending against him. Not to mention far away from the freak who liked to hire people to kill women who pissed him off and then blew up houses to cover up their shit.

"I need money, man," he told Winkie. Seeing his friend frown, he quickly added, "No, not askin' for it, bro. I can get some, just gotta figure out the best way."

"Don't be bringing any trouble into my house, Frankie. I let you in 'cause of the old days. But I don't want any street garbage coming to my door. I got my kids to think of."

"It won't," he insisted. "I just…gotta get some money somebody owes me."

Not that it was gonna be easy getting the guy who had tried to kill him to pay up. If he knew where the fucker lived, he'd go there at night and carve what he was owed out of the sonofabitch's skin. But he didn't.

There was one address he knew, though.

Where the woman lived. The writer. The one who'd fought back.

Frankie had nothing against her. She'd done what any woman would do, and he didn't take it personally. He just wondered if there was any way to get her to give him what he needed.

The man who'd hired him had given him a piece of paper with her address on it. He could get hold of her. He just wondered what somebody like her would pay big money for.

It didn't take long to figure it out. There was one thing she would definitely want.

Information.

And that Frankie Lee had a lot of. Like the name of the fucker who wanted her dead.

He just had to figure out how to safely get her to pay for it so he could get outta California forever.

* * *

By Sunday night, Rowan had grown so used to having Evie in his place that it felt like she'd been there forever, rather than a little over twenty-four hours.

She was the best houseguest, not that he'd ever had one here before. But if he had, she would definitely be the best. Especially because they had barely left his bed since the night before, getting up only to eat and drink before going right back to bed again.

She was tired, emotionally and physically. So she slept a lot.

Rowan watched her, liking the way her lips parted when she drifted off. Even liking her occasional little snore.

Most of the time, though, they had crazy, hot, sometimes slow and sweet, sex.

As soon as they finished, she would move a certain way, look at him from below half-lowered lashes, or laugh her soft, husky laugh, and he'd want her all over again. He wasn't entirely sure how his legs were still functioning, but in truth, he'd never felt better in his life.

"Okay, I have to take a bath," she said Sunday evening after they'd finished a spaghetti dinner. He'd cooked this time. There wasn't much to screw up about boxed pasta and canned sauce, and he even impressed her by chopping up some fresh basil and tossing it in the pot.

"You do that," he said. "I'll just get you dirty again later tonight."

"You could take a bath with me."

He chuckled. "Maybe if we were at Reece and his fiancée's place. They have that big sunken tub. Mine's much more standard."

She tilted her head in confusion. "Fiancée?"

"Yeah," he said, remembering the good news he'd gotten at lunch yesterday. The call from Candace had interrupted that lunch; he'd left within two minutes of receiving it. He'd never even gotten around to telling Reece what was going on. All he had been able to think about was getting to Evie. "They got engaged last weekend."

She smiled. "That's wonderful."

"It really is. She'll keep him on his toes…but down to earth."

"I think that's what wives are for. At least, that's what my mom has always done for my dad. He's a doctor; he's pretty cocky. But he scuffs his toe like a little kid when she catches him doing something stupid like washing reds with whites."

"They sound great."

"They are." A shadow crossed her face. "I sent them a text letting them know I was fine, but I guess I'm going to have to pick up the phone and call them soon. I know they're going to hate that all this is starting again."

"I don't know them, but just knowing you, I have no doubt they can handle it. They raised a strong, determined, powerful woman. I can't imagine they're not all of those things too."

She sighed a dreamy little sigh. "Do you ever not say the right thing?"

"Ha. Ask my brothers that question."

"I will. I'm looking forward to meeting them."

He nodded, realizing he really needed to finish the conversation he and his siblings had never gotten around to concluding yesterday at lunch. He wanted them to meet Evie, and wanted her to meet them, but not if they were mistrusting and she had no idea why.

"Okay, off to my bath."

He picked up the glass of wine he'd already poured for her and put it in her hand.

"I could get used to you, Winchester," she said before sipping appreciatively.

"That's my strategy."

"For what?"

"For getting you to keep me around. If I can't talk you into letting me be your bodyguard, I'll just have to ply you with wine." He grinned. "And sex."

She shivered lightly. "Ply away."

"Definitely." He turned her around and gave her a little push toward the bathroom. "Go. Bathe. Get those thigh muscles loosened up. I expect acrobatics tonight."

"Sorry, I never even tried out for the cheerleading squad."

"That's okay. You're very limber anyway."

Oh yeah. Very.

Laughing, she went back down the short hallway. Rowan cleaned up the dishes and put them away, and then got online to see if there were any updates on, well…anything.

One of the first things he spotted was an email from his twin. The subject line, *You're such an idiot*, gave him a pretty big hint as to what it was about.

He double-clicked, opened it, and read. The message was short and not very sweet:

Raine told me what's going on. You dumbass.

I'd say you were being led around by your dick, as usual, but Raine says you're different when you talk about this Evie. And Jess has her romantic antennae up and says you know what you're doing. Hope that's true, that this woman feels the same way and isn't using you for information. Because if she drags this all up again, I am gonna fucking kill you.

Talk soon—

R

Okay. Not as bad as he'd anticipated. Maybe being called away so quickly yesterday, before he could say what needed to be said, had been a good thing after all. Raine had spilled his guts, probably bearing the brunt of Reece's anger. By the time his minutes-older brother had written this email, he'd obviously calmed down. A lot.

"Thank you, Jessica," he murmured, sure that his future sister-in-law had a lot to do with this. She was, apparently, the one looking for any signs that Rowan had a love life. Knowing her, she'd almost certainly viewed this situation as a tragic conflict in the middle of a grand romance—she wanted to write films, after all. She must have convinced Reece to remain calm and give Rowan—and Evie—the chance to prove the situation wasn't a major calamity.

Which was exactly what he intended to do, and he put it on his list. That list was getting pretty fucking long. It included things like finding out who had broken into Evie's house.

Getting in touch with the prosecutors back East to see what could be done to keep Angstrom from contacting Evie again.

Helping her with her research for her book.

Finding out what new information Raine had found regarding Harry Baker's murder.

Continuing to work on this flower murder case, which had captured his thoughts and had his cop senses popping and his brain spinning.

Keeping Evie Fleming as safe and close as she'd let him.

Oh, and sex. Lots and lots of sex.

He'd just finished loading the dishwasher, thinking about that happy thought, when he heard a sharp knock at his door. Not expecting anyone, he approached it cautiously. His backup weapon was on his ankle, back where it belonged, and he immediately thought about it. Which said a lot about how on edge he had been ever since he had realized Evie was being stalked in her own damn house.

Peering through the peephole and seeing a familiar figure, he opened the door.

"This is a surprise."

Raine didn't wait to be let in; he simply walked past him. "I needed to talk to you. I was nearby and figured I'd come over and talk to you in person. You raced out of lunch so fast yesterday…"

"Yeah, it was an emergency."

"I figured. Everything okay?"

He gave his brother a quick rundown, seeing Raine's forehead furrow in anger when he heard what some psycho bastard had been doing to Evie. He didn't know her, had never met her, but Raine was a protector, with an especially soft spot for women and children.

Maybe it was no wonder, given what he'd seen and heard, starting the night Rachel had died. They all wanted to know the truth, which was why Raine had been trying to find the girl who'd also been in Baker's house that final, violent night.

"You need help keeping watch over her?" Raine asked. "I've got a couple of guys. We can take shifts."

Rowan shook his head. "Not now, but thanks. She's safe with me."

His brother's mouth opened, but then closed. He simply shook his head as he realized what Rowan was telling him.

"It'll be fine," Rowan said.

"Uh-huh. She here now?"

"In the bath."

"Okay. I'll get outta here."

"Why did you come by?"

"I wanted to fill you in on Marley, or whatever her real name is."

According to Steve, Marley had been the teenage girl his father had raped the last night of his life. She had outed herself to Steve, looking for money and pointing the finger of blame at the Winchester brothers.

Raine, Rowan, and Reece wanted to know why.

They also wanted to find out what else she knew. She might just hold the key to the mystery of who had killed Harry Baker.

She might even have done it herself.

"She keeps a really low profile. Goes by Sugar on the stripper circuit now."

"You think she's in hiding? Is she scared of us?"

"If she really believes we killed Harry Baker, she just might be."

Behind them, Rowan suddenly heard something shatter.

He swung around and saw Evie standing in the hallway, her eyes wide with shock. Wearing just a towel wrapped loosely around her body, the top tucked in above her breasts, she had apparently finished her bath. On the wood floor, around her bare feet, were the shattered remnants of her wineglass. She had been surprised into dropping it.

Surprised by what she had obviously heard.

"Evie, it's not what you're thinking."

She held up a shaking hand to her face, brushing back the wet hair. "You? It was *you*? That's why you don't want me writing about Harry Baker's murder, because you and your brothers were involved?"

"Oh shit," Raine muttered.

Rowan strode toward her. "Evie, you have to let me explain."

Her blue eyes were wet with tears, her face red from her hot bath or from shock. As he came toward her, she looked ready to turn and dart back toward the bathroom. With the glass around her bare feet, however, he wasn't going to allow that to happen.

He swung her up into his arms.

"Put me down," she snapped, smacking him hard on the shoulder.

"You'll cut your feet. Let me clean this up and then we can talk."

"I'll see myself out," Raine called.

"Yeah, you do that." Rowan knew it wasn't his kid brother's fault that Evie had overheard their conversation and come to the wrong conclusion. But he was still pretty fucking pissed off. The situation couldn't be much worse.

He carried her into his bedroom and put her down. Evie glared at him. "You lied to me."

Huh. He'd expected her to accuse him of being a murderer or something. So things were starting out a little better than he'd figured they would.

"I didn't lie…"

"Yes, you did. You said you didn't want me writing about Harry Baker's murder because of the reminders of your sister and how you would all feel being questioned about it."

Yeah. She was a writer. She took notes, and she had a good memory.

"Damn you for deceiving me, Rowan Winchester. I expected better."

"Um, you're not upset thinking that I murdered someone?"

She rolled her eyes. "For heaven's sake, you're no murderer." She put both hands on his chest and shoved him. "But you're a liar. You wanted to shut me up to protect whatever secrets it is you and your brothers are covering up. Is that why I'm here?

Did you make love to me so I'd fall even harder for you and would never give you up?"

Holy shit. Here he'd been congratulating himself that the woman he was crazy about knew him well enough to know he wasn't a murderer, and she'd just accused him of fucking her to shut her up. That was almost worse.

"Evie, listen."

"No, I'm not listening to you. Not tonight, Rowan. I've had about as much as I can take."

She shoved him again and he backed up toward the door. One more push and he was through it, standing in the hallway.

"Please, give me the chance to explain," he told her, his voice soft, as honest and open as he could be. "I'll tell you everything. I'd planned to anyway. But you have to believe that what's happening between us now had nothing to do with that."

She blinked a few times and those blue eyes looked wetter. He knew she was still shaking with anger, but there was a glimmer of heartbreak in her expression, and he knew he'd put it there. She doubted him, doubted his feelings for her.

Considering he hadn't told her how he felt, he supposed that was natural.

"I'm falling for you, Evie," he told her.

Obviously not expecting to hear that, she sucked in a surprised breath.

"I know it's only been a week. I know it's way too soon. I know right now you're feeling like you're on a roller coaster, not knowing when you're gonna be taken up or when you're going to plunge down. But, please, believe me. Making love to you was about how much I wanted you, and how much I've come to care about you. Nothing else."

She didn't respond. Not for a long moment. She simply

stared at him, trying to find the truth in his expression. She did not reveal what she was thinking or what she was feeling. Didn't ask any questions or make further accusations. No.

Instead, after a silence that seemed to stretch across a century, she slowly closed the door in his face. He was left standing outside his own bedroom, wondering how the hell things had gone from almost perfect to a fucking mess within a span of ten minutes.

One thing he knew—he had a new number-one thing on his to-do list.

He had to make things right with her. Had to explain and make her believe he didn't give a damn about the book or what she wrote. He wanted her. In his bed, in his life. Wanted to figure out what they had and where they were going to take it.

But first, he had to get her to talk to him again.

Which, he realized as he cleaned up the glass and then grabbed a blanket, tossing it on the couch, probably wasn't going to happen until morning.

Chapter 11

By all rights, Evie should have felt guilty about kicking Rowan out of his own bedroom.

She didn't. Not for a long while, anyway.

Instead, almost all of Sunday night, she had lain in his bed, tossing and turning, crying a little, wondering if he really was the man she'd thought he was...and being lonely.

When she woke from a short, restless sleep and saw it was almost four a.m., she realized he would have to go to work soon and could probably use some real rest. So, although she hadn't forgiven him for what he'd done, she went out into the dark living room. He was, as she'd thought, sprawled on the couch, a blanket tangled around his legs. His head was awkwardly bent to lay on the armrest, and she wondered how much his neck was going to hurt in the morning.

She bent over and nudged his shoulder. He woke instantly and sat up, almost whacking her head with his. "Evie, are you all right?"

"Come to bed, Rowan."

"Evie, I'm so sorry—"

"I said come to bed, not apologize. We have some talking to do. But I also suspect you have some sleeping to do." As he got up to follow her, she glanced over her shoulder. "*Only* sleeping."

She thought he mumbled something under his breath, but she couldn't tell what he said. She had a pretty good idea, though.

He crawled into his bed, and she got back in, too, staying far to one side, near the edge.

But not for long. Within minutes, Rowan was nearly asleep, breathing evenly. And another minute after that, he had rolled onto his side, put an arm around her middle, and tugged her back against his warmth. She swallowed hard at the feel of that powerful, naked body cupping hers, knowing that but for his brother's untimely visit, they would have explored this position hours and hours ago.

"No," she whispered. And she meant it.

But three hours later, when she awoke in that same position, feeling some serious morning wood pressed against her ass, she couldn't help regretting it.

She slowly shifted away and out from under his heavy arm, looking back at him to see if he was awake. His eyes were closed, his breathing still slow and steady. She didn't think he was faking, which meant he must be having a *very* good dream. Funny, once he had come to bed and curled up behind her, she hadn't had any more bad dreams, as she had earlier in the night.

Despite everything, Rowan made her feel secure and safe, like she could actually sleep without memories clawing at her, warning her to be ever-vigilant and to never trust anyone.

But she did trust him.

The man who'd lied to her.

Using the bathroom, she washed up and splashed cold water on her face. She might have had the comfortable bed, but she sure hadn't slept much.

Returning quietly to the bedroom, she went to her open suitcase, in search of her robe.

"Hey."

She jerked and saw him watching her, his expression not sexy-adorable-smiling-I'm-gonna-gobble-you-up like it had been yesterday morning, the first time they'd woken up in a bed together. This was tense. A little sad.

He rolled over and looked at his phone to gauge the time, and then lay on his back, an arm thrown over his face. "What a night."

She cleared her throat. "I'm sorry, I had no business putting you out of your own room. I should have taken the couch myself."

He sat up, letting the blanket drop onto his lap. He looked sleepy and rumpled, and so sexy he stopped her heart. Every bit of her tingled at the memory of how he felt entwined around her, both awake and in sleep.

"I wasn't talking about that."

"Oh."

His brother. Their conversation.

What on Earth were the Winchesters hiding?

Only one way to find out. "Do you care to explain his remark to me?"

He sighed heavily. "Can I have coffee first?" Another glance at his phone. He swiped to read a message. "Shit, I definitely need coffee. I have to go back to the Seventy-Seventh today. My partner's getting a little pissed about doing all of our paperwork by herself."

"Okay," she said, knowing Rowan was not the kind of man who would make up an excuse to avoid a conversation.

"You weren't planning on doing anything today, were you?" he asked. "I mean, I don't have anything on my calendar."

She shook her head. "No, I'm just going to call the DA, my own attorney, and my family." The last conversation would probably take hours. "And I have lots of notes and pictures to organize from last week." Plus for-rent ads to sort through and a real estate agent to call. "I'm sure I can keep myself busy."

He got up, stepping naked onto the floor, his big back flexing, his tight ass and strong legs making her weak in the knees. Putting his arms over his head, he stretched back and forth to work out what were probably boulders in his neck and shoulders.

"Gimme ten minutes to shower and then I'll meet you in the kitchen for coffee," he said, not attempting to touch her.

She missed his good morning kiss already, even having only had it yesterday.

"Then we'll talk."

She nodded, watched him go into the bathroom, and then headed for the kitchen. Making coffee, she couldn't help thinking about the incident at her house. The whole thing made her feel nauseous. She hated the thought that someone had been in her home, prowling around among her things, and she hadn't even been aware of it. He had touched her pillow and her sheets, her hairbrush, maybe even her toothbrush—which was why she'd had Rowan stop on the way here the other night so she could get a new one.

She felt completely violated knowing someone broke into her home for dark and dangerous purposes and had no desire to ever step foot in the place again.

"Shit," she mumbled, remembering the box of files she had left at the house. Everything she knew about Angstrom was in there, including trial transcripts, her own personal notes, and copies of police interviews. And his lackey had probably gone through it. Or maybe even taken it.

Rowan was as good as his word, coming into the kitchen dressed, with his hair damp.

"Here," she said putting a cup of steaming coffee down on the table. Right beside it was a travel mug she'd already double-filled.

"You're a lifesaver," he said.

"Don't," she said, not wanting to be charmed out of her anger. "I know you don't have much time, so start talking."

He looked at the coffee, blew on it, sipped it, and finally spoke.

"You're right. I didn't want you to write about the Baker case because of how it could affect my family."

She glared. But before she could say anything, he went on.

"I told you what he did to my sister, and I was very serious about how you bringing that up would drag us back into the spotlight. Believe me, being asked questions about how we feel about our 'very good family friend's' murder makes every one of us squirm."

She didn't doubt he was telling the truth—he had already told her that much. And she even understood his reasons for not wanting his family dragged back into that, which was why she had already agreed not to include the Baker story in the book.

But that wasn't all. Not by a long shot.

"'If she really believes we killed Harry Baker, she just might be,'" she said, repeating verbatim what his brother had said the night before. "How about you explain that part?"

He drank more coffee and shifted in his chair. The torment in his expression told her he was thinking *very* carefully of what to say.

Which made it *very* obvious that he wasn't going to tell her the whole truth.

"Forget it," she snapped. "It's none of my business."

He got up and put his hands on her shoulders. "I am just trying to figure out how much I can say without betraying any confidences."

"Raine's?"

"Both of my brothers'."

So they were *all* tangled up in something that involved Harry Baker. Considering what she knew about the man and his involvement in their older sister's tragic downfall, her mind went to several places. But not to murder. Not when it came to Rowan, at least.

"There was a girl there. The night Harry died."

She stilled, listening, curious in spite of her anger.

"She was young, which means she was his type. He was attacking her."

Her coffee churned in her stomach. "What happened?"

"Raine was there."

"Raine killed him?"

Rowan squeezed her shoulders. "No. He absolutely did not kill him. I swear that."

"Maybe we should sit down," she said. "You're hurting me."

He dropped his hands immediately. "I'm sorry. You just have

to know—and believe—that my brothers and I did not shoot that man. Harry and Raine fought, yeah. But Raine was just a teenager, and he was drunk for the first time in his life. He was no match for Harry Baker."

She thought about the pictures she'd seen of the burly man and remembered what the youngest Winchester had looked like as a teen—that is, absolutely nothing like the big badass he was now. She nodded in agreement, accepting that much of the story. "What about this girl?"

"She ran out. He had no idea who she was. But before Steve Baker died, he told Reece that he had found her again, and she had information about that night."

"Did she kill Harry Baker?"

"Honestly, I don't know. She wanted money, and told Steve that it was us. But it wasn't, Evie, I swear to God."

She knew he needed her to believe him. And to a certain extent, she did.

"Like I said last night, I know you're not a killer."

She did not say the same thing about his brothers, whom she didn't know at all.

"Thank you."

They sat down at the small kitchen table. Although he got a few texts, he did not take his attention off her, telling her more, offering what she knew were only pieces of the story. Pieces he felt he could share.

They were tragic enough. Tears came to her eyes when he revealed how Raine had walked in on "Uncle Harry" attacking a young girl, how he had suddenly remembered the last night of their sister's life, and how it had set him off.

He admitted Raine had fought with the man, gotten his ass kicked, staggered away and called his brothers in a drunken stupor. Admitted that they'd picked him up and taken him home and that he'd spilled the entire story about their sister, and Baker, and the fight.

"I'm sure you must have wanted to kill him yourself."

He shifted uncomfortably. "Maybe. But we *didn't*."

"*You* didn't."

"Neither did my brothers," he shot back. "I was with Reece all evening. Baker had been shot in the head, and I knew Raine had no idea how to use a gun, nor did he have one on him. Nobody in my family killed that man, despite how glad we all were that he was dead."

And there he stopped. He simply went silent and watched her, waiting for her to absorb what he'd told her.

He wasn't going to continue; she understood that immediately.

The question was, had he said enough? Could she accept not knowing the rest? Could she really trust and believe him?

Oh, she trusted him physically. She knew a decent man when she met one, and Rowan was the most decent man she'd ever been involved with. But he was still keeping something from her. Lying by omission.

God, she hated being lied to. Whether it was her parents lying to her about what had really been done to Blair—for her own good, they said—or her agent lying about revealing her address to the press, she just couldn't bear it.

"There's more," she said simply.

He didn't try to deny it.

"Are you going to tell me?"

After a pause, Rowan slowly shook his head. "I can't, Evie. Not without talking to my brothers first."

"What else could there be?" she asked. "You've gone this far.

You've already admitted Raine was in the house the night Baker died." She thought about it. "Wait, why didn't you call the police and tell them all this?"

He shook his head again. Not opening his mouth. Keeping his family secrets.

"You didn't want Raine dragged into it, right? Didn't want the eye of suspicion on him."

"Would you, if it were your younger brother?"

"No, I wouldn't," she admitted. "As long as I knew he was innocent."

"Raine *is* innocent."

"All right," she finally said. "Thank you for telling me as much as you did."

"I'm sorry, Evie. I'm really sorry I tried to steer you away from covering the case without telling you the real reason why."

So was she. Yes, she understood that his family didn't want to get tangled up in something so ugly, something that could destroy their sister's memory, that might put the youngest brother in legal danger. She even got why Rowan hadn't trusted her at first.

But then they'd spent nearly every waking minute together for a week. She'd shared her darkest memories and fears about Angstrom, had enlisted his help in searching for answers to the flower killings. She'd spent thirty-six hours having wild, intense, incredible sex with the man. And he still hadn't said a word. Not one word.

That was what she couldn't get over yet. Especially since she knew he still wasn't revealing the whole truth.

She admired loyalty. But she didn't like not being trusted by someone to whom she'd already entrusted her body and, she greatly feared, her heart. Because if she wasn't in love with him yet, she was on the downslope of that roller coaster, and getting there fast.

His phone buzzed again. Huffing a little, he finally looked at it. "Shit. I've really gotta go. It's Abby, my partner. She's catching shit about some reports I didn't sign. I need to get down there."

She nodded. "Okay."

"We'll talk later, all right?" He got up but stopped to take her hand. "I want to tell you the rest. I really do. Just give me a little time."

"Fine."

He leaned in and brushed a soft kiss on her lips. She wanted to remain stiff and rigid, hold on to her anger and reject him. But she'd done that last night. Now she just wanted to reassure herself that this *could* be worked out. At least, God, she hoped so.

So she kissed him back, gently and softly. And when it ended, she stared into his handsome face. "I am not over this yet."

"I know."

"But I can wait to talk to you about it later."

"Thanks." He kissed her again, gliding his tongue across the seam of her lips until she parted them and took him in. The kiss was deeper, wetter, but was still more about reconnecting than anything else.

Finally, they parted. He put his phone in his pocket, strapped on both his service weapons, and grabbed a jacket.

"Okay, as long as you're going to be staying in and don't need me to play chauffeur, I'll probably spend the day at my own station catching up on stuff."

"I understand."

"Be careful," he told her. "Don't open the door to anybody

you don't know. I'm not expecting any packages or anything."

"I don't think anybody could have tracked me here already."

"Neither do I. But better to play it safe." He pointed to a spare key hanging on a hook in the kitchen. "There's a spare set of keys in case you do need to go out. There's a couple of pretty good lunch places up the block. Just be—"

"Careful. I know."

After he left, Evie did what she had said she was going to. She made phone calls that ranged from tense, to difficult, to painful, to teary.

Her parents were devastated and wanted her to go into hiding. That was *without* them knowing anything about what had happened to her since she arrived in California.

Her brothers were furious and also wanted her to go into hiding. They also talked about pulling a *Prison Break*–like stunt, getting put into prison to take care of Angstrom personally.

It was crazy, and ridiculous, but she appreciated their worry on her behalf.

The prosecutor on the Angstrom case told her everything, including the one thing his office had messed up, which had gotten Angstrom's conviction overturned.

"It was one witness we didn't disclose. One person we didn't even intend to call. That was all it took."

"Unreal," she said in response. "But he won't be out until the new trial, right?"

"No way," the lawyer said. "Absolutely not. But listen, Miss Fleming, you know he holds you almost singly responsible for his conviction."

"I know."

There was a pregnant pause before he went on.

"He does communicate with the outside world."

"I know that too." Although she hated to get into it, she told the attorney about everything that had gone on over the past week.

"That's not good," he said. "Do you really think he got someone to harass you?"

Or worse?

"I think it's possible."

"You might want to consider moving."

"I have."

"Good. I'll get in touch with the LAPD and ask them to have somebody watch out for you."

"That's already covered. I have my own personal police escort wherever I go."

"Excellent." He called out to someone who came into his office, sounding harried and overworked. She had no doubt that he was and couldn't imagine that the oversight in the discovery phase of the trial had been anything but a mistake. But, wow, had it been a costly one.

After she finished the calls, she pulled up her research files for the book and began updating them with some of the impressions and information she'd gotten this past week. She really wished she had her journal, as well as all her printouts of documents she'd been collecting, but had to make do. She did have an electronic file for each of the cases she was researching, and the one for the Baker case caught her eye. She couldn't stop thinking about everything Rowan had told her about the night of Baker's death. How his brother had been there, the girl Baker had been attacking, the fight.

"The girl," she whispered, suddenly recalling a piece of information that could be important. She thought for sure she'd read something, somewhere, about a girl being seen running in the neighborhood that night. She couldn't, however, find anything about it on her typed notes in the Baker file. Which made her wonder if it had been somewhere in her print ones.

"Damn it," she muttered, her curiosity growing. She should have grabbed all of her paperwork before leaving the rental house, and definitely planned to ask Rowan to take her over there to retrieve the files tonight.

At about two, she suddenly remembered her promise to Candace. She was supposed to go into the office to go over the publicity plan for her new book. Although she had promised Rowan to be careful, she didn't see what going to a public place would hurt. Still, she texted him to make sure he knew what she was up to.

Can't she come to you? he texted back.

Don't think so, but I promise I'll take a cab over and straight back. Frankly, since she'd left her rental car at the house, she didn't have any other choice. She hadn't really been in any condition to drive here Saturday, after figuring out somebody had been stalking her in her own home. Now, though, she wished she'd had Rowan take her back yesterday to get the car. And the files.

I don't like it.

Yeah, no kidding. *I'll be fine.*

Can it wait till tomorrow? Looks like I'm gonna have a long day today, but after that I'm back on full-time writer's assistant duty.

Sweet, but she was already getting a little claustrophobic. She didn't like feeling imprisoned by someone else, didn't like going back to that place where she had to always be nervous, waiting for the other shoe to drop. She'd lived a big part of her life that way, after Angstrom. Damned if she was going to do it again.

I'm going. But I promise I'll text and let you know I made it safely there and back.

His response was slow in coming, but finally he texted back.

Please be careful.

I will.

She meant it. Yes, she hated feeling like Angstrom was a puppet master, again pulling her strings, this time from a maximum-security prison. But she wasn't stupid, either. Someone *had* been in her house last week. She was not about to forget that.

She took an Uber to Candace and Marcus's company office, a plush suite in a downtown high-rise, arriving by late afternoon. She'd called her agent to let her know she was coming, and had been relieved to hear that Marcus was out. True to her word, she texted Rowan that she'd gotten there safely.

As soon as the receptionist announced her arrival, Candace hurried out to the waiting area to greet her. "Evie, thank you so much for coming in. I've been thinking about you all weekend."

"I'm fine," she insisted, going into Candace's private office. It was a far cry from the crowded little place she'd had in New York, which, frankly, Evie had liked more. Candace had just seemed to fit in better there, all busy and crazy, with stacks of books and manuscripts crowded on every surface and in every corner. She'd lived a fast-paced life in a high-stakes world, with lunches with publishers and nonstop action.

California was very different. It had its own pace and seemed far removed from the frenetic energy that always vibrated in New York. This place was slick and glassy, immaculate and perfectly decorated. It screamed Hollywood and Marcus, not books and Candace. Absolutely the only thing that looked the slightest bit real and unpretentious was a big vase of daffodils standing on Candace's desk. There were dozens of them in bloom, the bright yellow of the blossoms providing a nice splash of color in the otherwise monochromatic office space.

"So, tell me everything that's happened."

Because Evie hadn't wanted to get into the details on the phone, Candace had no idea about the home intrusion situation. When Evie told her about it, her friend looked horrified. "Oh my God, did you call the police?"

"Well, I was with the police when I figured out it had happened."

Candace shook her head, her curtain of shoulder-length brown hair swinging. "Sorry, of course. But is anybody officially investigating?"

"Yes, and hopefully they'll find whoever did it."

"And you really think Angstrom hired him?"

She shrugged. "I don't think it would even be a question of 'hiring' someone. He has a lot of supporters. Did you know that? Some people actually become obsessed with these monsters. They want to become, I don't know, like pen pals, or even get involved in romantic relationships with them."

It was a bizarre phenomenon that had really shocked her when she'd looked into it. Men like Ted Bundy and Charles Manson had been more popular and sought after in prison than they had in their regular lives. She couldn't even fathom what would drive someone to form a connection and work toward building a relationship with a convicted murderer. A *monster*.

"My point is, if he found a way to get the word out to one of his fans, he could get somebody to do almost anything he wanted."

Candace shuddered. "I am so sorry this is all coming up again."

Yes, so was Evie.

She just wondered how it was going to affect her life going forward.

She liked Southern California and had been looking forward to spending the winter here. She especially liked the time she was spending with Rowan. Was it possible for her to stay here, though, if the word was out among Angstrom's followers that she was living here? Would she be better off going someplace else and not telling anyone, at least until after the new trial?

Damn it. There were those puppet strings again. They infuriated her.

That did not, however, mean she didn't have some serious thinking to do.

For her own safety, and the safety of those around her, she should probably leave Los Angeles.

Which meant leaving Rowan Winchester—and what they were creating together—behind.

* * *

Would nothing ever go right?

He should have had his problem taken care of Saturday. He had been positioned and ready, in Evie Fleming's house, waiting for her to come back. Having been staking out the place, he had seen her arrive home and, a few minutes later, walk down to the beach. Perfect. So he'd broken in, for the fourth time this week, and waited for her, busying himself by playing little games that would mess with her head as soon as she walked in the door.

She'd be confused. She'd be off-balance.

And he'd be there to *catch* her.

Plans made, he'd settled down to wait for her to return. But then a car had pulled up outside—that fucking cop. He'd parked, and then he, too, had walked toward the beach. There was little doubt that when Fleming came back, Winchester would be with her.

Which meant he'd had to leave in a hurry.

Once again, she had eluded his grasp. Which was simply unacceptable.

But she had to come back sometime. Sitting in his dark, bland car on the next block, he'd been watching her house all day Sunday and again today. Her convertible sat in the driveway, so of course she'd be coming back. He just prayed his "little tricks" hadn't scared her away for long and wished he'd been more subtle. Thinking the whole thing was almost over, he'd played tricks that would be a little more noticeable.

Dumb. She noticed; that's why she hasn't come back.

Maybe. But why would she leave her car? It was probably more likely that she and the cop had gone away for a couple of nights for some reason of their own.

He could guess what that was. *Slut.*

He had to believe she would be back. She wouldn't leave that convertible just sitting in the driveway. He'd seen mail being put into her mailbox this afternoon, and a package from Amazon was left on her doorstep.

Yeah, she'd be back. Maybe even tonight.

Which was why he'd moved his car over a block and taken his normal route in the high brush between two houses backing hers. A quick jump over the fence and he'd been at her back window.

The criminal crept up to the front porch, probably thinking his victim was at home, given the car's presence. He held a piece of paper in his hand. Looking over his shoulder again, moving as quietly as such a big man could, he got to the front porch. The piece of paper, dingy and scrawled on, started to inch in underneath the door.

That was when he flung it open, pointed a gun at Frankie's head, and ordered him into the house.

Chapter 12

Working together at a conference table in Candace's office, the two of them spent about an hour going over the marketing plan Evie's publisher had proposed. Evie appreciated the distraction, glad to have something else to think about. Despite everything going on around her, she still had a job to do and a career to maintain. Just as she wasn't going to let Angstrom keep her housebound, she wouldn't let him cost her her writing career.

The moving part she hadn't yet figured out.

By the time they finished, it was nearly five p.m. She texted Rowan to let him know she would be leaving soon, hoping he would say he'd meet her back at his place. They still had some real talking to do.

Unfortunately, his response was less than encouraging. *Gotta go back to headquarters. And then somewhere else with Raine. Sorry. I'll probably be late.*

"Darn," she mumbled.

"What's the matter?"

"I wanted to get my rental car from the house, but it looks like Rowan won't be able to take me over there tonight." She doubted he would want to go over there at night anyway. Well, *he* probably wouldn't mind, but she suspected he wouldn't want her being with him.

Candace was in the process of locking her desk, about to head home herself. "Let me run you over to get it."

Evie's brow shot up. "To my house?"

"Sure. Do you have the car keys with you?"

She nodded. "But honestly, I don't want to go back into that place." She shuddered lightly. "I'm not sure I'll *ever* be able to go inside again. I'm going to ask Rowan to get my files and the rest of my things."

"No, definitely not inside the house. But since you have the keys, you can just hop out of my passenger seat into your driver's seat, and away we'll go. Ninety seconds, tops."

That sounded reasonable, and she *did* want to get the car. Rowan might have said he'd be at her disposal for the rest of the week, but she still didn't like feeling entirely dependent on him.

Especially since they still hadn't cleared the air about whatever his family was hiding.

Until that was done, until she knew that he wasn't going to lie to her anymore, she just didn't feel comfortable being completely reliant on him.

But it was more than that. She didn't like this feeling that she was backsliding to where she'd been the year after Angstrom had killed Blair. She'd retreated from the world, she'd stayed hidden and frightened and withdrawn.

That wasn't going to happen this time. No, she wouldn't take any stupid chances. But she'd already had to move and might have to leave the state altogether, which really made her mad. Yes, it was probably smart to move, but enough was enough. She wasn't going to let that bastard rob her of her ability to drive herself around. He had taken too much already.

"You know what, that's actually a really good idea," she said.

"Excellent."

Although she knew Rowan would not be happy about this plan, she texted him anyway, not wanting to keep secrets. Promising she was only going for the car and would not walk through the front door, she waited for a huffing and puffing response. But he didn't respond at all. Apparently, he was in a meeting or something.

That was actually a good thing. Hopefully by the time he got around to calling to inform her that she was not, under any circumstances, to go near her house, she'd already have gotten her car and had it back in the parking lot of his building.

A short time later, sitting in Candace's Mercedes, Evie had to adjust her timeline. Traffic was a nightmare, as it always was in this city. Still, no response from Rowan. Hopefully that meant that when he got her message and called to insist that she not go, she'd be able to tell him it was too late.

"Damn I miss New York," Candace said as they sat through a changing streetlight, unable to go through the blocked intersection. "At least there you can scream and cuss at people. Here people all try to be so laid back. Ugh."

Evie laughed. "Yeah, it's a little different out here."

"Tell me about it. Everything's new, slick, shiny, and metallic." Candace wrinkled her nose. "Like my office. It's god-awful, isn't it? It's so…"

Marcus?

"So colorless."

away from her, leaving her completely alone in a sensory-deprivation chamber meant only for thinking.

A path of possibility rolled out in front of her. She took that very first step in her mind.

"No way," she whispered.

Was it possible? Could it be something as simple as that?

"What?"

"Birth flowers. Different for every month," she whispered, continuing to turn over this new idea. She let it flit and find fertile ground for the seeds to land, sprout, and grow.

She didn't know the birthdays of every victim off the top of her head, but she did remember some of the varieties of flowers either mentioned or shown in the crime scene photos. A couple had been very unusual, not a typical bunch of flowers someone would pick up in a grocery store, or even a florist. She suspected they might even require special ordering.

Her mind on fire now, she grabbed her phone and quickly looked up sites with information on birth flowers.

"Carnation. Violet. Daffodil."

"What are you muttering over there?"

"Birth flowers," she said, talking more to herself than to Candace as she continued to read. "Daisies, larkspur. Mine is gladiolus."

"Why are we still talking about birth flowers?"

She remembered the birthday of only one of the victims, because she had been born on Evie's own birthday, but ten years earlier. Try as she might, however, she just couldn't remember what kind of flowers had been in that victim's bedroom.

If it had been gladiolus…well, it wasn't 100 percent proof, but it would go a long way toward convincing her that she might have stumbled across an explanation for the varying types of flowers left at the crime scenes. Because really, who gave any-one gladiolus, except for a very specific reason? Like because that person had an August birthday.

"I need my files," she mumbled.

She had the basics of all the cases on her computer at Rowan's place. But the more in-depth stuff, including the crime scene photos, were in print. And her really detailed impressions of the crimes were handwritten in her journal, which was also at her place.

"What?"

They were nearing her street now, and she kept thinking, turning everything over and over. She did not want to go into her house. God, no. Though, when she thought about it, the po-lice presence there might very well have scared the prowler out of trying it again.

If Rowan were going to be home tonight and could bring her over, or even meet them, she would ask him to go in with her. If he couldn't do that, unless she wanted to go into the house by herself, it was going to *have* to wait until tomorrow.

That would drive her absolutely insane. Now that this possi-bility was spinning in her brain, she couldn't think of anything else.

"It's this one, right?" Candace said as she pulled up in front of the house. Evie's little rental convertible still stood in the dri-veway, looking exactly as it had when she'd left it.

It would be so easy. Just do what Candace had suggested. Get out of this car, into that one, and drive away.

But it would also be easy to go into the house and get the box of files and research documents. It was on the floor under a table in her room. And it wasn't like she was alone.

"Would you consider standing watch for me?" she asked, hating the idea even as she suggested it.

Candace looked over at her. "What do you mean?"

Licking her lips, she said, "The birth flowers. I can't stop thinking about them. I've been trying to figure out why the victims of the flower killer, as I've been calling him, all received different types."

Candace, who was the only person other than Rowan who even knew about Evie's side investigation—unless she'd told her husband—gasped. Her jaw dropped and her eyes rounded. "You think maybe they were their birth flowers?"

"Exactly."

"Oh my God, that's so fucking creepy!"

"Tell me about it."

If the killer knew the birthdays of his victims, that meant he had researched them. He had not chosen those women at random; he'd planned everything out. And he had come to the murder sites with the flowers on him.

If it was true, they were dealing with one incredibly organized serial killer…with a very obvious signature: birth month flowers.

She glanced toward the front porch. It was partially blocked by another of those overgrown bushes the landlady hadn't cut back, just like the ones in the backyard. Although Evie couldn't see the entirety of the porch, she could, at least, confirm that the front door was closed. The house looked quiet, normal.

Rowan will kill me.

Yeah, he would. Maybe she *should* wait and get him to bring her back here tonight. Or come himself. But she hated that idea too. It seemed safer for her to do it now, when it wasn't even fully dark yet, with Candace staying on the front porch acting as lookout and alarm system should something be wrong inside.

Besides, she realized, there was something else that might be very useful in her box of files. Something Rowan might be very appreciative of.

She knew she'd read something about a girl running in the neighborhood the night of Harry Baker's murder. If Rowan and his brothers had been searching for the girl, and Evie had more information about her, he'd probably be very grateful.

Not grateful enough to not go off about you going inside.

No. Probably not that grateful.

"I think I'd better text Rowan," she said.

Candace lifted a brow. "Seriously? I mean, there's two of us, it's daylight, you'll be in there for, what, ninety seconds?"

She nodded.

"Pfft. I wouldn't even tell him."

"You don't think he'll notice if I suddenly come back with a big box full of files?"

"Tell him they were in the car."

Nope. She was not a liar. Not ever, if she could help it. And given how she'd shut him out of his own room last night for lying to her, she would certainly never do the same to him.

"I'm going to text him. If he absolutely loses it, I'll ask him to come here and meet us."

Candace shrugged, then reached into her purse for her own phone and started checking emails. Evie, meanwhile, pulled up her message app and realized Rowan *had* responded to her last one. She simply hadn't heard the notification. Make that notification*s*.

Please don't go without me. I'll take you to get the car tomorrow.

"No, it can wait," she said. She had her keys in her hand. She quickly thumbed from the front door key to the one for the car. Decision made.

Candace frowned and rolled her eyes. But rather than getting back in her Mercedes and waiting for Evie to get into her car, she pointed toward the porch. "You've got a package."

Remembering she had ordered some books from Amazon, Evie nodded and started walking toward the house. Candace fell into step beside her.

"I can't believe I didn't get over to see this place before it became toxic," Candace said. "It's super cute. Tiny."

"Yes, just one bedroom. But it was big enough for me."

"Great location."

It really was. She doubted she'd find anything like it again and mentally cursed Angstrom for probably the millionth time in her life. Whether she was in danger here anymore or not, he had ruined the place for her. Knowing someone had been prowling around inside made it no longer hers. It was Angstrom's now, touched by his darkness through whatever surrogate he was using to frighten her. Or worse.

When they reached the porch, Evie bent down to pick up the box. It contained several hardback books and was heavy. She had to shift a little to hoist it into her arms. When she did, she dropped not only her keys from one hand, but also her purse from her shoulder.

"Let me help you," Candace said as she crouched down and started shoving things back into Evie's bag.

"Thanks," Evie said. Spying her phone, which had skidded to the exterior wall, she turned around and reached for it. And then she heard a clangy little jingle.

She looked up at her friend just in time to see Candace twist the key in the front door lock. "What on earth are you doing?"

"You wait here. I'll get the damn box."

"No, Candace, don't!"

But the brunette ignored her, shoving the door open and stepping inside before Evie had even gotten back up to her feet. Horrified, Evie stepped into the small foyer and grabbed the other woman's arm. "Come on, let's go."

"Where's the box? Just point the way."

"Out."

Candace was looking around, peering across the living room toward the kitchen. The house was utterly still, not even the drip of a faucet making a sound. The wooden floors in the old place creaked terribly when you walked across them, but right now, silence reigned.

"It's empty, honey," Candace said, patting Evie's arm. "We're in now, just grab the thing and we'll go, okay? You can tell Rowan it was all my fault."

"It was," she grumbled, though she knew Candace was right. They were already inside; the decision had been taken out of Evie's hands. "I really don't like this."

"Just go."

Sighing, she slowly nodded. "All right, it's in the bedroom. You stay right here by the open door. I'll be back in thirty seconds. If I'm not, scream the neighborhood down."

Candace laughed and pulled her pepper spray out of her purse. "I got your back, kiddo."

Evie walked quickly across the living room to the short hallway that led to her room, and the house's single bathroom. Everything seemed normal. Some things looked a little out of place, but that was to be expected since Rowan and the other cops were in here the other night.

And yet…and yet….

Her heart was pounding wildly, her nerves pinging and sparking.

"Nothing to worry about," she told herself as she walked into her bedroom. She beelined for the writing table she had been using for a desk, grabbing her journal from on top of it. Then she crouched down to pull out the file box from underneath. It was heavier than the package outside, and she had to get down on her knees to tug it out, sliding it across the carpet.

Wrapping her arms around it, Evie slowly stood up and tried to shift the box into a better position, bracing it on her hip. It really had been only thirty seconds, and she found herself feeling glad she'd gone for it. Rowan would not be pleased, of course, but hopefully even he would agree it had been worth the quick dash.

Ready to leave and walk straight out the front door, she stopped when something on her bedside table caught her eye. Something colorful and fragrant.

Something she had not left there.

Evie froze. Her entire body quaked in shock, and she dropped the box to the floor, hearing it thud from somewhere far away, like she was right back in that sensory-deprivation chamber.

"No," she whispered, moving beyond shock into confusion. "What…how?"

It couldn't be. She *couldn't* be seeing this. It made no sense. It…

And then she understood. The truth slammed into her brain, clicking all the puzzle pieces into place. She understood *everything*.

"Not him," she whispered. "Not Angstrom."

It hadn't been Angstrom at all.

Run. Go!

Spinning around, she darted out the bedroom door. "Candace, get out of the house!" she yelled. But before she'd managed the few more steps to the living room, she heard a distinctive pop and a loud thud. She tried to skid to a stop, but her feet got tangled in a runner and flew out from under her. She fell right into the living room, hitting the floor hard.

Which put her about face level with her friend.

Her friend with the bullet hole in her head and blood spreading out beneath her.

"Oh my God," she cried. "Oh God, Candace!"

"You shouldn't have brought her with you."

A man's voice. Above her. It sounded…familiar.

She saw a pair of dark, heavy-soled shoes move into view as he walked closer and stood over her. Beyond horrified at what had just happened to her friend—*oh Christ, Candace, I'm so sorry*—she forced herself to look up. Her gaze moved slowly, shock making her feel sluggish, as if she would be unable to lift her head enough to even see his face.

But she found the strength. She lifted her head. She looked. She saw.

She understood. Everything.

And as he aimed the gun at her head, she couldn't beg, couldn't ask any questions; she could only manage to whisper one word.

"Gladiolus."

* * *

Although he was in a meeting with one of the highest-ranking members of the LAPD Detective Bureau and some of his staff, when he read Evie's last text, Rowan got up and announced that he had to leave.

"Excuse me?" said the commanding officer of the Robbery-Homicide division. "This is your meeting, Winchester."

"Sir, like I've been saying, Evie Fleming is the one who stumbled onto all this. I am sure she can explain it better than I can."

The commanding officer, Captain Andochick, plus Captain Avery and the others in the room all stared at him. The senior-level staff members had gathered to demand answers about why he and Evie had been going around asking questions about a bunch of cold cases.

Rowan had fully expected it to come to this, just not so soon, and not in an ambush meeting he'd known nothing about. Apparently, they had stirred up a few hornets, one of whom was Captain Slaughter, who worked right here in this building and had registered a complaint.

He felt every minute that ticked by. He was supposed to meet Raine to try to find the girl they'd been looking for. Then had come the texts from Evie. Now Rowan was about as tense as he'd ever been in his life.

Raine he wasn't worried about. His brother had only asked Rowan to come along because he was good at handling people. They both thought he would have better luck getting the young woman to talk about what had happened the night Harry Baker died. *If* they found her.

But Raine could do it without him. Because all thoughts of going to meet his brother had evaporated when he'd taken a quick look at his phone and seen Evie's last few messages.

Going to the house to get her car was bad. He hadn't liked it at all and had told her so.

But going *into* the house to get some records?

That was absolutely out of the question.

"Sit down, Winchester," snapped Captain Avery. "We don't want to talk to the writer. We want to hear it from you."

"Sir, I'm sorry. As you might know, Ms. Fleming was attacked a few blocks from here one week ago. Since then, someone has broken into her house more than once and has been playing psychological games with her. You know about her involvement in the Angstrom case?"

A few nods.

"I just learned she has gone back to the house to pick up some things, and now she's not responding. I am concerned, sir."

Avery glowered, but Andochick nodded slowly. "You want to send a car out to check on her?"

"Yes, that would be a good idea. Her address should be on file with Captain Avery's office." Rowan was still standing. "But I'd also like to go myself. As I said, Miss Fleming can give you a lot more information about this than I can anyway."

Andochick looked around the table and then waved him off. "Fine. Go. But plan on being back in here tomorrow. And bring her with you."

Rowan mumbled something and then strode out the door. He was dialing her number before it even swung closed behind him.

No answer.

He redialed. It rang and rang. Back to voice mail.

"Evie, please, call me back right away and let me know you're all right."

He thought about all the other things he wanted to say. Things like *God, please be careful,* and *What were you thinking? And You're precious to me, don't take risks like that, you'll give me a heart attack, I'm falling in love with you, please be okay.*

But words weren't going to help her if she was in trouble. And something deep inside him, some intuition that had served him well throughout his life, told him she was.

"Uh, Winchester?" a voice said behind him.

He glanced over his shoulder, seeing Lieutenant Carlson emerge from the conference room. He hadn't had much to say during the meeting. Probably just absorbing everything he could so he could report back to his asshole uncle.

"I'm in a hurry."

"Just wanted to ask if you need some backup."

From this guy? Oh hell no. But he merely shook his head and started walking again.

Carlson fell into step beside him. "I'm really sorry to hear what's going on with Evie. I hope I didn't...I mean..."

Rowan stopped and looked at the other man, hearing a nervousness that he couldn't understand. "You hope you didn't *what?*"

Carlson quickly shook his head. "Oh, no, I didn't do anything."

Other than acting like an annoying jerk.

"I just meant, you know, I never gave out any information to anyone who wasn't completely trustworthy."

This time, Rowan didn't just stop, he swung around to face the man, grabbing the front of his starched uniform shirt. "What the hell does that mean?"

Carlson's face reddened, and he quickly stepped back, but Rowan had a tight grip on the shirt and he didn't go far. "I mean, it's not like I gave out her address randomly or something." His throat bobbled as he swallowed. "If somebody found out where she lived and was stalking her, that couldn't come back on me. I only told one person, and he's very trustworthy."

Rowan was torn between wanting to shake the guy and wanting to hear what he had to say. Although anger roared to life inside him that Carlson had given out Evie's private information, he kept it hidden, needing answers.

"Who?" Rowan inching even closer until he could smell the mints this dickhead sucked down after every time he kissed some ass to get ahead. "Who did you tell, and why?"

"Phil, that's all. Nobody else."

Phil? Who the hell was that?

"He's a fan. He wanted to thank her for looking at some cold cases he'd worked on, so I gave him her address. But nobody else."

He suddenly got it. "Phil Smith? The retired detective?"

Carlson nodded. "Yes."

Rowan's confusion mounted, but even as it did, he felt the blood surging harder in his veins. "When was this?"

"I guess about a week or so ago." He nodded. "Yeah, it was the first day she came in. She filled out some paperwork to get the files she was requesting, and her address was on it. He called that afternoon and asked me if I had it, and I did."

This was making even less sense. "A week ago? But she didn't even go see him until Friday."

Carlson shrugged. "But she called him before that to set up their meeting. He was excited to talk to her and wanted to be sure he had her address so he could send her a little thank-you."

A thank-you? For bringing up a couple of unsolved murder

cases to a retired detective, reminding him of failures that obviously still haunted him?

"He said he was gonna send her flowers."

Every bit of air left Rowan's lungs. He couldn't replace it, unable to draw in a breath for a few seconds, though his heart was pounding wildly. A rushing sound filled his head, like a massive wave washing over him, and he would swear the floor started to roll beneath his feet. It was like being on the deck of a ship during a storm, everything was off-balance, out of focus and dizzying, but for a few seconds, he couldn't even understand *why* any of it was happening.

"Flowers," he finally managed to mumble, trying to make sense of the thoughts spinning around in his brain. The words weren't connecting with the mental pictures; a suspicion was trying to formulate, but his reason and his memory were getting in the way.

"Uh-huh. That was it. No biggie, right? I mean, no harm done?"

"Phil…he was your uncle's partner."

"Right. He was with my uncle's family all the time when I was a kid. Didn't have any of his own, couple of bad divorces, I think. No kids, no other family."

Just a mother whose picture still stood in a place of honor in his living room.

"He was a good cop. Sad about the arthritis. If not for that, he'd probably outwork all of us."

"What about the other health issues?" he asked, remembering the oxygen tank, the weight, the slowness, the diabetes. "Isn't he pretty sick?"

Looking confused, Carlson shook his head. "Nah, he's healthy as a horse otherwise. Just his fingers went on him. But he's still strong as an ox—could probably out-bench-press me if he could keep a grip on the bar."

"Jesus," Rowan muttered, seeing the *real* man through the role Smith had been playing when they'd gone to see him. Good old slow-moving retired cop with his twisted fingers, his sad cookies, and an oxygen tank trailing him like a dog on a leash.

An act. All an act. Except for those hands he could not disguise.

Why? What possible reason could there be?

Only one. The one that had been trying to come together in his brain. Now it exploded with the power of a bullet, appearing with complete clarity and certainty.

"Flowers. Oh my God!"

Carlson opened his mouth to say something, but Rowan was already sprinting down the corridor. He knocked into people, mumbling excuses, but not slowing down for anyone. He was behind the wheel of his car within five minutes and out of the parking lot into traffic one minute after that.

When the phone rang, he glanced at it, praying he would see Evie's name. Instead, he saw Raine's.

"I need you. Now," he barked as soon as the call connected.

His brother didn't ask questions. He never would. "Where?"

"Evie's in trouble. I think one of the people we talked to last week is a murderer and he wants to shut her up."

"*Where*, Rowan?"

He snapped the street name but couldn't remember the house number. "Just look for my car out front."

"I'm thirty minutes out."

"I'm twenty," Rowan replied. "I won't wait for you."

"I wouldn't either in your position. I'll get there as fast as I can."

Twenty minutes.

He flipped his siren on. That would cut out five or six.

Not enough.

It had been fifteen since Evie had texted him that she planned to go into that fucking house and had then disappeared into radio silence. Whatever was going to happen may already have taken place.

She could be fine. She might be avoiding his calls because she didn't want to argue with him over the phone. Maybe hers had died. Could be she and Candace had gone to a bar for happy hour. Maybe she was packing up the last of her stuff.

Or maybe none of those things.

If Phil Smith really was the flower killer—and Rowan knew in his gut that he was—the retired detective would have planned on getting rid of Evie as soon as he found out she was looking into those old cases. He knew what she did for a living and had to fear she was about to shed light on murders he thought he had gotten away with. Which was why days before he even met her, he'd had good old Carl give him her address.

He wouldn't give up just because she was away from home for a while. He was a former cop. He understood surveillance. He knew people almost always came back around to the places with which they were familiar.

He would have watched her house. He would have been ready.

In which case he would have had Evie in his grasp for twenty minutes already, which was far less time that it had taken the bastard to kill some of his victims.

But not all. Not *all* of them had been lucky enough to die quickly. Rowan had no doubt some of them had been begging for death long before their murderer had granted their wish.

Crime scene photos he had reviewed at her own kitchen table just a few days ago exploded in his memory. If he weren't behind the wheel, he would have scrunched his eyes shut to try to force the images out of his vision.

"No, no, no, Evie, no."

Rage warred with fear for her. He couldn't tell which was making his pulse rocket.

He only knew he had to get to her.

And pray that not only was she still alive…but also that she *wanted* to be.

Chapter 13

I guess you aren't quite as weak and ill as you let on," Evie said as she watched Phil Smith drag a dead body into her bedroom.

The retired cop—no longer wearing baggy clothing that made him look overweight or shuffling when he walked, with no oxygen tube in sight—smiled at her, though only with his mouth. His eyes remained flat and dead. "Maybe in another life I was an actor."

"While in this one you're just a sick monster."

Smith dropped the body onto the floor beside her bed. That was fortunate; she could no longer see the remains. Tied as she was, unable to move from the center of her bed, she could see very little other than the hateful face of the man who had gotten away with murder for so many years.

Completely at his mercy, she tried hard to remain calm, to not show her fear. A man like this thrived on fear he inspired in others. So while deep down she was utterly terrified, she managed to watch, and even speak, calmly while he worked around her. That was a miracle, considering her heart was pistoning in her chest, and had been ever since she looked up into the barrel of his gun, certain she was going to die in one second.

But he hadn't pulled the trigger. In fact, his swollen finger barely fit in the opening, though it had worked well enough when he'd shot Candace. Instead of shooting her, he'd ordered her to the bedroom, tied her up, and gotten busy on whatever he was planning.

"You really shoulda minded your own business, you know. I was retired."

"From everything?"

"Yep."

"People like you don't just stop doing what you do."

He snickered, as if he were a little boy letting her in on a secret. "Well, maybe just once in a while."

Right.

"Not so easy these days, though." He lifted his hands with the swollen joints and bent fingers. "The mind is willing, the flesh…"

"I suspect they're not as twisted as your soul."

"Oh, clever with words, aren't you?"

"So I've been told."

He shrugged. "I've read your books. You're not *that* good. Oh, and by the way, you got Angstrom by sheer luck. But you won't get me."

"I believe I already did."

He looked at her, trussed up on the bed, and then at himself, moving around her room, stepping over the body he'd just brought in here, as spry as a teenager. "Doesn't look that way."

"But I figured you out. Right down to the birth month flowers."

For the first time since Phil Smith had ordered her at gunpoint to go back into her bedroom, he appeared startled. "Whad you say?"

"The flowers," she replied. She nodded toward the ones on her bedside table. "My birth flowers. You found out when your victims were born and left the appropriate flowers."

"Huh." His eyes narrowed and his jaw clenched. "Think you're smart, don't ya?"

She managed to hold on to a normal tone, despite how very much she wanted lightning to strike this man dead right here and now. "My friend, the one you killed?" She blinked rapidly but didn't let any tears fall. She would cry for Candace plenty in the future. Right now, she had to focus on staying alive herself. "She said something that got me thinking about it. When I saw the gladiolus, I knew for sure."

"Well, *she* wasn't that smart," he said, almost petulantly, like a child. "Not smart enough to run out the door when you yelled. She ran toward you instead."

Evie sniffed. *Oh God, Candace, I'm so sorry.*

"So why the birth flowers?" she asked, wanting to keep him talking for as long as she could. The longer he talked, the more time that gave Rowan to get here.

She knew he would come. Knew it down to her bones. Her last text would have upset him; the silence that followed must have signaled him that something was seriously wrong.

He's coming.

"My father had a shop. Used to give flowers to the whores he cheated with."

She was no shrink, but she got the picture, knowing enough about serial killers to know some of what drove them. "I bet that made your mother unhappy."

The mother whose picture still stood in a place of honor in his home.

"She was a *saint.*" His eyes, flat and lifeless, now sparked with anger. "He might's wella killed her himself. She died of a broken heart."

"I'm sorry," she murmured, trying to keep him calm. *Please hurry, Rowan.*

He mumbled something else, averting his eyes and crouching down to the body. "He's coolin' off. Don't have as much time as I'd hoped," he mumbled.

Evie still didn't understand how, exactly, the dead man on the floor tied in to all of this, except for the fact that she recognized him as the one who'd attacked her last week. How he'd gotten here—and gotten dead—she didn't know.

"Did you hire him to attack me?"

"Nah." Seeing her confusion, he gave her an evil wink. "I hired him to kill ya."

She swallowed hard. *Be cool, be cool, be cool.*

"I guess he let you down, hmm?"

"You could say that. You believe this guy came here to try to get you to pay him to tell you who he was workin' for?" He swung a leg back and kicked the corpse. She didn't see it, thank heaven. The thunk was enough. "Piece of shit. He was a CI for me back in the day, thought he could be relied on to finish a job."

If not for Rowan's arrival last Monday night, he would have. Bile rose in her throat at the thought of it. She had been thinking the attack was about robbery or sexual assault.

Murder hadn't really entered her consciousness. Not until now.

"So that's why you killed him?"

"Yep, he made it easy. Him showing up here just brought everything together all nice and neat. The flower killer came here to kill you but didn't expect you to be with your friend. So he had to shoot her. All true so far. Beautiful, isn't it?"

She didn't answer, merely staring at him.

"He got you, did awful things to you, but somehow you fought and got away."

Did awful things to you.

Oh God. She knew some of the *awful things* this man had done to his victims.

She'd been priding herself on being calm and smart, but right now a scream was locked in her throat, bulging and throbbing, dying for escape.

"Despite how fucked up you were, you managed to get his gun, staggered into the bathroom. He came in after you and you shot him. That explains all the blood in there. You were able to kill him just before you died of your horrible injuries."

Knowing he was trying to torture her mentally, she tried not to think of all the ways in which he hoped to make her suffer. Franklin Lee's body had been in the bathroom when she arrived home, not that she'd known it at the time. "Then why bring his...why bring him in here?"

"Oh, he's still got a role to play. Gotta make sure good old Firecracker's DNA is found right here in this bed where he did all those nasty things to you."

His grin and the expectant look in his eyes were enough to tell her what he wanted her to do, to say. He wanted her to beg, wanted her to scream and cry. Wanted her broken and terrified.

Maybe his poor victims had reacted that way. But Evie had seen evil before. Horror had brushed up against her life when she was very young, and she had soaked herself in research of it from then on. Somewhere deep inside her, in the hard, iron core of herself that had been forged by her experiences with Joe Henry Angstrom, she found the strength she needed.

She held his stare. She focused on appearing calm and rational. And not afraid.

It was one of the hardest things she had ever done. Looking into the face of pure and unfiltered evil should have been enough to break her; he'd been counting on that. But she'd looked into that face before, though it had a different shape, different eyes, hair, and mouth. She was on a first-name basis with evil, and it hadn't broken her yet.

Their stare-off lasted for almost a full minute.

He was waiting, mentally ticking off the seconds until she broke.

But fucked if she would break.

Finally, he looked down at his first victim of the day. "Wish I'd held off a little longer killing him." He smiled at her again. "Can't let his body temp get too much colder than yours since you killed each other. I guess you and I won't get to have *too* much fun."

Gagging silently, she forced herself to reply, "What if I hadn't come back here today?"

He shrugged. "I was betting you would, but it didn't really matter. If you hadn't, I woulda dumped Frankie somewhere and gotten at you another way. But this works out so well. Franklin Lee was responsible for all those unsolved murders, and brave little Miss Fleming figured him out, which was why he had to kill her."

"Neat and tidy," she said, not pointing out the many flaws with his plan. Not least of which was the fact that Rowan would *never* believe it.

Leslie A. Kelly

"Yep. Gets all those cases off the books and takes care of my problems."

"All those cases. Twelve, right? Did I get them all?"

His eyes narrowed. He obviously wasn't happy that she'd figured him out and connected so many of his crimes when nobody else ever had. "Not quite."

"How many did I miss?"

"You got 'em all in this area," he admitted. "But you didn't really look out of state much, did you? Guy's gotta go on vacation once in a while."

Obviously, Phil Smith's vacations included killing innocent women. That could be why he was able to spread his local crimes far enough apart so they wouldn't draw a lot of attention. He could go more than a year between kills here in Southern California if he was committing murders elsewhere in between. That would be the only way a sadist like him would be able to keep himself from killing more frequently right in the city where he lived.

"So how many?" she asked, not certain she wanted to know but still anxious to burn up every possible moment. With any luck, Rowan would have gotten her last message right away and come straight over when she didn't answer his calls. That meant he could be here at any time. She just had to hold on a little longer.

Smith tapped the tip of his finger on his chin and looked up, his brow furrowed in concentration. He seemed like someone trying to solve a tricky math puzzle. Knowing he was tallying up the number of women he'd murdered over the years gave the performance a depraved quality.

"Twenty-seven," he finally said.

She swallowed a gasp. "Being a police officer must have made things easier for you."

"It sure didn't hurt."

"You knew to choose victims in different jurisdictions and to vary means of death."

"Stop actin' like you know anything about me. Just because you write about crazy fucks who kill 'cause they're psychos doesn't mean you can get into my head and figure me out."

Oh, he was *beyond* easy to figure out. Almost laughably, textbook easy when you ran down the checklist of what serial killers had in common, starting with the Madonna/whore attitude toward women. Not that she was about to say that out loud.

"Did anyone ever suspect you?"

He glared at her, again making it clear he did not like that she had actually done so. "No."

"What about your partner?"

"Slaughter? He only cared about getting promoted. He saw what I wanted him to see."

The arrogance was another sign of an organized killer.

"There's something I've been curious about."

Crossing his thick arms over a broad, not-at-all-sunken-in chest, he said, "I know you're trying to buy yourself a few extra minutes to live, but sure, I'll play. What?"

Not letting him see he'd scored, she calmly replied, "I've been wondering how you got the women to let you into their homes. Of course, now that I know who you are, I suspect you used your badge."

He shrugged. "Yep. Show 'em a badge and say there's a sick sex pervert in the neighborhood and sluts always open up and welcome you right in."

Of course they did. He had played on a single woman's cautious nature, not to mention their trust in the police. It was a very cruel ploy, an utter betrayal.

"And you chose them in advance. You must have, since you came prepared with their birth flowers."

"Uh-huh."

"I don't imagine they opened the door to you if you had flowers in your hand."

"Nah, they stayed in the car until…after."

After.

"Well, it's been fun chatting, but I think we need to move on now."

She couldn't prevent a shiver from rolling up her body.

He noticed and grinned. "Ahh, you know what? I just thought of something that might be fun. Never had a chance like this before, so let's change things up a bit."

Having no illusions that the "change" would make things in any way better for her, she remained silent.

"I have to go get something." He headed for the door. "Be back in a few. Don't go anywhere, now."

As soon as he walked out of the bedroom, turning left out the door and heading into the main part of the house, she began pulling to test the strength of the bindings holding her in place. Her feet were bound at the ankles, the rope connecting to the metal bedframe. She could barely lift them off the mattress, he had her down so tight.

Her hands were also constrained, tied together above her head. The end of that rope was looped through the slats of the wooden headboard. She twisted and flexed, feeling only a small amount of give in the rope itself. But the bed wasn't exactly a high-quality, solid-wood piece. As she strained and pulled, she heard a cracking sound from one of the slats.

She froze, praying he hadn't heard the noise. Listening closely, she heard him moving around in the living room, on that squeaky wood floor. He was whistling, sounding almost cheerful. The monster who lived in his skin was being given free rein and he obviously intended to enjoy himself.

She bit her lip, not letting herself think that way. Whatever he was up to would not take long. He was already worrying about the time difference between Franklin Lee's death and her own. She had no time to waste.

Stretching her hands as far as she could above and behind her, she clasped the slat and wrapped her fingers tightly around it. Using every muscle she had in her arms and shoulders, she pulled again. The cracking sound was a little louder. Her heart beat out a rapid rhythm, half because of her hope that she might get out of this and half out of terror that he'd hear her.

He didn't come charging in. She could actually hear him still whistling from out in the living room. She forced herself to relax. *You can do this.*

Once more. One more pull to give herself a fighting chance against someone who was going to kill her, but only after he made her suffer first.

Taking a deep breath and then pushing it out, she tightened her fingers, arched her back, and *pulled*. Her arms screamed, her shoulders felt like they were about to pop out of their sockets, and tears came to her eyes as she strained every muscle in her upper body.

The slat cracked again, and this time actually moved in her hands! Hope exploded inside her, but she forced it aside. This was merely the first in a long line of steps that, combined with more luck than she'd ever dare to dream of, might let her live through the night.

But it was something.

Unable to contort herself into a position that would allow

her to see what headway she was making, Evie ran her fingers down to the bottom of the slat to determine just how far the break extended. She wiggled the inch-wide piece of wood and felt a jagged edge of it poke into the tip of her index finger.

It was definitely broken, probably at least halfway through. One more solid yank, or even a hard push to wear it down in the other direction, might very well finish the job.

But if it wasn't done in utter silence, it also might finish her.

"Not up to anything bad in there, are you, girlie?" called the monster in her house.

She froze, moving her hands off the slat, back into a prone position above her. Shifting the pillow with her head, she pressed it against the headboard, hoping it would disguise the break. Wanting to keep him off guard, she cried out, "Please, please, let me go. I won't tell anyone. I'm begging you."

It was, she knew, exactly what he wanted to hear, and his loud chuckle told her he believed it. Her terror sweetened his experience.

She had no idea what he was doing out in her living room, but when something thumped and he grunted, she took a chance of making one more noise of her own.

She wriggled as far up as she could, grasped the slat again, and counted to three.

"Please let me go!" she yelled at the exact moment when she pushed and twisted with all her might.

He wouldn't have heard anything but her terror. *She* heard—and felt—the snap as the piece of wood broke away from the headboard.

Tears came to her eyes as she gripped the roughly eighteen-inch-long wooden spike. Her situation was still dire, but at least she had something to fight with. God, she would love to plunge it into that man's heart and destroy him like the monster he was.

Be smart, think, think!

She had to hold the stake right where it was, not tipping him off that she had it. Nudging the pillow with her head, she pushed it against her hands to try to disguise the way she gripped the makeshift weapon.

It was something…but it wasn't enough. Her wrists might no longer be hooked to the bedframe, but they were tied to each other. And her feet…well, she couldn't move them at all.

They wouldn't stay that way for long, though.

She knew from all the reading and studying she'd done of the flower killer that he would untie her legs. Maybe not right away, maybe not until after he'd done other things. But at some point, he would want her legs apart.

Vomit rose in her throat. Gulping, she forced herself to swallow it back down, not wanting to draw him back in immediately, or choke to death right here in her bed.

"Ready for your surprise?" he called, laughter in his voice.

She was running out of time, her panic building, the fear she'd held at bay roaring like a volcano inside her.

And then a voice whispered in her mind.

It sounded like Rowan's.

If you can help it, don't do a thing until he unties your legs. When he's bent down on the floor beside the bed to unfasten the rope, use the stake. Don't go for his heart; the wood won't go through the breastbone. Go for his eyes.

Another voice whispered. Softer, feminine.

You can do this, Evie.

Blair.

Hurt him bad, kiddo.

Candace.

She didn't believe in ghosts, and she knew the inner voices were whispers from her own subconscious. But right now, at this moment in time, she almost believed she was not alone in this fight. She had been given strength by people who cared about her.

There was another thump and a muttered curse. The floorboards groaned even louder than before, and his footsteps were very heavy and slow. Like he was hauling something.

Or someone.

Suddenly suspecting what he'd been doing, and what he would be carrying when he came back into the room, she steeled herself for the horrors she might see. And a few seconds later, when he walked in holding the naked body of her dead friend, she was filled with a kind of rage that she hadn't even known herself capable of.

"You sick fucking son of a bitch," she snarled. "I'm gonna kill you, do you hear me?"

He was still whistling as he stared down at her, Candace hanging limply in his arms.

"She didn't look very comfortable out there on the floor. I thought it would be better to have her in here with us." He kissed Candace's pale cheek. "What do you know? My first three-way."

This time, Evie was unable to swallow the vomit that rushed up her throat. She turned her head away from him and threw up on her pillow, shaking with horror and grief and fury.

"Now look what a mess you've made," he said with a tsk. "You can't expect her to lie in that." He stepped over to a lounge chair by the window and lowered Candace onto it, gently and carefully, like a father putting a child to bed.

Walking around the bed, to the side on which she lay, he

looked down at her. Evie tried to meet his stare defiantly, but she was so close to the edge, so close to panicking and begging—for real—that she closed her eyes.

"Better clean you up, huh?"

When she felt him pushing her hair out of the way and then lifting her head, her eyes flew back open. "What—"

"Can't let you lie here in this mess, now, can we?" He smiled that evil smile that went well with those black, inhuman eyes and began to move the pillow.

Her whole body stiffened as she realized what was about to happen. He would take the pillow, and then he would see the way her hands were gripping the wood stake behind it. The broken one.

She knew waiting until her legs were free was the best way to go. But it looked like she might not have the chance.

"I wish I had time to wash your pretty blond hair," he murmured as he leaned closer. "I like women's hair. You didn't even notice that when you were snooping into my past, did you? I always took a few strands with me."

The "gift" he'd left on her pillow the other day now made even more sickening sense.

"Yours isn't as long as I like, and I do prefer redheads. But it's still nice and soft."

She felt the heat of his stale breath on her forehead, and her skin crawled like it was being walked on by spiders.

No time, no time. Do it, just do it!

Now or never.

For you. For Candace.

For all of them.

She did it.

Yanking the wood completely out of the headboard frame,

she swung it up, and plunged it into the murdering psychopath's face.

"You bitch! You miserable fucking bitch!" he bellowed as he staggered back, his hands clutching his face, blood already drenching his fingers. He tripped over what she assumed was his hit man's body and fell back, still screaming in pain and fury.

Evie immediately sat up, shimmying toward the end of the bed. Her wrists were still bound, but without the slat between them, she had a bit more freedom. She tried to unknot the thick rope securing her ankles. It was *so* tight. If she had ten minutes, maybe she could do it.

She didn't have ten seconds.

"I'm gonna make it worse than you ever dreamed about," Phil Smith promised as he staggered to his feet and came toward the bed.

She'd missed. She'd hurt him, yes. But it had been no incapacitating blow.

All she had done was enrage the bull.

The long shaft of wood was embedded in his cheek, just below his eye. Blood gushed from the wound, and he was almost foaming at the mouth as he reached up, grabbed it tight, and pulled it out. In his incoherent anger, he threw it at her, striking her on the head.

Like a desperate animal, Evie scurried back out of his reach, bumping into poor Candace's body. When he walked around the bed, following her like a shark circling a raft, she grabbed the splintered piece of wood and jabbed it at him.

He sneered; there was little damage she could do with the thing now that he was watching for it. She had taken her one chance and had blown it.

"I'm gonna enjoy this." He tried to stretch his hands, those swollen, mangled hands, and absently rubbed one with the other. The grip he'd taken on the stake when he'd pulled it out had apparently hurt him. A lot. "Oh, how I wish I could choke the breath right out of you. But I guess the blades will have to do."

Evie wasn't listening. She was focused only on his hands, the way he moved them so gingerly, the massively swollen knuckles and permanently bent fingers.

Those hands had brutalized dozens of women. Whatever pain he suffered from them now wasn't nearly enough. Not nearly.

She wanted to add to it. If it was the last thing she did on this earth, and it probably would be, she wanted to punish him for what he'd done to Felicity Long, and Amy Nolan, and Candace, and all the others.

He reached for her. She gripped the stake. This time, though, instead of jabbing it at him, she slammed it down, with all her might, directly onto the fingers of his right hand.

He screamed, a high-pitched howl that nearly deafened her.

"Oh holy Jesus, oh God, you bitch, you evil whore!"

The screams were accompanied by sobs. From the sound of it, the pain she'd just inflicted on him was worse than when she'd stabbed him in the face.

Good. It was a small satisfaction in this, the last minute of her life.

"Bitch, I'm gonna shove that thing right up your—"

"Get your hands up, you son of a bitch, or I'll put a matching hole in the other side of your face," a cold, hard voice snarled.

Phil Smith froze, completely shocked, but no more than Evie.

"Rowan!" she cried, seeing him standing in the doorway, gun in hand, aimed directly at the man who'd been within seconds of killing her.

He didn't take his eyes off Smith, not even to assure her that everything was gonna be okay. Which was just fine with her.

It *was* going to be okay. He'd come, just as she'd prayed he would.

Just as she'd known he would.

Smith didn't say anything. He didn't try to make up a fast story or ask for mercy, and he certainly didn't put his hands up. They were still clutched at his chest, curled protectively together, as tears of pain ran down his face.

"Hit me, she hit me," he mumbled to himself. "Hit me, Mama, she hit me."

It sounded as though the man was dissolving into his own little world, his mind splintering. Evie had done something no woman had ever done before: she'd hurt him. Badly. First by discovering his secret, and then physically.

Which *shouldn't* have made him cry, no matter how much pain he was in.

Given his hatred of women, she would not expect him to be feeling sorry for himself. He should be filled with volcanic anger. He should want revenge. The voices in his mind weren't consoling him; they were screaming at him to lash out and hurt the person who'd actually damaged him.

"Rowan, watch—"

She didn't even get the last word out before the killer lunged at her. His hands were a witch's claws, grabbing her throat and digging in.

It hurt for less than a second. Because before he'd even managed to cut off her last breath, Phil Smith flew off his feet and landed on the floor. Her ears were ringing as the sound of a gun-shot echoed in the room.

Rowan rushed to the bed, casting a quick, sad look at poor Candace and then cupping Evie's face. "You're okay. You're gonna be fine, Evie. It's over."

Unable to even speak, she simply nodded, knowing he needed to assure himself of that before he went back to work.

He shifted from worried lover back into alert cop, crouching down to the floor to check Phil Smith's vital signs. She watched, seeing the blood all over the man. From the look of it, Rowan's bullet had hit him in the chest, dead center in his heart.

Dead, she believed, being the key word.

When Rowan stood up and turned his back on Smith, she knew the monster's evil heart had beaten its last.

"Rowan!" another man's voice called.

"Here."

Raine ran into the room, a gun in his hand, a glower on his face. He immediately sized up the situation, his dark gaze assessing the three dead people and then the two living ones.

"Are you both okay?" he asked.

Evie nodded.

"You got a knife?" Rowan asked.

Raine pulled a utility knife out of his pocket and tossed it over. Catching it, Rowan knelt on the floor at the edge of the bed and sawed away the ropes at her feet. When she extended her hands, he cut those away too.

Then, and only then, did Evie allow the dam that had been holding her emotions in check to collapse. She had never really understood the expression *burst into tears*, having always just started crying when she was sad. This, though, was an utter eruption of sobs and tears. She shuddered and shook, her face was instantly wet, and a wail that she didn't even realize had been trapped inside her emerged from her mouth.

Rowan didn't say a word. Instead, he scooped her up into his powerful arms and carried her out of the room. And then right out of the house.

He took her to the front lawn and sat down in the grass, still holding her tightly. His mouth close to her temple, he whispered, "I've got you. I've got you, Evie, you're fine. It's over."

She let him rock her like a child, let the cool evening breeze coming in off the ocean fill her lungs and blow away the remnants of terror from her mind. The night was starry, the moon bright. Such a beautiful sky shining down. Gradually, she let herself believe his whispered words and feel safe in his embrace.

But she wasn't sure how long she would allow herself to believe it.

Because life could smack you anytime it wanted.

"Why is there such evil in the world?" she eventually whispered, once she felt capable of speaking without bursting into ugly sobs again. "And why do I keep finding it? Do I attract it or something?"

"You know that's not true, Evie."

"Tell that to Candace." She closed her eyes and buried her face in his neck. "And Blair."

"There are horrible, awful people in this world, honey. You know it and I know it. That just means that the really good ones—like you—matter even more."

She merely shook her head.

He squeezed her tighter. "Evie, what you do, the way you can look at things and see them in a different way than anyone else ever has before, that's a gift. You're smart, and you're tenacious, and you're curious, which is something a lot of people aren't anymore."

"It hasn't exactly paid off for people around me, though, has it?"

"Don't do this to yourself. I'm so sorry about Candace and Blair. But you can't carry that weight. They died because two evil monsters decided to kill them. That's all."

"But if I—"

"No. No buts. Thanks to you, and the fact that you noticed some damn license tags, Angstrom wasn't able to hurt anyone else. And again, thanks to you, neither will Phil Smith. Nobody even knew he existed until you put it all together."

"Not in time to save Candace," she whispered, knowing that wound would be a long time healing. "He was in there, waiting. We walked right into a trap."

"Evie, don't do this to yourself. You couldn't have known he was there."

She blinked and looked up at him. "I did, though. Something inside me *did* know, which is why I changed my mind and refused to go in."

He gave her a quizzical look.

"I went to get a package off the porch and dropped my purse. Everything spilled out."

"So that's why I found your phone outside when I got here. It put my guard up. Then when I heard that screaming, I broke the door down. Guess you didn't even hear."

"Not over his howling."

"You hurt him."

She nodded.

"Good."

He brushed a kiss against her cheek. "Sorry, you weren't finished. You dropped your purse?"

She explained to him what had happened, how and why she had ended up going inside, even after she'd decided not to. It didn't, by any means, relieve the guilt she felt over Candace's death, but it was the truth.

"Sorry to interrupt."

Hearing Raine's voice, Rowan said, "Hey. Didn't mean to abandon you in there."

In that house of horrors, he meant.

"Just did a sweep," Raine said. "All three DOA."

From somewhere nearby came the sound of police sirens. They were drawing closer.

Raine looked in that direction. "If it's all the same to you, I'd rather not get caught up in this if I can avoid it. Especially since I came in after it was all over."

Rowan nodded. "Go. And, Raine, thanks for coming."

Evie managed a tiny nod. "Yes, thank you."

"He's the hero," Raine said, nodding at his brother. "Good job, brother."

Getting on a motorcycle parked in the street, Raine drove away just as two police cars rounded the corner and pulled up out front. A few neighbors had come outside, probably because they'd heard the gunshot and the sirens, but so far nobody had approached Evie and Rowan.

Two uniformed cops got out of the first car. "Are you Winchester?" one of them asked.

Rowan removed one arm from around her and pulled a badge out of his pocket, flipping it open to show the two officers. "Yeah."

"Everything all right here?" one of them asked, approaching

them across the lawn. "We were asked to come do a health-and-safety check at this house."

A half laugh, half cry came out of Evie's mouth. Rowan continued to hold her, not getting up.

"No. It's definitely not all right," he said. "It's a triple."

The cop, who'd been pretty casual about finding a detective holding and rocking a disheveled, bruised, bloodied woman on his lap in the middle of the lawn finally came to attention. "What?"

"Three. All in the bedroom. You'd better call it in and get forensics out here."

"Can you walk me through—"

"Fewer people going through the scene the better. We'll just wait here for a while."

She rested her head on his shoulder and closed her eyes, knowing they faced a very long night. But until all that started, they would sit here together, cooled by the night air, tasting the salty breeze, wrapped around each other.

Just for a little while.

* * *

Over the next several days, with the national press focusing nonstop on the woman who had solved not one but two serial murder cases, Rowan did what he could to shield Evie from the spotlight. She didn't want it, hated it, in fact, and was content to stay in his apartment, the two of them separated from the rest of the world. No one other than immediate family knew where they were. That's how they both preferred it.

They had left only once, to attend Candace's funeral.

Despite everything Rowan thought he knew about the widower, Marcus Oakley's grief was sincere and painful to witness. His anguish had turned him into a pale and silent shell. Crying onto her shoulder during the service, Marcus had made it clear he didn't blame Evie for what had happened.

Perhaps someday Evie would stop blaming herself too.

Rowan took some time off, not wanting to leave her alone. Her cuts and scrapes healed quickly, much faster than her spirit. Gradually, though, as the days passed, the real Evie began to emerge from the heartbroken shell.

They ate and they talked. They made love and they talked. They slept and they talked.

She cried a lot. He cried with her once.

Then, one day, she laughed out loud.

That was the day he let himself really believe she was going to be all right. Not undamaged by what she had gone through, but okay. She was strong, she was smart, she was determined. And she had him.

"So what did the DA have to say?" he asked her one afternoon, about a week after everything had gone down so badly at her old house. They'd just finished lunch when her phone rang. She'd gone out of the room to talk to the prosecutor in the Angstrom case. He'd busied himself washing dishes, waiting for her to come back.

"The judge set a trial date for next spring. I'll definitely need to be there."

He dried his hands and went to her. Crouching down beside her chair, he took her hand. "You okay?"

She smiled a little. "I think so."

Noticing the way her lips struggled to retain the smile, he

twined her fingers in his. "You are one of the strongest people I have ever known, Evelyn Fleming. You can handle anything. But you don't have to do it alone. I will be there with you, if you want me."

"I want you," she insisted, gripping tightly. "I definitely want you."

The words weren't flirtatious or sexy. She was assuring him that she wanted him in her life, just as he wanted her in his.

"Then you've got me."

Although Angstrom hadn't been responsible for what had gone on over the past couple of weeks, he was certainly a cloud on the horizon. But Rowan would make sure that cloud was never able to darken her life again.

They hadn't made long-term plans, beyond her deciding that, no matter what, she wasn't going to go into hiding because of a possible future threat. She was staying here in LA, at least for the new few months, writing her book, determined to remain in control of her own destiny.

Frankly, he hoped she decided never to leave. Or if she did want to go, that she wouldn't mind him coming with her. It really didn't matter where they went. He liked his job, and had, indeed, been offered a promotion, but it wasn't like he couldn't be a cop somewhere else. Or hell, maybe he'd even go back to law school.

After all the years of uncertainty about his own future, and the crazy shit still to be dealt with by his family, the one thing he was sure of was how he felt about Evie.

He loved her. He wanted her. He wanted *them*. Everything else was secondary as far as he was concerned.

"Thank you." She leaned forward and pressed her mouth to his. "But let's forget about that, about him, for now. I don't want to give him one more moment of my attention than I have to. We'll deal with it next year."

"Sounds like a plan."

They kissed again, and he saw her shake off the dark thoughts that had hit her when she saw the number on her phone screen.

"You know, there's something else I've been wanting to discuss with you," she said.

"About how addicted you are to having sex with me?"

She waved a hand. "That goes without saying." She nibbled her lip, and then said, "It's about the Harry Baker case."

Although his go-to reaction when that name was mentioned was to clench and heave, he merely nodded. Sliding up to sit on the other kitchen chair, he said, "I know. We never did get back to our conversation about that."

He had talked to his brothers. They knew what Evie had gone through, and they also knew what she meant to Rowan. They weren't exactly offering their blessings for him to tell her the whole story, but they weren't threatening his life about it anymore either.

"Evie, I want you to know what happened. *Everything* that happened. But before I tell you, I want you to hear me when I say this. I did not kill Harry Baker. Neither of my brothers killed Harry Baker. His blood is *not* on my family's hands."

"I never really thought you—"

"But we were there."

Her mouth fell open, and she simply stared at him.

"Everything I told you about Raine waking up, finding Harry assaulting that girl, all his memories coming back—every word is true." He swallowed hard. "It's just not *all* the truth about that night. After Raine left…after he told us what had happened both that night and the night Rachel died, Reece and I went over there."

It was her turn to reach out and clasp their hands together. "And he was already dead."

"Yes."

"What if he hadn't been?" Rowan stared steadily into her face and told her the truth. "If he'd still been alive, I don't know what would have happened. Could I have killed him? Could Reece have? Sometimes I think…yes. But we'll never know."

She nodded, her eyes narrowed in thought. "What did happen when you went there and found him dead?"

"What do you think?"

It took her less than a second. "You thought Raine did it."

"Of course."

She took that final step on her own too. "And you covered it up so he wouldn't be charged."

Ding ding ding, she won the prize.

"It's not something I'm proud of, Evie. You have to believe that."

"Of course I believe it." She lifted a hand and ran it through his hair. "I know you, Rowan. I know who you are."

He caught her hand in his and kissed her palm. "It was years before Reece and I found out that Raine was actually innocent. Can you believe we were assholes enough to never actually ask him? Steve Baker is the one who told us that. Meanwhile Raine had thought all along…"

"That you two did it."

"Right."

She blew out a slow breath as she took it all in. "And I thought *my* brothers didn't communicate."

It wasn't precisely a joke, but it wasn't too far out of that ball-park.

"And how did Steve Baker find out?"

He told her about the stripper who'd paid Steve a visit, demanding money for information on the night his father had died. And what she'd said about teenage Raine staggering away while Harry was screaming after him on the front porch.

"That's why you need to find this girl."

"Yes. She told Steve something else—that she saw a car come back. And despite what she thought—or thinks—it wasn't us. We showed up even later."

"So either the girl came back and killed him for what he'd done to her—and lied about it to blame it on you and your brothers—or someone else showed up and did it."

"Right. That's where I was supposed to be going with Raine last Monday night. He thought he'd tracked her down finally. He's been looking for her for months—Steve gave us a first name, a description, and said she's a stripper."

For the first time since he'd started talking, Evie frowned, looking confused.

"That doesn't sound right."

"What do you mean?"

"I mean, one of the reasons I went back for my file box that day was because I knew I'd read something, somewhere, about a half-naked girl running screaming down Baker's street the night he died."

Rowan sat up straight, stunned. "What? Where? I haven't seen anything like that."

Evie bent down to dig into a box of papers she'd been reading before they'd cleared the table to eat. When she found what she was looking for, she handed it over. It was a printout of an email, sent to Evie about three months ago, from someone named Mike Dillon.

"What is this?"

"He was Baker's neighbor. He heard I was writing a book on the case—which I'm *not*—and contacted me with some information he thought I might find interesting. I guess he's a fan; he asked for some autographed books."

Rowan read the brief email.

"Holy shit, he knew her? He knew the girl? He recognized her?"

"Yes."

"Chelsea Voss," he murmured. "Her name is Chelsea Voss."

"Uh-huh. She was another neighbor. He saw her running away, her clothes torn, crying. He thought she'd had a bad breakup or a boyfriend had hurt her."

Rowan continued reading. This neighbor had reached out to the girl's widowed father, who said he would find out what had happened.

"How could he not have associated it with Baker's murder that same night?"

She shrugged. "Some people aren't like us, Detective. Harry Baker was everybody's favorite Hollywood neighbor. Never a whiff of scandal. Such a tragedy. What would that have to do with the fourteen-year-old girl up the street having a fight with her boyfriend?"

Fourteen. Jesus.

"It wasn't until a couple of years later, when the neighborhood starting whispering that there'd been child porn found on Baker's computer, that Mr. Dillon started wondering if it was relevant. But by then he felt like it was too late to go to the police. The girl was doing well, and he didn't want to mess up her life."

That confused Rowan. From the sound of it, this girl, Chelsea, wasn't doing well at all. She was scarred, she went by the name Marley, she was a stripper. Not the ideal life for any twenty-year-old who'd grown up in the neighborhood where Harry Baker had lived.

"It just doesn't compute, not with what we learned from Steve."

Evie pulled out another sheet of paper and pushed it over. "That's because you've been looking for the wrong person." She tapped on a black-and-white photo of a pretty young woman wearing a graduation gown. "This is Chelsea Voss. She graduated top of her class and is now a college student...in Chicago. No scar. And she's most definitely *not* a stripper."

What the actual fuck? It made no sense. Could there have been two girls of about the same age and appearance traumatized on that block that very same night? It defied the odds.

"You've really been working on this," he said as he skimmed the information Evie had found about the young woman.

"Yes. I wanted to help if I could. You know me, I always like digging into mysteries."

That sounded like the real Evie. The confident, smart, determined one.

"You helped. You definitely helped," he said. "Can I show this to my brothers?"

"Of course. I even have her address at school if one of you feels like taking a trip to Chicago."

"It should probably be Raine," he said. "I'm sure he'd relish the chance to talk to somebody at a private college rather than staking out every seedy strip club in LA."

She glowered. "Is that where you were going to go with him

last Monday night? To a strip club? Rowan Winchester, I'm shocked!"

"It's part of the job, babe. Believe me, I wouldn't have liked it." He pulled her off her chair and onto his lap. "I don't even want to look at any other woman but you."

He kissed her hard, and she responded in kind. Their tongues came together in a hungry dance, and he felt her excitement rise. They'd made a lot of slow, sweet love in recent days. It was always good. *Always.* But he sensed her mood had changed.

This was the wild woman from that first day on the beach.

She turned to face him, straddling him on the chair, and he pushed up into her, letting her know how much she turned him on. She had since the night they'd met. He suspected she always would.

"So, how do you feel about being the feast on the kitchen table?" he asked as he lifted her from his lap and put her up onto the butcher block. He didn't even want to take the time to go to the bedroom, and swiped a hand across the pages there, sending them spinning to the floor.

She reached for his shirt, pulling him to her. Twining her fingers in his hair, she licked her lips and gave him a coy little look. "That depends on how hungry you are."

He laughed. "I'm starving, honey. Absolutely famished."

Then there was no more laughing, only hot, wet kisses, steamy touches, and needy gasps. Their clothes were on the floor in seconds, and he pushed her onto her back so he could kiss her from top to toe, stopping at several particularly delicious places in between.

"Oh, God, Rowan," she moaned as he pleasured her, bringing her to her first climax quickly. He knew her body so well, knew what she liked and how she responded. There were, of course, many more things to discover, and he looked forward to doing that. But right now, he just wanted to make her feel *good*. And judging by the way she cried out and arched toward his mouth, he succeeded.

"Aren't you full yet?" she asked as he continued to kiss and sample her inner thighs and everything in between. "Because I *want* to be."

Laughing softly, he straightened and look down at her. Her blue eyes were glazed with pleasure, her lips red and parted, her hair strewn about her on the table.

She was perfect. So beautiful she stole his breath. Just like she'd stolen his heart.

Wrapping her legs around him, she tugged him closer, arching toward him in welcome. Rowan pulled her to the very edge of the table. His hands tightly around her hips, he lifted her a little and then plunged into her body, hard, fast, and deep.

She let out a cry of pleasure, one he was becoming very well used to.

"Yes, yes, oh, God, nothing ever felt as good as this," she whispered. She reached up and stroked his chest.

"No, nothing ever did, Evie," he said as he pulled out and then drove in deep again.

She met him thrust for thrust, until she came again, hard, and this time he went with her.

A few hours later, after they'd napped, showered, had sex in the shower, and eaten something for dinner, they curled up together on the couch for a Netflix-and-Laugh marathon, as they'd once joked about doing.

Suddenly thinking of something, he said, "Wow, I just remembered. Do you know what this Thursday is?"

"No, what?"

"It's Thanksgiving."

Evie's mouth rounded. "Oh goodness, I completely forgot about that too."

His arm draped across her shoulders, and he squeezed her. "Have any mad turkey-making skills I don't know about, Ms. Author?"

"No. Do *you*, Mr. Cop?"

"Uh-uh. And, uh, I kind of hate turkey," he admitted.

"Yeah, not a big fan either."

"So…pizza?"

"Pizza sounds perfect."

She smiled at him.

That smile, that beautiful smile.

He could get lost in that smile forever, and he never wanted her to lose it again.

"Why are you looking at me?" she said, shifting out from under his arm to study his face.

"Because I love you."

He hadn't planned to say that, but it was only the truth. He wasn't a game player; he wasn't smooth and controlling like Reece or dark and dangerous like Raine. He was just himself. The normal one, if there was such a thing. He believed in being forthright and telling it like it was. So, he'd told it like it was.

And he didn't regret it.

He expected her to be surprised, to question how he could know such a thing so soon. He half wondered if she would try to argue him out of it, pointing out the dark cloud she thought she walked under.

Instead, with a gentle kiss, she simply replied, "I love you too."

Epilogue

"Are you sure you're okay with not having pizza?"

Getting out of the car in the driveway of Reece's house, Rowan was thinking pizza with pepperoni and green peppers was sounding better and better.

But he'd agreed to this. When his dad had called and said the whole family was getting together for Thanksgiving dinner at Reece's place, and they all looked forward to getting to know Evie, there really was no way to refuse.

"Just don't leave me alone with your brothers, okay? They might want me to sign a blood oath not to write my book."

Coming around to her side of the car, Rowan pulled her into his arms. "Don't worry about my family. They're going to love you."

She nibbled her lip. "Even knowing what I do?"

"Are you kidding? Especially knowing what you do. The last time I talked to Reece, he warned me that Jess was probably going to pick your brain about writing a script based on some of your work."

She lifted a brow.

"Don't worry. She's really nice. If you say no, she'll back off…for a half hour or so."

She was actually laughing at that when the garage door opened and the stunning redhead herself appeared. "I told you I heard a car!" she shouted to someone inside.

Darting toward them, she grabbed Rowan and kissed him on the cheek, and then turned her back on him, giving all her focus to Evie.

"I'm Jess," she said, looping her arm through Evie's. "I've heard all about you, and am so excited to hear more."

He could see Evie stiffen a little and knew she was worried Jess might immediately start asking questions about the flower killer case, or Angstrom—the dark shadow still hanging over her. But it seemed his future sister-in-law was talking about something else altogether.

"Tell me how you met. You were mugged? And he brought you here? Were you okay? Did he stay the night? When did you guys go out again?"

Evie was smiling, and then laughing as the other woman continued asking questions and poking fun of Rowan. He knew her well enough to know she was overdoing it, intentionally, of course. She was trying to put Evie at ease, not have her worrying that they were all going to treat her with kid gloves or ask her about her experiences with serial killers.

Not for the first time, he thought that his brother Reece was one hell of a lucky man. Jess was the lively, bright breath of fresh air his twin needed.

Evie, meanwhile, was the cool, smart, strong, and loving partner Rowan had always wanted.

Who'd have ever thought it? A year ago they'd been three

happy bachelors. Now they were two down, and one to go.

Of course, Raine was still pretty young. He had just turned twenty-five and had time. Rowan only hoped that their kid brother was able to wear off some of his hard edges, and maybe put down some of his baggage, by the time he met the right woman.

Inside the house, Evie was quickly surrounded with hugs and kisses on the cheek from his dad and Aunt Sharon. Raine nodded, Reece shook her hand. And with every minute that passed, Evie relaxed and grew more animated. Soon she was chopping vegetables in the kitchen while Jess set the table and Aunt Sharon brined the turkey. The house was filled with laughter.

It was the first Thanksgiving he could remember that had been genuinely warm and happy. Which made it more of a damn shame when he told his brothers that he'd like to talk to them on the patio right after their father and Aunt Sharon had left.

Evie met his eye. She knew he was about to tell his siblings what he'd learned about Chelsea Voss, the girl they should have been searching for. When they learned she was not who they thought she was, they would probably be as stunned as he had been.

But not for long.

That was the thing about the Winchesters. They bounced back. And once his brothers got over their surprise, the three of them would put their heads together and figure out what to do next. Because none of them was going to give up on this quest for answers.

Not Raine, who'd had his darkest, most tragic memories poured back into his mind by Harry Baker.

Not Reece and Rowan, who'd cleaned up the crime scene and thought for years that their baby brother was a killer.

They would find out the truth for themselves. For Steve. For their mother.

And for Rachel.

"So," he said as they sat down in lounge chairs, Rowan closest to the house, as usual. "I think it's time we talk about the girl."

Dying for a sneak peek of the next book in the exciting Hollywood Heat series?

Keep reading for a preview of

Waiting for You

Available early 2019.

Former Child Star Assaults Reporter

Hollywood Tattletale Reporter R. Carlisle

February 5, 2019

LOS ANGELES—Former child actor Raine Winchester, of the famed Hollywood family dynasty, is in the news for assaulting reporter James Federer on the set of *Locked and Curled*, currently filming at Paramount.

The hulking owner of the protection company Hollywood Guardians was at the side of nine-year-old star Brittany Blake during a backstage press tour of the set. Federer, a reporter with this organization, insists he accidentally stumbled among the crowd and instinctively grabbed the girl for balance, inciting the professional bodyguard to action. Federer was bodily picked up and thrown aside by the former Army Ranger, incurring a broken rib and a dislocated shoulder.

Scandal and violence are no strangers to the Winchester family, and yesterday's incident is sure to raise questions about family once again, especially since no charges were filed, or are expected, against Raine Winchester, despite the violence of his attack and the injuries to Federer.

Are the Winchester brothers just incredibly lucky?

Or has their fame and influence allow them to escape justice time and time again?

Chapter 1

Sadie Allen remained awake late into the night, tense and anxious, despite her state-of-the-art security system and safe neighborhood.

After four years of hell, the threats, the phone calls, the vandalism, and the stalking had finally come to an end. It had been eighteen months since any of *them* had made contact, and she had grown confident that that part of her life was in the past.

Oh please, don't let this be starting again. "They wouldn't. Not now."

Her daughter couldn't possibly be taken without the entire world hearing about it. Not when Charity was protected by professional bodyguards paid for by powerful studios, and was watched constantly, by a camera, a director, a film crew, a security team.

And by her mom.

Sadie was no longer a helpless, broke, desperate single mother running from a pack of fanatics. She had allies. She had help. Most of all, she had strength. Unlike six years ago when she'd escaped and fled to California from the wilds of Montana.

If they thought she was still that desperate, frightened girl, they had a lot to learn.

She rolled onto her side and punched her pillow, aching for rest but unable to find it. "Damn reporters," she whispered as she gave up on sleep, reached for her iPad, and tapped on the screen. Ever since the incident on the lot, when her little girl had been assaulted by a creepy reporter from a creepy tabloid, Sadie had been watching the story unfold in the press.

Her anger rose as she read the latest article from James Federer's rag about it. Rather than casting blame where it belonged—on a sleazy, middle-aged man who had grabbed a nine-year-old girl's arm to get her attention, his grip hard enough to leave bruises—they were blaming Raine Winchester.

Raine, who had been doing his job protecting Sadie's daughter.

Raine, whose eagle-sharp eyes missed nothing, and whose threatening presence was usually enough to stop any fan from getting too close to his charge.

Raine, who was, without a doubt, the strongest, most protective man she'd ever known.

Not to mention the hottest.

Good Lord, the bodyguard was traffic-stopping. Tall, broad, with muscles other men's muscles aspired to be. Always dressed in camo pants and form-fitting black T-shirts, his body was a textbook example of masculine. His dark hair was kept military short, which only emphasized the male beauty of his face. The deep-set eyes, the cut cheeks, the square jaw, all combined to set a woman's heart pounding, heart fluttering, and legs trembling.

The guy was steamy sex on two feet.

Sadie didn't know that firsthand, of course, despite the fact that she spent so much time around him. Not sexy time, definitely not. Everything between them was professional.

That didn't mean she hadn't thought about kissing him, touching him. More.

"Lots more," she whispered, wishing fantasies weren't all she had.

She had had sex with only two men, ever. Sadie had been a teenage virgin on her wedding night. *God, who was that girl?* And after running away from her sham of a marriage and her ex's insane life, she'd been too gun-shy to allow anybody to get close.

She'd also had her daughter to take care of. Once Charity had become a superstar, now known to the whole world as Brittany Blake, Sadie's protective mom duties had quadrupled. Hollywood wasn't exactly a safe place for kids. It had taken a long time for Sadie to agree to go out with someone—an aspiring actor.

Big mistake. Because after the very first time they'd slept together, he'd had the nerve to ask her to use Char's status to get him a job on "Brittany's" new movie.

No more dating for Sadie. Definitely no more sex. Just fantasies about the strong, silent, devastatingly attractive bodyguard, who was never anything more than polite and professional.

After all, why would a man from a famous Hollywood family, who was drop-dead gorgeous, strong, and successful, have any interest in a boring single mom? Not only that, a single mom who was older than him by a couple of years?

He wouldn't. The end.

She tossed the iPad onto the other side of the bed, still fuming at the article, wishing the movie business wasn't so filled with sharks and barracudas and defined by who devoured whom.

Something scraped against her window, and Sadie flinched, forgetting all about sexy bodyguards. Although she knew it was just a branch from a tree right out front, the creaky scratch reminded her that, even though strong professionals watched over her little girl by day, Sadie alone was responsible for Charity's well-being when they were in this house.

And even though the security system remained silent, she could no longer ignore the alarm in her brain.

Sadie threw back the covers, grabbed her robe, and left her room. She turned right, heading for the next door down, needing to see that Char was safe and sound.

She edged the door open a few inches, her gaze moving past the Brittany Blake movie posters toward the bed. Spying the dark curls and sweet face pressed against the pillow, a thumb resting close to the bow-shaped mouth—her daughter had been a thumb-sucker—Sadie let out the breath she'd been holding. She wanted to go into the room, draw the blue down comforter up over the child's bare shoulders, and give her a soft kiss on the cheek.

But she didn't, fearing she would wake Char up. She needed to go check the rest of the house. Right now.

Softly closing the door, she continued to prowl, looking in the rest of the upstairs bedrooms and bathrooms. Nothing. She walked carefully down the curved staircase. Her bare feet made no sound on the slick wood, and she listened for any noise from downstairs.

You're being paranoid.

The creepy-crawly sensation wouldn't go away, though, no matter how much she tried to tell herself all was well. Sadie had lived too much of her life knowing all was *not* well to fall for mental games, even if she was playing them all by herself.

Reaching the marble-tiled foyer, she shivered a little. It was drafty down here.

Something moved. She caught a glimpse of a shadow out of the corner of her right eye.

Her heart leapt, and so did she, spinning to race to the formal dining room, where she'd seen the movement. She immediately managed a tiny laugh at her own expense. The sheers over the windows were wafting as the heat kicked on, sending warmth from the vent above.

Just the curtains, nothing more.

Nothing more. Nevermore. Nothing more. Nevermore.

"No," she groaned. The memory of that singsong voice made her instantly queasy.

She went to the alarm panel and double-checked that everything was in working order. "Fine," she whispered. "Everything's fi—" The word died in her mouth as the floodlight in the backyard came on.

It was triggered by movement. And there was movement.

"Oh my God," she whispered once she could speak.

A quick glance through those softly billowing sheers revealed several dark shapes moving from the fence across the back lawn toward the house.

Five shapes. Five people. At least that she could see.

"No," she moaned, even as she willed her brain to kick into action.

They'd prepared for this, hoping it would never happen, but knowing that with Sadie's history, and Charity's fame, it could.

"Charity," she whispered. Finally getting the lead out of her butt, she turned and raced up the stairs three at a time, her toes slipping on the stupid slick surface.

"Baby, wake up," she said as she burst into the room. She made no effort to be quiet and gently wake her daughter. The clock was ticking. She knew what they had to do, where they had to go.

Charity blinked at her, sitting up and letting the covers drop onto her lap. "What's wrong, Mommy?"

"It's time to play the hide-and-seek game, honey."

The little girl's big, blue eyes widened in excitement. "In the secret room?"

"Yep."

Charity leapt out of the bed. "Can we slide?"

"You bet we can."

"Yay!"

This was a game to her. A game they'd rehearsed as soon as the special construction had been completed, although never in the middle of the night.

"I gotta bring Coconut!" Char said. She reached for the fluffy white cat who'd been sleeping on the foot of the bed.

"Of course you do." Sadie flung open the doors to Charity's large, walk-in closet. She pushed racks of clothes aside and found the concealed control panel. She slammed her palm into the large red panic button that even Charity knew was to be used only in the direst of emergencies.

"You pushed the button," her daughter whispered from behind her.

Sadie glanced over her shoulder, seeing Charity's jaw drop open. "Yes, I did."

"It's real?"

"It's real."

Charity nodded, her expression solemn and mature as she grasped the true situation. She displayed no fear, only the slight tightening of her arms around the cat, revealing her rising tension.

"Should I shut the door? Like we practiced?"

"Yes, please. And shift the clothes back."

Her daughter immediately did as instructed so anyone opening the door from the bedroom would see nothing out of the ordinary, not until they dug into the back corner and spied the control box. That would buy them some time.

Sadie punched the six-digit code into the electronic keypad. Before her eyes, the wall slid open, a cleverly concealed panel gliding out of the way.

"Ready?" she asked.

Charity moved past her, slowly and calmly. "Ready."

Brushing a strand of hair off her daughter's cheek, Sadie whispered, "It's gonna be fine. Slide down, just like we practiced. I'll be right behind you." She pressed her lips on Charity's forehead. "I love you."

"I love you too," Char said, and then she dropped to her bottom and scooted toward the edge of the opening. "Now don't scratch me, Coconut, it'll be over quick."

Comforting her cat. God love her.

Charity didn't make a sound as she shimmied farther, reaching the top of the slide. And then she shot down it, disappearing on the quick ride directly down into the safe room.

Trying to remember everything Raine Winchester had told her during the many times they'd gone over this plan, Sadie did a quick mental rundown. The safe room was incredibly secure, but nothing—not even the most well-thought-out plan—was entirely foolproof.

Buy as much time as you can. Cover your tracks, don't make it easy for anyone to find you. Don't leave a single clue that will lead them to you.

The lights were off in their bedrooms. Beds unmade, yes, but she couldn't do anything about that now. Closet door closed and nothing hinting that they'd disappeared inside it.

Behind her, a ring alerted her to an incoming call on the control panel. She spun around and swept up the receiver.

"Sadie." The crisp, strong voice immediately calmed her.

"Raine. They're here. I saw five."

He didn't waste time asking her anything except, "Are you in the safe room?"

"Char just went down. I'm going now."

"Good. Hang up and go right now. Don't forget to hit the Secure All button when you get down there. I'll make sure police are dispatched."

"Thank y—"

A shrill shriek suddenly pierced her eardrums. The house had been breached.

"Oh God, they're inside!" she said, her heart thudding, her whole body shaking.

"Stay calm. The alarm might scare them off."

No, it wouldn't, though Raine wouldn't understand how she could be so certain of that and there was no time to explain.

This was no random robbery. Not with five people all dressed in black, moving so deliberately. If they were who she suspected them to be, no alarm would stop them.

"Go, Sadie. Go now," he said, his strong voice cutting through the sound of the alarm and her panic.

"The police will be here in fifteen minutes?"

"Yeah," he replied. "But I'll be there in ten."

About the Author

Leslie A. Kelly is a *New York Times* and *USA Today* bestselling author of more than fifty novels and novellas. Known for their sexy humor, Leslie's books have been honored with numerous awards, including the National Reader's Choice Award, the Aspen Gold, the Golden Quill, the Write Touch, the Romantic Times Award, and four RWA-Rita nominations. Leslie is also a Career Achievement Award winner from *Romantic Times* magazine.

Although she has spent most of her life in Maryland and Florida, Leslie currently resides in Colorado with her husband and two fluffy, yappy little dogs, one of whom is now officially called the Coyote Warrior.

CPSIA information can be obtained
at www.ICGtesting.com
Printed in the USA
BVHW03s0826190818
524653BV00005B/16/P